About the Authors

Author of more than 100 novels, **Gina Wilkins** loves exploring complex interpersonal relationships and the universal search for 'a safe place to call home.' Her books have appeared on numerous bestseller lists, and she was a nominee for a lifetime achievement award from *Romantic Times* magazine. A lifelong resident of Arkansas, she credits her writing career to a nagging imagination, a book-loving mother, an encouraging husband and three 'extraordinary' offspring.

In 2002 **Janice Maynard** left a career as a primary teacher to pursue writing full-time. Her first love is creating sexy, character-driven, contemporary romance. She has written for Kensington and NAL, and is very happy to be part of the Mills & Boon family – a lifelong dream. Janice and her husband live in the shadow of the Great Smoky Mountains. They love to hike and travel. Visit her at www.JaniceMaynard.com

New York Times and *USA Today* bestselling author **Barbara Dunlop** has written more than fifty novels for Mills & Boon, including the acclaimed *Whiskey Bay Brides* series for Mills & Boon Desire. Her sexy, light-hearted stories regularly hit bestsellers lists. Barbara is a four-time finalist for the Romance Writers of America's RITA® award.

Christmas with the Boss

GINA WILKINS

JANICE MAYNARD

BARBARA DUNLOP

MILLS & BOON

First Published in Great Britain 2020
By Mills & Boon, an imprint of HarperCollins*Publishers*
1 London Bridge Street, London, SE1 9GF

CHRISTMAS WITH THE BOSS © 2020 Harlequin Books S.A.

The Boss's Marriage Plan © 2015 Gina Wilkins
Billionaire Boss, Holiday Baby © 2017 Janice Maynard
Twelve Nights of Temptation © 2017 Barbara Dunlop

ISBN: 978-0-263-29841-3

MIX
Paper from
responsible sources
FSC™ C007454

Printed and bound in Spain
by CPI, Barcelona

THE BOSS'S
MARRIAGE PLAN

GINA WILKINS

As always, for the family that gives me strength and my reason for living, my husband of more than thirty years and our amazing son, two daughters, son-in-law and precious grandson.

Chapter One

Tess Miller stood quietly nearby as her older sister, Nina Miller Wheatley, made a minute adjustment to an impeccably set Thanksgiving dinner table. Nina's formal dining room glowed not only with the light from a crystal chandelier but from multiple candles on the table and antique sideboard. Fall flowers spilled over crystal vases onto Pilgrim figurines and pumpkins nestled beside them. Calligraphy place cards rested in little turkey-shaped holders beside the brown-and-orange plaid place mats. Tess didn't know why they needed place cards when the entire dinner party consisted of Nina, her husband, their three kids and herself, but her overachieving sister never did anything halfway.

There was enough food for another six people, at a minimum. Turkey and dressing, several side dishes, salads and four choices of desserts crowded the serving tables. Tess had brought a casserole and a cake, both of which Nina had proclaimed "very nice" and had then set at the back of the buffet.

Nina wore a rust silk blouse and dark brown slacks that showed off her gym-toned body. Not a salon-tinted blond hair was out of place in her stylish do, and her makeup was perfect despite the hours she'd spent in the kitchen. She'd given a critical once-over to Tess's black wrap top and slim charcoal pants, but her only comment had been that maybe Tess should consider adding more red highlights to her hair, just to "spice up" her shoulder-length auburn bob. Tess was perfectly content for now with the color nature had given her, but she hadn't wasted breath arguing.

The sisters didn't look much alike. Tess's brown eyes had a more golden tint than Nina's, her face was more oval and she'd inherited their father's shallow chin cleft. At five-four, she was two inches shorter than her sister, though she'd always wondered if being taller would have made any difference in Nina's still treating her like a child.

"Everything looks beautiful, Nina," she said, knowing just what to say to make her sister happy. "I can tell you've worked very hard."

Nina heaved a long-suffering sigh. "You have no idea. All the chopping and mixing, cooking and baking, not to mention keeping up with all the kids' extracurricular activities and volunteering at two different schools. I'm utterly exhausted, but of course it's all worth it for my family."

Through her mental sigh, Tess heard a football game playing in the den. She knew her brother-in-law, Ken, and her nephews, thirteen-year-old Cameron and nine-year-old Austin, were parked in front of it, though both boys were probably engrossed in handheld video games. Almost fifteen-year-old Olivia was in her room, likely risking carpal tunnel syndrome with marathon texting to her bazillion friends. None of them had offered assistance to their mother, though Nina wouldn't have accepted if they had. She loved being a martyr to her overly indulged family.

Nina shook off her air of selfless weariness to replace it with a sympathetic smile toward her much younger sibling. "You wouldn't understand, of course, not having a husband and children of your own to take care of."

She didn't add the uniquely Southern, artfully patronizing "bless your heart," but Tess heard it anyway. Ever since Tess turned twenty-one eight years ago, Nina rarely missed an opportunity to voice her concern that her sister would remain single and childless. It didn't help that her only semiserious relationship during those years had crashed and burned.

While Tess wanted a family of her own, she was increasingly resentful of her sister's condescension, making every holiday gathering progressively more uncomfortable. That was a shame, because she and her sister were the only surviving members of their immediate family. Their parents, who'd been in their mid-forties when Tess was born thirteen years after Nina, had both died within the past six years. Now Nina always made a big show of including Tess at every holiday table because as she said, "Tess has no one else to share the special days with."

Tess drew a deep breath before asking, "Would you like me to call everyone to the table?"

"In a moment. First I want to ask if you'd allow me to

give your number to Cameron's orthodontist, Dr. Mike. He's really quite nice, if a bit socially awkward. He's been divorced for almost a year. He seemed interested when I showed him your photo on my phone, but after that little fit you threw last time, I knew better than to give him your number without asking." Nina rolled her eyes, as if making it clear she thought it unreasonable that Tess objected to Nina handing out her number to just any single stranger.

"Seriously, Nina, stop trying to fix me up," Tess said with a firm shake of her head. She didn't mind her friends arranging the occasional blind date, but she'd rather her meddlesome sister stay out of her love life, such as it was. The thought of her photo being shown to random men made her very uncomfortable. "I don't need you to arrange dates for me."

"Well, someone should. I don't see how you're going to find anyone sitting in that office working for your taskmaster of a boss. I mean, sure, you meet construction workers and architects and suppliers, but you're too professional to flirt with them on the job and you're never *not* on the job, so where does that leave you, hmm? Needing a little help meeting someone, that's where. And because I'm actually out in the community mingling with nice, successful people, who better to direct a lead or two your way?"

"If I want your help, I'll let you know, all right?"

Nina didn't quite growl her frustration, but she seemed to be making an effort to restrain herself. "You haven't forgotten about Dana's party the second Saturday in December, have you? You have to be there. Everyone's expecting you. You can come alone, of course, but you know how snooty some of our cousins would be if they think you can't find a date. Perhaps that would be a good time for you to spend an evening getting to know Dr. Mike?"

"I'll find my own date, thank you." Tess wasn't sure where or how, but she'd bring a date if she had to hire someone!

Maybe she shouldn't let Nina get to her this way. Maybe she should go to the family gathering alone as she usually did, with her head high and her shoulders squared. Confident, composed and contentedly independent. But then she'd have to endure everyone trying to set her up with their dentists, accountants and gynecologists.

Before her sister could demand details, Tess turned toward the dining room doorway, which was decorated with a garland of autumn leaves and just-too-cute little gourds. "I'll call everyone in to eat. It would be a shame to let this delicious food get cold."

It was probably the only threat that could have derailed Nina's attention from Tess's personal life. At least for now.

Tess must not have known anyone else was in the office at 6:00 p.m. on the Saturday after Thanksgiving. No other reason she'd be chatting on her cell phone with her office door open, so her words drifted out very clearly to Scott Prince in the lobby. He didn't mean to eavesdrop, really. It was simply that while he hesitated, trying to decide if it would be rude to interrupt her, he heard a bit more than he intended.

He'd just quietly entered the reception area of Prince Construction Company, Inc., the Little Rock enterprise into which he'd invested all his time, sweat, money and dreams for the past nine years. It had been a struggling little local-only construction company when he'd purchased it from the retiring owner, with whom Scott had interned while he'd obtained a master's degree in construction management. His family and friends had been concerned to see him take such a major financial risk, considering him too young and inexperienced at twenty-seven to successfully run a complicated business. It had taken almost a decade of personal sacrifice and unwavering determination to prove their doubts unfounded, but he was now owner and CEO of a successful, multistate enterprise specializing in small to medium commercial construction projects.

Tess had started working for him as a clerk over six years ago and had become his office manager and valued administrative assistant. No one got to him except through her. Some people said he was gifted when it came to surrounding himself with the right people. Tess was a prime example of that. He admitted freely that the whole operation would fall apart without her to oversee the office.

But this was Thanksgiving weekend, not an official workday. Shouldn't she be spending it with family or friends—at least unless he needed her for some crisis or another, as he confessed he so often did?

"It was the usual painful family meal," he heard her say from the other room, almost as if in answer to his silent question. "My sister tried to fix me up with every single male she's ever met, because she says I'm incapable of finding eligible men on my own. My brother-in-law finally told her to lay off because as he said, 'Some women are just meant to be single.'"

Scott grimaced, knowing now why Tess had chosen to work on the long weekend rather than to spend more time with family. He almost spoke up then to let her know he was there, but she started talking again.

"So, anyway, Nina nagged me about bringing her son's orthodontist to Dana's big Christmas bash, but I told her I'd find my own date, thank you very much. No, I don't know who it will be. You know my lousy luck with the online dating sites I've tried lately. Maybe I'll just take Glenn. Yes, I know you keep telling me he's boring, but maybe we've been too critical of him. He's a nice enough guy. Makes no secret that he's ready to settle down and start a family. Maybe I've just been too—"

Scott opened and closed the front door. More loudly this time. He'd suddenly realized that he'd been standing in one place for too long, hearing more than Tess would surely want him to know.

He heard her mutter something quickly, followed by the thud of her phone, then the squeak of her chair. Moments later she appeared in the open doorway looking slightly flustered, though she almost instantly assumed her usual calm and collected expression. She was dressed more casually than on weekdays in a blue-and-black patterned tunic with black leggings tucked into flat boots. She'd left her hair down rather than in the neat twist she usually wore for work. He'd seen her weekend look many times before, of course—but he thought she looked particularly pretty today. The slight flush that lingered on her cheeks was definitely becoming.

"Scott? What are you doing here? I thought you and your dad and brothers were driving to Missouri for the Razorbacks game today."

"We were. But Eli had to be on call because one of

his partners broke an arm in a Thanksgiving biking accident. Then Jake's son came down with a virus and our plans all fell apart. We gave our tickets to Mom and Dad's neighbors and their kids. They were happy to get them."

"I'm sorry your plans were canceled. You really needed a break from work."

He felt his mouth quirk into a half smile. "Are you saying I've been surly lately?"

"Not surly, just… Okay, maybe a little surly," she said with a quiet laugh.

He could count on Tess to be honest with him, sometimes brutally so. Somehow she always managed to do so without crossing boundaries of the employee-employer relationship, even when she was annoyed with him. And she had been annoyed with him on several occasions.

He cleared his throat. "Sorry about that. You have to admit, the past few months have been challenging." They'd dealt with a couple of big, complicated jobs, a burglary at a job site that had cost them several expensive tools, even a break-in here at the office earlier in the year. Speaking of which…

He frowned. "Why was the security system turned off? You shouldn't be here alone on a weekend, especially after dark, without that alarm activated. As I've just proved, anyone could have walked in."

She lifted an eyebrow. "Didn't you have to use your key?"

He was still surprised she hadn't heard him enter the first time, which only illustrated how focused she'd been on her conversation. "Well, yes, but still…"

Relenting, she smiled. "I've had the security system

on almost the whole time I've been here. I turned it off when I ran out to my car for something I'd forgotten and I was going to turn it back on after I finished a phone call in my office."

He kept his expression as unrevealing as he could manage. He knew she'd be embarrassed if she thought he'd overheard too much of that call. "I want you to be safe when you're here alone. Keep the blasted thing turned on."

Sending a salute toward him that was just short of impertinent, she said, "Yes, sir. I'll do that."

He sighed and shook his head. "Insubordination. Remind me again why I keep you around?"

She laughed easily, slipping back into the comfortable relationship they'd forged during their years of working side by side. "Because you know this entire enterprise would collapse without me."

He chuckled after she pretty much echoed his thoughts from earlier. He had to concede her point.

She'd made her mark on every aspect of his business, from the state of the reception area to the total of the bottom line.

Speaking of the reception area... He suddenly noticed decorations that hadn't been there a few days earlier. A Christmas tree sat in the front corner, decorated with gold-and-white ornaments and tiny white lights. A strand of garland wound with gold ribbon draped the front of the reception desk, matching the wreath on the door. On the tables sat frosted glass holders with fat white candles. All very subtle and tasteful—very Tess, he thought with a faint smile. She could have assigned one or two of the clerical workers she now supervised to decorate, but she'd no doubt taken care of it herself,

as she had every Christmas since she'd started working for him.

"You came in today just to decorate?"

"I thought I'd get the decorations up while I had a
quiet afternoon to work on them. I'm almost finished."

"Looks nice. Is there anything I can do to help?"

"I've got it, thanks. There are only a few more things
I want to do."

Nodding, he moved toward the closed door of his
own larger office to the right side of hers. "Let me know
if you need anything. I'm going to review the paperwork for that Springdale job we start Monday, just to
make sure everything is lined up."

"I left a couple of contracts on your desk for you to
look over and sign. They could have waited until Monday, but since you're here..."

"I'm on it."

He glanced over his shoulder as he opened the door
with his name engraved on a brass plaque. Tess stood
half-turned away from him, frowning in concentration
at the Christmas tree, which looked perfect already to
him. She really did look pretty today. He thought fleetingly about telling her so, but something held him back.

He made a cup of coffee with the pod brewer on
his credenza. "Would you like a hot drink?" he asked
through the open doorway as the enticing aroma filled
his office. The rack beside the pot always included a variety of herbal teas that he knew Tess liked. They often
shared drinks at his desk as they discussed business.

"No, thank you," she called back without making
an appearance. He told himself he wasn't disappointed
that she was too busy for a cozy chat, which meant he

had no excuse to procrastinate any longer with the work he'd come in to see to.

Taking a seat at his desk, he tried to concentrate on paperwork for the next twenty minutes. Despite his resistance, his thoughts kept returning to the one-sided conversation he'd accidentally overheard, and the glimpse of insight it had provided into Tess's personal life. Of course, he couldn't have worked so closely with her for six years without knowing some things about her.

Through night classes and online courses, she'd completed her business degree and had earned postgraduate hours since she'd started working with him. He knew she took pride in those accomplishments. During that same time, he'd seen her deal with the illness and loss of both her parents. He'd gotten the impression the majority of the caregiving had been on her shoulders because her sister had been so busy with her young children. Yet he'd never once heard Tess complain. Whatever she dealt with in her off-hours, she'd always reported to work with her usual serene efficiency.

Serene. He repeated the word in his head, thinking how well it suited his assistant. Throughout several major work upheavals, when he'd been edgy and bad-tempered amid the confusion and mayhem, Tess had remained…well, Tess. She came in every morning with a smile, an encouraging word and a roll-up-her-sleeves attitude that let her tackle each day's tasks with single-minded focus.

One would think someone so agreeable would be a bit of a doormat, easily intimidated, perhaps. Not Tess. He'd witnessed her hold her own with even the most belligerent, disgruntled employees and clients. One of his

job foremen had confided to Scott that Tess reminded
him of a nun who'd taught his junior high math classes.
"Nice lady most of the time," he'd clarified. "But get
out of line, and you'd get a ruler across the knuckles
before you could spit."

Scott could imagine Tess wielding a mean ruler if
necessary. But he'd never thought of her as a nun—
had he?

He cleared his throat and reached hastily for his
quickly cooling coffee, almost knocking over the cup
in his clumsiness. He salvaged the papers on his desk
at the last moment and with a muttered curse.

"Everything okay in there?" Tess called from the
other room.

"Yes, fine, thanks."

Maybe he hadn't thought of Tess as a nun, but before
that overheard conversation, he'd had no idea she'd tried
online dating, or that she'd been actively looking for a
match. Meeting strange men online was dangerous, he
thought in disapproval. Sure, people did it all the time
these days, but it just didn't seem right for Tess.

He knew she'd been in a relationship about three
years back that hadn't worked out. That was about
the same time he'd been briefly engaged to a stunning but capricious woman who'd understandably—
and angrily—chosen to pursue a career in modeling
over marriage to an often-neglectful workaholic. He
still winced when he remembered the scene Sharon had
caused when she'd broken up with him in a crowded
restaurant, and all because he'd been a few minutes late
meeting her there. Okay, twenty minutes late, but he'd
texted to let her know he'd been held up—again—by
yet another work crisis. She'd known going into the

relationship that his business required a great deal of his time, but like others he'd dated before her, she'd expected more from him than he'd been able to give. She'd stormed off furiously when she'd finally concluded that his construction company meant more to him than their relationship. The split hadn't been amicable, but then for some reason, his breakups never were.

He wondered if Tess had remained on good terms with her former flames. He wouldn't be surprised if she had. Unlike the volatile Sharon, Tess was the practical, pragmatic type. In the years she had worked for him, he'd never heard her carry on about romance and unrealistic fantasies.

Of course, he rarely allowed himself to think of Tess as a vibrant, available single woman. After all, she worked for him, and he'd never even considered overstepping their professional boundaries and risking their comfortable work relationship. She had just turned twenty-three when she'd applied for the clerical job with him. He'd been a couple months shy of thirty-one, and had already owned the business for over three years. Perhaps that was why he'd thought of her all this time as much too young for him, though the actual gap was only seven years. She would soon turn thirty, he mused, surprised by how quickly time had passed. He supposed it was only natural that she would now be considering marriage and children. After all, he'd given quite a lot of deliberation to those things lately, too.

She strolled in through his open doorway. "I thought I'd put this candle on your table. I know you don't like a lot of froufrou in your office, but this isn't too much, is it?" She held a hurricane glass candleholder with a little garland around the base. "You've got a few meetings scheduled in here during the next couple of weeks."

He often eschewed the main conference room in favor of the cherry table in his office. Everything he needed was available to him in here—a projector and screen, whiteboard and display easels and blackout shades to hide the distracting views of the Arkansas River and the distant rolling hills. He loved his office. It was exactly what he'd envisioned back when he'd first started building his own business.

"I don't mind a candle on the table," he assured Tess, making her smile.

"How was your Thanksgiving?" she asked as she fussed with the garland.

"Nice. Noisy. The kids were wound up from all the attention."

Both his brothers were happily married fathers. His older brother, Eli, a family practice physician, had twin girls, Madison and Miranda. Cute as little bunnies, they were almost five years old and full of energy. He was their "uncle Scotty," and he adored them, just as he did his little nephew, too. Six-month-old Henry was his younger brother, Jake's, kid. Both his brothers had been lucky enough to find their soul mates—Eli and Libby had started dating when both were in medical school, while Jake, an attorney, had met psychologist Christina at a cocktail party a couple years ago.

As much as he'd enjoyed the gathering, Scott had been painfully aware that he was no closer to having a family of his own than he'd been during the last solo holiday season. None of his relatives was actually nagging him to marry—after all, the next generation of Princes was already well established—but he couldn't help wondering if they thought something must be lacking in him. Increasingly, he wondered the same thing about himself.

Without arrogance, he could admit he'd accomplished a great deal in his almost thirty-seven years. Valedictorian in high school. Summa cum laude college graduate. A master's degree. His own business. He had a nice home he'd remodeled himself, with a couple of empty bedrooms he hoped to fill someday. All his life he'd heard about biological clocks, but he'd never quite understood the term until he found himself only a few years from forty without any immediate prospect of a wife and kids. During these past twelve months, he had attended cocktail parties and professional mixers— more than he would have liked, actually. He'd gone on blind dates, been to clubs and bars and charity fundraisers. He'd met a lot of nice women, had some good times, made a few friends…but he'd yet to find anyone he thought would be a lifelong partner.

After his brief engagement to Sharon had ended so disastrously, he'd wondered privately if he was destined to remain a workaholic bachelor. He was accustomed to success, to achieving the high-reaching goals he set for himself. His only experiences with failure had been in the romantic area of his life. He really hated failure.

Tess stepped back to critically study the centerpiece she'd created. Apparently deciding it would suffice, she turned to the door, asking over her shoulder on the way out, "Have you signed those contracts?"

He reached hastily for the stack he'd yet to touch. "On it."

He wondered half seriously what she'd have said if he shared that he'd been fretting about how to find a mate.

Knowing Tess, she'd set her mind to solving that issue for him. He'd probably come in on Monday to find a line of qualified applicants standing outside his office door. Having trouble in her own quest wouldn't stop her from setting to work on his if he asked.

His smile faded as it occurred to him that maybe he was on to something here. Oh, not the part about asking Tess to find candidates for him, but the idea that he'd been going about this all wrong. Perhaps he should approach this endeavor with the same attitude he'd used in establishing his successful business. Practicality and analysis were his strengths. Romance obviously was not. There had to be nice women out there who didn't require all the fancy trappings of courtship, but simply wanted to marry an upstanding, decent guy and start a family. Surely a union based on common goals and values, preferably even friendship, would appeal to someone besides himself. Maybe if he spelled out from the start what he had to offer—and what he didn't—there would be no artificial expectations that could only lead to another disappointing failure.

When he'd drawn up his original business plan, he'd made lots of lists. Where he needed to focus his efforts, how he wanted to solicit clients, specific steps for growing the business in a sensible, feasible manner and at a reasonable, sustainable pace. Perhaps he should approach his marriage plan in a similar vein.

He visualized a mental list of the type of woman he thought would suit him best. It should be someone organized and efficient, much like himself. Practical— the kind of woman who would understand he was never going to be a smooth-talking Romeo, but that he would be loyal, generous, committed, dependable. That was the type of husband and father his dad was, and that his brothers had become. Maybe they had married for more emotional reasons, but that didn't mean he couldn't make his own future partnership just as successful. Middle kid that he was, he'd always had his own way of doing things, as his mother had pointed out on many occasions. His way had turned out well for him in business, so why not in marriage?

His wife didn't have to be model beautiful, as his ex-fiancée had been, but it would be best, of course, if he was attracted to her. He'd always been drawn to kind eyes and a warm smile, and he had an admitted weakness for dimples…

He heard Tess moving around in the other room. She had nice eyes, he thought, along with a generous smile with occasional flashes of dimples in the corners. She never wore much makeup, but he'd noted some time ago—just in passing—that her skin was creamy and flawless without it. He supposed she would be considered girl-next-door attractive rather than strikingly beautiful—but then again, there was nothing he'd have changed about her appearance. On more than one occasion, especially during the past year or so, he'd found himself admiring her attributes in a manner that had made him immediately redirect his thoughts, chiding himself that it was inappropriate to even notice those things.

A muffled thud and a disgruntled mutter drifted in from the lobby. Curious, he stood and walked around his desk to stand in the open doorway. "What are you doing?"

Tess was on the floor beneath the big artificial tree, propped on one arm as she stretched to reach something he couldn't see. "I knocked off an ornament when I was trying to straighten a branch. Oh, here it is."

Holding a sparkling gold orb in her hand, she swiveled so that she was sitting cross-legged on the floor looking thoughtfully up at the tree. After a moment, she leaned forward and hooked the ornament to a branch, then leaned back on her hands to gaze upward. Tiny white lights glittered among the thick green branches, their reflection gleaming in the dark red highlights in her hair.

"How does that look?" she asked.

"Looks good," he murmured slowly, his eyes on her. "Really good."

She pushed herself to her feet and brushed absently at her slacks. "Do you think a candle in a snowflake-shaped holder on the reception desk would be too much?"

He cleared his throat. "I'm sorry. What?"

When she realized he was staring at her, she cocked her head to eye him with a frown. "Scott? Are you okay?"

"Yeah, fine. Just…absorbed with a dilemma."

"You'll figure it out," she said encouragingly. "You always do."

Her steadfast confidence in him had bolstered him through some of his most challenging periods during the past six years. Her absolute dedication to the company had been instrumental in its success. She understood why it was so important to him in a way that perhaps no one else did, because it seemed almost equally valuable to her. In some ways, he thought she knew him better than anyone outside his immediate family. Even some of his longtime friends were unable to read him as well as Tess. She was more than an employee, more than a professional associate. Not exactly a personal friend—but whose fault was that? His or hers? Both?

Tess had often teased him about being "blessed with strokes of inspiration," in her words. Solutions to thorny problems tended to occur to him in sudden, compelling flashes, and he had learned to respect his own instincts. They had let him down only on very rare occasions.

He had just been staggered by another one of those brilliant moments of insight. In a near-blinding flash of awareness, he'd realized suddenly that the woman he'd mentally described as his perfect mate had just been sitting under the Christmas tree.

Chapter Two

Tess wasn't particularly concerned about Scott's sudden distraction. This was an expression she knew very well, the way he always looked when he'd been struck with a possibly brilliant solution to a troublesome dilemma. She would wait patiently for him to share what he was thinking—or not. Sometimes he had to mull over details for days before he enlightened anyone else about his latest inspired idea.

Glancing around the reception area, she decided she'd finished decorating. The offices looked festive and welcoming but not over the top. "I'm calling it done," she said, more to herself than Scott, who probably wasn't listening anyway. "Any more would be too much."

He gave a little start in response to her voice—honestly, had he forgotten she was even there?—then cleared his throat. "Um, Tess?"

Picking up an empty ornament box to stow away in a supply closet, she responded absently, "Yes?"

When he didn't immediately reply, she glanced around to find him studying her with a frown. The way he was staring took her aback. Did she have something on her face? Glitter in her hair? She thought he might look just this way at finding a stranger in his reception room.

"Scott?"

He blinked, then glanced quickly around them. "Not here," he muttered, apparently to himself, then addressed her again. "Have you eaten?"

"I was going to stop for takeout on my way home."

"Want to share a pizza at Giulia's? There's something I'd like to discuss with you."

It wasn't unusual for them to share a meal after working late, and the nearby casual Italian place was one of their customary destinations. Because she had no other plans for the evening, she nodded. "Sure. I'll just grab a notebook."

"You won't need to take notes. We're just going to talk."

That was odd, too. They'd worked through shared meals but never just talked.

He was still acting peculiarly when they were seated in a back booth in the restaurant.

Sipping her soda while waiting for their pizza, Tess studied Scott over the rim of the glass. He was visibly preoccupied, but she knew occasionally it was possible to sidetrack him from his musings, at least briefly. She gave it a try. "Tell me a funny story about your nieces," she suggested, leaning back in her seat. "I could use a good laugh this evening."

He blinked a couple of times before focusing on her from across the table. Candlelight gleamed in his dark blue eyes. His hair, the color of strong, rich coffee and a bit mussed from the winter evening breeze, was brushed back casually from a shallow widow's peak. A few strands of premature silver glittered in the dark depths. There was no denying that her boss was a fine-looking man, trim and tanned with a firm, square jaw, nicely chiseled features and a smile that could melt glaciers when he turned on the charm.

Sometimes she still thought of the first time she'd met him. She'd been struck almost dumb by her first sight of the great-looking, intensely focused man sitting behind a cheap, cluttered desk in his first office. She still cringed a little when she thought of how incoherent she'd been during that awkward interview. She wasn't sure what he'd seen in her to take a chance on hiring her, but she was so glad he had. She loved her job and took great pride in the success of the business.

Scott thought for a moment before complying with her impulsive request. "During breakfast Thanksgiving morning, Madison reached for the butter and knocked over an entire glass of cold milk directly into Eli's lap. Eli jumped and knocked over his cereal bowl, which landed on their shih tzu. The dog went tearing through the house scattering milk and Cheerios all over the floors while the girls chased after it, smashing the cereal underfoot. Eli was laughing when he told us the story over Thanksgiving dinner, but his wife was not amused."

Tess laughed. "That sounds like a scene from a TV sitcom."

"Right? Eli said it's pretty much life as expected with energetic almost-five-year-old twins."

"I can imagine. It must be exhausting."

He smiled up at the server who set their pizza in front of them, then continued the conversation as Tess reached for a slice. "Eli and Libby put on the long-suffering act, but they love every minute with those girls."

She'd met all the members of Scott's family, most recently in September, at the annual PCCI picnic at sprawling Burns Park in North Little Rock.

She doubted he got the same kind of grief from his family that she did from hers just because he hadn't yet found his own life mate. From what she knew of them, she thought perhaps they'd tease him a little, but probably not in the insultingly patronizing tone her sister used toward her. With Thanksgiving behind them, the holiday season was now well under way. Parties, traditions, family gatherings loomed ahead. She wished she could feel a little more enthusiastic about what was to come in the next month.

"You like children, don't you, Tess?" Scott asked unexpectedly.

"I love children." She hoped her quick smile hid the wistfulness that underlaid her reply.

"Yeah, me, too."

Looking down at his plate, Scott toyed with his food, seemingly lost in his thoughts again. With silence reigning, she took another bite of her veggie pizza.

He cleared his throat and she glanced up. Her eyebrows rose in response to his expression. "What?"

"You remember when I had that unexpected appendectomy last year and you had to come to my house to work the next day because we had that big deadline?"

She was rather surprised he'd mentioned that incident. He'd seemed to try very hard to forget that day since. "Of course I remember."

Hypersensitive to the painkillers, Scott had spent a few hours rambling somewhat disjointedly until the effects wore off. He hadn't said anything too far out of line, but he'd been amusingly whimsical and had continually heaped praise on her, telling her how important she was to him and how he couldn't get by without her. Even knowing his effusiveness was fueled by medication, she'd taken the compliments to heart.

The only seriously awkward moment had come as she'd prepared to leave. Though Scott wasn't a "hugger," he'd hauled her into his arms for a somewhat clumsy embrace, thanking her too heartily for her help. She'd convinced herself afterward that he had surely intended to kiss her cheek, but he'd missed. His lips had landed squarely on her mouth.

It had lasted only seconds. Hardly long enough to be called a kiss. Even under the influence of the medicines, he'd been aware enough to jump back immediately, stammering apologies, flustered, his face uncharacteristically flushed. Tess had laughed it off, attempting to mask her own reactions behind indulgent humor. Despite her assurances the next day that he'd said nothing untoward, Scott had been embarrassed by his lack of control and obviously concerned that he'd crossed professional lines. They had implicitly agreed to put the incident behind them and never refer to it again. To be honest, though, there'd been times when she'd found herself reliving that almost kiss and wondering what it might have been like had it been real.

Scott cleared his throat, bringing her abruptly back

to the present. "So, the thing is, I'd like to handle this conversation the same way we did that incident. Though I am completely clearheaded and unaffected by any outside influences tonight, feel free to forget anything I'm about to say, if you want, and to pretend it never happened next time we see each other. That's why I wanted to talk here, away from the office."

Lifting her eyebrows in confusion, she looked at the tall, thin glass in his hand. "You've only had a few sips of your beer, so that's probably not the reason you aren't making any sense."

Setting the glass aside, he shook his head. "As I said, I'm not under the influence of anything. Just not quite sure how to begin this conversation."

Swallowing a bit nervously, she touched her napkin to her lips, then lowered her hands to her lap to toy with the checkered tablecloth. Since when had Scott ever had trouble talking with her? This couldn't be good. "Just say it, Scott."

He nodded. "Your job means a lot to you, right? I mean, it matters to you that the company is successful. Reputable."

Her chest tightened. A cold, hard knot formed in her throat, forcing her to clear it before she could ask, "Have I done something wrong? Have I messed up somehow? Is that what you're trying to tell me?"

He shook his head quickly. "Of course not. Just the opposite, in fact. You've gone above and beyond this past year. I'm not exaggerating when I say I don't know what I'd do without you."

Relief flooded her. Her hand felt just a little unsteady when she tucked a strand of hair behind her ear. "Then, what...?"

"I overheard some of a phone conversation you had earlier," he blurted. "You were talking about the upcoming holiday parties, and about problems you've been having with online dating."

She felt warmth spread across her face. He'd heard her conversation with her friend Stevie? How humiliating!

"So anyway," he continued before she could speak, "I've got a bunch of holiday events coming up, too, and no one to attend them with me. Which made me wonder why we couldn't go to some of those parties together."

Of all the things he could have said, this was the least expected. Surely he wasn't suggesting…

"You mean…as coworkers?" she asked in a tentative attempt at clarification.

"No, nothing to do with work. I guess you could say I'm asking you out."

She stared at him, her mind going completely blank with shock. "Oh. Ah."

"I've been thinking about how you and I get along so well and always have," he said, cutting into her stunned stammering. "About how much more comfortable it could be if we attend these things together rather than going alone or trying to deal with early-dating drama with other people during the holidays. So, what do you think?"

She moved his glass firmly to the other side of the table, symbolically out of his reach. "I think you had too much of this on an empty stomach. It must have gone straight to your head."

He made a sound that was half amusement, half exasperation. "I've had maybe three sips of the beer. I'm not intoxicated. I had this inspiration at the office and

I've been trying to figure out how to bring it up to you. I guess I'm not doing a very good job of it. I'm really bad at this sort of thing."

"After hearing me complain about online dating, you decided we should attend holiday parties together?" She still wasn't sure she entirely understood where he was going with this. "And you're not just talking about business-related events?"

"No. There are several events coming up very soon that I'll be expected to attend with a plus one. I'll admit I've been putting off thinking about them until the last minute because I didn't know who to ask, but I suddenly realized there's no one I'd rather go with than you. And wouldn't you rather attend your parties with me than with some guy you think is boring?"

So he'd heard her talk about Glenn. She resisted an impulse to hide her face in her hands as she understood exactly how much of her conversation he'd unintentionally overheard. She wasn't angry with him for his eavesdropping; after all, her door had been open and she'd made no effort to speak quietly. But that was because she'd thought herself alone in the office. Remembering the way he'd announced his arrival with excessive noise, she figured he must have been uncomfortable with what he'd overheard. But that hadn't stopped him from mulling it over afterward, had it?

After clearing her throat, she said, "The holidays can be difficult for singles. Trust me, I know. My older sister is a champ when it comes to dropping patronizing hints and comments, especially since one of my two best friends just got married and the other is in a steady relationship. Even though I'm mostly okay with going to parties and other events on my own, sometimes I think it would be nice to have someone to accompany me. Someone I like and enjoy spending time with. But—"

"You don't feel that way about me?"

"Of course I do. But—"

"You like me. You're certainly comfortable with me. You seem to enjoy spending time with me."

"Well, yes, but—"

"So what's the problem? You attend a few things with me. I'll go to your gigs. It'll take a lot of pressure off both of us."

He was on a roll now, a mode she'd seen him in many times. He'd had what he considered a brilliant idea and he was running with it. True, his "aha" moments had served him well in the past, earning him a reputation as a business genius. But he'd really gone off the rails this time.

"May I speak now?"

He grimaced. "Oh. Sorry. Go ahead."

"As I was trying to say, I understand what prompted your suggestion and it makes sense in some ways. But," she said quickly when he started to speak again, "I don't think you've considered all the ramifications. Showing up together for professional gatherings wouldn't raise eyebrows because we're usually together in that capacity. But in social functions, with families and friends… Everyone's going to wonder if there's something going on between us other than the construction business."

"Would that be such a bad thing?"

Maybe he'd misunderstood what she was trying to say. "To have people speculating about us? It's not that I care so much about gossip, personally—well, not too much—but I'm not sure how good it would be for the company."

He shook his head. "I wasn't talking about the gossip. I meant the part about our relationship being more than a professional one."

She stared at him across the table, trying to read his face. Was he joking? It wasn't his usual style of humor, but surely he wasn't suggesting that they should start... dating?

"Okay, maybe I'm getting a little ahead of myself," he said quickly, probably in response to her stunned expression. "But think about it, Tess. We make a hell of a team. Everyone says so. How many times have we been teased about being so in sync that we're accused of communicating telepathically?"

She could hardly count the number of times during meetings when she and Scott had exchanged thoughts with little more than a glance and a nod, to the bemusement of their associates. "Well, sure, but—"

"We both love children," he reminded her. "We want families of our own. We share many of the same values. I always respected the way you took care of your parents, even though it meant a great deal of sacrifice for yourself. That's the same kind of family loyalty my own parents instilled in me and my brothers."

Children? He was talking about kids now? "I've, um, always admired how close you are with your family. But—"

"I'm pretty sure we've both tried all the conventional dating methods. We've had relationships we hoped would lead somewhere, only to end up single again. It occurred to me that maybe we've both been going about the process all wrong, ignoring the obvious solution right in front of us. We've been successful partners for more than six years, longer than any other relationship I've ever had."

She bit her lip. He was doing it again. Enthusiastically barreling along without giving her much chance to respond. She knew how to break in, how to get his attention and make her point. Even if he didn't agree, he always listened and respected her opinion—but she didn't for the life of her know what she'd say if she stopped him just then. She was literally struck speechless.

After a moment, Scott grimaced and made a little sound that seemed self-chiding. "You're completely gobsmacked by all this, aren't you?"

"That's one way to phrase it," she managed to say fairly steadily, though her pulse rate was still fluttering like crazy.

He reached across the table to lay his hand over hers. "Sorry, Tess. You know how I get when I'm inspired by an idea."

She knew exactly how he got. Which was why she was suddenly so nervous.

He squeezed her fingers. "It's just something to think about. You have to admit it makes sense, but I won't take offense if you decide you don't want to try it. Nothing will change between us, if that's what you prefer."

Her attention was drawn to their joined hands. His was strong, tanned and very warm. She'd always admired his hands, secretly studying them as his capable fingers had flown over the keyboard or tablet screen. Her own felt suddenly small and soft beneath his, feminine to his masculine. She found herself mesmerized by the contrasts, the sensations, the intimacy of that contact.

What on earth was wrong with her? Though that

medicine-fueled embrace had been a definite glitch, it wasn't as if Scott never touched her. He was in the habit of patting her shoulder when he was particularly pleased with her or high-fiving her when a job was completed satisfactorily. But now, with just this casual hand-holding, she was suddenly transported back to inarticulate appreciation of just what an attractive and compelling man he was. The thought had always been present at the back of her mind, but she'd kept it firmly locked behind professional boundaries she had never expected to cross.

Maybe they had both lost their minds.

"Why don't you think about it for a couple of days?" Scott suggested after another moment of silence. "We could start slow, attend a party or two together, see how it feels. We'd figure out what to say to anyone who questions us. Whatever happens, nothing has to change at work. This would be a totally separate experiment."

Experiment. The word cut through the daze that had temporarily engulfed her. She drew her hand from beneath his and picked up her soda again, holding the cool glass in a firm grip to control a slight tremor. "I'll think about it," she said evenly, "but I'm not sure it's a good idea to mix business with personal pursuits. From my observances, it's rarely successful."

"Maybe for people like us it's exactly the right way to go about this. Thoughtfully, practically, logically. As adults who share common goals and common interests, not starry-eyed kids too caught up in fantasy to give serious consideration to the future."

People like us. This could be the least romantic discussion of dating and potential marriage she'd ever had, she thought, frowning down at the now unappetizing food that remained on her plate. Not that she'd ever expected romance from her prosaic employer. Okay, maybe she'd let herself daydream a time or two, especially in those early years, but she'd long since convinced herself she was completely happy with her comfortable friendship with Scott. Now he was suggesting changing the parameters of their relationship, carrying the success of their business collaboration into a personal partnership. And while she was utterly—well, gobsmacked by the proposition, she had to admit that a part of her recognized the unassailable logic of his idea.

She'd tried romance. She'd crashed and burned. Scott had been engaged. It hadn't ended well. So maybe he was right that a union based on common goals and interests was much more fitting for, as he'd said, people like them.

He gave her one of the quick, crooked smiles that almost always made her melt inside, even when she'd been annoyed with him. "Or you could always go to your parties with boring, no-chemistry Glenn."

She pointed a finger at him. "It's not wise to tease me about something you overheard while eavesdropping on a private conversation."

He held up both hands in a gesture of surrender. "You're right and I apologize. But will you think about what I suggested?'

"I'll think about it," she agreed after a moment.

Looking satisfied that she hadn't shot down the idea out of hand, he nodded and pushed away his plate. "Great. Just let me know what you decide."

As far as he was concerned, apparently, the new business at this impromptu meeting was concluded.

She had no doubt that if she presented good reasons

why she thought it best to decline, he would accept her answer graciously and they would go on with their professional lives exactly as they had before. But maybe she needed to give his suggestion a bit more thought before she reached that conclusion.

Declining dessert, she gave the excuse that she had things to do that evening. The silence wasn't quite as comfortable during the short drive back to the office in Scott's car. She suspected that was why he turned on the radio to a station already playing nonstop holiday music.

"I left my tablet inside," she said after he parked next to her car. "I'll just run in and get it."

"I need to collect a few things, too. I'll walk you in."

She'd left the Christmas lights on when they'd gone out, so they were greeted by the cheery glow of the tiny white bulbs on the tree and garlands, an unnecessary reminder of the upcoming festivities. She glanced at Scott. It was all too easy to imagine herself walking into her cousin's party with him at her side. Her sister, especially, would be stunned to see Tess with her handsome, socially prominent boss.

Was that really a good enough reason to risk upsetting the solid working relationship they'd built between them during the past six years?

Needing a distraction, she glanced around the reception area and noticed a strand of garland had slipped from the light fixture behind the desk. She rose on tiptoes to fix it, but Scott stepped up to help her, reaching over her head to secure the end into the cluster of greenery and glitter.

"Thanks," she said, smiling automatically up at him.

Her smile faded when their gazes met and she realized just how close he stood to her. So close she could almost feel the warmth and energy radiating from him. So close she could see the sudden heat reflected in his dark blue eyes. It was a look she'd never seen there before during all the times they'd been alone in the office together, all the late nights and long weekends and holidays when they'd given up personal time to work toward the mutual goal of making the business successful and profitable.

He took a half step nearer, so that they were almost but not quite touching. His voice sounded deeper than usual when he said, "We've agreed that come Monday this conversation never happened, if that's the way you want to play it. With that caveat in mind, there's one more experiment I think we should try to help you make up your mind."

That was the only warning of his intention as he dipped his head down to hers. He stopped with his lips only a whisper away from hers. "Say the word and I'll back away now," he murmured, his warm breath brushing her skin. "Or we can satisfy our curiosity and give you just a little more to think about while you make your decision about my proposition."

She couldn't even argue about that "our curiosity" comment. He'd know she was fibbing if she denied that she'd ever wondered what it might be like to kiss him—a real kiss, this time, not an accidental brush of lips.

"This never happened?" she asked in a husky whisper, letting her hands rest against his broad chest.

His lips curved into a smile. "Totally your call."

The temptation was too great. A chance to find out what it would be like to share a kiss with Scott without worrying about the consequences? Maybe it wouldn't be quite as easy as he made it sound, but for once in her safe, responsible life, she gave in to a reckless impulse. It took only a shift of her weight to bring their lips together.

Chapter Three

Maybe Scott had intended for it to be a quick meeting of lips, merely a sample taste of what could be—but it turned quickly into a kiss that made her knees go weak. He wrapped his arms around her and drew her more firmly into his embrace. Gripping his shirt, Tess tilted her head to provide better access for both of them, her lips parting and softening beneath his. Heat coursed between them, surging through her veins to sizzle in her pounding heart. She felt her toes curl in her shoes, the kiss affecting her literally from head to heel.

Her pulse raced frantically by the time they broke apart. For a moment Scott looked as disoriented as she felt, blinking as if to bring their surroundings into focus. It seemed that he, too, had been surprised by just how good the kiss had been.

Maybe they shouldn't have conducted that particular

experiment here at the office, she thought with belated qualms. She might never again stand in this particular spot without remembering how it felt to be held against that hard, strong body, their mouths fused, their hearts pounding together.

Maybe once all the Christmas decorations were put away, once the place looked normal and completely businesslike again, it would be easier to wave this off as a holiday anomaly.

Maybe.

Scott tugged at the unbuttoned collar of his shirt as if to loosen it, then glanced up at the garland they'd just straightened. With a slightly lopsided smile, he asked, "Did you tuck a sprig of mistletoe into that thing, by any chance?"

Clearing her throat, she tried to speak in the same light tone he'd used. "No mistletoe. Just a little fake balsam and holly."

"The whole place looks great. You did a nice job decorating." He scooted backward as he spoke, looking around the office as if suddenly fascinated by the holiday touches. Did he regret the kiss, or was he giving them both time to mentally process what had just happened between them? She couldn't tell from his profile, and he wasn't meeting her eyes.

She pushed back her hair and took a steadying breath. "I'd better go now. I have some things to do at home."

After a moment, he turned to face her, his expression still inscrutable. "We're okay?"

"We're okay," she assured him, touched by the hint of anxiety she thought she detected in his voice, though it didn't show on his face.

"And you'll think about the things I said?"

"Of course I will." As if she'd have any other choice.

"You have to admit, we make a hell of a team, Tess. We always have."

She couldn't argue with that. There'd been a connection between them from that very first day. But was their professional bond strong enough to sustain a more personal relationship?

Making a hasty escape from the office that was as much her home as her own apartment, she decided to call an emergency meeting of her two best friends. She very much needed Stevie and Jenny to let her know if she was insane. Because she was suddenly thinking that maybe Scott's surprising proposition wasn't completely crazy.

"Wow."

Tess nodded ruefully in response to her friend Stevie's succinct response to being told about Scott's out-of-the-blue proposition. "I know. I'm still trying to wrap my head around it myself."

Sitting in the living room of Tess's place Sunday afternoon with cups of tea in hand, her friends Stevie McLane and Jenny Baer Locke stared at her with almost identical thunderstruck expressions. Tess figured her own face must have looked much like that when Scott had sprung his suggestion on her that they should try dating. Especially when he'd made it clear that he was looking beyond merely attending events together to potentially building a future as a couple.

"He really hinted you could have children together?" Jenny asked, her dark eyes wide.

"Indirectly. At least, I think he did." Tess held up

her free hand in a gesture of bewilderment. "The whole conversation was a little hard to follow."

"What did you say?" Stevie demanded with avid curiosity.

"I told him I'd think about it."

"Wow." This time it was Jenny who expressed the sentiment. "You must have been stunned."

"That's an understatement." *Gobsmacked* still seemed a more accurate description.

Stevie set down her teacup to study Tess intently. "This could make things awkward, to say the least, when you report to work on Monday."

"Scott assured me there would be no awkwardness. He said when we're at work, we can pretend the conversation never took place."

"Can you do that?" Stevie sounded skeptical. "Really?"

After only a momentary hesitation, Tess nodded. "I think so. Scott and I have never had trouble being completely professional on the job, no matter what was going on in our personal lives. We just focus on business."

Which didn't mean there wouldn't be complicated emotions swirling inside her next time she was with her employer, she acknowledged privately. She only hoped she would do as good a job of hiding them as she had in the past.

Stevie shook her head, making her blond curls bob around her pretty face. "I have to admit I wasn't expecting to hear this when you invited us here this afternoon. I thought you'd tell us about the latest aggravating thing your sister did to you. Hey, you don't suppose she somehow put Scott up to this, do you? She is determined to marry you off after all."

With a wry smile, Tess said confidently, "No, Nina wasn't involved. This was totally one of Scott's brain flashes. Apparently, something he overheard me say to you triggered it."

Jenny nodded thoughtfully. "That sort of makes sense. You said you were complaining about your bad experiences with online dating and wishing you had a companion for some upcoming events. If he's been thinking along the same lines lately for himself, I can see how he might make this leap."

Successful business owner Jenny always looked at all the angles. Until six months ago, Tess had thought Jenny the most practical of all her friends. It had turned out, however, that Jenny had a romantic and slightly reckless side she'd been suppressing for quite a long time, a side that had emerged when she'd been reunited unexpectedly with her college boyfriend after a decade apart. Jenny had been considering an offer of marriage from a wealthy, socially connected attorney most people had considered a perfect match for her. Yet only a couple weeks after a chance reunion with Gavin Locke, she'd surprised everyone by breaking off her relationship with Thad. Barely two months later, she'd married her police officer first love in a sweet, simple little ceremony that had been a far cry from the lavish, very public wedding she would surely have had with Thad.

Stevie swiveled in her seat to frown at Jenny. Both daughters of single mothers, Stevie and Jenny had become friends in high school. They'd attended the same college and had remained close since. Tess had met them two years ago in a yoga class, and she'd fit right in with them, so that they were now a tight trio. Each brought her own strengths to the alliance. Jenny was the friend who offered shrewd advice and blunt candor. Stevie was the embodiment of generosity and thoughtfulness, the one who'd do anything for a pal—to her own detriment, at times. As for Tess… Well, she'd been told she was the encourager, the one who always supported and bolstered the confidence of her friends. She could use a little of that encouragement herself as she faced this potentially life-changing decision.

"Surely you of all people aren't suggesting Tess should actually consider marrying His Highness?" Stevie demanded of Jenny, employing the nickname she often used when referring to Scott. Tess was actually surprised Stevie seemed so perturbed. Perpetually upbeat and positive, Stevie was an unapologetic romantic, and Tess would have thought her friend would be more intrigued than troubled by this development.

"I'm not saying she should start booking bands or ordering flowers," Jenny shot back with a shake of her head. "Just that maybe it's not such a crazy idea. I can understand why Scott thinks it's worth examining more closely. Assuming he and Tess really are able to compartmentalize their work and personal lives so it wouldn't affect their professional relationship, what could it hurt to go to a few parties together?"

"I don't think anyone's that good at compartmentalizing. I mean, seriously, could you work with Thad now after dumping him for Gavin? You don't think that would be awkward?"

While Tess swallowed hard at the images Stevie's question invoked, Jenny squirmed a bit in her chair. "I didn't dump Thad," she muttered, obviously uncomfortable with the blunt term. "When I told him Gavin and I had found each other again and realized we were still in love, Thad graciously bowed out."

"Okay, that's not dumping at all," Stevie said, her tone fondly mocking.

Jenny sighed. "Still, point taken. I've crossed paths with Thad a couple times in the past six months and we've been perfectly civil, but I can't deny it was awkward. I can't imagine spending eight hours a day with him now that I'm happily married to Gavin."

Jenny wasn't just happily married, she was blissfully married, Tess thought with a touch of wistfulness. Jenny would always fret about the dangers in Gavin's job, just as he occasionally became frustrated with the long hours her popular fashion boutiques required of her, but they were crazy in love.

"So even though you turned down a practical business-based marriage in favor of true love for yourself, you think this would be a good idea for Tess?" Stevie challenged.

Jenny tossed back her layered dark hair and lifted her chin in a familiar pose of obstinacy. "All I said was that maybe she should at least consider the possibility. And it wouldn't be such a bad idea for Tess to examine her feelings for Scott. It's not as if you and I haven't wondered—"

Stevie cleared her throat loudly, but not before Tess figured out exactly where that statement had been headed. "The two of you have talked about my feelings for Scott?"

With a chiding look at Jenny, Stevie sighed. "Okay, maybe it's crossed our minds that your total devotion to Scott isn't entirely due to employee loyalty. But we both know you'd never overstep any professional lines," she said hastily. "You've risen in the ranks of his company because you're damned good at your job—irreplaceable, really—and everyone knows it. You've always insisted you had no romantic feelings for Scott, but I couldn't help thinking sometimes you were denying those feelings even to yourself.

"It's not like I've made a secret of my suspicions," she added with a touch of defensiveness. "I've asked you several times if you've been so picky about the men you've dated lately because you've compared them to His Highness and they've all come up short. I just don't want you to get hurt if it should turn out his feelings aren't the same as yours."

Tess felt her cheeks warm. She had to concede Stevie had quizzed her about Scott on more than one occasion, and each time she'd laughed and brushed off the questions. "I wasn't comparing other men to Scott."

"Not consciously, maybe, but subconsciously?"

"We are not getting into amateur psychoanalysis hour," Tess grumbled into her teacup.

Jenny crossed her ankles and settled more comfortably into her chair. "You have to admit Scott has quite a few qualities you would naturally look for in a mate. Let's face it, if you didn't work for him and you met him online, you'd think he was exactly what you're looking for."

Tess looped a strand of her hair idly around one finger. "A workaholic confirmed bachelor with a noted weakness for busty blondes? Really?"

Jenny shrugged. "Obviously he's not that confirmed a bachelor if he's actively contemplating marriage and children. And he's never married any of the busty blondes he dated, so maybe it's not such a weakness after all."

"He did propose to one." With a slight scowl, Tess pictured the stunningly beautiful almost Mrs. Prince. Sharon had always been perfectly civil to Tess, though she'd had a subtle way of making it clear that as valuable as Tess might be to Scott in the office, he belonged to her after hours. Tess had never wanted to believe she'd thrown herself into an ill-fated romance of her own at about that same time as a reaction to Scott's engagement—but there had been times in the past couple years when she'd wondered...

Jenny made a face. "And his engagement lasted all of—what?—five months?"

"Four." Her own failed romance hadn't even made it that long before it crashed and burned, a year or so before she'd met Jenny and Stevie. James had accused her of always putting her job ahead of him, and he'd been jealous of her relationship with Scott, though she'd assured him repeatedly that there had never been anything personal between her and her employer.

Jenny gave a hint of a righteous smile. "So there you go. After realizing said busty blonde was the wrong match for him, he started thinking about a right match... and maybe he finally realized she'd been right in front of him for a long time. Is that so hard to believe?"

"What is easier to believe is that my newlywed friend is seeing everything through romance-tinted filters these days," Tess replied indulgently to Jenny. "It's very sweet, but..."

"*Was* there any romance to Scott's proposition?" Stevie cut in to ask.

"Not an iota," Tess answered, and though she'd tried

for wry humor, she was aware her tone came across more as grumpy. "Unless you consider 'we make a hell of a team' a passionate declaration."

"Not so much," Stevie said with a sigh. "Not even a kiss, huh?"

Tess took a too-hasty sip of her tea that made her cough. By the time she caught her breath again, both her friends were studying her much too closely.

Stevie leaned forward. "There *was* a kiss?"

"Well, yes. Sort of...coincidentally."

Jenny's cup hit the side table with an eager little *thump.* "Oh, this I have to hear. How did he coincidentally kiss you?"

"He, um, thought I'd hung some mistletoe in the office."

Neither of her friends bought that explanation for a moment, as their expressions clearly informed her.

She sighed. "Okay, we knew what we were doing. I guess it was an impulse. Curiosity. Scott called it an experiment. I'm not sure I can explain it completely."

Stevie waved a hand dismissively. "Forget explanations. We want details. How was it?"

"It was nice."

Her friends groaned in unison at the guarded reply.

Stevie cocked her head skeptically. "You're telling me that after six years of being pretty much joined at the hip with that undeniably great-looking guy, you finally kiss him and it's just...nice?"

Jenny tsked her tongue. "I don't believe it. Scott hasn't spent time with all those busty blondes without picking up a few tricks."

The image of Scott picking up kissing tricks from a series of blondes made Tess scowl when she realized just how intensely she disliked the idea. It was difficult to keep believing she wasn't harboring secret feelings for Scott when just the thought of him kissing another woman caused a knot to form in her stomach.

"Well?" Jenny teased. "Was it good?"

"It was better than good," she conceded with a sigh. "The man knows how to kiss. No surprise, I guess, since he's so successful at everything he does."

"Except finding a bride," Stevie added pointedly.

"That remains to be seen," Jenny murmured.

Tess made a sound like a strangled growl. "Can someone remind me why I thought it was a good idea to consult with you two about this?"

"Because we're your best friends and we love you," Stevie replied immediately. "Even if Jen and I don't necessarily agree on everything, we absolutely want what's best for you."

Tess could hardly continue to pout after that. "That is why I called you. I just needed to talk this through while I decide how to answer him."

"You didn't mention any of this to your sister?" Jenny looked as though she already knew the answer, but asked just for confirmation.

"I wish Nina and I had the kind of relationship that would make me feel comfortable discussing this sort of thing with her, but we just don't. I don't know if it's because of the age gap or her preoccupation with her family and her schedule, or maybe we're just too different to fully understand each other, but I don't think she'd be of any help at all with this."

Nina would probably tell her to stop waffling and latch on to this eligible bachelor before he got away, perhaps adding that it wasn't as if Tess could count on any other offers. Tess bit her lip as she could almost hear the words in her sister's blunt voice—or was that her own insecurity whispering at the back of her mind?

"It really is a shame you and Nina aren't closer. I always wanted a sister, myself," Jenny mused with regret. "I thought I'd missed out on something, being an only child. I was lucky enough to meet Stevie in high school, and she filled a big gap for me."

"That goes both ways," Stevie assured her. "I love my brother, but I certainly can't talk to him about relationship issues."

"And I'm lucky to have you both in my life now," Tess assured them, then quickly waved a hand. "That's enough of the sappy talk or we'll all end up sniffling. So I'm ready for advice. Stevie?"

Uncharacteristically somber, Stevie took her time deliberating her response. "I'd be wary," she said after a moment. "You and Scott work together so well, and you love your job so much. I'd hate for what could turn out to be an impulsive mistake to change everything for you."

"Jenny?"

Jenny shrugged. "As I've already said, I think it could be worth considering. You and Scott are mature adults with a great deal in common. You both know the personal and professional risks you'd be taking, so maybe you could take steps to minimize repercussions if it doesn't work out. Yes, it's a gamble, but isn't every relationship, in some way?"

Any other time, Tess might have been amused at the role reversal from her friends. Reckless Stevie advising prudence, practical Jenny encouraging a romantic gamble. Tess couldn't help wondering if the turnaround could be attributed to the state of her friends' own relationships—Jenny was so happy in her new marriage, whereas Stevie had been involved for some time with a moody musician who'd been spending increasingly more time with his moderately successful local band than with her. Tess and Jenny had worried lately that Joe was growing restless, perhaps even beginning to stray. Both suspected Stevie secretly echoed their concerns. Tess had never truly believed Stevie and Joe shared the kind of commitment that would last a lifetime, but Stevie always gave everything she had to making her relationships work, even when it became obvious to others that her efforts would ultimately fail. She was always so optimistic—which made Tess even more nervous that Stevie was the one urging caution.

"So what are you going to tell Scott?" Stevie asked.

Tess spread her hands in confusion. "I have no idea."

"And we haven't helped much, have we?" Jenny asked ruefully. "With our completely opposite advice."

"You've helped tremendously. You've listened without judgment while I expressed my concerns. I'll think about everything you've both said while I make up my mind."

"If you need to talk any more, you know where to find us," Stevie offered.

"I know. Thanks. And now, how about if we table this topic for a while and maybe order take-out?"

"I'd love to, but I can't stay," Jenny said with a glance at her watch. "Gavin has the night off and we're having a date night. We might even see a movie. In a theater. With popcorn and everything."

Knowing how rare a free evening was for them, Tess smiled. "Good for you. Stevie?"

"Sorry. I'm out, too. I promised Joe I'd drive him and his band mates to the airport this evening. They're catching a late flight to Austin for a gig there."

Tess and Jenny exchanged quick glances. Stevie spent a lot of time as an unpaid assistant for her boyfriend's alternative rock band, Eleven Twenty-Five. As busy as she was with her own kitchen design business, she still spent hours making calls for the band, dealing with printers and club owners, hauling supplies in her SUV, making flight arrangements. Tess wasn't entirely sure what Stevie received in return. But because it was none of her business and Stevie hadn't asked for advice, she kept her mouth shut. "Another time, then."

"Soon," Stevie promised. She jumped to her feet, tossed back her curls and carried her teacup toward the kitchen, looking suddenly restless. "I'd better get going. I promised Cole I'd feed his cat while he's out of town."

Cole McKellar was Stevie's next-door neighbor, a quiet widower who sometimes helped Stevie with home maintenance in exchange for occasional cat-sitting. Tess hadn't met him, but Stevie always spoke fondly of him. It was part of Stevie's charm, as well as her weakness, that she liked almost everyone, and she had a near compulsive desire to take care of her friends. She stopped to give Tess a quick hug on her way out. "Seriously, call if you want to talk more. I'm always available as a sounding board."

"Same here," Jenny seconded as she prepared to follow Stevie out. "We're here for you, pal."

Smiling broadly, Tess locked the door behind them. Her smile faded as it occurred to her that an entire Sunday evening of solitude stretched in front of her now that her friends had rushed off to be with their significant others. Maybe she'd do a little Christmas decorating of her own place.

Not much was going on this last day of the long holiday weekend. Her sister had invited her for dinner, but she'd begged off, having endured enough nagging this week. Usually Tess enjoyed an evening to herself with nothing to do but lose herself in a good book or catch up on TV shows she'd recorded. Tonight she felt too antsy to relax, too aware of the silence in her condo. There were too few distractions from her convoluted thoughts, and she was no closer to a decision now than she'd been before her friends had arrived.

As she retrieved her small artificial Christmas tree from the storage room attached to her condo's little balcony, she had to face the fact that neither Jenny nor Stevie could really help her with her personal problem. Sure, they could offer suggestions, advice—even differing opinions, as it turned out. Yet she was the one who was going to have to decide whether to take Scott up on his offer to explore new possibilities in their relationship or remain on the same safe, comfortable path they'd walked for the past six-plus years.

She'd never been a risk taker. The dutiful, responsible younger daughter—she'd always been so cautious, so careful. How could she possibly foresee all the potential pitfalls this time, when it affected every aspect of her future—her social life, her career…and maybe even her so-far-unbroken heart?

After the long weekend, the Monday workday hit the floor running. Phones were already ringing when Tess walked into the office, and the buzzing, beeping and bustling continued for hours. Before two o'clock she'd dealt with one panicky client, two surly vendors, three frantic contractors and a clerical job applicant who could barely articulate around the wad of gum in her mouth. Mentally marking that name off the list of potential employees, she sat back and drew a long breath. It felt almost like the first chance she'd had to breathe since she'd arrived almost six hours earlier.

At least she hadn't had to worry about what to say to Scott. He'd been in meetings and phone conferences all day, and she'd seen him only for a brief consultation about a business issue. There'd been no time for personal conversation, nor even for awkward pauses. Today had been all about work, catching up and looking ahead. As she'd assured her friends, compartmentalizing wasn't really that difficult for her and Scott. When they were in the office, nothing was more important to them than taking care of business.

As if in response to her thoughts, he stuck his head in the open doorway to her office. "What's Art Connolly's wife's name?"

"Debbie. And their son is Art Jr., but they call him Buzz."

"Debbie. Buzz. Got it. Heading out for the meeting. Shoot me a text if you need anything."

"Okay. Have a good—" But he was gone before she could finish the sentiment.

Her mouth twisted in a wry smile. If nothing else had demonstrated how efficiently Scott could put their Saturday-evening conversation out of his mind, that little exchange would have done the trick. There had been nothing at all personal in his tone or expression, no meeting of eyes, no more warmth in his voice than she heard when he spoke with the receptionist on his way out. She couldn't imagine any observer would even suspect that less than forty-eight hours earlier, Scott had all but asked her outright to consider having his children.

Had their conversation even crossed his mind this morning? Despite how busy she'd been, it had hovered constantly at the back of hers. Did that mean they were already unevenly invested in this looming decision? Was it really of little import to him if she accepted his offer or politely declined? Was he less concerned about the repercussions—maybe because he didn't believe he would be as deeply affected in the long run? Had he changed his mind, had later misgivings about his impulsive suggestions, or was he really too wrapped up in business today to give anything else a second thought?

"Um, Tess?"

Blinking, she glanced toward the doorway to find a heavily pregnant young woman standing there studying her with a slight frown. She got the distinct impression it wasn't the first time her name had been spoken. "I'm sorry, Heather, I was distracted. What can I do for you?"

"The next applicant for my job is here for her interview. And I wanted to remind you I'm leaving a little early today for a doctor's appointment."

Tess nodded. "I remember. I hope it goes well."

At almost eight months along, Heather had recently given notice that she would not be returning after her delivery. Now Tess was hiring a replacement.

"The applicant's name is Sofia Vasquez. She seems very nice—and she's not chewing gum," Heather added with a wink.

Tess laughed. "Good to hear."

"I'll send her in. And unless you need anything more from me, I'll see you tomorrow."

Tess couldn't help smiling as she watched Heather retreat in her pregnancy waddle. Which reminded her, she needed to pick up a gift for the office baby shower scheduled for tomorrow afternoon. She should have taken care of that already, but she'd been so busy lately.

Putting thoughts of tiny sleepers and pastel blankets out of her mind, she stood with a professional smile to greet the job applicant entering her doorway.

As was so often the case, Tess was the last person remaining in the offices that evening, well after darkness had fallen. She'd just completed the hiring of Sofia Vasquez, and sat back in her chair with a weary sigh. It had been a long day, with only a twenty-minute respite for a quick salad in the break room, and she was tired to her toes.

She cleared her desk and pulled out her phone, doing a quick check of her personal email before calling it a day. She frowned when she saw an evite to her cousin's holiday party. It was addressed to "Tess and guest," and she was expected to RSVP. She would deal with that later, she decided. It was after six, and she was ready to hole up at home with pj's and tea. Slinging the strap of her bag over her shoulder, she grabbed her coat and headed for the break room to retrieve her salad container.

Now, of course, she was reminded again about Scott's offer to accompany her to her holiday affairs. There certainly hadn't been time during the past couple of hours to think about his proposition—not much anyway. Scott wasn't the only one who could compartmentalize, she thought in satisfaction. And if he'd changed his mind, fine. They could agree to pretend the conversation had never taken place. After a few days, she probably wouldn't give it another thought.

"Yeah, right," she muttered, thinking she'd never convince her concerned friends if she couldn't even believe it herself.

Impatient with her own dithering, she collected her plastic salad container from the drying rack next to the sink. With big windows looking out over the now-dark river, the break room had been decorated by the office staff. Normally, Tess's spirits would have been lifted by the sight of the silly stuffed reindeer grinning from the top of the microwave, but she had too much on her mind this evening. Gripping her salad dish, she turned toward the door. She jerked to a stop when she saw someone standing there.

"Scott," she said when she caught her breath again. "I didn't hear you come in."

Leaning casually against the doorway, he smiled. "Seems as if that's becoming a pattern. And do I have to point out again that the security system isn't on?"

"Give me a break, everyone just left. I'm on the way out myself."

"Crazy day, huh?"

"Very." She filled him in on the new hire.

Scott nodded. For the past couple of years he'd given her free rein for hiring and supervising the office staff. She often joked that her official title should have several "slashes" in it—office manager/human resources director/customer service representative/personal assistant to the boss. While she enjoyed the variety of her duties, the challenge was doing them all well, a feat she thought she managed most days.

"I'm sure you made the right choice," he said. "Oh, and we got the Kilgo job today."

"Congratulations. I know you and Andy put a lot of hours into that bid." Andy Staples was one of the project managers, an architect who'd been with the firm from the beginning. If Tess thought of herself as Scott's right-hand woman within the home office, Andy was definitely Scott's second in command everywhere else.

"Yeah. We're both excited about the project. So you were about to leave for the day?"

Because she was wearing her coat and holding her purse and empty lunch dish, the answer seemed obvious, but she nodded. "Yes. Do you need anything before I go?"

"Want to have an early dinner somewhere? Talk awhile?"

His smile and the gleam in his navy eyes took her aback. That quickly, he'd transformed from work associate to would-be suitor. Was he really able to separate the professional from the personal that easily, or was he just that much better at masking his thoughts and feelings when he was in work mode?

"I, um—" It took her a bit longer to make the switch. "I have to stop by a baby-supplies store. We're having Heather's shower tomorrow afternoon and I haven't had a chance to get anything for her. So maybe we should—"

"Stop by there together," he finished for her. "I haven't gotten anything for her, either."

She blinked. "You want to go baby shower shopping together?"

"Well, there are things I'd rather do," he replied candidly. "But you need a gift and so do I, so it makes sense for us to go together, right?"

She bit her lip. She wasn't sure she knew what made sense anymore.

The phone in her hand beeped and she glanced down at the screen. Her sister had sent a text unnecessarily alerting her that cousin Dana's party invitations had gone out. Nina had also felt the need to remind her that Awkward Orthodontist was still available as a potential escort—though not in those exact words, of course.

Tess sighed, then glanced up at the doorway where her good-looking employer stood smiling at her. "Okay, fine. Let's go buy something cute and fuzzy," she said more gruffly than she'd intended.

His eyebrows rose and his smile turned a bit quizzical, but he merely nodded and moved out of the doorway, motioning for her to precede him.

Chapter Four

Had they done this even a week earlier, Tess thought it wouldn't have felt at all odd to walk into the baby store with Scott to find gifts for their coworker. Well, not very odd anyway. But now the comfortably established camaraderie that had previous existed between them had changed. Permanently? That remained to be seen.

She and Scott paused in the baby furniture aisle, their heads close together as she scrolled through the baby registry on her smartphone, showing him the check marks that indicated items already purchased by others.

"There's not a lot left," she said with a self-censuring frown. "I should have taken care of this sooner."

Scott glanced up from the phone screen to study her face. "That's not like you. You're usually ahead of schedule on stuff like this."

She gave a little shrug. "I guess it was Freudian," she

said lightly. "As happy as I am for Heather, I hate the thought of her leaving us. I'll miss her."

She didn't want to think there'd been an even deeper emotional reason she had been reluctant to peruse catalogs of baby supplies.

Before Scott could respond, a young man in a store uniform paused near them. "Can I help you find anything?" he asked cheerily. "Do you need help setting up a registry?"

"Oh, no, we're not—" Tess stopped her automatic and completely unnecessarily explanation with a slight grimace. "I mean, we don't need help right now. Thank you."

The young man moved on and Tess focused more intently on the list, avoiding Scott's eyes. "There are still a few nice things left. I'm sure we can each find something."

"Maybe we could go in together on a gift?"

Picturing someone reading aloud a card that said, "From Tess and Scott," she cleared her throat. "Maybe we'll just each buy our own."

She heard the amusement in Scott's voice when he said, "Or that. What should I get?"

She pointed to the screen. "No one's bought this fancy baby monitor set yet. That's about what you usually spend for this sort of thing."

"And no one would know that better than you," he murmured with a smile. "Okay, so I'll get the monitor. That was easy enough. What are you getting?"

"I don't know yet." She scooted past a giddy young couple who appeared to be choosing items for their own registry, so absorbed in the colorful displays that they didn't realize they were blocking an aisle. Tess couldn't really be annoyed with them; they looked so excited and eager, and they apologized sheepishly when they realized they were in her way.

She moved down an aisle, idly touching one cute little item after another, looking for something that spoke to her of Heather. Heather and her husband had chosen a nautical theme in navy, red and taupe. According to the registry, the bedding items had all been purchased, but the coordinating laundry hamper and changing table cover were still available. She chewed her lower lip as she debated between the two.

"Not exactly an exciting choice, is it?" Scott asked as he eyed the options. "A laundry hamper?"

"They're things Heather wants. That's all that matters. I'll get the hamper. But I'm going to get a nice little outfit to go with it," she added with a decisive nod. "Something not on the list for a surprise."

"Excuse me?"

In response to the voice, Tess glanced around to find an older, silver-haired woman eying Scott with an oddly assessing expression.

Scott smiled at the woman. "Yes, ma'am?" he asked, instinctively displaying the manners his Southern mother had drilled into him.

"Do you mind if I ask how tall you are?"

With a quick, amused glance toward Tess, Scott replied politely to the diminutive senior citizen. "I'm six-one. Do you need help reaching something?"

"No. I need you to stand right here by these strollers and tell me which one would be more comfortable for you to push. My grandson is about your height, and his wife's expecting. I'm here to buy them a stroller, but

I want to make sure the handle is high enough for my grandson to push comfortably."

"I think most of them are adjustable," he explained, reminding Tess of his familiarity with his young nieces and nephew. "There's usually a button to push to raise or lower the handle."

The woman still wanted him to pose with a couple of strollers, just so she could "get a mental picture" of her grandson with her ultimate choice. Obliging, Scott took down the display models the woman indicated, then stood behind each one. His mouth quirked into a wry smile, he waited patiently while she studied him from all angles. She narrowed her choices down to two, had him stand behind each for another look, then pointed. "I think I like that one best."

"That's the one I'd have picked, too," Scott assured her as he hoisted the display model back onto its shelf. Having enjoyed the entire encounter from close by, Tess couldn't help but admire his gracefully strong movements.

"Really?" His new friend beamed in pleasure. "Is that the same stroller you two are buying for your little one?"

Tess's smile faded. "We're shopping for a friend's baby shower," she blurted.

"Oh. Well, I'm sure you'll choose something nice. Thank you, young man," she said over her shoulder as she bustled toward the customer service desk. "I appreciate your help."

"You're very welcome," Scott called after her before turning back to Tess. "Well, that was interesting."

Ready to get out of this baby-obsessed place, Tess grabbed the hamper, then marched over to the clothing section with Scott behind her. Flipping through the outfits, she selected a three-piece set consisting of a red snap-bottom shirt, navy pull-on knit pants and a navy-and-white-striped hoodie with an embroidered sailboat. It was cute and looked comfortable, and it worked well with the nautical theme. "This will do. I'm ready to check out now."

They paid at separate registers for their purchases, then headed for the door almost at the same time. Still, she was a good three steps ahead of Scott when they reached their cars, which were parked side by side in the lot.

"Were we racing?" he asked ironically when he caught up. "If so, you win."

"Sorry," she muttered. A night breeze blew steadily against her face, but didn't seem to cool her overly warm cheeks. She couldn't have explained why she felt so uncharacteristically awkward and foolish all of a sudden. She hated this feeling of being not quite in control.

He took a step closer to her. The parking lot was well lit with tall security lamps decorated with holiday wreaths, but his eyes were shadowed from the light behind him. She couldn't quite read his expression. Still, she could see he wasn't smiling now.

He touched her arm. Even through the fabric of her coat and clothing she was intensely aware of that point of contact between them. She hoped he attributed her shiver to the weather.

"Tess, you've been tense and jumpy ever since I came back to the office. I'm guessing you're trying to figure out how to tell me you aren't interested in the suggestion I made the other night. I don't know if you're afraid of hurting my feelings or worried that I'll be upset with you or what, but really, you can relax. I promised I wouldn't let your answer affect our working relationship—or our friendship—and I'm standing by that promise."

A brisk gust of cold wind whipped a strand of hair out of her loose updo and into her eyes. She reached up to push it back. Were they truly going to have this conversation in a parking lot?

"We can get past this, right?" he asked quietly, the question barely audible over the drone of passing cars and the voices of shoppers milling in the lot around them. "We'll be okay?"

She moistened her chilled, dry lips. "Actually, you've completed misinterpreted why I'm so nervous tonight," she said. "I'm not trying to figure out how to turn you down, Scott. I'm trying to find the courage to tell you I'm willing to give it a try."

It wasn't often she saw Scott startled into immobility. She thought maybe she was viewing it now, as he went very still, his hand unmoving on her arm. After a moment, he said, "So it's a yes?"

She took a leap of faith and nodded. "Yes."

A car cruised past them in search of a parking space, bone-vibrating bass booming from the interior as the passengers gambled deafness in favor of volume. Roused into recognition of their surroundings, Scott glanced around with a grimace. "So…dinner?"

She nodded again. It was too late to bolt in panic now, she reminded herself, though she had to admit the thought occurred to her.

They dined at a barbecue restaurant within view of the baby store. First pizza and then barbecue, Scott thought after they were seated in the casual, noisy dining room. He made a mental note to take her someplace nice soon, now that they were dating…or whatever it was they were doing. For now he was aware of a deep sense of satisfaction that she'd decided his brainstorm wasn't so crazy after all.

Because it seemed to calm her, he kept the dinner conversation light and primarily centered on work. They discussed the new employee she'd hired, and he shared his enthusiasm for the apartment complex project he'd contracted that day. Though a bit quiet at first, Tess was soon chatting easily enough, helping him plan ahead for the holidays that always played havoc with schedules. Every year it seemed they ran into delays and shortages between the first of December and New Year's Day, whether because of vacations or weather or a half dozen other seasonal issues.

This was their strength, he reminded himself. Their common ground. He didn't have to try to woo her or put on a calculatedly romantic facade for her. He could simply be himself, which only confirmed his belief that they were uniquely suited as a match. Pushing his luck a bit, he took advantage of her more relaxed mood to say, "There's that thing Thursday night. The Holiday Open Home party."

He knew he didn't have to be more specific. His company had participated in the Holiday Open Home fund-raiser for the past five years. Each year, one of the area's most luxurious homes was lavishly outfitted for the holidays with donations from local builders and decorators. Tours were conducted during the first three weekends of December, with all the receipts given to a local women's shelter. In return for a monetary donation, Scott's company was listed in the publicity material. The event's organizers always hosted a cocktail party for donors on Thursday evening before the tours began on the first Friday. The gathering was covered by the media and attended by the professionals who considered the event part of their annual advertising and charitable budget.

The parties were usually rather dull, but Scott figured it was good to be seen at them, so he tried to make a regular appearance. Because Tess was in charge of the firm's charitable donations, she was always invited to the cocktail party by the organizers. It occurred to him only then that though she'd probably been invited to bring a guest, as he was, she'd always attended on her own. He wasn't sure why, unless she'd considered the event strictly business.

She toyed with a forkful of coleslaw. "Yes, I remember."

"Why don't I pick you up and we can go together?" It seemed like a good opportunity to make their debut as a couple. Their business associates could become accustomed to seeing them together outside the office so that it wouldn't cause quite such a stir when they made it clear their relationship had moved beyond professional.

"We won't be making any announcements about our personal plans or anything like that," he assured her when she didn't immediately respond. "Just attending together. You know, sort of kicking off the season."

She nodded. "All right. We'll go together."

He chuckled drily. "It's a party, Tess, not a tax audit."

A quick, rueful laugh lit her eyes and curved her lips. She had such a very nice mouth. Full and soft, perfectly shaped. He found himself transfixed by her lips now, remembering the feel of them against his. The taste of them.

"I was somewhat less than gracious, wasn't I?" she acknowledged apologetically. "I'm sorry, it isn't that I don't want to go with you. I'm probably just overthinking things. You know how I get."

"Having second thoughts?"

"No." Her answer was immediate and steady. "I've considered everything you said and it makes sense to me. We do make a good team."

"We always have," he agreed with a surge of satisfaction.

"And it will be nice to have you with me at some of the events I have to attend in the next few weeks. I can't wait to see my sister's face when she sees you at the parties with me," she added, almost as if to herself. "I dare her to find anything to criticize about you."

He was a bit taken aback by the glint in her amber eyes. Maybe she'd intended that as a compliment? But he wasn't sure he wanted to be used as a pawn in some sort of battle of wills between Tess and her sister. He was trying to decide how to broach the subject when someone called his name from nearby. "Hey, Scott, thought that was you. How's it going?"

He glanced up to nod warmly at the couple who paused beside him. An old friend of Eli's, Bryan Crawford, held a towheaded toddler on one hip while his wife, Jessica, held the little boy's golden-blond older sister by one hand. "Hi, Bryan. Jessica. Nice to see you both."

"This is a coincidence," Bryan said with a broad grin spread over his ruddy face. "We just saw Eli and Libby an hour ago. We were all attending an open house at the girls' preschool. Your nieces are growing fast, aren't they?"

"They are. It's been a while since I've seen you, Bryan."

The other man chuckled and ruffled the hair of the drowsy boy he held. "Yeah, I haven't had much time for pickup basketball games lately. You know how it is once you have kids, always something on their schedule."

Jessica rolled her eyes with a weary bark of a laugh. "Now, how would Scott know about that, honey? He's the carefree bachelor in the Prince family, remember? Libby says he's too busy running that company of his to settle down and chase after a couple of kids." As if on cue, their daughter, who was the same age as Scott's nieces, whined and tugged impatiently at her mother's hand.

"Yeah, lucky guy," Bryan said with a grin, but the way he patted his son's back made it clear he wouldn't change places with the "carefree bachelor."

His smile feeling a bit strained, Scott motioned toward Tess, who was sitting very quietly watching the exchange. "Bryan and Jessica Crawford, this is my friend, Tess Miller."

He very deliberately neglected to mention their work relationship. This was the start of their new phase. Step one of what he was beginning to think of as his marriage plan was successfully under way. Tess was willing to give it a try. Which meant this evening was officially a date, not a business dinner.

Neither looking surprised to have found him dining with an attractive woman, the Crawfords murmured their polite "nice to meet yous," then gave in to their daughter's increasingly insistent urgings and made their exit. The toddler waved bye-bye over his dad's shoulder, making Scott chuckle and wave back.

"Cute kids," Tess said, drawing his attention back to her.

"Bryan's an old friend of Eli's. His daughter's in school with the twins, at Miss Bitty's. I think Libby had the girls on a waiting list for the place while she was still pregnant with them."

"I've heard of it. It's supposed to be one of the best. I know my sister looked into it when her oldest was a toddler, but it was too expensive for them then. She didn't want to admit that, so she just told everyone it wasn't her favorite option."

Was that another little dig at her sister? As close as he was with his own clan, it bothered him to think about Tess being estranged from the only immediate family she had left. From what he'd heard her say on the phone, it sounded as though Nina's nagging was most of the problem. So if his presence at the parties helped alleviate that problem, then maybe he didn't mind so much after all. Wasn't mutual benefit the whole point of this dating experiment?

"So," he said, "we're on for Thursday night, right?"

She gave him a too-bright smile. "Yes. We're on."

"Great." Personal business out of the way, he turned his attention back to business. "Now, about those meetings tomorrow…"

Twenty minutes later, he walked her to her car. Their breath hung in the air as they continued the work-related conversation they'd started inside, finishing up with a list of tasks he wanted completed the next day.

"I'll have Heather and Lynne start on those things in the morning," Tess agreed with a brisk nod, drawing her coat more closely around her against the chilly night air. "They should be able to finish most of it before the baby shower at four. I'll make sure your office is set up for the ten o'clock meeting, and the conference room upstairs for the one thirty. You should have plenty of time between meetings for that lunch with Garvey and Hannity."

It occurred to him that she was so confident, so at ease with him when they spoke of work, in marked contrast to the hesitation she showed when they veered into their new personal arrangement. Of course, she'd had several years to grow comfortable with him in the business setting; he supposed it would take a little practice in this new arena. And because there was no time like the present to begin…

He caught her arm as she reached for her car door. When she looked up at him, he lowered his head to brush his mouth against hers. "Your lips are cold," he said, smiling against them. "Maybe I should warm them up for you before you leave."

"That would be considerate of you," she murmured, and tilted her head into a more accessible position.

With a muffled chuckle, he kissed her. After only a heartbeat's hesitation, she was a willing and eager participant in the embrace.

His powerful reaction to their kiss in the office Saturday evening had caught him by surprise. He'd tried shrugging it off as first-time novelty, though technically it hadn't been a first kiss between them, if he counted that embarrassing, medication-fueled buss after his surgery. He decided not to count that one.

He'd tried blaming mistletoe, even though Tess had assured him there hadn't actually been any in the office. He'd even wondered if maybe he'd exaggerated the kiss in his memories, that maybe it hadn't been quite as spectacular as he remembered. He knew now that he had not. Kissing Tess felt so damned good that he had to ask himself now what had taken them so long.

Only his awareness of their very public surroundings made him draw back reluctantly when he would have liked very much to deepen the kiss. He opened her car door for her and then moved back to watch her slide in. Even as they said their good-nights, he was tempted to ask her to come home with him for coffee—but maybe it was a bit too soon for that.

Step one, he reminded himself while he watched her drive away. He climbed into his own car with a mixture of frustration and satisfaction with the way the evening had gone. They'd get to step two when the time was right.

"I don't know." Tess craned her neck to study her back view in the full-length mirror. "Does it seem a little tight to you?"

Jenny and Stevie answered in unison. "No."

A bold red sheath, the dress was closely fitted to her body, ending in a flirty double kick pleat just behind her knees. It wasn't overtly revealing, just brighter and snugger than her typical outfits.

"Your butt looks amazing in that," Stevie said bluntly. "I wish I could wear it, but that bateau neckline would never work with my boobs."

Tess's gaze was drawn to the reflection of her bust. The dress was definitely flattering there. As the least endowed of the trio, she couldn't help but push her shoulders back and pose a bit, making her friends laugh.

It was Wednesday evening and they had gathered in Jenny's fashion and accessories boutique, Complements. The store closed at seven on weeknights, staying open until nine Fridays and Saturdays, so Tess and Stevie often met there after-hours on Wednesdays to play in Jenny's new deliveries. They'd even been known to pitch in hanging up garments and setting up displays, mostly because they had fun doing so.

Tonight both Tess and Stevie were looking for outfits to wear to the Holiday Open Home cocktail party the next night. Stevie was attending as one of the donors; she'd been selected this year to design and oversee the kitchen update. It was for a good cause, not to mention she'd make the most of the professional exposure.

They stood in the dressing room area where several cushy benches were grouped around a large, full-length, three-way mirror. Six stalls with floral curtains for privacy surrounded them, but since they were the only ones in the store, they weren't overly concerned with modesty.

"The color is amazing on you, Tess," Jenny assured her. "I told you it would be."

Tess had worried that the red wouldn't go well with her auburn hair, but she should have known to trust Jenny's eye. "It does look festive without being too Christmassy. Not too splashy for the event?"

"You know what those things are like." Jenny waved a dismissive hand. "There will be people there in designer silks and others in jeans. If Sandy's there she'll have on a few strips of cloth and a boatload of diamonds. Trust me, this dress is exactly right for a charity holiday cocktail party."

Tess bit her lip against a grin at the description of their mutual acquaintance's fashion tastes. A notorious man-eater, Sandy had once made a fairly blatant play for Gavin. Not that he'd had eyes for anyone but Jenny.

"I'll give you the usual bestie discount," Jenny added persuasively.

"Okay, I'll take it."

Jenny smiled. "Great. And since you're in a buying mood, there's another dress I want you to try on. I think it's perfect for you, maybe for your cousin's party."

"I'm sure I already have something that will work for that."

But Jenny was already headed out to the showroom, saying over her shoulder, "Just try it, okay?"

"And that," Stevie said with a giggle, "is why Jenny now has two successful stores in the state and is considering a third."

"She is good," Tess admitted with a shake of her head. Twisting to admire the red dress once more in the mirror—her butt really did look good—she asked absently, "Aren't you going to try things on?"

"Oh, yeah, sure." Stevie turned toward one of the stalls. "Jenny hung some things in here that she thought I'd like. I just wanted to see that red dress on you first. I knew it would be amazing."

"It is pretty, isn't it?"

"You'll knock Scott off his feet," Stevie remarked through the open doorway to the stall, her voice muffled as if she were pulling her shirt over her head.

Tess's hand froze on the side zipper of the dress. She moistened her lips. Yes, she'd wanted something nice to wear to the event, and she'd been pleased that the dress had suited her so well, but she didn't want to look as though she was making any special effort to knock Scott off his feet. She turned when Jenny returned with a green garment draped over her arm. "Does this look like I'm trying too hard?"

Jenny sighed gustily. They were close enough friends that she understood the question immediately. "No," she said firmly. "Looking nice and appropriate for an event—even looking as beautiful as you do in that dress—is not trying too hard. It's simply putting your best foot forward."

Stevie stepped out of the stall wearing a filmy black dress shot through with silver threads. The skirt fit snugly at her hips, then flared out around her knees. She did a little spin and the hem swirled around her.

Tess nodded. "Pretty."

Shorter and curvier than her friends, Stevie's blond curls and large blue eyes made her look younger than her thirty-one years. She tended to be a more bohemian dresser, so Tess wasn't particularly surprised when her friend looked in the mirror, then made a little face at the reflection. "I don't know. Maybe."

"No." Jenny thrust the green dress at Tess. "Try this on while I help Stevie find something that suits her better."

"Yes, ma'am."

Stepping into the stall, Tess changed into the dress Jenny had brought her. A rich, dark green, it was another body skimmer, ending well above her knees to make the most of her legs without being too short for comfort. The neckline was a deep scoop outlined with a thin line of gold fish-scale sequins, just enough to add a little holiday sparkle.

It was a wholly impractical purchase, of course. Like the red cocktail dress, it would be something she'd wear only a few times. It was kind of hard to justify buying two party dresses at one time, but she loved them both.

"Gold earrings," Jenny said appraisingly from the open doorway. "Thin black tights and those high-heeled booties I sold you in the fall."

"You're killing me."

Her friend laughed without compunction. "Every girl needs to splurge occasionally. Especially when she's seeing a new guy."

Tess groaned. "Come on, Jen. Scott is hardly a new guy."

"He is when it comes to your social life." Jenny winked. "And I'm going to help you make sure he sees you as more than his trusty office sidekick."

Warmth flooded Tess's face, but she couldn't help glancing once again at the mirror. She did look different dressed this way.

"Okay, I like this one." Stevie danced into view in a short rose silk dress with a filmy mesh overlay. Gray beads and sequins were worked into an overall art deco–inspired pattern on the mesh, which ended in a beaded, scalloped hem. "I feel like a flapper. Makes me want to do the Charleston."

"T-strap shoes. Silver bracelets." Jenny nodded as if it was all decided. "Do your hair in that little twist off the face I like so much."

"Do you know how to Charleston?" Tess asked curiously.

Stevie laughed. "Not a clue. But it would be fun to learn, wouldn't it?" She glanced in the mirror again. "Sold."

Tess laughed. "Hooray for bestie discounts!" she

cheered as she went in to change out of the green dress
that would be accompanying her home.

When she carried her purchases into the glittering,
holiday-decorated showroom, Stevie was already paying for her choice and looking forward to wearing it at
the charity event.

"I hope I'll get some new business," she added. "I
can't wait to show you the kitchen. The updates are gorgeous, if I do say so myself."

"Will Joe be back from Austin in time to attend the
party with you?"

Stevie's smile dimmed noticeably. "No, they're staying a little longer, making some good contacts in the
Austin music scene. Joe thinks they have a nice gig
lined up for next weekend."

"Good for them." Tess resisted an impulse to glance
at Jenny, though she suspected they were both thinking
the same thing—that this was the beginning of the end
of Stevie's relationship with Joe.

Tess had heard all about Stevie's romantic history
during late-night girls-only wine and confidences ses-
sions. She knew her friend had a weakness for musicians, several of whom had broken her tender heart over
the years. Would her heart be broken again, or was Stevie more prepared this time, more guarded?

At least she didn't have to worry about having her
own heart shattered if this experiment with Scott didn't
work out, she told herself. By approaching their relationship logically and cautiously, based on friendship
and mutual goals rather than capricious emotions, they
were protecting themselves against the sort of pain Stevie seemed to continually court with her impetuous
infatuations.

"Well," Jenny said brusquely, breaking into Tess's somber thoughts, "it's Joe's loss that he won't get to see you in this dress, at least not this time."

"That's okay." Stevie's usual glint of mischief lit her eyes as she grinned at Tess. "That'll free me up to spy on Tess and His Highness all evening. After all, Jen, I promised you all the juicy details."

Tess rolled her eyes as Jenny laughed. "There will be nothing to report. We're just going to make an appearance at this thing, do a little networking and schmoozing for the business, then get out of there."

"To go where and do what?" Jenny teased lightly. "Do you and Scott have plans for after the party?"

"We haven't talked about it."

They hadn't actually had an opportunity to talk about anything but business since they'd parted in the parking lot Monday night. The past two days had been one pressing situation after another. Scott hadn't even had a chance to attend the office baby shower yesterday.

Only once had she suspected Scott's thoughts had wandered into personal territory. She'd caught him looking at her lips as she'd stood beside his desk waiting for instructions while he'd listened to a long-winded caller on his phone. Something had told her he was remembering their kisses—which, of course, had sent her thoughts, too, in that direction. Her lips had tingled as she'd instinctively moistened them. His eyes had narrowed and darkened, his expression making her pulse rate jump. She hadn't quite known whether to be relieved or a little disappointed when Andy had rushed into the room with another decision to be made, pushing all private issues aside.

"Has he said anything more about, you know, wanting to have your babies and stuff?" Stevie inquired, a little too artlessly.

Tess gave her friend a chiding look. "It's been a very busy week at work. And honestly, Stevie…"

Stevie shrugged. "You know I'm still concerned that you'll settle for Scott because of all the pressure your sister has been putting on you, and maybe the biological clock thing. I remember that silly, panicky feeling just before I turned thirty. I met Joe not long after that," she added quietly.

Was Stevie acknowledging that Joe had been a "Mr. Right Now" who'd shown up at a time when she was vulnerable? It was what Tess had always believed, but she hadn't thought Stevie was aware of it.

"A lot of people might be surprised to hear you suggest Tess would be 'settling' for Scott Prince," Jenny commented. "You are aware that he's one of this city's most eligible bachelors?"

Waving a hand dismissively, Stevie said shortly, "I'm not denying that Scott's a great catch. I'm just saying Tess deserves more than being a means to an end for a guy who's already accomplished many of his life goals and now wants to check marriage and kids off his list of aspirations."

Both Tess and Jenny stared at Stevie in response to that rather astringent assessment. Tess swallowed past a hard knot in her throat, while Jenny frowned in disapproval. "That was kind of harsh. I can't imagine Scott sees Tess as just a means to an end. I think it's more likely he's realized how lucky he is to have her in his life."

After a moment, Stevie held up both hands in apologetic surrender. "You're right. That was a tacky comment. Sorry, Tess, I certainly didn't mean to imply that Scott wouldn't be damned lucky to have you. I just hope he knows it, that's all."

Tess cleared her throat. "We're just exploring possibilities, Stevie. I haven't even decided what I'm going to do yet."

"Don't listen to me, okay?" Stevie's eyes were suddenly a glittering bright blue, glossed over by unshed tears. "Just have fun and make up your own mind what you want, with or without Scott. I just want you to be happy. I want all my friends to be happy."

Visibly concerned, Jenny moved around the counter to catch Stevie's fluttering hands. "What's going on, Stevie? Is this about Joe?"

Pasting on a semblance of her usual sunny smile, Stevie freed one hand to dash at her eyes and shook her head. "No. I'm fine, really. Just… I don't know, I'm kind of out of it today. I didn't sleep very well last night and I had to get up early this morning to feed Dusty before I left for work. Sorry."

Jenny patted her shoulder. "Of course. Do you need chocolate? I think I have some in my office. PMS is a bitch, am I right?"

Stevie's smile flickered momentarily, but she nodded and laughed cheerily. "You're so right."

Stevie was smiling again, but Tess still had some doubts about her friend's state of mind. Still, she went along with the change of subject. "You're still feeding your neighbor's cat? When is he supposed to be back from his business trip?"

"Tomorrow, thank goodness. Dusty's a sweetheart, and I don't mind sitting with her to keep her company when I have extra time, but I know she misses Cole."

To avoid any further potential pitfalls, they kept the conversation breezy for the short remainder of their visit. They parted on their usual affable terms, agreeing to get together again soon, with Tess and Stevie saying they'd see each other at the Holiday Open Home. Just to make it clear there were no hard feelings, Tess added a little extra warmth to her smile when they waved good-bye in the parking lot.

Still, Stevie's words echoed in her thoughts as she drove home. *Tess deserves more than being a means to an end for a guy who's already accomplished many of his life goals and now wants to check marriage and kids off his list of aspirations.*

She had a few life goals of her own, which just happened to be aligned quite closely with Scott's. Yet she didn't actually see him as just a means to an end, did she? Which brought up the question—what, exactly, did she want from Scott?

She almost chose not to wear the new red dress after all. For some reason, only minutes before Scott was due to arrive at her door, she glanced in the mirror and was taken aback by the reflection of the polished woman in the bright red dress with a glitter of diamonds at her ears. It wasn't that she hadn't dressed up for an event before, or worn bold colors. But something about that woman in the mirror looked different tonight, and she couldn't quite define what it was. Telling herself she was being silly, and that Stevie would certainly report to Jenny if she didn't wear the red dress, she turned away from the mirror and carried her tiny purse into the living room to wait for Scott.

She tried to remember if he'd ever actually been inside the condo she'd purchased two years ago. Had he come in the time he'd stopped by in his four-wheel-drive truck to pick her up for work after a late-January ice storm? No, she recalled, she'd met him downstairs.

She cast a quick glance around her place, trying to see it through his eyes. Stevie had helped her decorate in a warm, cozy style built around classic pieces with unexpectedly whimsical accents. The colors were greens, grays and off-white, her favorite combination. It was so well suited to her.

She sat down on the cushy sofa and sighed, trying to release some of her nervous tension about tonight. When her doorbell rang, she found herself wishing she could exchange the snug red dress for comfy pj's and spend the evening at home with popcorn and hot cocoa. Alone? Maybe.

Or maybe not, she thought, opening the door to find Scott standing there looking like sex in a suit.

"You look very nice," he said. "Are you ready to go?"

Maybe it wasn't quite the reaction she'd hoped for from all the effort she'd put into her appearance tonight. Still, she told herself it would have been foolish to expect Scott to be knocked off his feet, as Stevie had predicted, by a snug red dress. Whatever she wore, she was still just Tess. She supposed he knew her too well by now to see her any other way.

Chapter Five

Maybe it was the dress. It looked amazing on her. It was all he could do to keep his gaze focused on her face, especially when she happened to turn her back to him. She did so again, to reach for a glass of champagne from a passing server, and he couldn't resist noticing how the snug dress cupped her shapely bottom. He was only human after all.

"Scott. Good to see you. How's it going?"

Drawing his attention back to the networking he was here to do, he shook a couple of hands and exchanged meaningless small talk before his gaze was drawn inexorably back to Tess mingling on the other side of the crowded room. Even among the other guests crammed in the almost overly decorated large living area of the Holiday Open Home, she stood out—at least to his eyes.

There was something different about her tonight. He

couldn't quite decide what it was. She'd chatted easily enough with him during the drive. She worked the room like the pro she was, making nice with people who were either potential clients or referrals for PCCI. He was quite sure she worked his name into every conversation, subtly extolling his business acumen. She'd always been his most loyal cheerleader—and his most bluntly honest critic. His most valuable asset. But there was something different about her tonight.

Maybe it *was* the dress.

Or maybe it was the knowledge that tonight he'd be taking her home when the party ended.

As if in confirmation, she glanced his way, saw him looking at her and smiled. He lifted his champagne flute in acknowledgment. He took a sip, but what he really wanted was to taste her lips again.

A surge of hunger swept through him, and for a moment, he was unnerved by the strength of it. He reassured himself with the reminder that sexual appeal was a plus when it came to choosing a compatible mate. He wouldn't examine too closely how long he'd been aware of his attraction to Tess, but now that they were dating there was no real reason to continue to suppress it. He could handle, even welcome, a mutually gratifying physical relationship. It was romance he simply couldn't seem to comprehend, and at which he'd proved so incompetent.

He didn't want to mess this up. There was too much at stake to take unnecessary risks. But fortunately he and Tess seemed to be on the same page in both their business and personal agendas. Her sexy red dress hadn't changed anything. But she did look damned good in it.

For the first time since they'd arrived an hour earlier,

he'd found a moment to himself, sipping champagne in a relatively quiet corner of the two-story living room. Between the Christmas music playing from cleverly hidden speakers and the chatter of milling guests, not to mention that he'd been too busy to eat more than a few bites all day, his head was beginning to ache dully. He hoped he'd hidden his discomfort behind his best social smile as he'd worked the event. They'd already been given the official tour through the impeccably styled and glitteringly festive six-thousand-square-foot house, and now it was just a matter of making sure his company was represented to maximum effect before they could make a graceful escape. No one had seemed surprised to see him enter with Tess at his side; everyone who knew them probably assumed they were simply attending in a business capacity. It would take a few more appearances to get the message across that their relationship had changed.

A movement next to him made him glance around to find a petite blonde in a sparkly dress frowning at him. She smoothed her expression quickly, but not before he'd seen the disapproval on her pretty face. "Is something wrong, Stevie?"

"I was just looking for Tess."

"She's over there, by the Christmas tree, chatting with the mayor and his wife. Apparently Tess and the mayor's wife are on some sort of civic committee together."

"I'm sure she's worked you and your company into the conversation a few times," Tess's friend murmured, echoing Scott's thoughts from only moments earlier. "You have to admit she's your most dedicated ally."

"No argument here. I owe a great deal to her. She's

a big fan of yours, too. I've heard her directing several people to look at your kitchen this evening."

Stevie nodded. "She's the most loyal and supportive person I've ever known. Always the one in the background quietly doing all the work and getting too little of the credit."

Okay, there was definitely a message here. He just wasn't entirely sure what it was. Was Stevie implying that he hadn't given Tess enough credit at work in the way of salary, title, promotions? Or was there a more personal implication to her comments? How much had Tess told her?

"Tess has certainly been instrumental in the success of my business," he said to reassure Stevie that he was fully mindful of that fact. "I've told her many times, both publicly and privately, that I don't know what I'd do without her."

"You're lucky to have her. She has plenty of options, you know."

He was well aware that Tess had been approached by other employers, some who'd met her through his business and coveted her organizational skills for their own enterprises. One of his own friends had recently offered her a position as human resources director for his trucking company, promising he'd add 20 percent to whatever Scott was paying her. Lane hadn't even bothered to be subtle about trying to hire her away; he'd made his move in Scott's own office. Scott had been gratified when Tess had made it clear she wasn't looking for a new job, and he'd tried to be good-natured about it with Lane. But come to think about it, they hadn't really spoken since, though Scott wasn't carrying a grudge. Still, if the truth were told, he'd been annoyed. Maybe even territorial in a way that hadn't been entirely business related. Had it been about that time that the seed of this marriage plan had been planted unknowingly in the back of his mind?

"Anyway," Stevie said when he sipped his champagne to avoid having to figure out a way to respond to her, "I'm just saying I wouldn't want Tess to be taken for granted. I would hate for her to be hurt. By anyone."

He lowered his glass and met her eyes. "So would I."

"Good."

"Hey, you two. Sorry I got detained for so long, I got caught up in a conversation about the chances of my nephew's basketball team making the state playoffs," Tess explained as she rushed up to join them. "Stevie, the mayor's wife wants to remodel her kitchen within the next few months. I told her she should be sure to talk with you before she leaves. Be ready to make a pitch," she added with a smile.

"I'll be ready. Thanks, Tess."

Only moments later they were interrupted by someone who wanted to question Stevie about a function of a trendy new feature in the impressive chef's kitchen.

Scott turned to Tess after Stevie had moved away. "What's with your friend?" he asked quietly. "She seems unusually subdued this evening."

On the few occasions when he'd met Stevie before, she'd always been laughing, animated, a bundle of barely suppressed energy in a compact package. Tonight she'd seemed more serious than he'd ever seen her, and he didn't know if it was only due to her doubts about Tess and him.

He saw concern flit across Tess's face as she glanced in the direction in which Stevie had just disappeared.

"I think she's going through some issues with her boy-friend," she murmured. "But I don't really know, so I'm only speculating."

That seemed to be all she was willing to say about Stevie's problems, so he changed the subject. "I think we've put in our time, don't you? How about if we duck out now?"

"Sounds good to me."

"Do you want to say good-night to your friend?"

She shook her head. "Stevie's busy. I'll send her a text later. Let's go before someone else corners us."

Smiling at her eagerness to escape, he moved across the room with her, exchanging nods and quick hand-shakes on the way out. Tess shivered as she slid into the passenger seat of his car. She grabbed her coat from the backseat and wrapped it snugly around her over the seat belt. "I think the temperature has dropped a few degrees since we went inside."

He started the car. "Some people know better than to wear sleeveless dresses in December without a coat."

She laughed. "I brought a coat."

"And left it in the car."

"I didn't want to bother with having to check it and then wait to reclaim it. It was worth a few minutes of freezing to make a faster getaway."

"That was a bore, wasn't it? I was expecting live music or some sort of entertainment other than just walking through the rooms, then standing around with cheap wine and dry canapés."

"I have a feeling there will be a new chairperson for the Holiday Open Home committee next year," she agreed wryly. "It's been so much better planned in the past."

"Oh, well, as long as they met their fund-raising goals, I guess that's all that matters."

"True. And I'm sure Stevie will get some new business from it. Her kitchen was gorgeous, wasn't it?"

"It was very nice." It still bothered him a bit to remember the way Stevie had frowned at him, as if she had some valid reason to worry that he would hurt her friend, but he shook off the concern. Maybe it was only that Stevie was having relationship troubles of her own, as Tess had implied, and was subsequently pessimistic about any new relationship. Maybe if they'd been in a place where they could have had a private conversation, he would have assured Stevie more forcefully that he had no intention of hurting Tess. Considering his belief that broken hearts were the result of unrealistic expectations, his plan was much healthier and saner than Stevie's idealistic and deliberately naive approach to the search for a life partner. Would Tess's friend see his point if he explained, or would she still disapprove of his prosaic tactics?

Not that it mattered. The only concern to him was that Tess approved.

Feeling a bit more cheerful now that their first official outing had been generally successful, he said, "I'm starving. I've hardly had time to eat anything today and those little nibbles at the party didn't fill me up. Want to stop for something to eat?"

"I ate before the party. But if you'd like to come in to my place, I'll make you an omelet or something."

His fingers tightened a bit on the wheel, but he made sure to keep any hint of surprise from his voice. "Sounds good, thanks."

Oh, yeah, he thought. This was all working out just fine.

* * *

"And this," Scott said, his head close to hers as they peered down at the phone in his hand, "is Miranda holding Henry after Thanksgiving dinner. She and Madison love being the older cousins and taking care of the baby."

"Do you just remember who this is, or can you really tell those girls apart?" Tess asked with a laugh and a shake of her head. It always amazed her that Scott's family seemed to so easily identify each twin, though they looked exactly alike to her.

"I can usually tell. Their personalities are different enough that their expressions sort of give them away, even when they're dressed alike, which isn't very often. Eli and Libby think it's important that the girls develop their own identities, so that they aren't just known as 'the twins.' Still, every so often I mix them up, and they call me on my mistake pretty quickly."

They sat side by side on the deep-cushioned sage-green couch in her living room, flipping through family photos stored in Scott's phone. He'd already eaten and effusively complimented the generous omelet she'd made for him, and he'd quickly accepted her offer of herbal tea afterward. He seemed to be in no hurry to leave, and Tess was enjoying this relaxed, private time with him.

"Your nieces are really cute. And Henry's a little doll. Thanks for showing me the pictures. It looks as though you had a great Thanksgiving."

"We did." Setting his phone to one side, Scott touched her hand. "I'm sorry you didn't have a good Thanksgiving with your family."

Her first instinct was to deflect the sympathy with a

shrug and an assurance that her gathering with her sister's family had been fine and she'd had a lovely time. It was a bit embarrassing to compare her strained situation with his close clan. But if Scott was going to become a part of her life, he might as well know everything he was getting into. "I guess you know that Nina and I aren't close. I can never seem to live up to her standards, and I think it annoys her that I'm not jealous of her. Does that make sense?"

"It does, actually. You being jealous of her would be a validation that she's important. Impressive. If you don't want to be her, she probably wonders what you find lacking. Needing to be envied is a common weakness for people whose sense of self-worth comes only from the amount of admiration they receive from others."

He sounded like an amateur psychologist, but he was right. "That does sound like Nina," she agreed slowly. "It sometimes seems as though everything she does is slanted toward impressing others. She pores over fashion magazines and trend blogs trying desperately to stay current. She's raising her kids the same way. Nina would pretty much pawn her soul to buy them the 'right' label. She and Ken aren't wealthy, but they try so hard to keep up with the Joneses that it exhausts me just watching them."

"I've had friends fall into that trap before they realize it's a game they just can't win. There's always someone with more money, more toys, more admirers. I like nice things as much as anyone, but I buy what I like, not because someone else would be impressed by it."

She knew that about him, of course. She couldn't have worked side by side with him for six years without learning something about his core values. It was another point in their favor as a budding couple that they shared so many of those principles. Smiling, she waved a hand around her living room. "Same here, obviously."

"I've always admired your sense of style."

The compliment pleased her. She smiled. "Thanks. But I have to give credit to my friends—Stevie with her flair for design and Jenny for keeping my wardrobe reasonably up-to-date."

Draping an arm casually across the couch behind her, he ran a fingertip along the bateau neckline of her red dress. "If this dress is an example of Jenny's contribution, then I applaud her advice. You look spectacular tonight. I could hardly take my eyes off you at the party."

The brush of his hand against her throat made her pulse flutter there. She wasn't sure he'd even noticed her appearance this evening other than the perfunctory compliment when he'd greeted her. "Thank you. And yes, I bought the dress at Jenny's boutique for the party."

"Then, I can see why her business is doing well."

"She deserves every bit of her success. And her happiness." Tess thought of her best friend. "You know, Jenny got caught up in that game we were just discussing when she dated a man before she met Gavin. Thad Simonson runs in an exclusive crowd, and with his political aspirations, everything he says, does, wears or eats is shrewdly calculated. Jenny said she felt as if she was losing herself in that life. She spent so much time trying to please Thad and his followers—not to mention her overbearing grandmother—that she wasn't even sure what she wanted anymore. Since she married Gavin, she's happier than I've ever seen her. She says she feels as if she's just getting to know the real her, pursuing her own dreams. She and Gavin are planning a camping trip in the Smoky Mountains next summer. It's something she always secretly wanted to do, but Thad wasn't interested in sleeping in a tent and her grandmother would have called it a waste of valuable time."

"Sounds like fun to me. My brothers and I have been on several camping hikes."

"I know," she reminded him with a smile. "I was the one keeping the offices running while you were gone, remember?"

He tapped the shallow cleft in her chin in a teasing gesture. "You've taken a few vacations, yourself. We struggled to stay in business while you were gone, but somehow we managed."

She laughed, though she was increasingly aware of his proximity on the couch, the way his thigh brushed hers when he shifted his weight, the air of intimacy surrounding them in the quiet room.

"How about you?" he asked. "Do you like camping?"

"I don't know. I've never been."

He looked surprised. "You've never camped?"

"No. You have to understand, my dad was almost fifty when I was born. He had his first heart attack when I was only nine. My mom was forty-five when they were shocked by her pregnancy with me. She was diagnosed with lupus when I was still in junior high and her health was never good after that. Neither of them was interested in outdoor pursuits. Usually we just went out to eat or to watch Nina perform in pageants or at college. She majored in music, though she only attended for two years before she left school to marry Ken. She has a beautiful voice, but she sings only in her church choir now."

"What were your extracurricular activities in high school and college? Do you sing, too?"

"Oh, no, not really. I can carry a tune, but I don't have Nina's talent. By the time I was in high school my parents were both in such poor health that I had to help out at home a lot. I was on the school newspaper and yearbook staffs, because those were activities I could do during the schoolday. Nina was a young bride with small children, so she couldn't help much at our house. I contributed as much as I could preparing meals and doing housework."

Realizing she might sound as if she was whining, she shook her head and spoke more brightly. "Don't get me wrong, I've had a good life. My parents made sure I had everything I needed. They paid for my tuition and made sure I had a little nest egg to set me up in this condo when they were gone. I have good friends. I have a job I love, thank you very much. My relationship with my sister isn't really close, but it's not as if we're actually estranged. Considering the age difference and the lack of anything in common, we get by okay."

He covered her hand with his and gave her fingers a warm squeeze. "I'm glad you feel free to speak candidly with me. I don't think you'd have said those things to just anyone—not even to me had we had this discussion just a couple weeks ago. Right?"

"No, probably not," she conceded. "I'd have just said everything was fine. But if you come to my cousin's party with me, I'm sure you'll see how it is with my sister and me, so I wanted you to be prepared."

"*When* I come with you to your cousin's party," he murmured, emphasizing the first word, "I'm sure we'll get along fine with your family."

"Oh, undoubtedly. We're all very civil when we get together." Mostly because she bit her tongue until it almost bled to keep from snapping when they criticized her, she added silently, choosing to keep that comment to herself.

He laced his fingers with hers. "Maybe you and I could go camping sometime. I think you'd like it."

Her heart gave a quick thump at the thought of spending a night in a tent—or anywhere else—with him, but she managed to smile. "Both of us out of the office at the same time? Sounds like a recipe for disaster."

"I suppose we'll have to figure out how to handle that situation in the future," he said with a slight shrug and a smile that almost made her sigh aloud. "We've both been working damned hard for a lot of years. Now our company is well established, we have good people on our payroll that we can trust to take care of things occasionally, and we can be reached in a multitude of ways if we're needed. I think we both deserve to take some time away from work occasionally, don't you?"

Several things about that little speech stood out to her, but his use of the plural possessive was particularly startling. *Our company. Our payroll.*

"I've been giving it a lot of thought lately," he continued before she could answer what must have been a rhetorical question. "I'm closer to forty than thirty now, and all my energy thus far has gone into the company. Buying it, growing it, securing its future. As you know, I pretty much ignored my personal life. I made the one attempt at getting engaged, but that would have been a mistake even if it hadn't fallen apart due to my own negligence. Now I'm ready for more. Commitment. Marriage. Kids. Soccer games and teacher meetings and dance recitals. Eventually cutting back on work to travel and see the world with my wife."

"That sounds very nice." She almost sighed in response to the lovely images he'd invoked.

"But first," he said briskly, "we have to get through the holidays. What's next on our social agenda?"

There was that word again. *Our.*

She moistened her lips and drew her attention back to the topic. "I'm sure you remember that tomorrow afternoon is the reception at the Best Burger home office to celebrate the holidays and the opening of their twentieth restaurant." The relatively new, locally based fast-food chain was rapidly expanding throughout Arkansas and two neighboring states and had contracted with Scott to handle its new construction. It was one of the more lucrative deals Scott had signed during the past few years. He spent a lot of time making sure the owner of the chain was happy with the construction, including one currently under way in Little Rock. The three-to-five drop-in reception was for store managers, vendors and other professional associates, and Scott was expected to make an appearance. "I don't know if you want me to attend that with you...?"

"Absolutely. This was the deal, remember? We're doing all the holiday stuff together."

The deal. Was that the way he viewed their dating agreement? She supposed it summed it up well enough. She cleared her throat silently and nodded to indicate she was on board.

"So we'll stop by the Best Burger thing tomorrow afternoon. Do you have plans for tomorrow evening?"

This felt so familiar, she thought with wry amusement. How many hours had they spent coordinating their office calendars, planning business commitments for weeks or months at a time? She supposed it was only natural that they'd handle their personal plans in much the same way. "No, I don't have anything specific planned for tomorrow night."

"I have tickets for the symphony's holiday performance. I know it's short notice, but would you like to go with me? You know—a real date?" he added with a crooked smile that was too charming to resist. "Just the two of us."

"I would like that. I love the symphony."

Looking pleased, he nodded. "We'll pop back in to the office after the reception, then leave from there to have dinner and go to the concert, if it's okay with you."

She made a quick mental note to choose a day-into-evening outfit for the next day, and to take a sparkly jacket to slip on for the concert. "That'll work."

"What about the rest of the weekend? Do you have personal plans?"

"Saturday is my niece's birthday, and Nina has made reservations at that popular new Japanese restaurant."

Should she ask him to accompany her? She supposed the reservation could be changed to add one more, but was it too soon for Scott to join her at a family celebration? Would it make the evening better or even more awkward to have him there with her?

The possibility of joining her didn't even seem to occur to him. "I've got family stuff Saturday night, too. I told Jake I'd go to his house to watch the SEC West playoff game with him tomorrow night. Have fun at the party."

She nodded. It seemed that she and Scott were already beginning to define their future together: they would be free to pursue their own interests as individuals even as they attended some events as a couple. Practical and independent. The two adjectives had always been applied to her, so it made sense that they defined her budding relationship, as well. "Have fun with your brother."

It occurred to her that he was still holding her hand. It felt nice. His fingers moved on hers again, giving another little squeeze as he said, "Next weekend is fairly busy, too. We have our office Christmas party Saturday night. But before that, on Friday night, I have a dinner thing. Would you be free to go with me to that?"

"A dinner thing?"

He waved his free hand. "It's an engagement party. The couple sent out invitations a couple of months ago, I think, and to be honest, I'd forgotten about it until I got a reminder by email today. You know how hectic everything has been the past few weeks. This dinner totally slipped my mind."

This was the first she'd heard of an engagement party. She didn't handle his personal social calendar, but usually he mentioned upcoming events at least in passing. It did speak to his state of mind lately that he'd forgotten a commitment. "Did you tell them you'd be bringing a date?"

"Oh, sure. I figured I'd ask someone. I can't think of anyone I'd rather go with than you."

She swallowed. Accompanying him to the Holiday Open Home had been a relatively innocuous first social outing together. If anyone had been surprised to see them enter side by side, Tess hadn't noticed. She figured the Best Burger open house would be similarly easy. It was possible they'd see people they knew at the symphony performance, but then again, perhaps they wouldn't, nor would they likely be expected to explain why they attended together. But an engagement party... Well, that was very different. This would most definitely be interpreted as a date. "Are these close friends?"

He shrugged. "Bethany, the bride-to-be, is the youngest daughter of my mom's college roommate. I've known her all her life, but I wouldn't call us close friends. The groom just finished dental school in Louisiana and Bethany's mom talked Dad into interviewing him as a potential associate."

"So is he going to join your dad's practice?"

"Yeah, I think so. Dad's been wanting to add someone who specializes in pediatric dentistry, which apparently this guy does."

So the daughter of an old friend and his dad's new business associate. Which meant the entire Prince clan would probably be in attendance at this party. "You haven't, um, mentioned to your family that you and I are..."

"I haven't talked about us with anyone," he assured her. "But they'll probably get the picture when we show up at the party."

She nodded.

"Haven't changed your mind, have you?" He spoke lightly, but she sensed he was serious.

"No." In fact, now that he'd laid out such an enticing future for them, she was even more committed to their tentative plan. "I have to admit I'm a little nervous, but I'll go with you."

"Why are you nervous?" he asked with a little smile, holding her hand between both of his now.

"Well, it's your family and friends."

"Many of whom you've met several times. They already know you and like you."

"As your office manager."

"As a person," he corrected firmly. "My family doesn't tend to label people by their professions. The dinner's at Trapnall Hall and it shouldn't last overly long."

"I always enjoy events there this time of year. I'm sure the Christmas decorations are beautiful."

He lifted one hand to her face, running a fingertip lightly over her lower lip. "I'm glad you'll be going with me. It'll make the event much more tolerable."

Warmth seeped through her in response to his nearness, his touch. In some ways it still felt odd to be snuggled with Scott on her sofa, yet beneath the novelty was a growing certainty that it was exactly where they were meant to be. He'd simply realized it before she'd acknowledged it herself.

She rested a hand on his chest, allowing her fingers to curl a bit against his shirt to savor the warm strength beneath. He'd removed his jacket and tie and opened his collar, so he looked casually at ease, gazing at her in a way that made her heart beat a little faster. His eyes had darkened to a gleaming navy and his lips were curved into a faint sexy smile that made her ache to taste him.

"I'll try my best to make the party tolerable for you," she said, smiling.

His gaze was focused intently on her mouth. A low rumble of laughter escaped him. "I appreciate that," he murmured.

Silence fell between them then. Looking into his eyes, she realized that the time for conversation had ended. It was time for him to go…or not. Which didn't mean they had to rush to a decision about those options. She slid her hand up his chest to the back of his neck, her lips parting in an invitation he accepted instantly, eagerly.

Gathering her against him, he kissed her with a thoroughness and urgency he'd reined in previously. His mouth was hot, hungry on hers, his tongue sweeping deep to explore and challenge. She gave a little moan of surprise and pleasure, her arms closing around his neck to bring them even closer. His hand moved on her leg, toying with the hem of the dress and then sliding under to caress her thigh. She shivered in response to an image of his hands moving higher. Her breasts swelled against his chest, and a restless ache settled there. Just the thought of his hands closing over them made her tremble.

Slowly breaking the kiss, he lifted his head only a couple inches, his gaze sweeping her flushed face. Still nestled snugly in his arms, she was aware that he was breathing rapidly, that his eyes were dilated, his heart beating hard against hers. He was as aroused as she was, in control but reluctantly so.

She touched her fingertips to his jaw almost wonderingly. "Does this feel weird to you? Shouldn't it feel strange?"

His lips curved upward. "Maybe it should. But it doesn't. It feels…good. Right."

"To me, too," she confessed. "Maybe the strange part is that it *doesn't* feel weird."

He chuckled and set her a couple inches away from him. "I'm not quite sure how to unravel that statement, but I think I'd better go."

She blinked. "You're leaving?"

His voice was just a little rough when he nodded and said, "It's either that or I'm going to start trying to get you out of that pretty red dress. I'm not sure we're quite ready for that step yet."

Though a surprisingly insistent part of her wanted to argue, rational discretion prevailed. She scooted back another couple inches and reached up with unsteady hands to smooth her hair. "You should go," she agreed, pleased that her voice was reasonably normal. "We do have to work in the morning."

She walked him to the door to lock up behind him. With a hand on the doorknob, she smiled up at him, giving in to an impertinent impulse. "Scott? For the record—you wouldn't have to try very hard. With the dress, I mean."

His eyes widened, then narrowed. "You're determined to make me suffer tonight, aren't you?"

She patted his cheek. "Just saying."

His smile was decidedly lopsided. "So this is how it's going to go, huh? You're going to make me jump through a few hoops to prove myself worthy?"

Even though his amusement was obvious, she grew serious. "I know you're teasing—as I was—but let me make this clear. I don't play games. I don't expect you to prove anything to me. Outside the office, we're not boss and employee, but equals. Full partners. Yes?"

He matched her serious tone when he replied, "Absolutely. I've said from the start this has nothing to do with business. I expect you to speak your mind, state your wishes, read me the riot act when I deserve it, without fear of any professional repercussions." And then he looked thoughtful. "Actually, that's pretty much the

way you act in the office, too. You've never been intimidated by me, have you?"

She thought fleetingly of that first interview so long
ago, but merely smiled. "Not that I'd let you see."

He chuckled, then leaned over to brush his lips
lightly across hers. "And now you know why I'm convinced we make such a great team, inside the office
and out. Thanks for the omelet, Tess. It was delicious."

"You're welcome. Good night, Scott."

He hesitated for just a few moments longer and then
gave a decisive nod and let himself out. Tess released a
long breath and listened through the door as he walked
away. Only when she could no longer hear him did she
head for her bedroom to change out of the red dress
and into her nightclothes. For the sake of her peace of
mind, she made a deliberate effort not to imagine what
it would have been like if Scott had been the one to remove the dress.

Chapter Six

As Tess had expected, no one seemed to find it news-worthy that she accompanied Scott to the Best Burger reception. It was their biggest regular client, and every-one knew she'd interacted frequently with representa-tives from the chain. Andy and Lana, their architect and cost estimator, had already left for the reception, so PCCI would be well represented.

The reception was drop-in and very informal. Tess had met most of the higher-ups in the fast food chain's echelon at one time or another. Aware of her function as valued assistant to Scott, they welcomed her warmly to their base of operations. The owner of the chain even introduced her to a district manager as "the glue that held PCCI together." Grinning, Scott said he couldn't dispute that assessment. He stayed by her side during the hour they mingled, but she doubted anyone thought they were actually there as a couple rather than a work team. Still, as Scott had said, it was good for people to get accustomed to seeing them together in a variety of settings. They stood by the food table—laden, of course, with snacks available at any local Best Burger restaurant—chatting with a variety of local business-people, and when they thought they'd accomplished their purpose in coming, they made a gracious escape.

"That went well," Scott proclaimed in his car on the way back to the office, sounding almost smug about it. "This whole dating thing is turning out just fine, wouldn't you say?"

Tess laughed. "Scott, I refuse to acknowledge that as a date."

He slanted a grin her way. "Was the Holiday Open Home a date?"

"More so."

"How about the baby shopping trip followed by the barbecue dinner?"

"Less so."

He chuckled. "So by your definition, we're just barely in the honeymoon part of this relationship."

Her heart gave a little jerk, though she didn't know whether it was in response to the word *honeymoon* or *relationship*. Maybe it was something about the words used in combination. But because he was kidding, she chuckled and said, "Yes, I suppose."

"But tonight definitely counts as a date. Just the two of us at the symphony, no professional obligations, nothing to do but enjoy each other's company and the music."

"That sounds nice," she agreed, relaxing again. She really was looking forward to the concert. As much as she loved music, she was sure she would enjoy it even more with Scott by her side.

By the time they'd finished returning calls, answering emails, signing paperwork and placing orders, Tess and Scott barely got away from work in time. They acknowledged wryly that they should have known better than to stop by the office. "A couple of hopeless workaholics," Scott said with a laugh as he locked up behind them. "That's why we get along so well. You understand me because you're just like me."

Straightening the short sequined jacket she'd donned over her day-to-evening black jersey dress, Tess smiled in return. "Was that supposed to be a compliment?" she teased.

"Just an observation." He placed a hand on her back as they walked side by side toward their cars. "I can count on you to understand that sometimes I get distracted or held up by obligations to the company. You won't expect me to apologize when unexpected problems crop up or when I have to cancel social plans rather than risk losing a valuable contract."

"Well, of course not." She suspected he was thinking of his ex-fiancée. Sharon had made her displeasure clear to everyone when she didn't think Scott was paying her enough attention. She'd even snapped at Tess a few times when Tess had answered the office phone and had to explain that Scott was in an emergency meeting and couldn't be disturbed. Even though she knew he was comparing her positively to his high-maintenance ex, she would just as soon not be compared at all. She deliberately changed the subject. "So you're following me home to drop off my car and then we'll have dinner before the concert, right? We'll have to choose someplace with fast service in order to make the start of the concert."

They did make it to the concert hall in time, but just barely. The lights were already dimming when they slid into their seats. Tess wasn't displeased by that. This way they didn't have to wait very long for the music to start, nor had they risked running into mutual acquaintances on the way in. The concert was wonderful, a charming mixture of classical pieces and Christmas favorites. She relaxed into her seat, letting the music wash over her, not worrying about work or family or the future, just enjoying the evening. After one particularly rousing number, she glanced at Scott to find him gazing back at her. Though the lights were very low, she could see well enough to tell that he was smiling at her, apparently enjoying her pleasure.

He reached over to take her hand, squeezing her fingers. "Glad we came?"

"Very much."

They'd both needed a couple hours away from work and expectations, she decided. True, they were on a date, and there was still the novelty of that—but it was Scott. With their demanding work schedule, they'd spent more time together over the past six years than most married couples. They communicated so well silently that she could even tell which musical numbers he enjoyed most without looking at him—which was probably also true in reverse. They were comfortable together…and yet underlying that familiarity was a new awareness that gave her a delicious buzz when he touched her. Knowing there would be more kisses later caused little ripples of anticipation to run through her.

Thinking of where those kisses would eventually lead made her breath catch in her throat.

But no. She wasn't thinking ahead now, she reminded herself. She wanted to enjoy every moment of this evening, just sitting beside him and listening to the music.

They each saw a few familiar faces on their way out, but the crowded rush to the exits prevented more than nods and waves. If there were any mutual acquaintances in the audience, she didn't see them, but then she wasn't really looking. She and Scott didn't linger in the hall, but made their way to his car as quickly as possible. They'd accomplished their mission. They'd enjoyed a concert while growing more accustomed to being out in public as a couple. Maybe by the time next weekend rolled around, she would be a little less anxious about attending the party with his family and friends. Had that been part of his reason for bringing her to this concert tonight?

They talked about the concert during the drive home, comparing notes on their favorite numbers, expressing their admiration for both the musicians and the vocal performers. Arriving at her place, he parked next to her little blue sedan. Each unit came with two designated covered parking spaces, leaving her with an extra for her guests. He walked her inside, and her heart beat more quickly with each step they took toward her door. Should she ask him in? Of course she should. Were they ready for that next step they'd alluded to when he'd left her here last time? Part of her was most definitely ready.

He started to automatically follow her inside, then seemed to realize he hadn't technically been invited yet. He hesitated. It briefly crossed her mind to send him on his way with weariness as her excuse, but she decided she didn't really want to say good-night just yet. "Would you like some tea?"

"Sounds good." His flash of a smile made her hands tremble. He closed the door behind them with a firm snap.

She set her bag on a table and draped her coat over the back of a chair. "Would you prefer tea or decaf coffee?"

"Actually, I'm not very thirsty."

She turned toward him. "Neither am I."

Scott stepped up to her and cupped her face gently in his hands. His palms were still cool from being outside, but her cheeks felt very warm against them. His eyes locked with hers, and she could almost imagine he could see her thoughts, her doubts as he gazed somberly down at her. "You can kick me out at any time," he reminded her gently.

"I know. The problem is…I don't want to kick you out," she replied, resting her hands on his chest.

His eyes heated, but still he kept his tone even. "Is that really such a problem?"

"I'm still trying to decide."

He moved his thumb against her lower lip, tracing the shape of it. His gaze following the movement, he murmured, "I've been trying to take it slow. Give you time to adjust."

Take it slow? It had been only a week since he'd sprung this proposition on her. She felt a slight frown crease her brows. "How are *you* adjusting so easily?"

His smile was warm, understanding. "You know me. Once I make up my mind about something, I rarely second-guess myself. Now that we've acknowledged how great we are together, it just seems as if it was inevitable all along."

Inevitable. Was that enough? She doubted Stevie would think so.

"And now that we've spent this time together," he added, his mouth so close to hers that his breath was a warm caress on her lips, "I can't believe it took me so long to see what was right in front of me."

Okay, that sounded a little more intimate. A little less deliberate. Not exactly a declaration of devotion, but that wasn't what she was looking for from Scott. She'd heard flowery speeches and passionate promises before, and those relationships had ended in disappointment if not actual heartbreak. Maybe this time she should put her faith in actions, not words. And speaking of action...

She wrapped her arms around Scott's neck when he gathered her closer, capturing her lips with his. Despite the five inch or so difference in their heights, their bodies fit very nicely together. Each time they kissed, the sensations grew more familiar—and yet more urgent. He'd said he'd been taking things slowly, so perhaps he'd held back in those previous embraces. He wasn't holding back now. He drew her closer, letting her feel his body's response, making her intensely aware of his growing arousal. His mouth was avid, his tongue insistent. Faced with a choice between pushing him away and doing what she really wanted, she gave in to temptation. She crowded closer to him, returning the kiss with an answering demand.

Take it slow? Hardly. This had been building in her for six years.

He was quick to recognize the silent invitation and

he accepted it with an enthusiasm that soon had them both breathing heavily, shoving impatiently at clothing to access the warm skin beneath. Scott's jacket and tie fell onto the couch. She left her shoes behind when she led him to her bedroom. He had his shirt untucked and partially unbuttoned by the time they reached the bed. She reached for the zipper at the back of her dress, but Scott's hands were already there as he gathered her into his arms for another hungry kiss. By the time the black dress fell to the floor, she was too deeply lost in the embrace, too eager for more, to be at all self-conscious.

She'd seen him without a shirt only once before. It had been the day they'd worked at his house after his surgery. Still loopy from the meds, he'd accidentally tugged off a corner of his bandage. She'd smoothed it back into place and then helped him don a fresh T-shirt. Other than the necessary touching, she'd kept her hands to herself that day, resisting the then inappropriate urge to run her palms over the firm planes and hard muscles of his chest, to follow a thin trail of hair down his ridged stomach to his shallow belly button and below.

She'd never forgotten how appealing he'd looked that day, all rumpled and drowsy and half-nude. Unbidden memories had haunted her more than once during lonely nights since, though she'd quickly and firmly suppressed them each time. She didn't have to restrain herself now. She gave her curious hands free rein to explore and savor every inch of him, even as he pushed her beyond coherence with his own bold forays of discovery.

They communicated with soft moans and approving gasps, with kisses and strokes and urgent movements. His mouth on her breasts made her arch with a choked cry of pleasure. Her hands closing around him tore a low groan from him. They rolled and writhed, shoving pillows to the floor, covers to the side. He dealt with protection swiftly and deftly before returning his attention to pleasuring her, which he did with even more practiced skill. Their hands were interlocked when he finally, finally thrust into her, filling an emptiness that seemed to have been waiting for him all her life.

For only a raw heartbeat of an instant, she was aware of a sense of panic, an overwhelming fear that this was too perfect, too powerful. The knowledge that everything would change after this night swept through her, and for just that second she fought to cling to the safe, cautious status quo. The comfortable camaraderie that had carried no risk of disappointment or heartbreak, no fear of losing what they'd found…of losing herself. But then he began to move, and any hesitation was replaced by an almost desperate need for release. Her mind emptied of any thought except that very moment, that very place, the two of them entangled in the cozy cocoon of her bed, their bodies joined, hearts pounding in unison. Her climax hit with a force that shattered any illusion that anything would ever be the same for them again.

He didn't stay the night. Referencing an early breakfast meeting with a couple of job foremen, he slipped from the bed and dressed to leave while she wrapped herself in a robe to lock up behind him. He paused before opening the door, and she got the distinct impression that he was trying to come up with the right thing to say. It wasn't like him to be at a loss for words.

To help him out, she said simply, "Good night, Scott. Drive carefully."

He kissed her lingeringly. "Sleep well, Tess. I'll call you tomorrow."

She nodded and reached around him to open the door.

His jacket over his shoulder, tie hanging from his pocket, his finger-combed dark hair tumbling onto his forehead, Scott turned just on the other side of the door to smile at her. "I knew we made a great team," he said in visible satisfaction. "I really am a genius."

That made her laugh, as he'd surely intended. "Yes, you are," she said.

Because she didn't want him to leave feeling too sanctimonious, she reached out to grab his shirt, tugged his mouth down to hers and gave him a kiss that turned his laughter into a groan.

"Okay, maybe I could stay a little while longer," he said rather hoarsely when the kiss ended.

She tossed back her tumbled hair and took a step backward. "Good night, Scott."

She closed the door almost in his face. Through the wood, she heard him sputter a rough laugh, then listened as his footsteps faded away. Only then did she allow herself to release a long, slow exhale.

After fastening the door locks, she turned toward her bedroom, then realized she was biting her kiss-swollen lower lip. She released it with a reassurance to herself that things really were going well between them. It was probably only weariness and lingering disorientation causing the heavy feeling deep in her chest. The sensation felt much like apprehension, but she couldn't fully explain it and didn't want to examine it too closely tonight.

* * *

The positive side of the showy dinner party Nina threw in celebration of Olivia's fifteenth birthday was that she was too busy being the hostess and mistress of ceremonies to have much time to focus on Tess. She'd reserved a private dining room in the restaurant for some thirty guests. Most of the guests were related to Nina's husband, Ken—his parents and two siblings and a few of their progeny—in addition to a few church, social and business acquaintances. More to Olivia's taste, there'd been a teen party the night before at the indoor pool of a country club. Though she visibly relished being the center of attention again, Olivia made it clear she'd enjoyed last night's bash much more than this dinner party. She huddled with her boyfriend and the few other friends she'd been allowed to invite while her brothers played handheld video games and Ken quietly did his part by standing at his wife's side, following her directions and bankrolling the event.

Tess would rather be just about anywhere else, herself. She loved her niece, spoiled little princess that she was, but this was not her idea of a fun evening. All in all, she'd rather have been watching the football game. Either alone…or not.

She wondered if Scott was having a good time. If he'd thought of her at all this evening. She'd never been one of "those" girlfriends, she mused. Though she both practiced and expected monogamy during her relationships, she'd never expected to know where her significant other was or what he was doing at all times, nor did she report her movements to him. But it would be nice to know that she'd crossed Scott's mind today as often as he'd hovered in hers. That he'd mentally replayed their lovemaking and relived the excitement, that he felt the same anticipation she did about the next time they'd be alone together.

She wanted to be confident that when he thought of her now, it wasn't only with a list of tasks he needed her to oversee at the office.

It was a relief when the dinner was over. She exchanged farewells with the other guests, most of whom she'd met previously, then lingered to say good-night to her family.

Holding her boyfriend's hand, Olivia sauntered up to her. "Thank you for the bag, Aunt Tess. It's really cool. I love it."

Pleased by the girlish delight in her niece's voice, Tess smiled. "I'm glad. Jenny helped me find it for you. She thought you'd like it."

They hugged quickly, and then Olivia and her lanky boyfriend hurried off to rejoin their friends. Satisfied that she could make her escape now, Tess looked around for Nina, finding her on the other side of the room saying goodbye to some departing guests. She made her way to her sister's side. "I'm leaving now, Nina. It was a great dinner. Thanks for inviting me."

"Of course you'd be invited," Nina replied with an impatient roll of her eyes. "We invited all Olivia's aunts and uncles."

Resisting an impulse to snap that she'd just been trying to be polite, Tess drew a deep breath and held on to her smile with an effort. "It was good to see everyone again."

"Don't forget next week is—"

"Dana's party," Tess finished in unison. "I haven't forgotten, Nina."

"You've responded to the evite?"

Nina was very much in "mama mode" this evening, treating Tess exactly the way she would one of her children. Again, Tess had to cling to patience. "I have responded."

"Did you tell her you'd bring a guest? Because if you haven't invited anyone—"

"I'm bringing a guest. It's already arranged, Nina."

Her sister's eyes widened in curiosity. "Who are you bringing?"

"Hon, we need to help Olivia carry out her gifts," Ken interrupted the conversation to say. "The room's booked for another party so they're ready for us to clear out."

Nina lifted her chin. "We have it reserved for another ten minutes. I will not be hustled out."

"It'll take us that long to gather everything up and get the kids out to the van. Come on, Nina, grab a couple bags, will you?"

Tess moved a step forward. "Can I help?"

Her brother-in-law gave her a quick wink. "We've got it, thanks. Get out of here while you can."

She took grateful advantage of his suggestion.

A particularly boneheaded play in the football game would have made Scott curse in exasperation had a baby not been asleep on his chest. As it was, he grumbled beneath his breath, making little Henry squirm and nestle his nose into Scott's shoulder. Scott hoped fleetingly that it wasn't a snotty little nose, but it wouldn't be the first time he'd been used as a tissue by one of his brothers' offspring. He patted the kid's diapered bottom and Henry settled back into a limp slumber. Sprawled on Jake's couch with his stocking feet crossed on the coffee table, Scott glanced at the canned soda on the table and wondered if he could reach it without waking his nephew.

As if he'd recently mastered the art of mind reading, but more likely correctly interpreting Scott's expression, Jake snagged the can and handed it over. "Game sucks, huh?"

With a nod of thanks, Scott took a sip of the beverage, which had gone rather flat in the past hour since he'd opened it. "Yeah. I thought the score would be closer than this."

"You okay there? Want me to take the rug rat?"

"He's okay. We wake him up, he's just going to want to eat again, and we promised Christina we'd give her a little more time to herself. Might as well stretch it out as much as we can after the week she's had."

The virus Henry had picked up at Thanksgiving had held on for several days. He was recovered now, but his parents were tired and frazzled. Scott's mom had helped out when she could, but as a full-time accountant, she'd been busy with end-of-the-year work for her clients. Today had been a day for Christina to get some rest, with Jake and Scott taking care of the baby.

His eyes on the big-screen TV on the opposite wall, Jake munched a handful of popcorn, then asked idly, "You going to Bethany's engagement party next Friday?"

"Looks like. You know Mom would pout if any of us skipped out without a damned good reason, and unfortunately I couldn't come up with one."

Jake chuckled wryly. "Yeah, us, either. We've got a

babysitter lined up, so I guess we'll make an appearance."

"Lousy time for an engagement party, if you ask me. This time of year, seems like I'm running from one party or fund-raiser or holiday reception to the next one. Bethany and what's-his-name aren't even getting married until spring, so I can't imagine why they thought they needed an engagement party now."

"Mom said Jeremy—that's the groom's name, by the way—has an aunt in poor health. They aren't sure she'll still be around for the wedding, but they wanted to have her at the engagement party."

"Oh, well, now I feel like a jerk." With a grimace, Scott set the soda aside and patted the sleeping baby again. "I'll be there. With a smile."

"Are you bringing someone?"

"Yeah. Tess is coming with me."

He wasn't sure how he'd expected his younger brother to react to that, but it hadn't been with a laugh. "Tess? Man, she really is on call 24/7 for you, isn't she? Do you pay her overtime for keeping you company at parties you don't want to attend alone?"

Scott shook his head. "She isn't coming as my employee. Tess has agreed to be my date for the party."

"Your date?"

"Yes."

"Like…a *date* date?"

Scott scowled, hardly pleased by the disbelief in his brother's expression. "So we're back to high school now? Really?"

Jake shrugged. "I'm just surprised, that's all. I didn't know you and Tess ever hung out outside the office."

"It's a recent development."

"You and Tess, huh? Wow."

Wow pretty much summed up the last few hours he'd spent with Tess, Scott mused, though of course he wouldn't say that to his brother. Henry wiggled and made a mewing sound. Scott bounced him gently while saying, "Yeah."

"Since when?"

"We've been out a few times." He smiled as he remembered the teasing conversation he and Tess had about how many real dates there had actually been.

"So is it, you know, serious?"

An erotic memory of deep-throated cries of satisfaction whispered in the back of his mind. Scott cleared his throat. "Getting there."

"Well, that's great," Jake said, still sounding surprised.

Henry squirmed again, then lifted his head from Scott's now-damp shoulder to blink up at him. He looked a bit surprised to find himself in his uncle's arms, but with his usual happy nature, he grinned broadly, displaying two shiny new teeth. Scott couldn't resist smiling goofily in response.

"What's great?" Christina entered the room looking considerably more refreshed than she had when Scott arrived. Short and somewhat square in stature, she had red hair, numerous freckles, warm green eyes and a smile that could melt glaciers. Henry had inherited her coloring. His wispy hair was already a bright ginger rather than Jake's dark brown.

"Scott's dating Tess," Jake blurted.

Christina blinked a few times, then nodded. "Good choice."

"You're not surprised?" her husband challenged.

"Not very much." She crossed the room to take her son, who'd reached out in response to her voice. She smiled at Scott as she relieved him of his charge. "I think you and Tess fit very well together."

Oh, yeah. He and Tess fit very well together indeed, he thought, shifting restlessly on the couch.

"I guess it makes sense," Jake said after a moment. "Tess is great, and everyone likes her. Not sure what she sees in you, bro, but you'd be lucky to keep her."

"Thanks a lot." Scott laughed as he carefully straightened his left arm. The pins-and-needles tingling of returning circulation told him he'd sat in one position too long holding the baby, but he wasn't complaining. He'd enjoyed bonding with his nephew.

"So, Scott, when did you realize you had feelings for Tess?" Christina asked while trying to extricate her eyeglasses from her son's grasp.

He wasn't quite sure how to answer. He remembered clearly that moment of recognition when he'd found Tess under the office tree and had suddenly realized how perfect she was for him. It had just made sense to him. Was that what Christina meant by "having feelings"— or was she imagining some sort of epic Hollywood romantic epiphany that hardly applied to two generally levelheaded adults with common goals and wishes?

Okay, so maybe last night had gotten pretty hot. Maybe he'd tossed and turned as he'd tried to sleep alone afterward, regretting that he'd made himself leave her bed. Maybe he was counting the minutes until he had her in his arms again. Physical chemistry was a good thing between a couple, especially when they'd agreed they wanted children, he considered as his gaze lingered on his giggling nephew.

Maybe the attraction had simmered beneath the surface for quite a bit longer than he'd realized, judging by how swiftly it had come to a boil when he'd finally been free to express it. Her heated responses reassured him that the attraction went both ways, though knowing Tess, she'd probably suppressed any such awareness in the past for fear that it would be unprofessional.

"Scott?" Christina looked at him quizzically over Henry's head, and he suspected the trained psychologist was trying to analyze his facial expressions. "You and Tess?"

"We've just started seeing each other," he said, choosing his words carefully. "It's occurred to us both how well we get along and how much we have in common, so we figured it was worth exploring on a more personal basis."

The couple looked at each other and then back at him. Jake broke the momentary silence. "Wow. What a romantic story. Almost brought a tear to my eye."

Frowning at his kid brother, Scott grumbled, "Bite me, Jake. We all know I'm no good at the romantic stuff. I don't have to put on an act for Tess. She already knows me better than anyone outside of the family. Anything that develops between us will be based on honesty and mutual goals."

Jake raised both hands in surrender. "Whatever works for you both. I just want you to be happy, bro. You know that."

"Yeah, I do. Thanks."

Henry was beginning to fuss. Christina bounced him in her arms to momentarily soothe him as she carried him toward the couch. "I need to feed him and give him his bath, then put him to bed. Say good-night, guys."

Both Scott and Jake rose to bestow hugs and kisses on the youngest Prince. He gave slobbery smacks in return, then waved bye-bye over his mother's shoulder as she carried him from the room. She paused in the doorway to look back at Scott. "I like Tess a lot," she said. "I always have."

"I'm glad to hear that."

She looked uncharacteristically fierce when she added, "Don't hurt her."

"I won't."

Nodding decisively, Christina swept out of the room with Henry.

While he appreciated the sentiment, Christina should know that hurting Tess was the furthest thing from his mind. Wasn't that the whole point of approaching her the way he had with his proposition?

"So when *did* you—"

"Halftime's over, Jake," he cut in flatly. "Let's watch the game, okay?"

"In other words, you don't want to talk about you and Tess any more this evening."

"Exactly."

Jake directed his attention to the television screen, obligingly bringing the conversation to an end. But even though they weren't talking about it, Scott figured his brother was still mulling over this new development. He knew thoughts of Tess would hover in his own mind until he saw her again.

Although rather hectic and borderline chaotic, that second week in December was nevertheless enjoyable, as far as Tess was concerned. The business problems that cropped up were no more than expected and fairly easily resolved. Sofia started training with Heather and was obviously going to fit in well with the staff. People seemed to be in a generally good mood during the week, because of the approaching holidays or perhaps because the weather had taken a nice turn.

As for her personal life—that was going nicely, too. Though both busy with previously arranged after-work obligations, she and Scott managed to find time together during the week. Scott had business plans Monday evening and she had a civic club meeting. He called her just as she was getting ready for bed and they talked about their respective meetings, sharing a couple of amusing anecdotes. Something else that was new for them, she thought with a smile as she climbed beneath her covers afterward. A chatty personal phone call made for no other reason than to hear each other's voices, to stay in contact despite their individual pursuits. It was nice that his was the last voice she heard before ending the day.

They dined at a restaurant following a long day at work Tuesday, slipping out after the rest of the staff left. Tess had rather hoped the evening would end back at her place, but the muted beep of Scott's phone just as they finished dessert dashed that fantasy. Scott looked at her in apology after disconnecting the call. "I'm sorry."

"Something has come up," she said, easily reading his expression.

He nodded. "Apparently a bunch of punks climbed the fence around the rental units we're building in Sheridan and had a little vandalism party before the cops rounded them up. Andy and I are going to look around and see if they've done any permanent damage. I guess Andy could go without me, but…"

"But you need to go check it out yourself," she said

matter-of-factly, knowing him too well to imagine otherwise.

He grimaced and nodded. "We were so close to finished with that project. I'm hoping there's nothing that'll hold us up too long. I need to put the crew on the fabric store job after the holidays, and I'm sure we'll have weather delays in January and February. We always do."

"You don't have to explain. Just go. Let me know if there's anything I need to do."

"You're the best, Tess," he told her warmly.

He might as well have given her a cheery knuckle-chuck to the chin. Even though he gave her a fairly heated good-night kiss when he dropped her off at her condo, his attention was obviously focused already on what he would find at the job site. Tess let herself in her door with a wry smile. She honestly didn't resent him at all for rushing off to work. How many times had she walked out on plans with her friends because something had come up at work and Scott had requested her assistance? Her ex-boyfriend James had accused her of being at Scott's "beck and call" 24/7…and worse, liking it that way.

Still, she thought as she prepared for bed in her quiet home, it would have been nice if the evening had gone the way she'd hoped.

Fortunately the damages to the Sheridan job hadn't been too extensive, so Scott was able to make arrangements for fairly swift repairs. They got a great deal accomplished in the office on Wednesday, to everyone's satisfaction. She didn't see a lot of Scott that day, only when he dashed in with barked instructions and scribbled his signature on whatever she slapped in front of him.

Though she had to silently chide herself a couple of

times when she found herself watching his sexy mouth instead of listening closely to his words, Scott seemed to have no trouble at all seeing her as the same efficient assistant she'd always been to him. She was fairly confident the staff saw nothing different in their professional behavior, which was a relief to her even though she was aware it wouldn't be much longer before the news got out. She wasn't looking forward to that part, mostly because she suspected everyone would watch them surreptitiously when they were together, at least until they got used to the idea that the boss and the office manager were more than business associates. Considering that it had taken her more than a week to wrap her head around the idea, she expected the transition to be a bit awkward.

It would have been nice to think Scott was having just a little trouble keeping his personal feelings for her, whatever they might be, so well hidden. She'd hate to think she was the only one having to work at that.

Scott was scheduled for an overnight trip Thursday to a job site in Joplin, Missouri, planning to be back just in time to make it to the engagement party dinner on Friday night, and there was a long list of things to do to prepare for his meetings there. The sun had long set by the time Tess and Scott wrapped up their work. Predicting it would be a wearing day, she'd left a beef-and-vegetable stew in the slow cooker that morning, and Scott eagerly accepted her invitation to share it with her.

At his suggestion, they didn't discuss work during the meal. Instead, they talked about their families and friends outside the office. He shared stories about babysitting little Henry last Saturday, making her laugh at his description of changing a soaked-through diaper and onesie. "Jake just stood there and laughed at me," he added with mock indignation. "Didn't even offer to help."

She laughed again. "Did he take video?"

"No."

"Then, consider yourself lucky. The whole episode could have ended up on YouTube, you know."

He chuckled. "There is that."

"You enjoy being an uncle."

It hadn't been a question, but he smiled and nodded. "Very much."

He'd be a wonderful father, she thought with a little ripple of wistfulness. He was already comfortable with kids and experienced enough through his brothers that he was prepared for the reality of parenthood.

"I told Jake and Christina that you'd be coming with me to Bethany's party," he said, somewhat abruptly changing the subject.

They'd been clearing away the dishes when he spoke, and she paused in the act of loading the dishwasher. "Did you?"

"Yeah." He closed the refrigerator door after stashing away leftovers. "Christina said she likes you very much."

It was nice to hear. "I like her, too. All your family seems nice. Have you told them that we're…um…"

"Seeing each other?" he supplied with a smile. "By Sunday morning the whole family knew. They're cool with it."

She wondered what, exactly, his family had said, but she assumed he would tell her when or if he was ready. For now, he seemed to consider the question of his family's reaction settled. "What did your sister say when you told her I'm coming to your cousin's party with you?" he asked.

"I haven't actually told her," she admitted. "She knows I'm bringing someone but there hasn't been a chance to tell her it's you."

That wasn't entirely true, of course. She could have made time to talk to Nina. She couldn't even explain why she'd hadn't.

Scott studied her face a bit too closely. "Will you mention it before we show up?"

"If I speak with her. Hand me that ladle, will you?"

He let the topic go, but she knew he didn't fully understand her relationship with her sister. How could he, when she didn't herself? He would simply have to see for himself when they spent time with her family. As close as his clan was, he would surely be aware of the difference in hers.

He wiped his hands on a kitchen towel. "So what had you planned for the remainder of the evening, if I hadn't come to eat your food?"

"Promise not to laugh?"

He grinned. "No."

She wrinkled her nose at him. "Okay, fine. *Rudolph the Red-Nosed Reindeer* and *Frosty the Snowman* are on tonight. I've watched them every year since I was a little girl. Usually I make hot chocolate and curl up on the sofa for an hour of Christmas nostalgia before I take care of anything else that needs to be done, like laundry or paperwork or laying out clothes for tomorrow."

He didn't laugh. Instead, she thought he looked almost charmed by her admission—which, of course, endeared him even more to her. He reached out to smooth her hair in a casually affectionate gesture. "Do you have any marshmallows for that hot chocolate?"

"Of course."

"Then, may I hang around and watch the elf become a dentist with you?"

"I'd like that."

He brushed a kiss over her lips. "So would I."

They made it halfway through the first show before teasing chocolate-flavored kisses turned to aching, impatient need. Tess tugged at his shirt, needing to touch him, all of him, and his hands were busy beneath her soft sweater, stroking and circling and tugging lightly until her breathing was fast and ragged.

"What about your Christmas specials?" he asked when she jumped to her feet and held out a hand to him, making sure he couldn't mistake the invitation.

"I know how they end." She smiled. "I can always watch the DVDs if I want."

Taking her hand, he turned with her toward the bedroom. "I'll buy them for you," he promised with a low laugh.

"I'll buy them for myself. There are other things I want from you, Scott Prince."

Grinning, he swept her against him. "Happy to oblige, Tess Miller."

They proved without doubt that the first time hadn't been a fluke. Their lovemaking this time was just as spectacular, just as breathtaking. As much as Tess hated clichés, she had to admit if only to herself that she'd honestly never felt anything like that before.

Because he'd be making an early start the next morning, Scott didn't stay long. He left her with smiles and kisses at the door.

"Be careful during your drive," she urged him.

"I will. You know how to reach me for whatever."

"Yes. See you Friday."

"Friday," he repeated, stepping out her door. He glanced over his shoulder with a rather odd expression. "I'll miss you."

Why did he sound almost surprised? "I'll see you Friday," she repeated and gently closed the door.

Was it really such a surprise to him to think he might miss her? True, they hadn't really talked about their feelings for each other—they'd talked about common dreams and goals and values, about families and children and other interests, but they hadn't said anything about love. They'd shared fiery kisses and mind-blowing lovemaking, but even in the throes of passion they'd whispered only encouragement and pleasure. She didn't expect flowery declarations from him; she knew him too well. But "I'll miss you" sounded innocuous enough. Why had it seemed so hard for him to admit?

And why hadn't she told him she would miss him in return? Because she realized now, as she climbed into the sheets still warm from his body, that she would miss him very much, even though she would see him again in only two days. And that was a bit daunting, indicating that she was investing a great deal in this budding relationship.

Apparently he wasn't the only one getting a little nervous with the speed and intensity with which this momentous development was taking place between them.

Chapter Seven

With Scott out of town and it being Heather's last day, Friday was particularly busy at work. By the time Tess arrived home, she was already tired, though she still had a party to get through that evening. A fairly momentous party, actually. She would be spending the evening with all of Scott's family for the first time since they'd become lovers. She doubted he'd shared such details with his relatives, but would they be able to sense the differences between her and Scott?

Scott arranged to pick her up at seven thirty, giving her just enough time to freshen up and change into the green dress she'd bought at Complements. He'd texted that he would be on time, but she knew he was rushing to make it after driving all afternoon from Joplin. She turned in front of her mirror. She'd followed Jenny's advice of thin black tights and heeled booties, and was glad she had. The dress was a bit shorter than usual for her, though perfectly appropriate for a party this time of year.

"Let me guess," Scott said when she opened the door to him a few minutes later. "Another purchase from your friend Jenny?"

Her coat draped over one arm, a small gold clutch in her hand, she smiled. "Yes. I bought it the same day as the red one. My holiday splurge for the year."

"And worth every penny," he assured her. "You look great. I suppose it would ruin your lipstick if I were to kiss you right now?"

She tilted her face up to him with a smile. "I can reapply it."

Grinning, he swooped in. "Always resourceful," he murmured just before his lips covered hers.

It was so good to kiss him again. Just to be with him again. Though they'd spoken by phone several times for business and once just for themselves, it still seemed as though the past two days had passed much too slowly. She'd had dinner with Jenny and Stevie last night and both had commented that she'd been unnaturally distracted.

"You're thinking about Scott, aren't you?" Jenny had accused her.

Feeling her cheeks warm, Tess had shrugged sheepishly. "A little."

"This courtship is moving fast, wouldn't you say?" Jenny had asked with raised eyebrows. Both she and Stevie had studied Tess's face closely when they'd gotten together, and Tess wouldn't be at all surprised to know that her friends could tell she and Scott had taken the next natural step in their relationship.

"It's not as though he's someone I just met," Tess had replied logically.

"True. It's just a big change, and it's happened almost overnight."

Tess could have responded that once Scott got a plan in mind, he rarely saw a reason to delay implementing it. She was his new plan, she'd thought a bit wistfully. And he seemed quite satisfied with how it was coming along.

Stevie, who'd been so perky and bubbly that Tess had wondered if there was some overcompensation involved in the cheeriness, grew a bit quieter when Scott's name came up. "I talked with him a little at the Holiday Open Home," she'd confessed. "I have to admit I was trying to read his feelings about you, just for my own curiosity."

Lifting her eyebrows, Tess had asked, "And…?"

"And I still don't know," Stevie had said. "He's a hard guy to read. He told me he values you highly. When I told him I'd hate to see you hurt, he assured me he would hate that, too."

Tess didn't know how she felt about Stevie issuing warnings on her behalf. She was certainly capable of taking care of herself, of course. Still, it was so characteristic of Stevie to feel protective of her friend. Hiding her annoyance, she'd let it go.

It was the same tonight, though as she entered the engagement party, it was nervousness she hid, this time behind a forced smile. Scott's hand at the small of her back was reassuring, reminding her she wasn't in this alone. They'd passed the test of whether they could continue to work efficiently despite their personal relationship. Tonight it was important they not be seen as boss and office manager, but as equals. To that end, she held her head high and her shoulders back as she and Scott entered Trapnall Hall, the historic antebellum home that had been rented for tonight's event.

Built in 1843, the Greek Revival–style brick house had been meticulously restored, and served as the Arkansas governor's official receiving hall. Tess had been here a few times in the past for various events—business gatherings, a couple of weddings, a charity fashion luncheon, among others—but it had been a while and she was struck again by the beauty of the place. Decorated for the holidays and the reception, it was undeniably the perfect setting for a momentous celebration. The guests mingled around impeccably set round tables with white cloths and glittering tableware, and Tess was secretly relieved to note that her green dress with its touch of glitter had been just the right choice for the evening.

She suspected that Scott's family had been waiting for them to arrive. The whole clan descended on them almost immediately, greeting them both with warm smiles and cheek kisses.

Short and plump, Holly Prince was towered over by her husband and three sons, adored and healthily feared by all of them. Tess had always liked the cheerful, gregarious woman, but suspected no one had better hurt anyone in Holly's family lest they feel her wrath. Her husband, Barry, like their sons, was tall and naturally slender. His thinning silver hair topped a face that Tess had always thought looked like Scott in one of those age-progression drawings. Eli and Jake bore a resemblance to their dad, but Scott was his younger duplicate.

"We're so happy to have you here with us this evening, Tess," Holly assured her. "You look lovely. What a pretty dress."

Scott's sister-in-law Libby studied the green dress with envious dark eyes. "I've been looking for something similar for a Christmas party next week. Do you mind if I ask where you got it?"

Tess was always happy to plug her friend's boutique. She chatted for a few minutes with the Prince women until Holly towed her into the room to present her to other guests, including the happy young couple. No one seemed surprised Scott was there with a date, reminding her that he'd never had trouble finding female companionship, an uncomfortable thought she immediately pushed away.

Tess and Scott dined at a table for eight with his parents, two brothers and their wives. Because she already knew everyone, Tess was able to join in the lively conversation easily enough, though it once again amused her that the Prince clan tended to talk over one another when they got deeply involved in a topic. They were so obviously close-knit, sharing quick grins and private jokes and good-natured insults, yet making Tess feel welcome among them.

She could see both Libby and Christina felt close to their in-laws, as comfortable in the circle as if they'd been born into the family. Tess suspected the ease was partially a result of Holly and Barry Prince's warm, laid-back parenting style. Scott had informed her his parents had been fairly strict when their sons were in their formative years, but they made it a practice not to get overly involved in their adult lives. They were always there for their sons and grandchildren, but they kept their advice and opinions to themselves unless asked—a policy that served them well with their daughters-in-law, Scott had added with a smile.

Dinner was followed by half a dozen heartfelt toasts from family and friends of the bride- and groom-to-be and then a twenty-minute performance by a smooth-voiced, Arkansas-born pop singer who'd performed well on a nationally televised talent show. The party pretty much ended with the resulting applause.

Scott gave her a sign that he was ready to slip out as soon as possible. She thought he was probably tired after being in meetings for two days, then on the road for four hours that afternoon. He got delayed for a few minutes of conversation with his father, and Tess hovered patiently nearby, watching in amusement as various starstruck party guests posed for snapshots with the singer.

Her attention lingered for a moment on the engaged couple, who were saying goodbyes to departing guests at the door. They were holding hands, she noted, their fingers interlocked at their sides. Every few minutes their gazes held and they smiled just for each other. They looked young and happy and visibly in love, she thought with a funny little pang she couldn't quite define.

"Tess, it was lovely to see you this evening," Holly said warmly as she, too, prepared to leave.

"You, too, Mrs. Prince."

The older woman patted her arm. "Please, call me Holly. There's no need to be so formal now that you and my son are seeing each other."

Was that Scott's mother's way of giving her blessing? Tess smiled but had no chance to respond before Scott returned to take her arm. "Okay, now we can leave. We've done our duty, right, Mom?"

Holly rolled her eyes comically. "Yes, Scott. You may go now. Thank you for coming. I know Bethany and her family were happy to have you here."

"As if I'd have had the nerve to skip it," he muttered, kissing his mother's soft cheek with a fond impertinence that displayed absolutely no wariness of her. "G'night, Mom."

She stroked his cheek. "Good night, sweetie. Drive carefully."

Tess bit her lip as another twinge rippled through her. Maybe she was just weary from a long, busy week, but she was feeling a bit more sentimental than usual tonight.

"You've been quiet since we left the party," Scott observed as he walked her to her door a short while later. "Is everything okay?"

"Of course." She tucked a strand of hair behind her ear and smiled faintly up at him as she unlocked her door. "Just tired, I guess. Probably not as much as you, though. You've had a very long day, haven't you?"

He didn't look entirely reassured. "No one said anything to you? Upset you in any way?"

"Of course not, Scott. Everyone was very nice. Frankly, I was expecting some personal questions or comments, but between dinner, speeches and the musical performance, there wasn't a lot of time for personal conversations."

"Yeah, that worked out pretty well, huh? Folks could get used to seeing us together without getting nosy about the details." He looked rather pleased with himself, as if he'd arranged that in advance.

She stepped inside her living room and looked over her shoulder. "Are you coming in?" she asked when he seemed to hesitate.

He took a couple steps forward, his smile faint. "Sorry. I'm a little slow this evening."

"You're tired." She studied his face, seeing dim shadows beneath his eyes, slightly deeper than usual lines around the corners of his mouth. To what lengths had he gone in order to get back in time for the party? "Go home, Scott. Get some sleep. I know you have that project manager meeting in the morning. Are you sure you don't need me to be there?"

"No, I'll text you if we have any questions for you. I'm sure you have things to do."

She nodded. "I do have shopping to finish and errands to run before Dana's party. Um, you're sure you still want to—"

"I'm going to the party with you," he said flatly, brooking no argument. "I keep my word."

She offered to drive the next evening, but he insisted that would be out of her way. "The party starts at seven, right? So I'll be here around six thirty."

"No rush," she assured him with a wrinkle of her nose. "It's not as if I care if we're the first ones there."

He chuckled and shook his head. "I'm not having your sister blame me for making you late. I'll be here on time."

He continued to stand in the center of the room, one hand squeezing the back of his neck. She got the distinct impression that he was torn between staying and leaving. But just as she hated sending him away, she knew it was best tonight.

"Go get some rest," she repeated quietly. "I'll see you tomorrow."

He reached out to pull her into his arms. "I am tired," he admitted. "I'm afraid once I get horizontal I'll be out for a while, and I do have that early meeting. So maybe it's best if I head home."

Nestling her cheek into his shoulder, she gave him a hug, savoring the feel of him before she had to let him go. "We'll see each other tomorrow."

He kissed her lingeringly, then took a step back. "Maybe we should start thinking about having only one place to go to when we're not at the office."

Was he really talking about moving in together? They'd been moving fast to this point, but that was kicking the relationship into hyperdrive!

He laughed wryly in response to whatever he saw on her face. "You don't have to respond to that tonight. Just leaving you with something to think about."

"As if you haven't given me enough to think about lately," she muttered with a shake of her head. "Go get some sleep, Scott."

"Yes, ma'am."

She moved to lock the door behind him. "Scott?"

He turned just on the other side of the doorway to look at her. "Yes?"

"I'm glad you're back. I missed you."

This time he was the one who seemed caught unprepared. After a moment, he said simply, "Good night, Tess."

He turned and walked away before she closed the door.

He'd been in an odd mood this evening, she thought

as she secured the locks. Maybe it was simply that he was exhausted.

It would have been nice if he'd said he missed her, too.

Tess's phone rang late the next morning just as she was loading a few bags of groceries into the backseat of her car. Slamming the door, she lifted the phone to her ear as she slid into the driver's seat. "Hi, Jenny," she said, having checked the caller ID screen before answering.

"I'm just calling to let you know that Scott's sister-in-law came into the shop this morning looking for a party dress. She ended up buying two outfits and some accessories, even a couple of Christmas presents. She said to tell you thanks for sending her to me, so thank you from both of us."

"You're both welcome."

"We were very discreet and didn't gossip about you and Scott."

Tess chuckled. "I appreciate that."

"She did, however, make it clear that the family approves of you and Scott dating."

"They seemed okay with it at the party."

"More than okay, I think. They think you and Scott are a good match."

A good match. A great team. Inevitable. The labels echoed through her mind.

Their relationship sounded so ordinary when described that way. Unexciting. Even calculated. Was that how their friends and families saw them? The way Scott saw them?

"I'm glad to hear they approve," she said, keeping her tone steady.

"You're okay? You sound a little funny."

"I'm in my car in a parking space. Just finished running some errands and buying groceries."

"Oh, sorry, I didn't mean to catch you at a bad time. We're going to have to get together soon, right? I want to hear details of how things are going with you and Scott, of course. And we need to talk about Stevie. I'm getting a little worried about her."

So Tess wasn't the only one who'd noticed that Stevie hadn't quite been herself lately. "I'll call you to set something up," she promised.

"Great. Gavin has three days off, so I'm planning to work here until three or so this afternoon and then he and I are heading up to the cabin until Monday evening. We're looking forward to a few days away. But as soon as I get back, you and I are making plans, okay?"

"Absolutely."

She put her phone in the console after disconnecting the call and backed out of the parking space. Her errands were done, so her intention was to head straight home and rest awhile before the party. Tonight was going to be a more emotionally stressful event than the previous ones. She expected her family to be much more nosy and critical than Scott's had been. Would her sister be able to tell by looking at them exactly how much had changed in the past couple of weeks?

Her concerns about the evening were driven from her mind a few minutes later when a car ran a stop sign in an intersection near her condo and crashed into the back-passenger side of her car. Her seat belt tightened, holding her in her seat, and she gripped the wheel with white-knuckled fists as she brought the car to a stop. The jarring, sickening sound of the impact rang in her ears, her heart pounded and her knees shook beneath the steering wheel. After a quick visual self-exam that told her she was still in one piece, she opened the door with trembling hands to assess the damage to her car and the other driver. To her relief, she could see that he was already out of his car and seemed unharmed.

She was grateful no one was hurt, but really she hadn't needed this today, she thought with a groan. As she leaned back against her dented car, one thought rang through her mind: Was this an omen for how things would go tonight?

"So meeting her family tonight, huh? The big audition."

Standing on a ladder outside his parents' home, Scott looked down at his older brother, who stood below him, steadying the ladder. "I've met Tess's sister before. They don't have much family left except for a cousin I'll meet tonight."

"You've met the sister as Tess's boss, not her boyfriend," Eli pointed out. "That's different."

"True." It was still a bit odd to hear himself referred to as Tess's boyfriend, but he supposed that was a close-enough description outside the office. For now. "Okay, the bulb's replaced. Mom can quit fussing now."

He and Eli had both just happened to drop by that afternoon. Taking advantage of their presence, their mother had talked them into replacing a burned-out bulb on the strand of Christmas lights strung over the portico entrance. That dark bulb had been driving her crazy for the past week since they'd paid a neighborhood teen to hang the strand. Scott's dad had wanted to take care of it, but only three months past knee-replacement surgery, he'd been forbidden by his wife and sons to climb the ladder.

Scott descended the rungs, then jumped the last couple of feet to the ground. He brushed off his hands on his jeans and reached for the ladder. "Grab the other end and help me carry this around to the shed," he ordered his brother. "Then I have to get out of here and get changed into my party clothes."

Eli chuckled and gripped his end of the ladder. "If you're anything like me, you're already tired of Christmas parties. I've lost track of the number of invitations Libby has accepted on our behalf. And that doesn't even count the open house we're hosting at the clinic next weekend."

"Know the feeling. Tess and I have already been to several."

"So the family's still trying to figure when and how you and Tess got together. It's as though one day you were business associates and the next day you're a couple. Unless it's been going on awhile and you've been keeping it quiet for some reason?"

"No. It's a recent development." He'd found himself using those words a lot lately. Maybe he should think of a new phrasing.

"Mom's a little worried."

Frowning, Scott stopped walking, causing his brother to stumble at his end of the ladder. "Why is she worried? I thought Mom liked Tess."

"Dude, give me a heads-up when you're going to stop like that, will you? Almost gave me whiplash. And Mom likes Tess very much. Which is why she's concerned."

"Because…?"

"She said you aren't acting like a man at the early

stages of a romance. She said she remembers how I was when I fell for Libby. Goofy. Distracted. Kind of hyper."

"Young," Scott added with a shrug. "You were just a kid when you met Libby."

"I was in med school. Not that young."

"A decade younger than I am now. I'm a little past the goofy, hyper stage."

"You and Tess are hardly a couple of senior citizens," Eli scoffed. "You're both younger than I am—and trust me, Libby still knows how to make me go all goofy."

Scott opened the door to their dad's backyard garden shed. "You can spare me the details, thanks."

Now that he thought about it, he was a little distracted today. He'd had to focus a bit more than usual on conversations because his mind kept wandering to a condo on the other side of town. He could hardly remember what he'd eaten at his breakfast meeting, but he still vividly recalled every touch, every taste, every sensation of making love to Tess. But that was only to be expected, right? He was a red-blooded guy with a healthy appreciation for great sex—and sex with her had most definitely been great. He wasn't the type to kiss and tell—or bag and brag, as a few of his buddies termed it—so he wouldn't discuss his intimate relationship with Tess even with his brother, but it had reinforced his certainty that he and Tess were well-matched in every way.

They stored the ladder, then brushed off their hands as they stepped back. "Anyway," Eli continued, seemingly determined to make his point, "Mom is worried that you aren't fully emotionally invested in this courtship, or whatever you're calling it. She thinks you're following your usual pattern of getting involved more because you think you should than because you've lost your heart."

Taking after their dad in personality more than appearance, Eli had always been the most sentimental of the Prince brothers. He'd had his heart broken, or at least painfully bruised, a couple of times before he'd found his Libby. So was he expressing their mother's concerns—or his own?

"You can tell Mom to stop fretting. My heart is exactly where it's supposed to be," Scott replied lightly. Losing one's heart—what a weird saying, he mused. His beat steadily in his chest. It had most definitely raced when he'd made love with Tess, but he'd never felt in danger of "losing" it. He knew what the metaphor meant, of course, but it had just never seemed to apply to him.

"She's afraid you're going to hurt Tess."

Scott heaved an impatient sigh. "Everyone keeps saying that. Isn't anyone concerned that maybe the opposite could happen?"

"No, not really."

"Thanks a lot. But you can all quit worrying. As I have said to anyone who's expressed concern, I'm not going to hurt Tess. I would never hurt Tess. She and I have talked extensively and we both know exactly what we want, what we're doing."

"So you are thinking long-term?"

"Yes," Scott replied simply.

"Okay, then." Eli nodded and locked the storage shed. "I'm happy for you, bro. Tess is a fine woman who'll fit right in with our family. You're damned lucky she's interested in you. Don't screw it up."

It might have been nice for his brother to have a little more faith in him, but still Scott was satisfied that his family approved of his choice. As Eli had said, Tess fit in well with the independent, capable women in the Prince family. Everything was falling into place very nicely. As he knew it would. When he had one of his brilliant ideas, he was very rarely wrong.

Which didn't explain the odd feeling that had hovered in his belly since he'd left her place after making love with her Wednesday night. He still remembered that moment when the words "I'll miss you" had left his mouth, before he'd even realized he was going to say them. When it had hit him that he would, indeed, miss her, even though he would be gone only one night.

He'd made trips before, several considerably longer than one night, and yet it seemed different now. Like an inconvenient necessity from which he couldn't wait to return. What the heck was that?

He'd done it again last night. Blurted out a thought he hadn't taken time to consider. He'd come close to suggesting that Tess move in with him. Granted, it was the logical progression of this courtship, but were they really ready for that just yet? He hadn't been flattered by the way she'd all but jerked back from him in response to his hint. She kept assuring him she was on board with his long-term plan—and she certainly seemed more than amenable to exploring all the possibilities—but there had definitely been doubts in her eyes when he'd even hinted that they give up their separate homes.

He and Eli walked into the kitchen to say goodbye to their parents—then both recoiled in exaggerated horror at finding their mother bent back over their dad's arm being soundly kissed.

"Jeez, I didn't need to see that," Eli grumbled, waving a hand in front of his eyes as if he'd gone blind.

"Get a room, people," Scott muttered, copying his brother's gesture.

Laughing, their parents straightened, though their dad kept his arm around his wife's soft waist. "Holly just said she'll make fettuccine Alfredo for dinner. I've had a hankering for that for weeks, and I've finally worn her down."

Shaking her head in exasperation, his wife muttered about all the rich foods they'd be eating during the holidays, but she was already pulling supplies out of the pantry.

"And garlic toast on the side?" their dad asked hopefully. "With plenty of butter? Maybe a chocolate cake for dessert. I'll make the cake."

"Don't push your luck." Their mom looked at her sons with a roll of her eyes. "You see what I have to put up with? Tomorrow I'll have to nag him onto the treadmill to make up for this meal and he'll pout like a toddler. Mark my words."

"She takes good care of me because she's crazy about me," their dad boasted, winking at his smiling bride. "I'm a lucky man."

His sons heartily agreed.

Dressed for the party in a sport coat and slacks, Scott drove into Tess's parking lot, eager to see her again. He frowned as he turned toward her unit and saw a dark compact parked in her slot. Frowning, he checked to make sure he hadn't made a wrong turn, but the painted numbers assured him he was in the right place. Noting a rental car sticker on the back bumper of the compact, he parked beside it. Was Tess's car in the shop?

She opened the door to him with a smile that showed no evidence of awkwardness. He kissed her in greeting.

"You look nice," he said with a glance at the boxy black jacket she wore with a silver tank, subtly striped black and charcoal pants and chunky jewelry. Another outfit from her friend's store? Wherever it had come from, it looked great on her. But then, everything did.

"Thanks. So do you," she returned with a cheeky pat on his jaw.

He chuckled, then asked, "So what's with the rental car downstairs? Where's your car?"

She groaned and rolled her eyes as she collected her bag and coat. "I was in an accident this morning. My car had to be towed to a body shop. I'm waiting to hear about the damage."

Scott froze, trying to process her words. "Wait. What? You were in a wreck?"

"Yes. Obviously I was unhurt, and so was the guy who ran a stop sign and hit me, but it was a nuisance to have to deal with it. I had groceries in the car that had to be salvaged and a few other things I had to take out before it was towed off. Now I'm sure I'll have to fight the guy's insurance company to get everything I should—you know how they try to pay as little as they can get away with. I hate that part."

He was still trying to wrap his mind around this. "How did you get the rental? Was it delivered to you at the scene?"

"No, I called Stevie. She came to pick me up and drove me to the rental lot."

His jaw going tight, Scott made a show of pulling his phone from his pocket and checking the log.

Tess raised her eyebrows. "What are you doing?"

"Just checking my missed calls. I thought maybe I hadn't heard you trying to reach me."

Something in his tone must have warned her he was annoyed. She eyed him guardedly when she said, "I didn't try to call you."

He stashed the phone again. "You had a car accident and you needed help. Why didn't you let me know?"

"I guess I didn't even think about it. I knew you had that meeting this morning and Stevie was—"

"You didn't even think about it," he cut in to repeat slowly.

"As I said, I knew Stevie was available and she wouldn't mind helping me out. She was just the first one I thought of."

He told himself he had no reason to be angry with her. No right, to be honest. But still it irked him that she'd turned to someone else for help. He drew a deep breath and touched her arm, searching her face. "You're sure you're okay? Any pain or discomfort?"

"I'm fine. Really, I wasn't hurt at all, just shaken up."

"So you still feel up to the party?"

"Of course."

"If you get a headache or anything…"

"Scott." She patted his hand on her arm. "I'm fine."

He nodded, trying to lighten his expression, though he wasn't sure he succeeded. "We should go, then."

She moved toward the door and he followed, still trying to decide why it bothered him so much that she hadn't even thought to call him after her accident.

Chapter Eight

Tess had always been able to read Scott's moods fairly accurately. Some of their coworkers claimed to have a hard time telling what he was thinking when he got quiet or preoccupied, but it had always been easier for her. She couldn't read his mind, of course, but she could usually tell when he was working out a problem in his head, when he was making mental lists or plans, even when he just wasn't feeling well. Tonight she could see he was annoyed—and his irritation was directed right at her.

It had never occurred to her that he'd be upset with her for not calling him after the accident. Stevie was almost always the one she called when she needed a hand, and Stevie knew, of course, that Tess would gladly return the favors. That was what one did in a personal predicament such as a fender bender—call a friend, a family member, a significant other.

Not the boss.

Apparently she was still in the process of adjusting to the major change in her relationship with Scott. Was that why he was so cross with her? He'd taken her unintentional slight as an indication that she wasn't invested in their relationship. But seriously, shouldn't the past week have convinced him otherwise?

She turned to ask him, but they'd arrived at their destination. Dana's party was being held in her west Little Rock home, a sprawling Mediterranean modern–style house built beside a golf course in a gated community. Dana had married into money, becoming the second wife of a considerably older investment banker who indulged her shamelessly. Though she considered her cousin rather materialistic and showy, Tess still liked her well enough. In small doses.

"Nice house," Scott commented as he parked among the other cars in the big circular drive. Knowing Scott as she did, Tess was sure he thought the place was overdone, particularly when it came to the holiday lights and decorations that covered nearly every square inch of the house and grounds.

"Dana does like her flash."

"I see that. I'm sure your sister approves."

"My sister is so jealous her brown eyes turn green here," Tess corrected him wryly.

He looked a bit puzzled. "So Nina won't be here this evening?"

"Oh, Nina will be here to spend time with her dear cousin Dana. Snuggly selfies will be taken and posted to Facebook before the evening is over. Probably in front of a sixteen-foot Christmas tree done up in real gold and crystal."

Scott laughed. "Okay."

"Trust me. My sister will bask in our cousin's social glory all evening, even as she secretly hopes every bite Dana nibbles goes straight to her thighs."

He laughed again. "Sounds like a fun party."

"Well, I can assure you the food will be amazing. Dana always puts out a great spread."

"That sounds promising anyway." He unfastened his seat belt and reached for his door handle. "Tell me again how she's related. Your mom's side or your dad's?"

"Her mother and my mother were first cousins. But they were very close, almost like sisters, so we saw Dana quite a bit growing up. She's five years older than I am."

"Got it." He opened the door and climbed out.

At least he'd seemed to have put her car wreck out of his mind for now, she thought. She needed to do the same. She'd worry about insurance and repairs and a man's prickly ego after the party.

She had to admit it felt good to walk into the soaring foyer with Scott at her side. The two-story entryway was anchored by a curving staircase laden with garland and lights leading up to a balcony-railed second floor. Beyond the staircase was the ballroom-size great room, from which guests could see into the formal dining room and elegant music room. The whole place looked as if Christmas had exploded inside, coating every surface with glitter and garland.

She couldn't help noticing the women whose eyes widened in appreciation at seeing Scott, then in surprise at recognizing her with him. It occurred to her that she'd attended the last social gathering here solo, and she'd been perfectly comfortable doing so—but she didn't mind having a polished, handsome escort, either. Was that shallow? Probably. She'd do some sort of penance tomorrow to make up for it.

Nina spotted them almost immediately, most likely because she'd been watching the door. Tess saw the startled expression on her sister's face when she recognized Scott. And then Nina shook her head. Tess knew her well enough to recognize the expression. Why was Nina exasperated with her now? Seriously, what could she possibly find to criticize about Scott?

Towing Ken in her wake, Nina made a beeline straight for them. "I'm glad you could finally make it, Tess."

It was all of five minutes past seven, Tess thought with a stifled sigh.

"And Scott. It's so nice to see you again." Nina offered her right hand with its gaudy profusion of diamonds. "Such a nice surprise."

He shook her hand lightly. "It's good to see you, too, Nina. It's been a while, hasn't it?" He'd met her a few times during the past six years when she'd dropped by the office.

"Yes, it has. Tess doesn't invite me to join her for lunch very often these days."

"Actually, I've invited you to lunch several times in the past few months," Tess refuted evenly. "You're the one who always has something else to do."

Nina heaved a sigh. "Oh, hon, I know. When you're the mother of three popular and active students, it seems as if there's always a demand on your time." She turned to Scott.

She turned then to Ken. "Scott, I don't believe you've met my husband, Ken Wheatley. Ken, this is Tess's boss,

Scott Prince. Wasn't it nice of him to do her a favor and accompany her this evening?"

Nina was really in a mood this evening. Tess didn't know what had gone wrong that day for her sister, but she was getting the sharp edge of it.

She glanced at Scott. He was still smiling, smoothly civil. Probably only she could tell that he was irked when he said lightly, "Actually, this party was just an excuse for me to spend an evening with Tess away from work."

Ken gave Tess a perfunctory kiss on the cheek. "You look nice tonight, Tess."

That drew Nina's gaze to Tess's clothes. "Pants? Oh, well, I suppose you're comfortable. Come in and say hello to Dana and Lloyd. Jolie and Cam are here, and Mary and Bill. Oh, and Glenn's here. He came stag. He asked about you."

She was not the only woman at the party in pants, Tess fumed with a quick glance around that showed her a wide variety of outfits. Hers fit in just fine.

"Glenn?" Scott murmured into Tess's ear when her sister turned away. "The guy you dated? Mr. Boring?"

She gave him a look. "I thought we'd agreed you weren't to mention anything you overheard during that phone call," she said, keeping her voice as low as his.

His smile was unrepentant. "I don't think I agreed to that at all."

She looked past him to smile and return a wave from an acquaintance just inside the doorway of the grand room. "I think I feel a headache coming on," she said to Scott through a forced smile. "It would be such a shame if we have to leave early."

He laughed softly and put a hand at her back as they

followed her sister and brother-in-law into the gathering. "Introduce me to our hosts, Tess. I need to compliment them on their very tasteful decorations."

This time a sputter of laughter did escape her. Perhaps the party wouldn't be so bad after all, not with Scott at her side.

The gleam of amusement in Tess's eyes was reward enough for the effort he'd made to come to this thing with her, Scott decided. No wonder she'd been so stressed at the thought of attending. Her sister treated her like a recalcitrant child, while their cousin was too busy showing off to make a real connection with anyone at the party. Tess seemed to know quite a few of the other guests, but not in a close way. Most of them mentioned how they rarely got to see her. When Nina made a point to introduce him as Tess's boss, they nodded knowingly.

He got the distinct impression that he was known among Tess's friends and family as a somewhat demanding employer. Totally unfair. He never required Tess to be at work all the time. She just happened to be as committed to the company as he was, as conscientious about her responsibilities there. Had Tess used him as an excuse to escape to the refuge of the work she loved rather than tolerate the condescension of her sister and cousin? Okay, he could live with that. He couldn't even blame her for latching on to any excuse she could find.

He did wish Nina would back off the "Tess's boss" introduction, though. His family had accepted that he and Tess were a couple now. Hers seemed to think she'd brought her employer as an escort for lack of another option. He was doing his best to change that impression. He stayed right by her side all evening. He deflected conversation away from work as much as possible. He mentioned other functions they'd attended together. He did everything but plant a kiss on her mouth to demonstrate that his presence at her side was anything but business related.

At least Tess didn't refer to him as her boss, but tended to say simply, "This is my friend, Scott Prince."

Friend. Better than *boss*, he supposed, but still he found himself vaguely dissatisfied by the introduction. But really, what else could she say, he asked himself as he shook the hands of yet another couple whose names he would surely forget. *Boyfriend* seemed juvenile. He supposed *friend* would have to do. For now.

Tess hadn't been wrong about the food, he thought as he popped a lobster puff into his mouth, followed by a spinach-and-goat-cheese mini quiche. Both were delicious, as was everything he'd sampled on the bountiful buffet. He already had his eye on the desserts table, his sweet tooth kicking into high gear at the sight of all the delicacies available there.

"You were right about the food," he said to Tess as they took a seat at one of the little tables artfully scattered about the great room. "Good stuff."

She smiled and picked up a wild-mushroom toast square from her own plate. "Dana would love hearing you say that. She takes great pride in her parties."

He could tell she was fond of her cousin despite their dissimilarity. "I'll be sure to compliment her when we take our leave."

"There you are, Tess. I saw you earlier but couldn't make my way to you."

Scott felt her stiffen a bit, though she turned in her seat with a smile in response to the male voice. "Hi, Glenn. How have you been?"

The portly, broad-faced man who appeared to be in his midthirties, perhaps a couple years younger than Scott, took Tess's outstretched hand and pumped it a bit too enthusiastically. "You look great tonight," he said, seemingly unable to look away from her. "It's been too long since we've seen each other."

"Oh, you know how it is," Tess replied, skillfully extracting her hand. "Work responsibilities get pretty crazy this time of year."

She turned to Scott, who rose to offer a hand to the other man. "Glenn Stowe, this is my friend, Scott Prince."

Glenn shook Scott's hand with an expression that made it clear he wished he was the one with Tess, instead. "Prince," he repeated, glancing from Scott to Tess and back again. "You own the company Tess works for?"

"Yes, I do."

He could almost see the change in Glenn's posture. It couldn't be more obvious that Glenn took encouragement from learning Scott's identity. "It's nice to meet you. Tess has spoken of you often."

In a business context, Scott silently finished.

Glenn had already turned back to Tess. "I'm so glad you weren't injured in that car accident this morning. You're sure you're all right? I can't help worrying that you should have had a doctor check you, just in case."

"I'm fine, Glenn, really. No sore neck or anything, just impatient to get my car back."

"So you knew about Tess's wreck?" Scott asked, working hard to keep his tone politely neutral.

Tess explained quickly, "Didn't I mention it? Glenn is my insurance agent."

"Yes, I see why you had to call him."

She cleared her throat, then glanced around. "Excuse me, guys, my cousin is motioning for me," she murmured, taking a few steps away. "I'll catch up with you later, okay, Glenn? Scott, I'll be right back."

"I'll guard your food," he assured her with a somewhat strained smile.

She gave a quick laugh. "That's leaving the fox in the henhouse. My crab Rangoon better still be on my plate when I get back."

Though it was hard to take his gaze from her as she moved so gracefully away, he turned back to the table. He was almost surprised to see Glenn still standing there.

"There are more of the crab things on the buffet table if you want your own," the other man offered helpfully.

"Thanks, Glenn, but she was teasing."

Glenn nodded. "It's hard to tell sometimes with Tess. She has a very subtle sense of humor."

Scott didn't think the reference to a fox in a henhouse had been all that subtle, but maybe Glenn just had a different sense of humor. "Yeah, I guess she does."

"Working so closely with her for so long, I suppose you've gotten to know her pretty well."

"Yes, I think I know Tess quite well." Was he being too subtle for Glenn, or had the other man picked up on the hint? He didn't consider himself the possessive type usually, but occasionally deeply ingrained male instinct just took over.

"She and I have been out a couple times," Glenn confided. "I'd hoped to attend this party with her tonight, but I guess I waited too long to ask. I sent her a text last week but she said she had already made plans. With you, I suppose."

Obviously, Scott almost said, but he merely nodded.

"Maybe I'll see if she's free for New Year's Eve. I should ask earlier this time. But it's nice that Tess wanted her family and friends to meet her boss this evening. We all know how much her career means to her."

Scott didn't know if this guy was doing some clumsy fishing or if he really was as socially clueless as he acted. But Scott was getting fed up with this "boss" crap. "Tess won't be available on New Year's Eve," he said bluntly. "She'll be with me."

"Oh?" Glenn blinked, finally catching on. "Ah. So you and Tess are…"

"I'm going to marry her," Scott replied clearly, succinctly.

He heard a gasp behind him. Maybe a couple of gasps. With a slight wince, he looked around to find Tess a few feet away, staring at him in disbelief. She stood between her sister and her cousin, with her brother-in-law only a few steps behind them. All of them were looking openmouthed at him.

"Oh, my gosh, Tess, why didn't you tell us?" Dana squealed, clapping her brightly manicured and bejeweled hands together. "You're engaged!"

Her head spinning, Tess stammered, "I, um—"

"Yes, Tess, why *didn't* you tell us?" Nina demanded, still looking as though someone had knocked the breath clean out of her. "How long has this been going on?"

"I want to see the ring," Dana insisted, snatching at Tess's bare left hand. "Oh…no ring?"

"Not yet," Scott supplied, giving Tess a look that was a mixture of sympathy, apology and...defiance? Daring her to dispute him, perhaps? "Maybe Santa will bring her one for Christmas."

"Oh, how exciting!" Dana giggled. "Bet it'll be a good one."

"Congratulations, Tessie." Ken kissed her cheek. "I hope you're both very happy," he added, reaching out to shake Scott's hand. "Welcome to the family, Scott. You've got yourself a treasure here."

Scott looked at Tess again when he responded, "Yes, I'm aware of that."

They were suddenly surrounded by well-wishers, hugged and congratulated and barraged with questions neither was prepared to answer. She noted that Glenn had disappeared into the crowd after unwittingly initiating this excitement. Standing at Scott's side, she gritted her teeth behind a bright smile and settled for a couple of stock answers. "It's a recent development" and, "No, we haven't set a date yet." She appeased her sister somewhat by promising to visit the next afternoon with all the details.

"We weren't planning to announce it just yet," she added with a chiding look toward Scott. "He just got carried away."

"My bad," Scott agreed. "I guess I'm just too excited to keep it to myself."

"Oh, that's so sweet," someone crooned while Tess fantasized about strangling him.

They took their leave as soon as they could politely do so. Dana's husband cracked a suggestive joke about the newly engaged couple wanting to be alone together, earning himself a cold stare from Nina that made him swallow visibly. Tess clutched Scott's arm in a white-knuckled grip and almost dragged him out the door.

A taut silence surrounded them in Scott's car as he drove through the gates of the neighborhood. Only when they were on the highway headed toward her condo did he sigh and say, "Okay, let me have it."

She twisted beneath her seat belt to face his profile. "I can't even come up with the words."

"Look, I'm really sorry, Tess. I know that was awkward for you—"

"Gee, you think?"

He winced. "It got away from me. That Glenn guy was grilling me about our relationship, talking about asking you out, brushing me off as nothing more than your boss, and I simply told him the truth. I didn't realize you and your family were within earshot, though I guess I should have checked before I spoke."

"Or maybe not have spoken at all?"

"Maybe."

She could tell he wasn't entirely sorry. Just what male ego button had Glenn pushed? Surely it hadn't been intentional; Glenn wasn't exactly the territorial type. For that matter, she'd never thought of Scott that way, either.

"Technically, I didn't say we're engaged," he added somewhat stiffly. "I told Glenn I'm going to marry you. I just didn't mention I haven't officially asked yet. You could have made it clear you haven't given me an answer yet if you didn't want everyone to start congratulating us."

"Oh, that wouldn't have been awkward at all."

"Sorry, Tess. But we knew when we started attending these things together that people would want to know what's going on with us. Like I said, Glenn asked about our relationship and I told him the truth. I want to marry you. I thought we'd already established that."

She couldn't quite define the emotions crashing through her. She wasn't surprised, exactly. Scott *had* made it clear that this was the direction in which his thoughts had been headed. All that talk of what a good team they made, what a brilliant idea he'd had about them, how nicely she fit in with his family, how well she understood his demanding obligations and responsibilities. Yet in all of that talk, not once had he mentioned love. He'd even had a hard time telling her he'd miss her while he was out of town.

She rode without speaking for the remainder of the drive, and he didn't push her to express her thoughts. He turned into the parking lot of her condominium compound. "Are you going to invite me in?"

With a little sigh, she reached for her door handle. "Of course. Come in."

They really did need to talk. The problem was that when they were alone together in her condo, talking was too often the last thing on their minds.

Inside her living room, she dumped her coat and bag on a chair, then turned to face him as he waited patiently for her to speak first. After a moment, she gave a wry laugh and pushed back her hair. "One thing about you, Scott—dealing with you is never boring. Neither at the office nor, it turns out, at parties."

"I hope that's a compliment."

"Not entirely. Every once in a while it might be nice to be prepared for what you're going to do next."

Taking a step toward her, he caught her hands in his, gazing somberly into her eyes. "I really am sorry I embarrassed you in front of your family, Tess."

She bit her lip, then couldn't resist saying, "Did you see Nina's face?"

A sudden grin tugged at his lips, though he seemed to be trying to contain it. "Yes. I'd say we surprised her."

"It's one of the few times in my entire life I've seen my sister struck speechless."

"How did that feel?"

"It didn't suck," she pronounced after another moment.

Scott chuckled. "She does like to get in her digs against you, doesn't she? I don't know how you keep from losing your temper with her."

She shrugged. "I have a few times. I learned long ago that it doesn't really accomplish anything. She gets all chilly and defensive and makes a grudging apology she doesn't really mean, and then everything goes back to the way it's always been. I've conceded that if I'm going to have any sort of relationship with my sister in the future, I just have to bite my tongue and accept the way she is."

He looked annoyed on her behalf. "But you don't have to let her push you around."

"I rarely do. I just let her speak her mind and then I pretty much do what I want."

Running a hand up and down her arm, he laughed softly. "Much as you do with me?"

She shrugged.

"I have always admired your quiet determination," he told her, and though his tone was still light, she could tell he was serious.

As always, his compliment touched her, weakened her resolve against him, dampened her annoyance. Releasing a low sigh, she shook her head slowly. "I guess you know word of this will be all over town by tomorrow. We had mutual acquaintances there, and Dana's love of gossip is second only to her passion for shopping."

"Then, we should probably tell my family. I heard you tell Nina you'd be at her house early afternoon tomorrow—why don't I join you for that and then you can come with me to my folks' house. We'll get it all out of the way in one day."

Out of the way. She frowned at him. "You're assuming quite a lot, aren't you?"

He grimaced. "I'm not trying to railroad you. I'm being clumsy again, I'm afraid. This really isn't my forte, is it?"

He drew a deep breath and asked, "What do you say, Tess? Will you marry me?"

She bit her lip.

"I'm lousy at the romance stuff, you know that," he said. "I'll probably forget birthdays and anniversaries and special occasions—hell, I've always depended on you to remind me of that stuff anyway. I'll cancel our plans when work issues come up. I'll get caught up in mulling over a dilemma and I won't hear your questions or comments. I'll be short-tempered and impatient sometimes when I let stress get the better of me."

"I'm used to all of that," she reminded him.

He smiled ruefully. "Yeah, I guess you are. I guess what I'm trying to say is you know me better than anyone. I can't be any different at home than I am at the office because that's just who I am. Other women didn't like that. They wanted more from me than I was able to give."

Lifting his chin, he added proudly, "And by the way, I think I have a hell of a lot to give. I can promise absolute loyalty and faithfulness. I'll be a good provider, a devoted father, a steadfast supporter of your dreams and ambitions. You can depend on me to be there for you whenever you need me. You and I have always gotten along amazingly well without either of us trying to be something we're not. We've proved that we have a strong, more than satisfying physical connection. I think we can carry our solid partnership into a marriage that will last a lifetime. I know what I want. But it's in your hands now. I can give you more time, even though I know I rushed things this evening. As much time as you need."

No, it wasn't a particularly romantic speech, but she couldn't deny that he'd laid out a very convincing argument. He was offering everything she'd looked for when she'd signed up with those online dating services hoping to make a connection. Well, almost everything. Maybe there was a bit more of the romantic in her than she'd realized. Most of the single women she knew would probably tell her she was crazy not to snap this guy up before he had even a chance to change his mind. And here she was dithering because there was some indefinable something missing from his earnest proposal.

Studying his face, she asked quietly, "What would you do if I were to tell you that I don't want to marry you? That I've decided we're not a good match after all?"

A muscle jumped in his jaw, but he spoke in an even tone. "I'd be disappointed. Very disappointed. But I would accept your decision and I'd continue to focus on my work. Maybe I was meant to be a workaholic bachelor. Whatever happens between us, I would still treasure our friendship and your contribution to my company."

"You honestly believe we could still work together if this experiment, as you called it, didn't succeed?"

"I'd like to think so. It could be a little awkward at first, but I think we could manage it. Which doesn't mean I wouldn't have moments of regret that it didn't work out," he added candidly.

Moments of regret. Hardly a description of a broken heart, but then they'd made a concerted effort from the beginning of this plan to avoid that drastic outcome, right? He'd steadfastly asserted that avoiding unrealistic expectations would protect them both from bitter disappointment. It sounded so logical and honest that she couldn't think of a sound argument.

"Is that what you're trying to tell me, Tess? That you don't think we're a good match?"

"I think we're a very good match," she replied, drawing a deep, bracing breath and lifting a hand to his cheek. "We'd never have made it through the past six years working together if we weren't. I'm willing to gamble with you that we're equally well suited outside the office."

The tension in his face eased. His smile broadened, as his face moved against her palm. "That's a yes?"

She swallowed. "Yes."

"We should seal the deal." He stuck out his right hand. "Put 'er there, partner."

A laugh sputtered from her. "I know you said you're no poet, but honestly, Scott…a handshake?"

Grinning, he swept her into his arms and spun her

around once. "I can do better than that," he said, and smothered her laughter with his kiss.

They took their time making their way to her bedroom. Whether because of their new status or because they were becoming more comfortable with their lovemaking, they weren't as frantic and impatient this time, but more deliberate, savoring every touch, every kiss, every slow caress. Clothes were smoothed out of the way rather than stripped off, falling softly to the floor beside the bed. Their bodies were illuminated by the dimmed light on her nightstand, an intimate circle of light in the otherwise shadowed room.

Scott frowned when he saw the bruise on her left shoulder that ran a few inches down onto her chest. He traced it very gently with one fingertip. "Does this hurt?"

"No, not really." Caught up in the pleasure of being snuggled against his warm, bare body, she couldn't care less about a couple of minor bruises.

"It's from your seat belt, isn't it? From the accident this morning."

"I guess. It locked up hard to keep me in my seat. I'm fine. I've just always bruised easily."

A lump formed in her throat when he pressed his lips very tenderly to the bruise. He lifted his head and smoothed her hair from her face, looking into her eyes with an almost fierce expression. "I don't want anything like that to happen to you ever again. But if it does, call me. Wherever I am, whatever I'm doing, I want you to call."

She'd had no idea it would bother him so badly that she hadn't called him that morning. She'd planned all along to tell him about the accident, of course. But she hadn't realized he would take the delay so personally. "I'll call," she promised.

He gathered her closer, lowering his mouth to hers. "Good."

Scott lay on his side, propped on one elbow as he looked down at the woman sleeping on the pillows beside him. He'd smoothed the covers over her and she'd snuggled into them, drawing them to her chin in her sleep. It was the first time she'd slept with him there. Was she growing more accustomed to his presence in her bed, or was she simply tired after a long week, a long day? He thought of the bruise on her shoulder and scowled, hoping she hadn't underplayed the physical effects of the accident. Should he be monitoring her sleep? No, he was overreacting. She hadn't hit her head. Even the bruise was mild, just a smudge of purple against her fair skin.

He was satisfied that she would remember to call him now should anything similar happen in the future. Now that they were engaged, he wanted to be the first one she thought to notify in an emergency, even a minor one.

Engaged. To be married. Tess Miller had agreed to be his wife.

He mulled the words over in his mind, getting used to the feel of them. They felt…pretty good, he concluded. Really good, he added, his body still warm and heavy with satisfaction.

He was still a little dazed by the way the evening had progressed. He hadn't intended to propose tonight, certainly not to announce their engagement before he'd even confirmed it with Tess. Hell, she'd have had every right to toss him out on his ear for his arrogance. Why hadn't she? Considering that Tess wasn't one to allow herself to be railroaded—not at work or in her personal life—he could only conclude that she'd accepted his proposal because she wanted to marry him. He'd made some good arguments in his own favor. Presented his case with the same enthusiasm and persuasion he used when making a pitch to a potential client. And he'd convinced her to say yes.

He always reacted to victorious presentations with pride, gratitude, personal validation. He supposed he felt those things now, but in a deeper, quieter way. Losing a bid, even a big one, was hardly devastating. Disappointing, perhaps, but there were always more jobs, more opportunities to make money. Having Tess turn down his proposal would have been harder to swallow. Since he'd concluded she was the perfect mate for him, he couldn't imagine anyone else in her place. He'd set his sights on convincing her and he'd been persistent. And now it was going to happen. He'd won again.

So why was there a nagging feeling deep inside him that something could still go wrong? That maybe he was forgetting something or overlooking some detail?

Perhaps it was simply all too new. Hadn't sunk in yet. Maybe it was the abrupt way the engagement had come about, as opposed to his usual practiced sales style. He'd been left with the feeling that something was still unfinished.

She stirred in her sleep and tugged the covers to her ears. He smiled. Tess was a cocooner. She'd probably nestle into his arms if he settled in beside her. Because that sounded so appealing, he did so, finding that she did, indeed, fit perfectly into the hollow of his shoulder. He hadn't intended to spend the night, but what the heck. He had no plans in the morning. It seemed like the right time.

He brushed a kiss across her warm forehead and closed his eyes. By tomorrow, he was sure this funny feeling inside him would be resolved.

Maybe he was just tired.

Tess wondered how long it would take for the novelty of waking up with Scott to wear off. She thought it might be a while. As for the novelty of having him join her in the shower and linger there with her until the water ran cold…well, she couldn't imagine that ever growing mundane.

They cooked breakfast together. She made French toast while he sliced fruit and brewed coffee. They didn't talk much as they prepared the meal, but worked in companionable silence in her small kitchen.

"So what time are we supposed to go to your sister's?" he asked.

"She sent me a text this morning. She ordered me to be there at two. I told her you'd be joining us."

"What did she say to that?"

"'Don't be late. I have plans for the evening.'"

"I can tell she's very happy for us."

She gave him a look over her coffee cup. "Delirious."

"Okay, two o'clock. That gives us time to stop by my place so I can change into clean clothes." He was wearing the slacks and shirt from last night.

"Plenty of time."

"Maybe we could run by the office, too. I have a couple of things I need to take care of there."

"Fine. But if we're late, you'll have to explain to Nina."

"Trust me. We won't be late."

She laughed in response to his fervent tone. Apparently Scott had decided it was best not to be on the receiving end of one of Nina's icy looks.

An hour later he ushered her into his house, a three-bedroom traditional-style home in a peaceful development filled with upscale professionals with families. Because it had begun to rain, and occasionally heavy downpours were predicted all day, he'd parked in the garage and brought her in through the kitchen. She had always admired the granite counters, the cherry cabinets, the state-of-the-art appliances. The room was almost exactly what she'd have designed herself, given the choice. Scott hadn't employed Stevie for the kitchen remodel because he hadn't yet met her at the time, but Tess doubted her friend would have any criticism of the beautiful and functional space.

Scott had bought the house at about the same time he'd been involved with Sharon, though Tess had gotten the impression even back then that Sharon hadn't been particularly enthused about living in this neighborhood with its families and minivans. Saying they could always flip the house for a profit and invest in something more to Sharon's tastes, Scott had boasted about having gotten a very good deal on the place. He'd had it remodeled to his own satisfaction after Sharon had taken off. Sharon had never lived there. Tess doubted Sharon had ever even spent a night in the house.

She was ruefully aware she found that fact gratifying.

The high ceilings and open floor plan gave the first floor an airy, inviting feel. Having toured the home previously, Tess knew a private office and the master suite were located downstairs while two smaller bedroom suites and a media room made up the second floor. He favored a traditional style inside, too, with matte walls, clean lines, leather and wood and stone. Not too masculine, but well suited to a nesting bachelor.

"You have a new sofa," she said as they entered the great room, nodding toward the large oxblood leather sectional positioned to face a big stone fireplace. Behind the sofa, glass doors led out to a travertine patio with teak furniture, a large fountain and a tidy expanse of privacy-fenced lawn beyond. He'd done little holiday decorating, but an artificial tree with multicolored lights and coordinated red and silver ornaments stood in one corner with wrapped gifts stacked neatly beneath. "Nice."

"Thanks. I'd had the old couch for ten years. It was ready to be retired." He motioned back toward the kitchen. "Can I get you anything?"

"No, I'm good. Go ahead and change. I'll make myself comfortable on your new sofa."

He moved toward the doorway. "Feel free to explore, if you want. After all, this will be your home, too, soon. Unless you want to sell both our places and find a different one," he added, pausing with a thoughtful expression.

She waved him on. "We'll talk about that later. Go change."

She pressed a hand against a little flutter in her stomach after he left. Glancing around the room, she pictured herself living here. Waking in the mornings, having breakfast with Scott, perhaps riding to the office together. Sleeping in that big master suite. She'd bet he had a nice big shower in there.

She cleared her throat and sank onto the new sofa. Very comfortable. Maybe she wouldn't have chosen leather, but she could get used to it quickly enough. She looked around. A beautiful house with a couple of extra bedrooms waiting to be filled, a handsome husband… Yeah, she could fit in here nicely, she assured herself.

He rejoined her a few minutes later wearing a royal blue shirt with khakis, clean shaven, his hair neatly combed. Her very own Prince Charming, she thought with a little smile, thinking of Stevie's nickname for him. "So what do you think?" he asked. "Do you approve of the couch?"

She patted the soft leather. "I approve."

He leaned over for a quick kiss. "We could always break it in," he murmured, waggling his eyebrows.

"Mmm." She ran a fingertip from his throat down the center of his chest to his belt buckle. And then she flattened her hand on his chest and pushed him away. "Later."

Scott groaned. "So cruel."

She stood and spoke with determination, "Okay, let's do this. We'll stop by the office and then find out exactly how our engagement is complicating my poor sister's life."

Scott gave one last wistful look at the new sofa, then turned with her toward the door. She paused on the way out to glance over her shoulder at the house that would be her home soon. She was sure she'd be very happy here. After all, she asked herself again, what more could she want?

Chapter Nine

The softly glowing numbers on the nightstand clock read 2:25 when Tess rolled over in the bed to check the time. She groaned and pushed at her pillows, trying to fluff them into a more comfortable position. It was a futile gesture and she knew it. Her sleeplessness wasn't caused by physical discomfort. It was too bad she couldn't unravel the tangled thoughts in her head as easily as she could smooth out the lumps in her pillow.

The sound of the rain hitting her windows should have been soothing, but it was only annoying instead. It had been raining on and off for hours. Turning over to put the clock behind her, out of sight, she found herself gazing instead at the empty pillow on the other side of the bed. She rested a hand on it, wondering fancifully if she could still feel Scott's warmth there. But no, it was cold. Claiming apologetically that he had a list of things to do to prepare for the to prepare for the busy upcoming workweek, he hadn't stayed tonight after they'd returned from dinner with his family. He'd left her with kisses and reluctance and a comment that he was looking forward to the time when they made their home together.

They still hadn't talked about a date for their wedding. Scott had implied that he'd like for it to be soon, which was no particular surprise to her. Once he had a plan in place, he was always impatient to get it under way. They'd talked about a wedding, both with her family and his, but had made no specific plans as of yet, agreeing that they should wait until Christmas was behind them to focus on the logistics.

Something about the word *logistics* made her wince. It was such a…businesslike word, taking the practicality of their engagement to an uncomfortable extreme. Scott could make her head spin with how smoothly and easily he transitioned from teasing, affectionate, even passionate to briskly realistic and deliberately prosaic. He claimed not to be the romantic type, and seemed to even take pride in the fact, but it was almost as if he were afraid of taking that final step into deep intimacy. Was it fear of being hurt? Of doing something wrong?

Now that she'd agreed to marry him, shouldn't he be more confident about it? Should she really have seen the faintest hint of panic in his eyes yesterday whenever anyone in their families had alluded to how romantic it was that their working relationship had turned into an engagement?

She thought about her sister. Maybe Ken had given Nina one of his rare lectures about how she should act that afternoon, because she'd been on her best behavior.

She'd served tea and pretty little cakes to Tess and Scott in her parlor and congratulated them on their engagement. True to form, Nina hadn't been able to resist a few complaints that she'd been left out of the loop and that she'd heard about their engagement in such an abrupt, public manner. Tess couldn't totally blame her sister for feeling slighted, which made her more patient in dealing with the censure. Nina had regally accepted Tess's apologies, then proved no more resistant than most to Scott's charming smiles and winsome contrition.

Nina had insisted she would do everything she could to help with the wedding—though of course her schedule was so very full, her presence so in demand, that she wasn't sure how much she could physically contribute. "We'll try to arrange lunches during the weeks ahead," she'd said to Tess. "You can bring photos and samples and I'll be happy to give you my input."

Tess could easily imagine how those meetings would go. She would potentially spend hours choosing colors and dresses and music and other details, and Nina would shoot down every option with an indulgent comment about how Tess's ideas were "cute," but perhaps she should consider Nina's much more fashionably inspired suggestions instead. Tess had smiled noncommittally and politely promised her older sister she'd let her know when she needed advice.

The only truly personal moment between her and her sister had come just as the visit was ending. Scott had dashed out in the downpour with an umbrella, having chivalrously volunteered to bring his car close to the front door for Tess. Waiting just inside the door with her sister, Tess had been surprised when Nina gave her a firm, apparently impulsive hug.

"I am pleased for you, Tess," she'd said. "I hope Scott will make you very happy. You deserve to have someone take care of you for a change."

Startled, Tess had almost replied that she was more comfortable taking care of herself, but sensing a rather touching sincerity in her sister's words, she'd said only, "Thank you, Nina."

Dinner with Scott's family could not have been more different. The whole Prince clan had been there, including the twins and baby Henry, all gathered around the big farm table in Holly's dining room, all talking at once, laughing, teasing, treating Tess as if she was already part of the family. They, of course, had already been aware of the change in Tess and Scott's relationship, so it was easier for them to process the announcement of their engagement.

"When's the big day?" Jake had demanded.

"We haven't set a date," Scott had replied, squeezing Tess's thigh beneath the table, "but I'd like for it to be soon."

"It takes a while to plan a wedding," Libby had warned. "You have to reserve a space for the ceremony and the reception. Caterers and florists and cake decorators and musicians are often booked well in advance, so as soon as you choose a date, you should start putting down deposits. I have a friend who's an excellent florist, Tess. I'd be happy to go with you to talk with her, if you like. Bet I can get you a discount."

"My cousin is a caterer," Christina had chimed in. "She did our wedding and it was great, wasn't it, guys? And I'll get you the number for our videographer and photographer. Jake and I were very happy with their services."

"I would love to help you with whatever you need from me," Holly had added eagerly. "I can make calls or address envelopes or anything else you want me to do. And I have a connection with a cake decorator who does some of the most beautiful work I've ever seen. I'd be pleased to introduce you to her, though of course I won't be offended if you decide to use someone else."

They had all been so excited, so eager to help, yet Tess hadn't felt at all as if they were trying to take over. They were just making themselves available to her in any way she needed them. She'd found that incredibly sweet.

All in all, it had been a very nice day. So why was she lying awake in the middle of the night, thinking back over the gatherings and trying to analyze why the more thrilled everyone seemed to act about them, the more Scott had seemed to withdraw into himself? Oh, nothing of the sort had shown in his behavior. He'd laughed and conversed as heartily as anyone else at his mother's table. He'd participated in the discussion of possible wedding venues and teased Tess about hiring an '80s-revival heavy-metal band for the reception. He'd kissed her good-night with the same heat and hunger that had made their previous embraces so exhilarating and he'd looked genuinely regretful when he'd made himself leave her.

Was she only imagining that he was holding a small part of himself back? Was she mistaken in sensing a tiny kernel of doubt deep inside him—or was that a projection of her own lingering misgivings? It had all happened so fast. She'd been swept along by his enthusiasm for his brilliant idea, his enticing verbal pictures of an ideal future together, her own yearnings and long-suppressed attraction. And now that everything seemed to be settled, now that everyone knew about their plans, now that it would be incredibly awkward to call it all off, now that she couldn't imagine not marrying Scott—a tiny part of her feared that she'd made a mistake.

With a groan, she punched her pillow again. She really was an idiot.

Maybe she was just tired.

Pulling the covers to her ears, she sank into the bed and squeezed her eyes shut, trying to push those silly doubts and foolish fears away. And wondering why she, who almost never cried, felt suddenly on the verge of tears.

Scott spent most of the following week out of town visiting job sites and attending planning meetings for the new year. Their hectic work schedule prevented them from spending much time together, but they spoke by phone every evening and managed to share a couple of pleasant nights together. By the beginning of Christmas week, both were tired and looking forward to the end of this hectic holiday season. Tess was ready to focus on their future together outside the office, something they'd barely had time to even think about since they'd become so unceremoniously engaged.

The shortened workweek ahead made Monday ridiculously busy in preparation. Wednesday was Christmas Eve, and Scott had announced the offices would close at noon that day and wouldn't officially reopen until the following Monday, which would also be a short holiday week. If any crises occurred, essential personnel could be called in, of course, but they all hoped the holiday would be problem-free.

The stressful day finally over, she was driving to Stevie's for a pre-Christmas celebration. But her mind was preoccupied by what had happened that afternoon.

Scott had called an early staff meeting to confirm the week's schedule. Then he'd wished everyone a merry Christmas as he handed out generous gift cards to an upscale local restaurant. End-of-the-year bonuses were included in their paychecks, but this was a little treat he'd been in the habit of providing on his own behalf for the past few years, telling his employees they deserved a nice night out to relax after working so hard and so loyally for him.

"Before we adjourn," he'd added, holding out a hand to Tess, "there's one more announcement I need to make. I'm sure the rumors have already begun and I want you all to hear the news from Tess and me."

Moistening her lips, Tess had pasted on a confident smile and taken her place at his side. Some of the staff looked puzzled, and she figured they wondered if a promotion or resignation was being announced. A couple others smiled knowingly, which meant the gossip had already made its way to the office.

After a slight nod of approval from her, Scott turned back to their team. "Tess and I are engaged," he said simply. "We haven't determined a date yet, but we're going to be married."

Amid the startled cries and happy claps, Scott held up a hand to add, "You all know how valuable Tess is to this company. Just so you know, we aren't making any immediate changes in her responsibilities here in the office. So carry on, and here's to another great year for all of us who make up PCCI."

She'd appreciated his attempt to make sure she was

treated no differently by the staff now that she was marrying the boss, but she knew some changes were inevitable. If there was any resentment, she didn't see it at the moment. Still, she and Scott would have to be very careful in the future to keep their personal life clearly separate from work, just as they had to this point.

The phones had begun to ring and everyone went back to work. Scott left soon after the staff meeting and was out of the office most of the day, though a series of terse phone calls and texts from him kept Tess and the rest of the staff busy trying to keep up.

He hadn't returned by the time Tess had to leave, so she sent him a text reminding him that she had plans with Jenny and Stevie, and that she'd see him at work in the morning.

I'll call you tonight, he texted back. Have fun with your friends. Tell them hello for me.

She arrived at Stevie's place for their own little Christmas celebration. A cozy bungalow, Stevie's house was the one in which she'd grown up with her mother and brother, located in a neighborhood that had briefly declined and was now undergoing a revival. Her white frame home sat on a corner lot, so her nearest neighbor was a '60s-style brick ranch on her west side, the one in which the widowed cat owner lived. Tess glanced automatically that way as she parked at the curb in front of Stevie's house. A dark car sat in the carport and lights burned in the windows, so she assumed Stevie's neighbor had returned from his business trip, though she caught no glimpse of him. She'd bet Stevie was glad to be done with her cat-sitting duties for now.

The neighbor hadn't decorated for the holiday, but other houses on the block were festooned with festive lights and oversize Christmas inflatables in their yards. Stevie had arranged a string of white lights around her little porch, and a Christmas tree with white lights was visible through the lace curtains at her front window. A big wreath with a red velvet bow decorated the front door, which was painted blue to match the shutters at the windows.

Stevie and Jenny both greeted Tess with such expectant expressions that she shook her head wryly. If they were trying to be subtle, they failed miserably at it. She'd told them individually about the engagement, sending messages to them both before they heard through the grapevine, and she'd promised to give them details tonight.

"At least let me set this stuff down before you start pelting me with questions," she said, handing over two wrapped gifts before peeling off her coat.

Jenny set the gifts beneath the tree while Stevie stashed away Tess's coat and bag. "Did Scott really blurt out that the two of you were engaged at Dana's party?" Jenny asked avidly. "Before you'd even told your sister?"

"Even worse," Tess replied with a groan, glad she could finally speak frankly about that night. "He told everyone we were engaged before he even got around to asking me."

"Oh, we definitely need to hear this whole story," Jenny said after a moment of stunned silence.

"Tell us while we eat," Stevie ordered. "I didn't cook all this food to serve it cold." She loved to cook, and she'd insisted on preparing the meal without any contributions from her friends.

An hour later, stuffed with delicious food and emotionally drained from talking, Tess sat with her friends in the living room, preparing to open gifts. Stevie was leaving the next morning to spend Christmas with her brother in Tennessee, while Tess and Jenny both had plans with their families here in Little Rock, so this had been the only night they could get together for their own little celebration.

"I'm so glad we decided not to have a big party this year. I prefer that it's just us," Jenny said as she leaned back against a throw pillow. "Though I would like for us to all get together soon to get to know Scott better. Gavin met him briefly when he responded to that break-in at your office earlier in the year, but they should get to know each other socially since I'm sure they'll be seeing quite a bit of each other through us. And Stevie will bring Joe, of course."

Stevie cleared her throat. "That's not an 'of course.'"

Tess and Jenny exchanged looks.

"Are you and Joe breaking up?" Jenny asked quietly.

"Looks like it." Stevie raised both hands to stave off any comments. "Would you mind if we talk about this later? After Christmas? I need some time."

"Absolutely."

"Whenever you're ready," Tess assured their friend.

Blinking rapidly, Stevie nodded. "Thanks. Besides, tonight is all about you, Tess. Jen and I hope you and Scott will be very happy together."

"Thanks, Stevie." But now it seemed completely wrong to discuss her engagement when her friend was obviously in pain. "You know, I have an idea. Let's not talk about men or relationship issues for the remainder of the evening. Let's focus on ourselves. Our friendship. Our jobs. Stevie, I want to hear all about this busy season for you. I know it's been great for your reputation and your bottom line. And, Jenny, tell us about your idea to open a store in Fayetteville. How exciting would it be to own a chain of three boutiques, maybe more? And I need to tell you about the new accounting clerk I hired this month."

Her eyes brightening, Stevie smiled. "I'd love to talk about my business, but first," she said, tugging impatiently at the red mesh bow on the gift Jenny had brought for her, "I have just got to see what's in here. I can't wait any longer to open presents!"

Laughing, Tess and Jenny ripped into their own gifts. They were still laughing two hours later when the night came to a close.

Stevie gave her a warm hug as Tess prepared to leave. Jenny had stepped into the restroom, so Tess and Stevie had the moment to themselves.

"Merry Christmas, Tess," Stevie said, pressing a kiss to her cheek. "Thank you so much for the bracelet. I love it."

"And thank you." Stevie had given her a hand-thrown pottery serving bowl. "It's gorgeous."

Her friend smiled with a little wrinkle of her nose. "I knew you'd like the colors. I hope they work in the new kitchen you'll be sharing with Scott."

She could already picture the bowl on the big island in Scott's kitchen. "It will work just fine. I'm sure he'll like it, too."

"I hope so." Stevie hesitated a moment, then blurted, "I know we said no more talk of relationships tonight, but I have to ask. Just for my own peace of mind..."

"What is it, Stevie?"

"Do you love Scott?"

"I—" It was such a simple question. It shouldn't have taken her by such surprise. And yet it occurred to Tess only then that Stevie was the first one since this had all begun to even think to ask.

"Tess?"

"Yes," she whispered as sweet memories of laughter and kisses, long conversations and leisurely lovemaking, flashed through her mind. "I love him."

Should that answer really make Stevie look only more worried? Shouldn't she have found it reassuring?

"Just one more question," Stevie said. "Does he love you?"

Tess swallowed. "He said there's no one else he'd rather marry."

Stevie held her gaze for a moment, letting her silence express a great deal, and then she reached for the door. "Thanks for being honest with me. I hope to God you're being honest with yourself. Good night, Tess."

Placing the bowl from Stevie and a beautiful spring cardigan from Jenny on the passenger seat beside her, Tess fastened her seat belt and started her car, her movements deliberate. Her gloved hands gripped the wheel tightly enough to cause pain in her knuckles as she drove away from Stevie's little house.

I hope to God you're being honest with yourself.

"So do I, Stevie." Her strained voice echoed hollowly within the darkened interior of her car. "So do I."

It wasn't uncommon for Scott to stumble into his house past 10:00 p.m., weary and ravenous yet satisfied after a long day of business operations. Particularly at this time of the year, he hardly had a minute to himself. Fortunately most of the professional and social obligations were out of the way now, with this week being reserved for family celebrations. He opened the fridge and drew out a container of yogurt, a little hungry but too tired to make a meal. He hadn't forgotten that he'd promised to call Tess that night, but he needed to catch his breath a minute first. He hoped she would still be awake by the time he finished his snack.

He was sure she'd had a good time with Jenny and Stevie. The three women had formed a tight friendship. A man would do well to keep in mind that he'd better not attempt to come between them, not that he would even want to try. He remembered before Tess met Jenny and Stevie. Though he hadn't given it much thought at the time, blindly ambitious as he'd been back then, he realized now that she must have been lonely, working long days while attending classes and taking care of her parents until she'd lost them so close together. He'd tried to be a supportive employer to her during those days, a good friend, even though he'd worked to keep the friendship professional. Perhaps getting involved with that guy James not long after her mother died had been a result of her loneliness. She'd done well to dump the jerk; Scott had met him only a couple times, but he hadn't liked him.

It was only during the past couple of years that Tess had really come into her own as a strong, competent, satisfied adult. Earning her degree, buying her condo, meeting her friends, taking on more supervisory responsibilities in the office, establishing her independence from her overly critical sister—all those things had contributed to a new confidence in her, a difference he'd observed and admired. She'd been looking for companionship on her own terms, unwilling to settle despite her expressed desire for home and family, and he was damned lucky she'd considered his proposal worthy of her. That she considered him worthy of her, despite his limitations when it came to romance.

How many women would have forgiven him for that boneheaded blunder at her cousin's party? Or would be so patient with his crazy schedule and his sometimes unpredictable moods? He hadn't showered her with compliments or gifts, as Sharon had pointedly and repeatedly informed him most women desired from a man. In fact, he hadn't given Tess anything at all, including an engagement ring, he thought with a frown. Hell, he hadn't even given her one of the restaurant gift cards he'd distributed to the staff.

Tossing the empty yogurt container in the trash and the spoon in the sink, he carried a glass of water into his bedroom to make the call he'd promised. He could at least do that, he thought guiltily.

"How was your evening with your friends?" he asked after they'd exchanged greetings.

"We had a wonderful time. Great food, good conversation, and we exchanged gifts. How was your day?"

"Long," he said with a sigh, and gave her a quick summary of what he'd accomplished since he'd last seen her. "Tomorrow's going to be just as long," he warned.

"Yes, I figured. I have a lot to do tomorrow myself. I'm hoping to finally have time to finish wrapping gifts and do my Christmas baking. I always take stained glass cookies and pear tartlets to my sister's house for Christmas dinner, and I haven't even started them."

"I've had your pear tartlets," he reminded her. "You made me a batch last year, remember? They were out of this world."

"I thought I'd make extras of everything to take to your family's house Christmas. Do you think they'd like them?"

"Are you kidding? They'll love them. Jake and Eli will probably arm wrestle for those tartlets."

She laughed musically in his ear. "That won't be necessary. I'll make plenty. Your mother was so insistent that as a first-time guest I shouldn't have to bring anything this year, but I feel as though I should take something."

"That'll be fine. It feels kind of strange to work around two family schedules for Christmas, huh?"

"It does. My social calendar was much busier this year than usual." Fortunately her family celebrated together on Christmas Eve, while his gathered for a big Christmas Day lunch, so the traditions hadn't overlapped.

"Mine's been packed, too," he said. "But I'm not complaining. I've enjoyed the past weeks with you."

"So have I," she said.

Had he heard something a little odd in her voice just then? He wished he could see her face. He wished he could touch her. Kiss her. The intensity of the hunger that shot through him so unexpectedly shook him. It had only been a few hours since he'd seen her, but here he was missing her as if it had been days.

"Tess? We can have as big a wedding as you'd like, but I'd like to put it all together fairly quickly. I don't know about you, but I'm hoping for a short engagement."

She hesitated only a beat, as if surprised by the abrupt change of subject, then replied, "I don't need a big wedding. Family and a few close friends are all I really want to be there."

"That sounds about perfect to me. The sooner the better."

"We'll talk about it."

"It's late. I'm sure you're tired. I'll see you tomorrow—though maybe only for a few minutes at a time."

"Okay. Good night, Scott."

The pause then felt oddly heavy, as if she was waiting for him to say something more, while he felt as though there was something he should say. He settled for "Sleep well."

And then he disconnected, feeling vaguely unsatisfied with the call's conclusion.

Don't screw this up.

Why did he feel the need to keep saying that to himself?

Chapter Ten

Christmas Eve was a great success so far, at least where Scott was concerned. For the first time, Tess had brought a bag and had spent last night at his house, a momentous occasion for both of them though they hadn't expressed it in so many words. They'd made dinner together in his kitchen, then watched a Christmas movie afterward while her pear tarts for the next day baked in the oven. They'd held hands during the movie like giddy teens in a theater. Afterward, she'd stashed the tarts in the fridge, playfully slapping Scott's hand when he tried to pinch a few. She had distracted him easily enough from the Christmas sweets by enticing him into the bedroom. It had been quite a while before they'd fallen asleep.

They'd talked of wedding plans that afternoon, and they'd agreed that a spring ceremony in his parents' sprawling backyard would suit them nicely. It was where Jake and Christina had exchanged vows, and Scott said theirs had been a very nice little wedding. Eli and Libby had married in the big Catholic church in which she'd grown up and had treated themselves to a lavish celebration with a couple hundred guests. Also nice, Scott had admitted, but not to his taste. He'd been relieved, but not particularly surprised, when Tess had heartily concurred.

Now, as it grew closer to time to leave for her sister's house, Tess donned the red dress she'd worn to the Holiday Open Home, and he was still struck by how good it looked on her. "You got your money's worth out of that dress," he assured her, looking at her in the mirror as he fastened his tie. "It's really pretty."

"Thank you. Sorry about the tie. Nina insists on fancy dress for her Christmas Eve meal."

He chuckled. "I don't mind. But tomorrow we get to be comfortable. My family's not nearly so formal."

"No surprise. I'm crazy about your family, by the way."

He grinned in pleasure. "Thanks. They feel the same about you."

It was all going so well, he thought in satisfaction. He must have misinterpreted whatever funny tone he thought he'd heard in her voice the other night. She seemed perfectly content with him now, visibly enjoying their time together. If there were moments when he caught her studying him with an expression he couldn't quite interpret, fleeting impressions that she was waiting for something he couldn't explain—well, this was all still very new for both of them, he assured himself.

It was only natural that it would require a bit of adjustment on both their parts.

When they were dressed in their finery, he asked her to wait a moment in the living room before they left. They'd already loaded his car with the gifts and baked goods they were taking to her sister's house, so all they had to do was collect their coats and her bag. She looked at him with a question in her expression.

"Have you changed your mind about going?" she teased, obviously knowing he hadn't.

Still, he gave an exaggerated shudder. "And risk Nina's wrath? I wouldn't dare."

She laughed. "Well, as least you're getting to know my sister. Since she's going to be your family, too, now."

"I can deal with your sister."

"Right."

His smile fading, he bent to pluck a small gift box out of the stack beneath the tree. "There's something I want you to open before we leave," he said, his heart beating just a bit more rapidly than usual.

Her eyes widened as she studied the gold-and-white wrapped box in his outspread hand. It would have been hard for her to mistake the size; he hadn't bothered with clever camouflage. She accepted it from him when he held it out to her, but didn't immediately open it.

"I have a gift for you, too," she said, her voice a little breathless. "I put it under the tree if you want to—"

Aware that she looked a little nervous—as he was himself, for some reason—he spoke gently. "I'll open mine later."

Moistening her lips, she nodded and tugged at the ribbon on the box. Moments later, she opened the hinged lid of the small velvet box she'd unwrapped to reveal the ring displayed in white satin inside. He'd selected a traditional round diamond engagement ring mounted in a platinum setting with three smaller diamonds on each side.

"I hope you like it," he said, growing a little anxious when she didn't immediately say anything. "It looked to me as though it would suit you—elegant but not too splashy, fashionable but not trendy." Again, he was quoting the jeweler, but the words had seemed to fit Tess. "If you'd rather have picked out your own rings—"

"This is beautiful, Scott. I can't imagine I'd have picked one any more perfect for me."

She looked up at him then and he was shaken by the sheen of tears in her eyes. He hoped they were happy tears. She'd said she liked the ring, so…

"Um, should I have gotten down on one knee?" he asked with a grimace. "Sorry, I—"

"No." With a misty smile, she placed a reassuring hand on his arm. "Please don't. We've said we aren't playing games, remember?"

Had he gotten on one knee when he'd proposed to Sharon? He couldn't remember. But come to think about it, he wasn't sure he had officially proposed at all to his former fiancée. He sort of suspected that an engagement had been mostly her idea. He'd just gone along for the ride because he'd thought himself ready to settle down and…well, because he'd been dazzled by her skills in the bedroom. A fascination that had worn off rather quickly when lust had turned to almost constant fighting.

But why was he thinking of Sharon now? Tess was nothing like his ex. He couldn't imagine his feelings for her ever turning as bitter and angry as he and Sharon had eventually become.

"No games," he promised. "We've already done the proposal and acceptance, even if I was fairly clumsy about it. But I will do this part right," he added, taking the diamond ring from the box. He slid the ring on her finger, then lifted her hand to his lips to kiss it in place. "There."

"It fits perfectly," she said in wonder.

"I guessed at your size, but the jeweler said it would only take a couple days to size it if it needs adjustment."

"I don't think it will. It's beautiful, Scott. I love— I love the ring."

He heard the little stammer and he attributed it to emotion. He thought that had gone very well. He believed Tess when she said she loved the ring. Seeing it on her hand gave him a wave of deep masculine satisfaction. From now on, he thought, all other men would know she wasn't free for New Year's Eve or any other night.

It occurred to him again that it wasn't like him to be the possessive type. At least he knew better than to say it out loud to Tess.

Don't screw this up.

"Let's see that ring! Oh, my gosh, it's so beautiful!" Clutching Libby's hand, Christina Prince turned to motion expressively. "Libby, Holly, come see. Scott gave Tess her ring and it's gorgeous."

While the men watched indulgently, Tess held out her hand for Scott's mother and sisters-in-law to examine the ring. All of them pronounced it exquisite, and just perfect for Tess.

"You picked it out all by yourself, Scott?" his mother asked in surprise.

"With a little help from the jeweler you've always used," he admitted.

"Patrick? Oh, yes, he has wonderful taste."

Tess couldn't help comparing this family's reaction to Nina's last night. Nina had studied the diamond with the shrewd eye of a well-trained jeweler, all but pulling out a loupe to assess the color and clarity before pronouncing it "very nice."

"Tess wouldn't have liked a big, gaudy diamond," she had assured Scott. "You were wise to choose such a pretty little stone for her."

Amazingly, Scott hadn't displayed any desire to strangle her tactless sister. He'd merely agreed that the ring seemed to suit Tess well.

Christmas Eve dinner with her family had been very nice, on the whole. With a newcomer in the midst, and with gifts on the line, the kids had been mostly on their best behavior. Scott had chatted easily enough with Ken, who was another college football fan caught up in postseason bowl hype, and it wasn't long before they'd drawn the boys into the conversation. Nina and her teenage daughter had spent the evening offering increasingly extravagant ideas for the wedding, from Nina's outlines for possible themes to Olivia's television-inspired suggestions of a Cinderella carriage with white horses, and doves for the guests to release after the ceremony. Tess had simply smiled and nodded a lot, mentally vowing to stick to the plans she and Scott had made.

Scott's family, on the other hand, seemed genuinely enthused about the ideas Tess and Scott presented, all agreeing that a wedding should reflect the individual couple's tastes and wishes.

"Both my sons had perfect weddings for them," Holly declared happily. "I know you and Scott will have just as nice a celebration."

"The wedding is just a party, really," Barry agreed, wrapping an arm around his wife's shoulders. "It's much more important to plan a marriage than a wedding. Holly and I were married by a justice of the peace in front of her grandmother's fireplace three days before I shipped out to Vietnam. We'll be married forty-four years next month. And I love her as much today as I did then," he added without embarrassment.

As if in echo of the sentiment, Eli and Jake hugged their wives. The love in the room was almost palpable. Tess swallowed a lump in her throat that seemed to be sharp edged. She glanced through her lashes at Scott and found him studying the back of his hand as if there were something fascinating to be seen there. He was obviously avoiding her eyes.

She was grateful when Madison—or was it Miranda?—interrupted the awkward moment. "We want to open presents," the little girl insisted. "Please, Grammy. May we please open presents now?"

"Lunch first and then presents," their grandmother said, smoothing the child's fine hair.

At the resulting protest, their parents reminded the twins that they'd already opened presents from Santa that morning and they had to be patient before opening the family gifts. They weren't happy about it, but the girls acquiesced and the family moved into the dining room to begin the meal.

Tess couldn't help watching the individual family members as they ate. She noted the little things—affectionate touches, shared smiles, teasing pats and pinches. She even heard a murmured "I love you" between Jake and Christina when they thought no one was listening.

As the day passed, she found herself working harder to keep smiling. She wasn't sure why, because she was having a lovely time with this endearing family.

"Tell us about when Scott gave you the ring," Libby said when the women were alone in the kitchen later. "Was it romantic? Did he get down on one knee?"

Tess forced a laugh. "I asked him not to do that. We've agreed that there's no need for pretense between us. We're just ourselves with each other. That has always worked well for us."

"Good idea," psychologist Christina approved. "You know each other so well after working together for so many years. It would be counterproductive to start acting differently with each other now. As long as you love each other for who you are, there's no need to try to change for unrealistic reasons."

"It's such a romantic story, though," the more sentimental Libby said with a sigh. "The boss who falls in love with his valued assistant and finds that she loves him in return. All these years you must have had secret feelings for each other. Now you can openly admit you're in love. That must be so liberating."

Tess twisted the ring on her finger, which suddenly seemed heavier than it had before. "Scott and I agree that we're very well suited," she said.

The brief silence that followed her words let her know it hadn't been an ideal response.

She was relieved when Jake barreled into the room.

"Tess, you have got to give us the recipe for these pear things. Man, they're good! Eli's been into them all afternoon, so I've hidden a couple for myself for later. Scott suggested we arm wrestle for the rest of them, but I know Eli would cream me at that, so I'm not taking the chance."

She was so relieved by the interruption that she spun to him with a too-bright smile. "I'd be happy to send you the recipe. They're really not that hard to make."

"These are good, too," Eli said, munching on a stained glass cookie as he followed his brother into the room.

His wife planted her hands on her hips. "Just how many sweets have you had today, Dr. Prince?"

Her husband grinned. "Calories don't count on Christmas, remember?"

"Sounds good to me," Christina said, heading for the dining room. "I'm having one of those pear things. You better not have hidden all of them, Jake."

Tess was smiling again until she looked around and accidentally locked eyes with Scott's mother. There was no mistaking the concern on Holly's face. It hadn't been there before that awkward conversation about Scott's feelings.

A hand fell on Tess's shoulders. "I told you your baked contributions would be a hit," Scott said with a laugh. "My brothers would marry you themselves if they weren't already taken."

She tried to laugh, failed, turned it into a cough. "I think I need a glass of water," she said, avoiding Holly's eyes as she moved toward the sink.

"You've gotten very quiet," Scott said in his car on their way back to her place. "You must be tired."

"A little," she conceded. She realized she was holding her hands in her lap, twisting the ring again, and she made herself stop before he noticed.

"Want some music?" He tuned the radio to an adult contemporary station, knowing from past conversations that she had a weakness for pop music, though his own tastes leaned toward classic rock. "I think we've had enough Christmas carols for a while, don't you?"

"Yes. This is fine, thanks." She was glad for the music, actually. She could pretend to listen and avoid having to make conversation for the duration of the drive.

Looking out the window at the passing holiday decorations, she let her head fall back against the headrest. A song ended and a new one began. She bit her lip when she recognized the opening piano notes to A Great Big World's "Say Something." The lyrics expressed the singer's longing to hear that his love was returned before he gave up on the relationship. He'd have swallowed his pride and followed his lover anywhere, he insisted in audible pain. All he'd needed were the words.

Say something, I'm giving up on you.

Funny. She'd heard this song dozens of times during the height of its popularity. She'd always liked it.

Only now did she fully understand it.

The last mournful note faded away just as Scott parked in the space beside the rental car. She'd have her own car back next week, she thought in relief. It was taking longer than she'd have liked, but that was probably to be expected this time of year.

Her car, at least, could be repaired. Brought back to its original condition, she'd been told, with no one the wiser at a glance to the damage that had been done to it. As for herself—well, maybe the damage wouldn't be visible at a glance, but she wasn't sure it would ever be fully repaired.

She and Scott both had their arms full of bags and gifts when they entered her condo. "Just dump it all on the couch," she said. "I'll put everything away later."

He turned to face her, his now empty hands planted on his hips. "All right, Tess. Spill it. What's wrong? Did someone in my family say something to upset you or make you uncomfortable?"

"Of course not." Not intentionally anyway. "Your family is wonderful. They were all so gracious to me."

"Then, what is it?"

She pushed a hand through her hair, her restlessly wandering gaze pausing on the Christmas tree. She hadn't turned on the tree lights so it was dark, the symbolism not lost on her. Should she wait? Was it horrible of her to do this on Christmas? But no. It would be worse to lie and tell him everything was fine. She and Scott had insisted on honesty from the start.

With her back to him, she slid the beautiful ring from her finger and looked down at it for a moment, struggling for composure. Only when she was sure she had her emotions under control did she turn to him, the ring closed in her fist.

"I asked you once what you would do if I told you I didn't want to go along with your plan. If I decided I'd rather not marry you."

His eyes wary, his expression guarded, he nodded. "I remember."

"Do you remember what you said?"

He nodded again. "I said I would be disappointed but I would do everything I could to put it behind me. I said I wouldn't let it affect our work relationship or our friendship. We could agree that it had been worth a shot and then go on with our lives just as we've been doing for the past six years."

She swallowed in pain before asking softly, "Do you still think you could do that? Even now?"

"Tess—"

He took a step toward her but she held up her free hand, palm out, and stopped him. "Please answer my question."

Lifting one hand to squeeze the back of his neck, he gave it a moment's thought before replying slowly, "I'm not saying it would be easy. As close as we've been the past month, as much as we've shared—hell, it'd be hard. But yeah, eventually, I could do it. Whatever happened between us, I would do anything I could to make you comfortable at the office, to assure you that your job would not be affected by any personal decision you make about us."

"And you'd be able to go back to seeing me as your office manager? Your employee?"

Again, a lengthy pause followed her question.

Say something, Scott.

"Yes," he said finally, the word a knife straight through her heart. "I could get to that point again. It might take a while, but we're adults, right? It would serve neither of us well to mope about our plans not working out."

"That's very…practical of you," she whispered. "You've always been so proud of your ability to compartmentalize your life. I guess that's part of what has made you so successful in your business."

She thought back to the end of his previous engagement. How long had it taken him to get over Sharon? A week? A day? She'd thought at the time he'd seemed almost relieved the relationship had ended, freeing him to concentrate again on the business he truly loved. Maybe it would take him a little longer this time.

But maybe not.

"Tess, you're really confusing me." He dropped his arm to his side. "I don't know where this is coming from."

She took pride in the fact that her eyes were dry when she looked at him. "I'm so very sorry, Scott. I wish I'd understood sooner what I wanted. What I needed. It wasn't your fault that I let myself get swept up into a fantasy. You did everything you could to warn me. You were nothing but honest with me from the beginning."

His eyes were wide now. Dark with dawning comprehension. "What are you saying?"

She held out her hand. Turned it palm up so that the ring was visible to him. "The life you've described would be a very good one. I'm sure you'd work as hard at being a husband and father as you have at running a business. Only a romantic idiot with totally unrealistic expectations would turn you down."

"You aren't an idiot, Tess."

"Apparently, I am."

The ensuing silence was almost suffocating. She drew a ragged breath into her aching lungs, her hand shaking a little as she continued to hold out the ring to him.

Say something. Please.

"What do you want from me?" He sounded honestly bewildered.

"Everything," she answered simply. "I needed to know that losing me would break your heart. But that's not something you were either able or willing to offer. And this pretty diamond isn't enough to make up for that."

"Tess, you don't understand. I can't... I'm not the kind who... I've tried before and I failed. And if I've hurt you now, I've failed again. I'm so sorry."

She took his hand and made him accept the ring. "It's not your fault," she repeated, tormented by his obvious distress. "You did nothing wrong. You offered everything you had to give. I'm the one who got greedy. Like I said, I'm an idiot. I fell head over heels in love with you, Scott. I've probably been in love with you for six years. Isn't that pathetic?"

"No." His voice was a little choked as his fingers closed hard around the ring. It would probably leave a mark on his palm. "Not pathetic."

"But foolish."

He couldn't seem to argue with that.

"I think you'd better go now," she said with a strained, sad smile. "I'd hate to complete my humiliation by bursting into tears. Neither of us would care for that."

"I don't want to leave you like this."

"Please." She almost flinched at the entreaty in her own voice. The one thing she was determined not to do was to beg. "Just go."

He walked slowly to the door. "Will I see you at the office next week?"

"I'll come by to get my things and to make arrangements for a replacement. Maybe Damaris could take over my duties until you can hire someone permanent. Actually, you'll probably have to hire a couple of people to replace me," she added with wry candor. "You'll need an office manager and a human resources manager."

"You're quitting?" So many emotions swirled in his face that it was hard to identify them all, but she saw the first glint of anger then. Good. Maybe it would make this easier if he got mad. At least that was a real, honest emotion. "You're seriously giving notice?"

"Yes. Unlike you, I can't go back to the way it was before. I can't just stop loving you. And I won't punish myself for it by working with you every day and watching you get over your disappointment and then move on. I deserve better than that."

"Yes. You do. You deserve everything you want." With that quiet statement, he turned and let himself out. He didn't look back as he closed the door behind him.

She didn't know how long she stood there just staring at the door, unable to move, unable to cry, unable to think beyond the dull realization that she had just ended her relationship with Scott and quit her job. She knew which loss was more devastating—but she'd loved her job, too. She would miss it almost as much as she would him. Or had she loved the job so much because of him?

The numbness began to wear off and the pain came in waves that crashed through her, slammed the breath from her lungs. A sound escaped her that was part sob, part moan. Nothing had ever hurt her as badly as this.

She needed not to be alone. But Stevie was out of town and she couldn't crash Jenny's first Christmas with her new husband. On an impulse she snatched up the keys to her rental car, tucked her bag under her arm and headed for the door.

Somehow she made it to her sister's house without being in another car crash. Shivering in the cold that seemed to be coming more from inside her than outside, she huddled into her coat and rang the doorbell.

Having checked through the security window, Nina opened the door. "Tess, what on earth are you doing here? It's nearly ten o'clock. On Christmas night! We're already getting ready for— Oh, my God. What's wrong? What's happened?"

The tears had started, and there was no way she could stop them now. "Can I—can I come in? Please."

"Of course." Nina took her arm and drew her inside. "Let me make you some tea. You're freezing. You can tell me all about it once you're warm."

Tess allowed her big sister to lead her toward the kitchen, even though she wasn't sure she'd ever be warm again.

Chapter Eleven

Scott hated failure. Hated it. He'd spent his entire life doing everything he could to avoid dealing with it, which meant he'd never really learned how to handle it. Failure had been such a rare thing in his life. Oh, sure, there'd been the broken engagement to Sharon, but that had been easy enough to wave off. Maybe because he'd never really considered that failure his fault. Sharon had demanded too much from him, made it impossible for them to continue. She might have been the one to officially call it off, but he would have done so eventually if she hadn't. So he'd always told himself that had all been more of a misstep than a failure. Still, it had left a few scars, along with more determination than ever to avoid future potential failures at all costs.

He'd been so confident that he'd minimized all the risks with Tess. That he'd looked at every angle, foreseen every potential problem, dodged any complications. With the experienced skill of a successful entrepreneur, he'd presented his case, brought her on board with his plan, followed a step-by-step progression from first date to engagement, a path that should have continued on to the cozy little wedding and a couple of kids to fill those empty upstairs bedrooms. He'd pretty much won over her sister, and his family had all but adopted Tess. The staff at work seemed okay with their arrangement, so that potential complication had been avoided. He'd done everything right. She'd said so herself.

But still he'd hurt her, the one thing he had vowed from the start not to do. He'd lost her as a fiancée, as a friend, even as an office manager. He hadn't just failed, he had failed spectacularly.

On Saturday, two days after Christmas—a month after he'd come up with that so-called brilliant idea—he sat in his empty office staring at a phone that wasn't ringing, looking at a doorway no one would be walking through today. The job sites were idle, his business associates all busy with their holidays, so there was nothing to distract him from his glum thoughts.

He hadn't broken the news to his family yet. He'd managed to avoid calls and respond to texts in brief, nonspecific replies, so they probably thought he and Tess were utilizing the time off to celebrate their engagement. Which was exactly what they should be doing, had it not all fallen apart.

He shoved himself to his feet, unable to sit still any longer. He didn't know what he was looking for when he wandered into the lobby. Everything was as tidy as they'd left it at early closing time on Wednesday.

The garland and other decorations still hung in place. He'd always thought there was something forlorn about Christmas decorations hanging around after the holiday passed. Today was no different. The tree sat in the corner, lights off because he hadn't wanted them on. Tess had been sitting right there under that tree when his brainstorm had hit.

The door to her office was open. Her desk was clean, organized. He tried to picture Damaris sitting there, or some other future employee. His brain just couldn't process it. Tess was the only one who'd ever sat at that desk. How could he ever find anyone to replace her? Here—or in the rest of his life?

Why would he want to replace her?

He could go on, he told himself. He could put it behind him. Shake off this misstep and focus on what he was good at. His business. He didn't need a wife he'd probably just neglect, or kids he didn't have time for anyway.

For Tess and the kids they'd have made together, he'd have made time.

He thought of the upcoming Kilgo job, the new Best Burger restaurants on the long-term plan, the apartment complexes and strip malls and other construction jobs waiting to be bid on and won and implemented. Maybe he'd get back his enthusiasm for the projects before long, once he figured out how to tackle them without Tess at his side.

Maybe he just had to get through that stages-of-loss thing. He'd already dealt with shock and denial. He was still struggling with bouts of anger.

What the hell more had she wanted from him? He'd

offered her his home, his business, his family, his future. What more could he have given her?

I needed to know that losing me would break your heart.

There wouldn't have been any need for heartache if she'd just gone along with the plan. She'd said she wanted the future he'd outlined, the same things he desired. Why had it mattered so much to her to hear the words, the things so many people said and didn't really mean? How many of his friends had tumbled into love, rhapsodized about their undying devotion to their new someones, thrown themselves headfirst into fairy-tale weddings, only to end up angry and disillusioned, bitter and resentful? Words held no guarantees. Actions were what counted. And he'd been prepared to follow through on all his promises.

I fell head over heels in love with you, Scott. I've probably been in love with you for six years. Isn't that pathetic?

What was more pathetic? The one who confessed love—or the one who was too cowardly to surrender to it?

I deserve better than that.

Yes. You do. You deserve everything you want.

He'd meant what he'd said. He wanted her to be happy. She did deserve it. He was sure there were plenty of men who'd be more than willing to offer Tess everything he had held back. Men who would think they'd just won the lottery of a lifetime if they were lucky enough to earn Tess Miller's love. Scott doubted that the boring Glenn was the only other man smart enough to figure out what a treasure she was. And choosy as she was, she would find someone worthy of her someday.

Maybe someday soon. And then he'd have lost her forever. That stupid plan of his would have cost him everything. More than he'd even known he'd placed at risk.

He leaned his throbbing head against the doorjamb of her office and pressed a hand to his aching chest. He'd never had his heart broken before, so he didn't know what that felt like. He suspected it felt a hell of a lot like this.

"You didn't turn on the security system. Don't you know just anyone could break in?"

He froze, his wounded heart clenching in his chest. And then he turned, very slowly, wondering if he'd only imagined her voice because he'd wanted so badly to hear it.

But no. She was here, standing in front of him looking a little pale, a little worn, but her chin held high and her shoulders square. Tess might have been hurt by his stupidity, but she would spring back to her feet. She was a survivor. He suspected she was a hell of a lot stronger than he.

"Why are you here?"

"I thought I'd start cleaning out my desk," she said quietly, dashing his hopes that she'd come to find him. "It's not something I want to do in front of the staff."

"You're really quitting."

She nodded. "I think it's best."

"I don't want you to go."

"I know. It won't be easy for you to replace me," she said with a frank shrug. "But you'll manage."

"And if I don't want to manage?"

"I'm sorry," she said, but he could tell she wasn't going to change her mind.

He pushed his fingertips into the pockets of his jeans. "I respect your decision."

"Thank you."

He moved to one side to allow her to enter her office. She set a tote bag on the desk. He hadn't even seen it in her hand. She opened her desk drawer. "Are you going to stand there and watch me?"

"Tess." Exploding into action, he reached around her and slammed the drawer shut. "Damn it, this is wrong. You can't do this."

He heard the edge of desperation in his tone, but there was nothing he could do about it.

She looked for a moment as though she was about to snap at him, but something in his expression must have caught her attention. She went still. "Why can't I do this?"

"The company needs you."

She shook her head. "Not good enough."

"*I* need you."

Her expression didn't change. "You'll find another office manager. No one is irreplaceable."

"You are," he said roughly. "Maybe I could replace you here in the office, though I'd never find anyone as competent and dedicated. But I could never replace you in my life. I don't even want to try."

"Why, Scott?"

"Because I love you, damn it. I don't want to lose you."

The words echoed in his ears as she studied him in silence. He grimaced. He'd screwed up again. That was probably the least romantic declaration she'd heard since…well, since he'd made such a mess of proposing to her.

"I really am hopeless at this," he muttered. "I can't

blame you for wanting to get as far away from me as you can, but I'm asking you to stay. If it means getting down on one knee—hell, on both knees—I'll do it. Don't give up on us, Tess. Don't give up on me."

She'd said she loved him. Had she changed her mind? Had she come to her senses?

She took a step toward him, searching his face intently. "You've really suffered the past two days, haven't you?"

"Yes," he admitted in a growl. "Hell, yes."

Incredibly, she smiled. "Good."

"Well, I'm glad that makes you so happy," he grumbled.

She threw her arms around his neck so abruptly he staggered backward. He righted himself quickly, gathering her close. "Tess?"

She drew back just far enough to gaze fiercely into his face. "I don't want to be married because we make a great team. I don't want to be the one you choose because I'm practical and sensible and fit in well with your family. I don't want you to marry me because I'm low maintenance or easygoing or understanding. I want the romance, darn it, just like any other woman. You don't have to get down on your knees, but you'd better be willing to admit you don't want to lose me. You'd damned well better fight for me if you want me."

He studied her flushed face and wild eyes, utterly fascinated by this new side of her. How could he ever grow bored with Tess or take her for granted when she never ceased to surprise him?

"I'd fight dragons for you," he said in growing wonder. "I'd give up everything I own to keep you, including this company. I'll give you every material thing I own because none of that matters. You already have the rest of me."

"Including your heart?"

"You're the only one who's ever had it. I was just too damned scared to admit it."

Rising on tiptoes, she lifted her mouth to his. He kissed her thoroughly, intensely, pouring all the emotion she demanded from him into the embrace. All he wanted to give her.

"You'll have to be patient with me," he said when they could finally speak again. "I'm going to make a lot of stupid mistakes."

She nodded. "I'll probably make a few myself. We'll deal with them together."

He set her a few inches away and dug into his pocket. Holding out his hand, he offered her the ring on his palm. The ring he hadn't been able to put away since she'd returned it to him. She hesitated only a heartbeat before smiling and reaching for it. Scott caught her hand and slipped the ring on her finger himself. Once again, he kissed it into place.

"This time it stays," he said in steadfast resolve.

Cupping his face in her hands, she brushed her lips against his. "This time it stays."

Feeling whole again for the first time since she'd sent him away, he grinned and swept her into his arms.

They really did make the perfect team. In business. In love.

It turned out he'd had the perfect plan all along.

* * * * *

BILLIONAIRE BOSS, HOLIDAY BABY

JANICE MAYNARD

For Charles, who makes every
Christmas special…

One

December 23

The calendar might say otherwise, but for Dani Meadows, *today* had been the longest day of the year. The morning started out okay. Business as usual. Her taciturn but oh-so-handsome boss had not by any stretch of the imagination been exhibiting a holiday mood.

She'd spent several hours locating hard-to-reach suppliers who were already in vacation mode. While most of the country was shutting down for a long end-of-the-year break, Nathaniel Winston, president and owner of New Century Tech, was looking for ways to increase the bottom line in the upcoming months. He worked hard. Dani, his executive assistant, matched him email for email, working lunch for working lunch.

The only place their schedules differed was in the fact that Dani left for home at five every day, while Nathaniel sometimes worked well into the evening.

He didn't expect that of her. In fact, he was an extremely fair boss who never asked anything of his employees that was out of line. If there were occasionally situations where the company needed an extra measure of devotion, Nathaniel never demanded it. Such assignments were strictly voluntary. The employees who participated were compensated well.

Dani glanced at her computer screen and sighed. She'd just received another out-of-office reply. That made a dozen in the last two hours.

Nathaniel should give up and go home himself. That, however, was as likely to happen as the snow-pocalypse forecast to hit Atlanta tonight. The capital of the Peach State got ice occasionally. Sometimes a dollop of snow. But never in December.

Yesterday had been a balmy fifty-five degrees. Today, though, a cold front was predicted to move through. In Dani's experience, that meant a miserable rain event and temps in the upper thirties. No worries. She kept her rain boots in a tote under her desk. A sprint to the MARTA station during a downpour wouldn't hurt her.

She raised her voice to be heard above the whoosh of the heat kicking on through the vents. "Nathaniel? I'm not having any luck. Do you want me to keep a record of these calls and emails and try again the first week in January?"

A tall, dark-haired man appeared without warning in the doorway to her office. He was overdue for a haircut, but his tailored suit was pristine. Intense brown eyes and a strong jaw shadowed with the beginnings of late-day stubble contributed to an appearance that was unequivocally male.

He raked a hand through his hair, for a brief moment appearing frazzled. The show of emotion was so unlike him, she blinked. "Um, you okay, boss? Is there anything else you want me to do before I leave?"

He leaned a shoulder against the door frame and frowned. "You've worked as my assistant for almost two years, right?"

She gulped inwardly. "Yes." Customarily, she went to his office and not the other way around.

Instead of answering, he glanced around her cramped quarters and frowned. "We need to do something in here. New carpet maybe. And furniture. Make that a priority when you get back."

"Yes, sir."

When he scowled, she backtracked quickly. "Yes, Nathaniel." His name threatened to stick in her throat.

In the privacy of her own thoughts she often referred to him as Nathaniel, but it was another thing entirely to say it aloud, even though he insisted that all his employees call him by his first name.

She noted he had said when *you* get back, not *we*. Which probably meant he would be working in this building all alone during the holidays. He didn't have any family that she knew of, though anything was possible. He was a private man.

It was ridiculous to feel sorry for him. The guy was a gazillionaire. If he wanted a homey, cozy Christmas, he could buy himself one.

After a long, awkward silence, Nathaniel glanced at his watch and grimaced. "I suppose I have to make an appearance downstairs?" The tone of his voice made it a question.

Dani nodded. "They'll be expecting you." She indicated a manila envelope on the corner of her desk. "I have the bonus checks right there."

"You could give them out."

She sensed he was only half joking. Just in case, she

answered seriously, "Your employees like hearing from you, Nathaniel. Getting a perk from the boss himself is a nice way to start the holidays."

"What about you?"

This conversation was taking a turn that made her palms sweat. "Payroll put a check in there for me, too," she said.

He grimaced. "You deserve more. This place wouldn't run half as well without you."

"I appreciate the sentiment, but the usual bonus check is fine. Let me shut down my computer, and I'll be right behind you."

"I'll wait."

She took that terse statement to mean *in the reception area*. But no. Nathaniel watched her every move for the next five minutes as she took care of the brief routine she repeated at the end of every workday. She decided not to take her purse and tote to the party. It would be easier to pop back up here before she went home. Because the office contained sensitive information as well as her valuables, she slipped a key card that opened the executive suite into her pocket. If the boss got trapped at the party, she didn't want to have to wait.

At last, she stood and smoothed the skirt of her simple black dress. She'd chosen sophistication over traditional holiday colors. At five feet four inches and with plenty of curves, she tended to look like a perky tomato when she wore all red.

Nathaniel studied her in silence. There was nothing insulting or offensive about his regard. Still, she knew without a doubt that in this moment he saw her as a woman and not simply a piece of office equipment.

She picked up the envelope with the checks and handed it to him. "Shall we go?" Her heart beat far faster than it should. It was becoming more and more difficult to act normally. Feeling so aware of him rattled her. Something had to change, or she was going to end up embarrassing herself.

No one would blink an eye if she and her boss entered the large conference room downstairs together. Nathaniel Winston might as well be a monk. His reputation with the opposite sex was not only squeaky clean, it was non-existent.

That fact shouldn't have pleased her. But she was attracted to him, and in some tiny corner of her psyche, a fantasy flourished. It wasn't as if she had any real shot at a relationship with him. Even so, his single status kept her reluctant fascination alive. It was impossible to be near him day after day without wondering what it would be like to share his bed.

Dani felt on edge as they walked toward the elevator and then headed twelve floors down in silence. Nathaniel had his hands jammed in his pockets. More than once she had wished she could read his mind. In the beginning, it was only because she wanted to know if he thought she was doing a good job. Now that she had a serious crush on him, her curiosity was far more personal.

Why didn't he date? Or maybe he did go out but in secret. Not likely. What woman would put up with his work-aholic schedule?

On impulse, she blurted out a clumsy conversational gambit. "Will you be traveling for the holidays?"

He shot her a sideways glance tinged with incredulity. "No."

Poor man. She had probably shocked him. No one asked the boss about his personal life. Dani was the closest employee to him, yet she managed to be remarkably circumspect despite the many questions she had. At this point, the deliberate choice to avoid any hint of intimacy, even conversationally, was the smart thing to do.

She wanted to learn everything there was to know about Nathaniel—of course she did. Keeping a professional distance was a matter of self-preservation. By relegating the man at her side to a box labeled *boss*, she told herself she could keep from getting hurt.

The elevator dinged as the door opened. The unmistakable sounds of merrymaking drifted down the carpeted hallway. "Well," Nathaniel muttered. "Here goes."

As bizarre as it sounded, Dani thought he was nervous. Surely not. Her boss was well educated, well traveled and wildly successful at a young age. There was no reason at all for him to dread this momentary formality.

Just inside the doorway of the crowded room, Dani abandoned the man who drew attention with no more than a quick, guarded smile.

As people greeted him, she found a group of women she had known from the beginning of her employment at NCT. Several of them shared a Pilates class. A couple of others had bonded over their young children. Ever since Dani became Nathaniel's assistant, though, her coworkers treated her with a certain deference.

She didn't particularly like it, but she understood it.

As she sipped a glass of punch and nibbled on a cheese straw, she noted the men and women who had already imbibed to the peril of their careers. Dani had nothing against alcohol. Sadly, though, some employees lost all circumspection when they enjoyed the office party a little too much.

Nathaniel was socializing, though his posture betrayed his lack of ease. At least it did to Dani. He was playing the genial host, but he would rather be most anywhere else. She'd bet her last dollar on it.

Nathaniel was never too excited about the office Christmas party. He wasn't a warm, fuzzy kind of guy. On the other hand, he was no Scrooge, either. At his urging, Dani had planned this lavish, catered affair complete with an open bar. The festivities had begun at four o'clock and were still going strong two hours later.

At last, Nathaniel made his holiday toast and passed out bonuses to key players of the various divisions. His speech was wry and funny and remarkably charming. Dani had to step forward when he called her name. "Thanks," she muttered.

Their fingers brushed briefly. "Merry Christmas, Dani," he said gruffly.

"Thank you." Her throat tightened inexplicably. Boyfriends were a dime a dozen. She needed a good job more than she needed a fling with her boss. But for the last year and a half—the length of time she had been fantasizing about Nathaniel—the idea of a physical relationship, no matter how unlikely, had made it increasingly uncomfortable for her to work with him. So much so that she had actually polished up her résumé and sent out half a dozen applications already.

During her five years working at New Century Tech, she had completed an MBA at Emory. She was definitely overqualified for the job she now occupied, however working as Nathaniel's executive assistant paid extremely well. Not only that, but watching him operate in the business world, learning from him, was invaluable experience.

Time moved on. People did, too, or they stagnated. It made perfect sense to extract herself from the temptation of a possible affair with the boss, and even more sense to pursue opportunities that would advance her career.

Unfortunately, all the pep talks in the world didn't make it any easier to do what she *knew* she had to do.

A couple of weeks ago—as soon as she emailed the first batch of job applications—the guilt began. NCT was a great place to work. Nathaniel had been a phenomenal boss from day one. Maybe she was jumping too soon.

Still, something was beginning to change, ever so slightly. She didn't think she had betrayed her intense fascination. Even so, she was getting a vibe from Nathaniel recently that was more personal than business.

Or maybe it was the mistletoe and her overactive imagination. If those feelings were real, she was in trouble.

A commotion on the far side of the room derailed her wistful thoughts. The maroon and navy drapes had been drawn before the party to shut out the gray December day. The heavy cloth panels, festooned with lighted garlands, gave the room a festive feel. Just now, someone had peeked out and received a big surprise.

A rain/snow mix had already begun to fall. The usually crowded thoroughfare in front of the building was alarmingly empty. Though local snowstorm forecasts were often disregarded because of one too many near misses, apparently this one might be the real deal.

Nathaniel assessed the situation in a glance and acted with his customary confidence.

"Let's wrap this up, folks. Unless some of you want to spend the holidays sleeping at your desks, I'd suggest you head for home ASAP."

He didn't have to tell them twice. It was Friday on a holiday weekend. A number of the staff had saved vacation days so they could be off until after the New Year. Suddenly, there was a mass exodus.

As Dani watched, Nathaniel said a quiet word here and there, making sure that anyone who was impaired ended up in the charge of a designated driver.

In half an hour, the room was empty except for Dani

and the boss, who stood in the doorway saying a few last goodbyes. Without thinking about it, she began to tidy the tables. Fortunately, there was not much food left. She chucked it all in a large trash container and stacked the trays. New Century Tech used a nearby catering company for all their events.

As she began folding the soiled tablecloths into a neat stack, Nathaniel startled her by speaking from behind her shoulder.

"Leave that alone," he said abruptly. "That's not your job. The janitorial staff will take care of it in the morning."

Dani turned slowly and lifted an eyebrow. "If the snow does what they're saying it will, I doubt anyone is going to go anywhere anytime soon."

"That's a lot of *anys*," he teased.

"Well, I'm right," she grumbled. "Besides, nobody wants to look at this mess when it's three or four days old."

"Do you honestly believe the storm is going to be that bad?"

The Weather Channel was headquartered in Atlanta. Dani knew the forecasters by name. At one time in high school, she had actually thought about going into meteorology as a career.

"They say it's possible. Moisture is riding up from the Gulf of Mexico and colliding with the cold air. Even when the snow tapers off, we may get ice on top."

Nathaniel grimaced. "That sounds lovely."

His sarcasm made her grin. "Look at it this way. We only get hammered a few times a decade. Apparently, we're overdue."

"Well, in that case, shouldn't you be getting out of here?"

"I'll catch the six-thirty train. I'll be fine."

"What if they shut down the system?"

For the first time, a trickle of unease slid through her veins. That thought had never occurred to her. Her car was parked at a commuter lot four stops north. What was the likelihood she'd be able to drive home even if MARTA took her where she needed to go?

This time, riding the elevator up and back down was more about expediency than anything intimate. While Nathaniel grabbed what he needed from his office, Dani shrugged into her coat, tugged on her boots and adjusted the strap on her purse so she could use it as a cross-body bag. She wanted her hands free to hang on to stair rails if necessary.

Outside, the city was eerily quiet. The snow was heavier now, blanketing buildings and muffling sound. Nathaniel cursed quietly beneath his breath when he saw the conditions. "I'll drive you to the train station," he said, his tone brooking no opposition.

"Thanks," Dani replied, not even bothering with a token protest. On a normal day, the half-mile walk was pleasant exercise. Under these conditions, she'd never make it in time, not to mention the fact that she'd be a frozen mess.

New Century Tech's main parking facility was a three-level garage attached to the back of the building. For VIPs, a private side-street lot big enough for a dozen spaces provided easy access and the assurance that no clumsy drivers would back into a high-end vehicle.

Nathaniel drove a shiny black Mercedes with all the bells and whistles. Dani had been inside it only once, when she and the boss had gone together across town to present a proposal to a clothing firm seeking to update their on-line presence and ordering capabilities. Today, when they rounded the corner of the building and spotted Nathaniel's car—the only one in the lot—she had a sinking feeling that Nathaniel's offer of a ride had been premature.

The Mercedes was coated with snow, and there were no marks on the ground. Either the various vice presidents had parked in the garage today, or they had left long enough ago for the storm to cover their tracks. Something about the solitary car looked odd.

Nathaniel was the first to respond. "What the hell?"

He jogged the last few feet, Dani close on his heels. They stopped abruptly in tandem. Dani blinked. "Is that a car seat?" she asked, her voice rising an octave in disbelief.

Nathaniel lifted the wooly blanket covering the oddly shaped lump. "Good God. It's a baby." His head snapped around, his gaze scanning the immediate area. The blanket was peppered with tiny bits of snow, certainly not enough to indicate the child had been there more than a few minutes.

Dani, too, peeked under the blanket and gasped. An infant, maybe six months old, slept peacefully in a baby carrier. The child was covered from head to toe in a fleecy one-piece snowsuit, but even so, the temperatures were dangerously cold.

"Call 911," Nathaniel said, his voice as icy as their surroundings. "I'm going to look around. Whoever did this must be close. My guess is they're watching us to make sure we retrieve the kid."

Dani was afraid to unfasten the straps and take the baby out. The heavy carrier was offering at least some protection from the elements. As long as the baby slept, he or she must not be terribly uncomfortable. The snowsuit was pink. Dani took a wild shot that the child was a girl. The baby's cheeks were a healthy color. Her chest rose and fell at reassuring intervals.

Hoping she was doing the right thing, Dani removed her gloves and dialed the authorities.

* * *

Nathaniel was pissed. He'd received several texts in the last few days from a number he recognized all too well, offering veiled threats. Never in his wildest imagination had he imagined something like this happening to him. The escapade had his ex written all over it.

Ophelia wasn't actually an "ex" anything. Nathaniel had met her at an in-town conference over a year ago and spent two nights in her hotel bed. That had been the end of it. Or so he thought.

He'd used protection. No way in hell was this baby his, despite what Ophelia's rambling emails had insinuated. If she had ever come right out and accused him of fathering her child, Nathaniel would have secured a lawyer and taken the necessary steps to pinpoint the baby's paternity.

He stood in the shadow of his own building, covered his eyes to keep the snow out of them and scanned windows near and far. Damn it. Ophelia could be anywhere. What was she trying to pull?

At last, he gave up his futile search. Dani stood where he had left her, one hand resting protectively on the edge of the car seat. "I found a note," she said, holding it out to him. "I read it. I'm sorry. I guess I shouldn't have."

Nathaniel unfolded the elegant card with a sick feeling in the pit of his stomach. The contents were much as he had expected:

Dear Nathaniel:
I cannot care for our baby right now. You're my only hope. When I get my life back together, we'll talk.
Yours always,
Ophelia

He closed his eyes and took deep breaths, trying not to overreact. Women had tried to trap men with this ruse since the beginning of time. He'd done nothing wrong. He had nothing to fear.

Crushing the note in his fist, he shoved it in his pocket and opened his eyes to find Dani staring at him with a stricken expression.

"It's not mine," he insisted. "I went out with a crazy woman a time or two. She's trying to blackmail me or something. I don't know. What did the police say? How soon can they get here?"

Dani hunched her shoulders against the wind. "They weren't very encouraging. The snow is causing pileups all over the city."

His heart pounded in his chest. "What about the foster care system? Surely they can send someone."

"Do you really want to entrust a baby to a stranger on the Friday afternoon of a long holiday weekend? Most foster families are wonderful, but you hear horror stories…" Dani trailed off, her expression indicating that she was upset. Maybe with the situation. Maybe with him.

"Fine." He sighed. "What exactly do you think we should do?"

"We?" She stared at him as if he had grown two heads. "I'm walking to the MARTA station. If I'm lucky, my route will still be open."

Atlanta's transit system was only partially underground. Unlike other major cities, Atlanta did not have enough snow-removal equipment to deal with a weather event of this size. Blizzards were so rare the expenditure would be wildly extravagant.

Nathaniel's palms started to sweat inside his gloves. "You can't go yet," he said. "I need help." The words threatened to stick in his throat. He wasn't a man accustomed to needing *anyone*. Dani wasn't just anyone, though. He was counting on her soft heart and her overdeveloped sense of responsibility to sway her.

"What exactly do you think I can do?" she asked. Her eyes held a mix of dubious suspicion and the urge to run.

Nathaniel recognized the urge. He felt it in spades. "You're a woman. Help me get the kid to my condo. Let's get her settled. After that, I'll call a car service to take you home." Without waiting for an answer, he unlocked the car and leaned in to toss his briefcase on the back seat.

Dani thumped him on the shoulder, hard enough that he jerked and hit his head on the door frame. "Ouch, damn it. What was that for?" he asked, whirling around.

"Are you crazy?" Dani asked. "You can't drive around with an unsecured infant carrier, especially with snow on the ground."

In all his emotional turmoil over realizing Ophelia had dumped a baby in his lap, Nathaniel had lost track of the weather. Now he blinked and focused on the world surrounding them. The snow was at least two inches deep already and showed no signs at all of letting up. "Good God," he said weakly. "This is a nightmare."

Had he said that last bit aloud? Maybe not. Dani wasn't giving him any more of those disapproving looks. Instead, she huddled miserably against the side of his car, using her body to keep the falling snow from reaching the baby.

"We're out of options," he said, his brain whirling like a hamster on a wheel. "I'll put the seat belt around the carrier. My condo isn't all that far. Three miles. Come on. The longer we stand here, the colder we'll be." Without waiting for his unflappable executive assistant to protest, he retrieved the infant carrier, covered it with the blanket and scooped it up.

Holy hell. How did new mothers do this? The thing felt like it weighed fifty pounds.

Strapping it into the back seat was an exercise in frustration and guilt. To be honest, he half expected Dani to turn around and trudge away in the opposite direction, heading for the train station and home. But she joined him in the car.

The wave of relief he experienced was alarming. Was he honestly that afraid to be stranded alone with a baby, or did the idea of spending time with Dani outside the office hold a certain appeal?

She was a very attractive woman always, but today— dressed up for the office party—she exuded a warm, sexy charm that made him want to forget every one of his self-imposed rules.

Though it probably wasn't wise, he took one hand off the wheel and loosened his tie. Having Dani sit so close to him tested his patience and his self-control.

New Century Tech was located in a trendy section of Atlanta known as Buckhead. Elegant glass office buildings stood amongst quirky restaurants and specialty shops selling everything from expensive watches to high-priced real estate. Nathaniel's penthouse condo offered him the privacy he demanded along with an unparalleled view of the city.

Unfortunately, today's drive was not going to be easy. Though he managed to back out of the parking space and exit onto the street, he felt the tires slip and slide beneath him. He barely managed to avoid sideswiping a fire hydrant.

With his eyes on the road and a firm grip on the steering wheel, he focused on the objective at hand. Reach his condo. Rest and regroup. What he hadn't expected was to have Dani tug at his arm several blocks before their destination. "Stop," she cried. "That one's open."

That what?

At her insistence, he eased the car off the road and parked beside a chain drugstore. She didn't pause to explain. Before he could protest, she was out of the car and headed inside. With a shrug, Nathaniel retrieved the baby and followed Dani into the store.

The kid still slept. Had it been too long? Was she unconscious? His stomach knotted. What the hell did he know about babies? Even a bad foster family might be better than what Nathaniel had to offer.

Every inch of the infant's body was covered except for her rosy cheeks. Still, she wasn't wearing high-tech fabric rated for low temperatures. The little girl might be cold. How would *he* know?

Just about the time he had worked himself into a frenzy of doubt and frustration, Dani reappeared, her triumphant smile a blow to his stomach that took his breath and squeezed his heart.

Was he simply damned glad to have her help, or was the prospect of spending time with Dani enticing him to do something stupid? Every logical cell in his brain shouted at him to send her away. He was fine. He could cope.

Besides, though it was true he wanted Dani, he didn't "want" to want her. As long as he kept that in mind, he'd be okay. Despite his confusion and the alarm in his gut, he didn't tell her to go. That was undoubtedly his first mistake.

Somewhere, she had found a shopping cart. It was loaded with diapers, wipes, formula and bottles. He stared at the bounty of baby supplies, incredulous. He'd been so focused on getting the kid to his condo, he'd never even thought about the fact that he had nothing—zero—with which to care for a child, especially one this small.

If this were a test to see what kind of father he would make, he was already failng miserably.

Two

Fortunately, Dani didn't appear to notice his turmoil. "I did a lot of babysitting in college," she said. "I've tried to remember everything you'll need, but I don't know if I have it all. It's hard when you're not used to taking care of an infant."

"Tell me about it," he muttered. He wasn't going to admit he would have forgotten half of the items in that cart. "We're lucky somebody's still open," he said. This was a hell of a time to feel arousal tighten his body. Dani was irresistible with her pointed chin and her flyaway hair.

She gave him a cute little half frown that said she thought he was an idiot. "You should unbutton your coat," she said. "Your face is all red. We need to hurry."

"I was hoping to be home before she wakes up. If she starts crying, I don't know what we'll do."

Dani looked better than any woman should while negotiating the beginnings of a blizzard with her brain-dead boss and an unknown baby. She was average height for a woman, though her snow boots lent a couple of extra inches. Her body was curvy and intensely feminine. The clothing she wore to work was always appropriate, but even so, in recent months, Nathaniel had found himself wondering if Dani was as prim and proper as her office persona would suggest.

Her wide-set blue eyes and high cheekbones reminded him of a princess he remembered from a childhood story-book. The princess's hair was blond. Dani's was more of a streaky caramel. She'd worn it up today in a sexy knot, presumably because of the Christmas party.

While he stood there, mute, with melting snow making the wool of his overcoat steam, Dani fussed over the contents of her cart. "If the baby wakes up," she said, "I'll hold her. It will be fine."

"I hate to be the voice of reason in the midst of your impressive knowledge of babies, but the Mercedes trunk is small. We'll never fit all that in."

Dani's tired grin was cheeky. "The guy back at the pharmacy said they'll be making deliveries until ten tonight in a four-wheel drive. Right now, you and I will take only the essentials. I stressed to him how important it is that we get our order. He swears he won't let me down."

It was no wonder. Dani's smiling charm would be hard to say no to under any circumstances. She was an appealing mix of girl-next-door and capable confidence. In that moment, Nathaniel realized he relied on her far more than he knew and for a variety of complex reasons he was loathe to analyze.

Clearing his throat, he fished out his wallet and handed the cashier his credit card.

Baby paraphernalia was remarkably expensive. Once the transaction was complete, the clerk gave Dani a large plastic bag. The two women ripped open packages and assembled an only-the-essentials collection that would hopefully suffice for the next few hours until the delivery arrived.

"I think that's it," Dani said with satisfaction. "Let's get this little angel home."

Unfortunately, their luck ran out. The baby woke up and let the world know she was hungry and pissed. Her screams threatened to peel paint off the walls.

Dani's smile faltered, but she unfastened the straps of the carrier and lifted the baby out carefully. "I'm so sorry, sweetheart. I know you want your mommy. Nathaniel and I will have to do for the moment. Do you have a wet diaper? Let's take care of that."

The clerk pointed out a unisex bathroom at the back of the store, complete with changing station. Nathaniel found himself following in Dani's wake. The tiny room was little bigger than a closet. They both pressed inside.

For the first time, Dani seemed frazzled. They were so close he could smell the faint, tantalizing scent of her perfume.

"You'll have to stand in the door and hand me things," she said. "We can't both fit in here."

"Sure," he said, feeling guilty for not offering to take charge of the diaper change. On the other hand, the baby's needs should be paramount. God knows Nathaniel was the last person on the planet qualified for the task.

Was it weird that being this close to Dani turned him on? Her warmth, her femininity. Hell, even the competent way she handled the baby made him want her.

That was the problem with blurring the lines between business and his personal life. He couldn't let himself be vulnerable. On the other hand, he would be lost without Dani's help, so he didn't really have a choice.

It was clear Dani hadn't overstated her experience with

children. She extracted the baby from the snowsuit, unfastened the romper and made quick work of replacing the baby's extremely wet diaper with a clean and dry one. Fortunately, no poop...at least not yet.

Then it was everything in reverse. When they were ready to go back out into the cold, Dani hesitated.

"What's wrong?" he asked.

Dani grimaced. "I'm wondering if we should try to feed her before we start walking again."

Nathaniel brushed the back of his hand over the baby's plump cheek. Her skin was warm against his chilled fingers. "I think she can make it. She's a trouper."

"Are you basing this on your personal DNA?" Dani asked wryly.

"I told you, she's not mine," he said sharply. "The only reason we're taking her home is because of the storm and Christmas and the fact that every emergency worker in the city is covered in snow...literally."

"Okay. Calm down."

He bit his tongue to keep from making a cutting remark. Dani was helping him. He couldn't afford to alienate her, and he definitely couldn't risk wondering what it would be like to kiss her.

Outside, they faced the next hurdle. Three cars had slammed into each other right in front of the drugstore, effectively blocking the only exit from the parking lot.

Nathaniel cursed beneath his breath. "Well, that's just great."

"We can't wait," Dani said. "Besides, aren't we close to your condo?"

"I don't like leaving my car."

She grinned. "Might be safer here than out on the road."

He squared his shoulders. "I suppose so. I'd forgotten how insane drivers can be when this happens."

To be fair, the streets were a mess. Road crews hadn't been able to salt anything more than the interstates, and the swift drop in temperature had added a layer of icy danger to the situation.

In the short time he and Dani had been inside the store, the situation had grown exponentially worse. People in other parts of the country couldn't understand, but Atlanta was particularly vulnerable to weather events like this one.

After retrieving their personal items from the car and consolidating their purchases, he and Dani struck out for the final leg of their journey.

They walked in silence, negotiating sidewalks they could no longer see and trying to move as quickly as possible.

Dani had the baby tucked inside her coat for extra warmth, which had to be a damned awkward way to walk. Nathaniel lugged the carrier and the supplies. When he offered to take the child after several minutes, Dani shook her head. "I'm fine."

It was a miserable, soul-crushing slog through ice and snow. He could barely feel his feet. Dani must have been equally miserable, but she didn't complain. Thank God they didn't have far to go.

When they finally arrived at Nathaniel's building, he had never in his life been so glad to see the doorman or the elaborately decorated lobby.

They dripped their way onto the elevator with Dani juggling an increasingly fractious baby. On the top floor, Nathaniel found his key, unlocked the door and ushered his unexpected guests inside. "Home sweet home," he said.

Dani was frozen to the bone. Her feet had long since gone numb. Though her coat and boots were nice, they were never meant to trek through deep snow for any length of time. She had struggled to keep up. Nathaniel, by all indications, was naturally athletic. He probably played multiple sports in high school and college.

They took turns holding the baby while shedding their outerwear. Dani's chic black dress was damp and rumpled. What she wouldn't give for a roaring fire and a cozy robe.

At the drugstore she had paid for a handful of personal items just in case. It seemed unlikely she was going to make it home tonight, though she still held out hope. Right now, all she wanted was her own bed, a warm nightie and something fun to binge-watch on Netflix.

Now that she had stripped off her black tights with the silver sparkles and was barelegged, she began to shiver. Nathaniel noticed immediately.

"If you're going to feed the baby, we've got to get you warmed up first. Come with me."

Clutching the little girl like a life preserver, Dani followed her boss down the hall.

The first thing she noticed was that Nathaniel's condo was three or four times the size of her own modest apartment. It was decorated in soothing shades of blue and gray with occasional pops of color. Coral cushions. An abstract painting that called to mind a Gauguin nude in the tropics. The space was silent and perfectly appointed in every way. Not a magazine out of place. No dirty socks.

Dani wanted to like Nathaniel's home, but she couldn't. It looked more like a magazine spread than a peaceful sanctuary at the end of a long day. She stopped in the doorway to his bedroom, unable to take another step.

Nathaniel, clearly unconcerned, rummaged in his dresser and came up with a pair of cream woolen socks and some faded gray sweatpants that looked ancient. He lifted one shoulder and lowered it with a sheepish grin. "I was smaller back in high school. These will still be too big for you, but at least they'll stay up. I think."

After that, he flung open his closet and found a soft cotton shirt in a pale blue. "Here we go," he said triumphantly. "Will this do?" She caught a brief glance of neatly pressed dark suits and crisp white dress shirts before he closed the closet door again.

She nodded. "Of course."

"Use my bathroom," he said. "I'll entertain the little one."

Dani frowned. "What should we call her? The note didn't say."

"How about Munchkin? That's generic enough, isn't it?"

"What kind of mother leaves her baby in a snowstorm?"

"I think Ophelia was probably watching us from somewhere nearby. She's a little weird, but not crazy enough to bring harm to a child."

"Why would you get involved with someone like that?" Dani wanted to snatch the words back as soon as they left her lips. It was none of her business.

Nathaniel's neck turned red. He avoided her gaze. "We weren't exactly involved. It was more of a physical thing."

"Casual sex." She said the words flatly, oddly hurt to know that Nathaniel was no better or worse than any other guy.

"I think we should change the subject," he said tersely. "Hand me the munchkin."

Dani passed off the baby and scuttled past man and child, already regretting that she didn't have the little girl for armor. Using Nathaniel's bathroom felt oddly decadent and personal. Everything was sybaritic and gorgeous. Marble. Brass. And mirrors. Those mirrors were her downfall. She looked as if she had been on an all-night bender at the North Pole.

Wincing at her reflection, she quickly took off her dress. At least her bra and panties were dry. The sweatpants were fleece-lined, and the socks were thick and warm. The shirt was miles too big, but she rolled up the sleeves. Though she was still chilled, the borrowed clothes made her feel more human.

Nathaniel smothered a grin when she reappeared in his bedroom. Wise man not to make any smart remarks. She was in no mood to be teased about her appearance, especially when it was Nathaniel's fault she was in this predicament.

"I bought a few bottles of premixed formula," she said. "It's expensive, but I didn't want Peaches to have to wait any longer than necessary?"

"Peaches? I thought we were calling her Munchkin."

"Well, we found her on Peachtree Street, so it seemed fitting."

"Fair enough. If you girls want to get settled in the den, I'll change and join you in a minute. Then it might be time for the grown-ups to eat. Are you hungry?"

"Starving," Dani said.

She made her way back down the hall and found the den. It was a more appealing room than anything she had seen so far. And hallelujah, there was a gas-log fireplace. One flip of a switch and the flames danced.

"Oh, Peaches," Dani said. "What kind of mess have we gotten ourselves into? These are pretty fancy digs, but you should be with your mama, and I'm supposed to be going home for Christmas tomorrow."

The baby whimpered while Dani shook the bottle and removed the protective cap. The formula was theoretically room temperature, but it might still be chilled from being outside. Fortunately, the child was too hungry to care.

Dani settled deeper into a cushioned armchair and propped her feet on the ottoman. The baby suckled eagerly. Was she old enough to take any other foods? This was a heck of a mess. Maybe they should try another call to the authorities. Or even to social services directly.

Then again, it was after nine o'clock, and tomorrow was Christmas Eve.

The child was a sweet weight in her arms. Enough to wonder what it would be like if this were really her child. Dani envied her sister at times. Angie and her husband were happily married and hoping to start a family soon. Then again, her sister was thirty-five. Dani was only twenty-eight. There was still plenty of time.

She didn't know what was taking Nathaniel so long, but did it really matter? She couldn't imagine leaving him in the lurch, even if this situation was his fault. Could the baby really be his? Contraceptives failed all the time. He acted like the kind of man who would live up to his responsibilities, but did she really know him that well? He seemed very sure he wasn't a father.

What alarmed her was how content she was to spend this time with him. Though the moment was fraught with emotional danger, she was happy to be here. Against all odds, Nathaniel had shown her his human side. Seeing him in this situation made her feel woozy inside. He was visibly shaken and yet so very determined to seize control.

His masculinity was in stark contrast to the baby's helpless vulnerability. Dani's regard for him grew, as did her need to explore what was sure to be a doomed attraction on her part.

She was almost asleep, her head resting against the back of the chair, when her boss finally appeared.

Nathaniel surveyed the sleeping child. "She seems like a pretty easy baby, doesn't she? If all she needs are food and diapers, maybe it won't be so bad to wait it out until someone shows up to claim her."

"I burped her a couple of times halfway through the bottle. She took it like a pro. I still feel bad, though. Peaches should be with her family at Christmas."

"Fortunately, she's too young to remember any of this," Nathaniel said.

"Maybe. But she has to know we're strangers."

"I called 911 again. They asked me if the baby was in any danger. I said no. They wanted to know if the mother was someone I knew. I had to say yes. The officer apologetically insisted that they're completely at the end of their resources and recommended I preserve the status quo until Tuesday."

"Tuesday?" Dani cried, startling the child. "That's four days."

"I don't know what else to do." Nathaniel ran a hand across the back of his neck as he prowled the confines of the den. "It's already the weekend now. Sunday is Christmas, which means everything will be closed Monday. If the snow has melted, we should be able to get some answers on Tuesday."

Dani stroked the little girl's back. "Poor Peaches. Grown-ups can be so stupid sometimes."

"Was that a dig at me?" Nathaniel asked. He slouched in the chair across from hers. He looked very different in jeans, a navy sweatshirt and leather moccasins. Different and so very moody and sexy.

"Not at all," she said.

"I'm innocent until proven guilty. Ophelia's note means nothing."

"Relax," Dani said. "I'm not judging you. Besides, it's Christmas. Everybody deserves a little miracle this weekend."

"It will be a miracle if I don't find Ophelia and wring her neck."

"Poor Nathaniel. Everyone at works thinks you have no social life at all. Now you may have a child."

"I'm *not* the father," he said. "Quit saying that."

"So you don't want children?"

He huffed in exasperation. "Not now. Not today. Certainly not with Ophelia. I have no idea why she thought palming a kid off on me was a good idea. I haven't a clue what to do with Peaches."

"It's not so hard," Dani said, yawning. "The worst part is the sleep deprivation, or so I've been told," she hastily. "I'm not ready to be a parent, either."

The room fell silent after that. Nathaniel had clearly nodded off. With his eyes closed, she was free to explore him visually to her heart's content. For years, she had seen him in suits. He was a very handsome man who wore tailor-made attire well. But here in his home habitat, tired and discouraged in comfy clothes like any other American male, he seemed more real to her.

She didn't want to care about his well-being. She didn't want to worry about him. And she most assuredly did not want to get involved with him. Life was complicated enough without adding drama and heartbreak.

Time passed. She must have dozed off herself. The drowsiness was the aftermath of being so cold for so long and then getting dry and warm. Now, though, her stomach growled when she roused. If she stretched her leg, she could barely touch Nathaniel's toe. "Wake up," she whispered. "Nathaniel, wake up."

He yawned and stretched, revealing a few inches of tanned, taut abs. "What's wrong?" he grumbled, only half-awake.

"You promised to feed me."

His eyes shot open. A look of stupefaction flashed across his face before he got ahold of himself. "Right."

Dani rolled her neck to get the kinks out of it. "Sorry, it wasn't a dream. The kid and I are still here."

"Very funny." He rolled to his feet. "I usually order in, but somehow I don't think that's an option."

"I'd settle for peanut butter if you have any."

"That I can do."

After Nathaniel left the room, Dani stood carefully and cradled the sleeping baby against her shoulder. Her body ached from sitting in one position. More than that, she needed to walk around, anything to break the spell of intimacy that came from napping in her boss's den. Too cozy. Too weird. Too everything.

Built-in bookcases flanked the fireplace. Books of every genre were mixed in together with no apparent regard for organization. Interesting pieces of glass and pottery shone in the illumination from can lights overhead.

Nothing about the library or the art matched what she knew of Nathaniel. Curiouser and curiouser.

He returned silently, startling her badly. The baby whimpered when Dani jumped. Nathaniel didn't seem to notice. He set the food on the coffee table. "I have coffee or soft drinks. Which would you prefer?"

"Black coffee if it's decaf."

"It is."

The tension in the room increased exponentially along with the vivid awareness that Dani didn't belong here. Her presence was an accident of weather and timing. She bore no responsibility, either moral or otherwise, for Nathaniel and his surprise Christmas gift. Even if the little girl truly wasn't his, Dani was not involved in that fight.

Then why was it so painful to think about leaving this sexy man and adorable baby tomorrow?

As if he had picked up on her tumultuous thoughts,

Nathaniel shot her a look as he poured coffee. "Is there someone you need to call?"

"My family will be expecting me tomorrow afternoon, though with the weather, I'm not sure we'll all be able to make it."

"Where do they live?"

"My parents are in Gainesville. My sister and her husband settled in Chattanooga for work and because they love the area. My only brother, Jared, lives in Marietta. He's probably the one who will have to come get me if I can't drive my car. Mine's a VW Beetle, so not really snow-worthy."

"I see."

It wasn't much of a response. She gave up on chitchat and managed to eat one-handed. Either Nathaniel made a habit of buying gourmet peanut butter, or Dani was hungrier than she realized.

Her dinner companion prowled while he ate. The tension in his body broadcast itself across the room. Dani could understand his frustration.

When he pulled back the drapes and stared out into the night, Dani joined him at the window. All they could see in the beams from the streetlights was heavy, swirling snow. Nathaniel pulled out his phone and tapped the weather app. "Good Lord," he said. "Look at the radar."

The storm was far from finished. In fact, there was every indication it would still be snowing until the wee hours before dawn.

The scary situation had turned into an actual blizzard. It didn't matter that by Tuesday the temps were supposed to be in the midfifties again. For now, they were well and truly stranded.

Nathaniel left her and began prowling again.

The silence built until Dani couldn't bear it anymore.

"Are you Jewish?" she asked, blurting it out before realizing that was not the kind of question one asked a work colleague.

He paused in his pacing to stare at her. "No. Where did that come from?"

Dani shrugged. "No Christmas tree. No decorations." It was a logical conclusion.

"I live alone," he said, his tone indicating a desire to shut the door on this particular line of conversation.

"So do I," Dani pointed out. "But I have a tree and other stuff. It makes the season fun."

"That's a lot of work for only me to see. Can we change the subject?"

"Sure." Maybe Nathaniel was a certified Scrooge. The idea made her sad. But she couldn't very well persist in the face of his disinclination to explain. His lack of December frivolity was well documented and would remain a mystery. "I *am* worried about one thing," she said.

"What's that?"

Nathaniel had finished his sandwich and now cradled his coffee cup between his big, long-fingered hands. *Oops. No thinking about hands, Danielle.*

"Well," she said slowly, hoping she wasn't blushing. "I'm afraid this little one has slept so much during the evening she'll be up all night. I've heard about babies who get their days and nights mixed up."

"I can get by on a few hours of sleep. I'll take the night shift. You deserve some rest." He stood up. "Let me show you the guest room. I guess you'll need a different shirt to sleep in?"

Three

He made it a question. Having Dani wear his clothes and wear them so damned well made it hard for him to think about babies and responsibility. He'd been attracted to her for a long time, but he knew better than to get involved with an employee. He'd learned that lesson the hard way. It wasn't one he would soon forget.

It was imperative that he get rid of Dani before he did something stupid—imperative for two reasons. One, he didn't need the temptation of having his charming, cheerful, cute-as-the-proverbial-button assistant underfoot outside of office hours. And two, he felt guilty as hell for ruining her holiday plans. Maybe they were still salvageable. She said she hadn't planned to leave until tomorrow, and Gainesville was not even two hours away.

Unfortunately, the massive and almost unprecedented winter storm was the wild card in this scenario. And then there was the baby. If he did the right thing and sent Dani home for Christmas, he'd be stuck caring for an infant. The notion was more than a little terrifying.

"Another shirt would be helpful," Dani said quietly, not meeting his gaze.

"Follow me," he said gruffly. The condo had two guest rooms. One he used as a home office. The other was furnished simply and elegantly in shades of amber, chocolate and ivory.

He'd hired a professional to do the whole condo when he bought it. Everything but the den. That was his and his alone. The huge comfy couch, big-screen TV and gas fireplace were things he had purchased on his own. Except for sleeping, he spent most of his leisure hours in the den. Ah, who was he kidding? He worked in there, as well. Creating boundaries had never been his strong suit.

In the guest room, Dani explored, the baby still in her arms. But the little girl was waking up.

Dani grinned and kissed the baby's head. "Hey there, Peaches. Mr. Nathaniel is showing me around. You want to sleep in here with me?"

It was tempting, very tempting, to let Dani rescue him. But such cowardice would be wrong on several levels. He took the baby from her and shook his head. "Take a shower if you want to. Get ready for bed. Then you can help me get everything set up in my bedroom for the night."

"Okay." Dani's eyes were big as saucers. Maybe she was worried about the innocent baby.

"I won't let anything happen to her," he said. The defensive note in his voice was unavoidable. As unpalatable as it seemed, he had to at least acknowledge the possibility, however slim, that Peaches was his. "We'll give you some privacy," he said. "When you're ready, come find us."

* * *

Dani returned to the foyer and gathered all her things. If she hung the dress and tights carefully, they might be wearable again. At the drugstore, she had bought toothpaste, a toothbrush and some facial cleanser. Fortunately—because of the Christmas party—she had made sure that morning to put mascara and other makeup in her purse for touch-ups.

After a quick shower, she rinsed out her bra and panties and hung them on the towel bar. Then she put on the sweatpants sans undies and spent a few minutes blow-drying her hair. It was thick and shoulder length, maybe her best feature. Because it was still a little damp when she was done, she left it loose. Whenever Nathaniel remembered to give her a second shirt, she would change into that for the night.

Barely half an hour had elapsed by the time she went in search of her host, forty-five minutes at the most. It wasn't hard to locate him. All she had to do was follow the sound of screaming. Little Peaches had a great set of lungs.

Dani stopped dead in the doorway of Nathaniel's bedroom, taking in the scene with openmouthed awe.

Nathaniel's head shot up and he glared at her, his expression hot enough to melt steel. "If you dare laugh, you're fired."

She swallowed hard, schooling her face to show nothing more than calm interest. "I wouldn't dream of laughing." It was maybe the biggest lie she had ever uttered. Poor Nathaniel.

Peaches had experienced what those in the parenting world not-so-fondly call a *blowout*. A poop so big and messy it squirts out the sides of the diaper and into every crevice imaginable. It was clear Nathaniel had made a heroic effort to remove the dirty diaper and replace it with a clean one, but he was taking too long, and poor Peaches was mad.

Dani grabbed several wipes out of the container and began cleaning the spots Nathaniel had either missed or hadn't gotten to yet. The baby was stark naked. Nathaniel had poop on his hands, his sweatshirt and if she weren't mistaken, a smudge on his chin. He was wild-eyed and flushed.

Her heart squeezed in sympathy. Most parents had nine months to get used to the idea of a baby. Nathaniel had been tossed in the deep end. If Peaches weren't his at all, this whole experience was even more unfair.

"I'll pick her up," Dani said. "You start getting rid of all the nasty stuff and throw your comforter in the washer." She was afraid the bed covering was beyond redemption.

Carrying the baby into the bathroom and using the sink as a miniature bathtub was her next step. Fortunately, the little one stopped crying when she saw herself in the mirror. Dani adjusted the water temperature and grabbed a washcloth.

The bottle of liquid hand soap on the counter would have to do for now. Moments later, she wrapped the sweet-smelling infant in one of Nathaniel's big, fluffy towels and returned to the bedroom.

Nathaniel had just finished cleaning up the mess that was his mattress. He held out a fresh diaper. "You can do the honors."

"Of course. I can't believe this Ophelia person left you with nothing. We don't even have another outfit for the baby."

"I turned up the thermostat. And I put her sleeper in the wash with all the rest. It will be ready in a couple of hours."

"I guess that will have to do." Since Peaches was suck-

ing on her fist, it seemed another bottle was in order. "I'll
feed her again. Your turn in the bathroom."

When she turned to walk away, Nathaniel put his hand
on her shoulder lightly. "Thank you, Dani. I know my
thanks is not enough, but I want you to know I'm grateful."

They were standing so close together she could see the
dark stubble on his chin. It was the end of the day. That
made sense. His brown eyes were deep pools of melted
chocolate. He smelled of soap and a tiny hint of aftershave
and maybe even a whiff of baby poop. Dani bit her bottom
lip. Why had the baby chosen now to be docile? A diversion would be helpful.

"You're welcome," she said quietly. "I know this isn't
easy. You're doing the right thing."

He shrugged. "It's not as if I had a choice."

"Even without the snowstorm, I think you would have
taken the child. Because you have to know…one way or
another."

"Who made you so smart?"

"Not smart. Just realistic. You're not the kind of man to
walk away from a responsibility, unpleasant or otherwise."

"It's more that that," he said.

His hand was still on her shoulder, fingers splayed,
though she wasn't sure he noticed. "How so?"

"What if Peaches *is* mine? Birth control is never a hundred percent. What if this little girl is my only shot at having a child?"

"You don't think you'll get married one day?"

The hour was late. It had been a very strange day. Nathaniel was practically embracing Dani and the baby. She
wanted to lean into him and rest her head. She was tired
and confused and very afraid of doing something she
would regret.

It took everything she had to step back and break the

spell. "I shouldn't have asked you that," she said hastily. "I'm sorry, Mr. Winston." She used his last name as a shield, but it was flimsy armor at best.

You can't put a genie back in the bottle, though. Nathaniel gave her a pointed look as if he saw right through her attempt to be businesslike. "I think we have to concentrate on what's important here. If you and Peaches are really okay for the moment, I'll jump in the shower. I still smell like a diaper pail."

"No, you don't," Dani protested, laughing. "But yeah, we're fine. Take your time."

On her way to the den, the doorbell rang. No one could come up without going through the reception desk downstairs, so this must be the delivery from the drugstore. She pressed the intercom button and waited for confirmation just to be sure.

After the young teenager unloaded all the baby paraphernalia in the foyer, Dani tipped him well and sent him on his way.

"This is it, Peaches," she said, bending down to pick up the smallest package of diapers. "I hope I did the math right. This has to last us until the snow melts or your mama shows up, whichever comes first."

Of course, it didn't take a genius to guess that Ophelia was probably snowed in wherever she was hiding out. It was creepy to think a woman like that had been watching as Nathaniel and Dani spotted the infant carrier for the first time. What would she have done if the two of them had walked away? She must have been relying on the decency of human nature. Even so, Dani would never have left her own baby in such circumstances. It was too risky.

She wandered back to the den and spread an afghan on the thick carpet so the baby could have tummy time. Peaches was very mobile already and trying her best to sit up. No signs of any bottom teeth poking through. Dani guessed the little girl was about five months old, maybe six.

As the baby played with a rattle from the drugstore, Dani stretched out beside her and leaned back on her elbows. It was a strange feeling to be a guest in her boss's home. Definitely outside the parameters of their usual interactions. Up until today, she'd had no clue where he lived.

Now, suddenly, everything was different.

When Nathaniel reappeared, his hair was damp and he had ditched the clothes the baby had desecrated.

"Much better," Dani teased, telling herself her heart wasn't beating faster.

He grinned, the sudden smile taking her by surprise. Her boss was more serious than playful as a rule. "Is it still Friday?" he asked, leaning a hip against the arm of the sofa. "I feel like we've fallen through the rabbit hole."

"Still Friday. I'm guessing your life isn't usually so tumultuous?"

"You could say that." He raked both hands through this hair. "I shouldn't have dragged you into this."

"Look at it this way. You probably saved me from being stranded on the side of the road. At least I'm safe and warm and dry."

"What a testimonial. Have you called your family yet?"

"Yes. I told them I was staying with a friend and that I would check in again tomorrow."

"Let's hope we don't lose power."

"Bite your tongue. That's not even funny."

"I wasn't joking. If we do get ice on the back end of this thing, the situation could get dicey."

"Oh, goody. Something to look forward to."

He cocked his head, his lips twitching. "How have I never noticed what a smart mouth you have?"

"I'm always deferential in our work environment." She smiled demurely, astonished to realize they were flirting. Of course, with a baby between them nothing could happen. But still…

Nathaniel stood up to pace. She was beginning to recognize his signature mood when he was agitated. He did it occasionally at work, but it was more pronounced on his home turf. "Is she getting sleepy?" he asked. "When should we put her to bed?"

"How should I know? Do you have work you need to do? You might as well let me take care of her for the moment. It's not like I can go anywhere."

"I know, I know. And I'm sorry."

"Quit apologizing, Nathaniel. Humility doesn't become you."

"Ouch." He squatted and rubbed the baby's tummy, his gaze pensive. "She doesn't look like me, not even a little bit."

The non sequitur betrayed his inner turmoil. Dani felt her heart squeeze. "In my experience, babies this age rarely look like anybody but themselves, Nathaniel. Don't torment yourself. Until you know for sure, she's just a baby."

"I suppose." He glanced sideways at her. "Go on to bed, Dani. I'll come get you if I get in trouble."

"You promise?"

"I do."

Nathaniel sighed beneath his breath. Hopefully Dani didn't realize how completely out of his element he was. He had learned long ago—while earning his stripes in the business world—never to show fear. He could negotiate with the baddest of the badasses. What he didn't know how to do was take care of a helpless human. Little Peaches was so damned fragile.

He scooped her up. "Here's the thing, kiddo. I need you to cut me a break tonight. I'll feed you and change your diaper, but you need to sleep. That's what babies do."

The little girl stuck a thumb in her mouth and stared up at him, unblinking. What was she thinking? Did babies think about anything?

After turning out the lights, he carried Peaches to his bedroom and surveyed the furnishings. As far as he could tell, the most important thing was to keep the kid confined. He knew it was dangerous to put her in his own bed. After getting out of the shower earlier, he had spread a sheet on the soft carpet and surrounded it with several wooden chairs. He'd probably be awake all night worrying about the kid, but he'd survive.

Fortunately, the baby had worn herself out playing with Dani. All it took was a few circuits around the bedroom with Peaches on his shoulder, and gradually her little body went limp. He crouched and laid her in the makeshift bed. Poor kid. She should be with her mother right now. It was impossible not to think about the marked differences between Ophelia and Dani. One woman was self-centered and flighty...the other generous and dependable.

At one time in his life, he had assumed all women were self-centered. His mother had taught him to believe that. It wasn't true, though. God willing, this little sweetheart would grow up with kindness in her heart.

On a normal evening, he was awake until after one. Tonight, that was a luxury he couldn't afford. Stripping down to his boxers, he climbed into bed, stretched out on his back and exhaled. What a hell of a day.

It was impossible not to think about the fact that Dani was sleeping in his guest room just down the hall. He liked and respected her. In recent months, he'd stumbled upon another feeling he couldn't, or wouldn't, acknowledge.

Dani deserved to find a man who would put her first, a man who would be happy to settle down with her and create a normal family life. That man wasn't Nathaniel. He'd certainly never experienced such a thing as *normal* in his formative years. All he knew was work and more work. That focus had propelled him to the top of his career. Given his long hours and his absolute refusal to date anyone remotely connected to New Century Tech, his options for meeting women were limited.

Loneliness and sexual hunger had been to blame for his hookup with Ophelia when they met at a conference. It had taken less than forty-eight hours for him to figure out that she was a narcissist and incredibly high maintenance. He'd broken off the relationship before it started, but perhaps the damage had been done.

The prospect of co-parenting with Ophelia for the next twenty years was daunting. Depressing, even. But if Peaches were his daughter, he would suck it up and be the best damned dad he could be. Never would he make that sweet little girl endure the kind of childhood he had experienced.

Unbidden, his thoughts returned to Dani. After seeing his father's life ruined years ago, Nathaniel had forged ironclad rules for his own business relationships.

That line in the sand had never been difficult to preserve until Dani walked into his life. She had become necessary to him. He told himself it was nothing more than a good working partnership.

Now, in the darkness and privacy of his bedroom, he acknowledged the possibility that he had been lying to himself. She was here. Now. Sleeping under his roof and making him think about things that were definitely not conducive to relaxation.

Arousal tightened his body and fractured his breathing. *Damn it.* He rolled onto his side and told himself he wasn't a slave to his urges.

Yawning, he tried converting foreign currencies in his head. It was better than counting sheep. Eventually, exhaustion claimed him…

The waning hours of the night turned into a long, wretched dream. The baby woke him every forty-five to ninety minutes. He knew she was disoriented and unsettled. Thankfully, each time he picked her up and cuddled her, he was able to coax her back to sleep.

At 5:00 a.m., though, the volume of her cries told him she was hungry again. Carrying her into the kitchen, he found one of the premixed formula bottles and uncapped it. He would have to learn how to mix the powder, but not while it was still dark outside.

Earlier, he had thrown on a robe with his boxers. Now he and Peaches settled on the sofa in the den. Pulling an afghan over both of them, he leaned back and watched as the baby gobbled down her meal. He remembered Dani mentioning the need for burping. When the bottle was half-empty, he hefted the baby onto his shoulder and patted her back. Peaches didn't like being interrupted, but her loud belch told him he'd done the right thing.

While the infant finished her formula, he reached for the remote and turned the TV on with the volume muted. He had a million channels to choose from, but nothing interested him. He wanted a distraction…some assurance that the world still spun in its normal orbit. Skipping over infomercials and weird sports channels, he landed on an old movie, a Christmas film.

He had never seen it all the way through, but he knew the general premise. A man unhappy with his life wished he had never been born and then had a chance to see what the world would have been like without him.

The scenario hit uncomfortably near home for Nathaniel. He had no close friends by design. As head of the company, he knew better than to build relationships that might backfire on him. Because he worked all the time, there was no opportunity for socializing even if he had wanted to. Other than a couple of guys he occasionally played racquetball with at the gym, he was a loner, and he liked it. Mostly.

By following a rigid set of rules for his personal life, he kept his days running smoothly. This blip with Ophelia only proved what it cost to deviate from his usual behavior.

Again and again, he wondered what he would do if Peaches were his. Again and again, he shut down that line of thinking. Until the truth came out, speculation served no purpose.

Too late, he realized he should have changed the kid's diaper *before* giving her a bottle. Now she had sucked down the last ounce of formula and was out cold. Fortunately, Dani had already stocked most rooms in the house with diapers and wipes. Thank God for her babysitting experience. At least one of them had some exposure to infants. Otherwise, the situation would have been far worse.

Luckily for him, Peaches slept through the diaper change, even though he fumbled and cursed and struggled with the seemingly simple task. He was able to return to his room, tuck her back into the little protected corner and fall into his own bed, facedown, unconscious in seconds.

The next time he surfaced, the clock said seven. He had a hangover headache, and he hadn't even had a beer last night. Stumbling to his feet, he visited the bathroom and then moved stealthily toward Peaches's corner on the floor to check on her.

The nest was empty. Panic flooded his chest for half a second before common sense intruded. The chairs were intact. Dani must have the child.

He found them both in the kitchen. Dani had fixed a pot of coffee, God bless her, and she was sitting at the window, baby in arms, drawing pictures in the condensation on the glass.

She looked up when Nathaniel entered the room. "Good morning. It sounded like this little stinker gave you a rough night."

He winced. "You heard us?"

"I'm a light sleeper." She shrugged, her expression guarded. "I decided that if you wanted help, you would ask, so I didn't disturb you. You're a very capable man."

Pouring himself a cup of coffee and gulping it with no thought for scalding his tongue, he snorted. "Didn't feel like it last night."

"Poor Peaches. I guess she knew she was in a strange place."

"Getting stranger by the minute. Have you heard a forecast?"

She nodded glumly. "The official totals are twelve to fourteen inches so far, with more, north of the city. It's supposed to change over to freezing rain in the next couple of hours. The governor has declared a state of emergency. All roads are virtually impassable because of abandoned cars, including major interstates."

"So you're stuck with me?" He tried to smile, but the knot in his chest made it hard to breathe.

"It looks that way. But on an up note, I've already talked to my family. They're all stuck, too, except my Chatta-nooga sister. The storm stayed south of them. My par-ents have decided we'll simply postpone Christmas until at least the twenty-seventh. It's supposed to be sixty-two and sunny then."

"Welcome to winter in the South."

"Exactly."

He had no clue how to act, what to say or do. This bizarre scenario was unprecedented. Nausea swirled in his belly, and he felt light-headed.

Blaming it on the lack of sleep was less worrisome than admitting he was afraid to be trapped with Dani. Sitting there with a warm smile on her face, wearing his shirt and holding a child who was possibly his baby, she personified everything he feared, everything he had avoided for so long and so well.

He hoped like hell his unease wasn't visible. He didn't want to give in to temptation, but he sure as hell didn't want to hurt her, either.

Four

Dani cocked her head, her smile dimming as a knot of *something* settled like a rock in her stomach. Nathaniel was acting very strangely. Despite her misgivings, she forged ahead with the idea that had come to her while she waited for him to wake up. "I have a question, Nathaniel. You can say no if you want to."

As she watched, he took two steps backward, set his empty cup on the counter and shoved his hands in his pockets.

"Ask away," he said. But his gaze didn't meet hers. His body language was one big keep-off-the-grass sign.

Sighing inwardly, she nuzzled the top of the baby's head. "It's Christmas Eve," she said flatly, as if he didn't know. "And tomorrow is Christmas Day. Your condo is virtually empty of any sustenance, holiday or otherwise. I checked around online and found a small market about a mile from here that's opening up from ten to four today. If I make a grocery list, will you go shopping for us?"

His lips quirked in a reluctant smile. "That's doable."

"I'm not the greatest cook," Dani admitted. "I don't think I'd be confident preparing a turkey, even if they have any. But I could do a pot roast with all the trimmings and some kind of fancy dessert. Are you allergic to anything?"

"No." He didn't look happy.

She was even tempered as a rule, but his silence grated. "Do you have an objection to observing the holiday with good food?" The words came out more sharply than she had intended. Still, she didn't regret them.

Nathaniel sat down on a bar stool at the counter and grimaced. "My family was not as warm and fuzzy as yours, Dani. My mother was diagnosed with schizophrenia, but not until I was in high school. I don't know if you can imagine what my childhood was like."

Suddenly Dani felt small and mean. "What about your father?"

"He loved my mother in spite of everything—and he loved me, I'm sure. But he wasn't the kind of man who could keep gluing bits of our life back together and making things work. His solution was to spend all his time at the office."

"I see." In fact, she saw more than she ever had before. Nathaniel had layers upon layers, it seemed. The more she learned about him, the more it became apparent he was destined to hurt her if she let herself get too close. The man didn't want a girlfriend or a wife. In fact, he seemed to be rabidly opposed to human emotion in general.

Squashing her disappointment, she managed a light tone. "So is that yes or no to the dessert?"

Finally, she coaxed a smile from him. "I may not know how to properly observe Christmas, but I do like to eat."

"Well, there you go." For no apparent reason, Dani felt like crying. She didn't want to see Nathaniel as a person, a man with hidden vulnerabilities. She didn't want to like or understand him anymore than she already did. Liking him led to fantasizing about a future that would never be hers. Fortunately, Nathaniel was oblivious to her turmoil.

"Your grocery store plan still doesn't help us with the baby's clothing situation, or lack thereof," he said.

Dani nodded. "I have a lead there, as well. Your poor doorman made it into work this morning, but he's bored, because clearly there's not much action in the lobby. I phoned down to him earlier with a question or two. In the process, he told me his daughter has a little girl who's a year old. He thinks they might have some hand-me-downs we can use for Peaches. And they live close enough he can walk to their apartment tonight after work."

"Do you make friends with anyone and everyone?"

His tone didn't sound as if the question was a compliment. Dani chose her words carefully. "The world can be a difficult place. We're all interconnected. I see no harm in being open to other people and experiences."

"Maybe you were a hippie flower child in another life," he muttered.

"I can go, Nathaniel," she said sharply. "You asked for my help. But if you're going to act like a horse's ass all weekend, I'd just as soon leave."

Her accusation found its mark. For a moment, Nathaniel turned icy and distant. She wanted to run from his disdain, but she held her ground. The standoff felt interminable.

Gradually, his posture softened. His chest lifted and fell in a huge sigh. "I apologize," he said. "Apparently, I'm not as good at sleep deprivation as I thought."

"You're forgiven. I know you're exhausted." Dani didn't hold grudges. Life was too short. A change of subject was in order. "I'm worried that if you get everything we need at the market, it will be too heavy to carry."

"I have an old army-surplus duffel bag. It's practically indestructible. I can load it up, cinch the top and drag it back, if necessary."

"That could work." The thought of filling Nathaniel's somewhat-sterile condo with the appealing scents of Christmas excited her.

"Is there anything else Peaches might need that I could get at the store?"

"We covered the basics last night. She's old enough to begin sampling simple foods, but since we don't know if Ophelia has given her anything yet, I'd be afraid to try. The formula will be enough for now."

"You're the expert."

"Hardly. I'm just grateful Peaches is an easy baby. I've heard stories about colic and other stuff. This situation could have been much worse."

"It *would* have been," Nathaniel said bluntly. "Without you."

She flushed. "I was an extra pair of hands, that's all."

"No," he said carefully. "It's more than that. I see it at NCT all the time. People come to you with problems and questions. You triage. You offer solutions. You give support. You're an extraordinary woman, Dani. Don't ever underestimate yourself."

With that, he turned on his heel and walked out of the room.

Dani put a hand to her hot cheek. *Wow*. That was the warmest and most personal testimonial she had ever received from her boss. And it told her he actually noticed what she did for the company. Sometimes she wondered. He became so absorbed in his work, she'd been convinced at times that he saw her as no different from a computer or the copy machine.

It was disarming to know he was watching.

Peaches had drooled all over the shoulder of Dani's shirt, which was, of course, Nathaniel's shirt. At this rate, she would have to borrow half a dozen to keep up with the baby's tendency to destroy clothing.

This was the strangest Christmas Eve Dani had ever experienced. Over the last decade, she had dated a number of men, but none of them long enough to warrant spending the holidays with their families or vice versa. The only Christmases Dani had ever known were celebrated in the bosom of her family.

Though Nathaniel's condo was a far cry from her parents' warm and welcoming home, Dani was determined to make this day memorable. For Peaches. For Nathaniel. Heck, for herself.

Someday, God willing, she would be marking the holidays in a house of her own with a husband, two as-yet-to-be-named kids and maybe a dog. *She* would be in charge of the meals and the decorations and the Santa gifts.

Maybe this odd Christmas was a testing ground. Did she have it in her to make the holiday special under these circumstances? Would Nathaniel even care?

One glance at the clock on the stove told her she had no time to spare. Presumably Nathaniel had disappeared to suit up for his foray into the winter wonderland. Dani loved playing in snow as a rule, but she didn't have the appropriate clothing, and it was too cold for the baby even if Dani had wanted to go along.

With Peaches in one arm, she quickly scanned the contents of the cabinets. They were mostly empty. One set of salt and pepper shakers. An out-of-date container of cinnamon. Half a bag of questionable flour. But at least the basics of cookware were represented. Maybe a woman had furnished the kitchen.

She found a pen and started writing. By the time Nathaniel returned carrying the big empty duffel bag, Dani had filled three pages of a notepad advertising a well-known realty company. "I hope you can read my writing," she fretted. "I'm not good at one-handed penmanship."

Nathaniel grinned. "We have these things called cell phones…"

"Well, that's true. But what if I'm changing a diaper at the exact moment you need to call me?"

He shrugged. "Then I'll wait." Even bundled from head to toe, he managed to look ruggedly handsome.

"What about eggs and bread?"

"I'll put them on top. It will be fine. Quit worrying. You should know, though, that walking a mile and back in a foot of snow won't be quick. Not to mention how long it's going to take me to find all this stuff." He waved the list in the air.

"Sorry," Dani said. "I guess I got carried away. Maybe I was making sure you didn't have to make a second trip."

"Maybe," he chuckled. He kissed the baby's cheek, his lips dangerously close to Dani's, close enough to give a woman ideas. "You girls stay out of trouble while I'm gone."

On the elevator ride down to the lobby, Nathaniel started to sweat. He'd put on clothes from his last Colorado ski trip. When he stepped outside, he was glad he had kept the heavy winter gear. As useless as it normally was in Atlanta, today it was going to come in handy.

The snow had turned into a nasty drizzle that froze on contact. Soon, he couldn't feel his cheeks. He wrapped his fleece scarf around all of his face but his eyes, and picked up the pace. It wasn't easy. Snowshoes might have been a good idea if he had owned any.

He relished the physical exertion. Despite his lack of

sleep the night before, he *wanted* to push himself to the limits, anything to keep from thinking about Dani. She was his very valuable assistant, not a lover. He had to remember that, no matter how great the temptation.

He'd never seen Atlanta like this. It was a ghost town, a frozen ghost town. Occasionally, an official vehicle passed. There were a few intrepid explorers out, like himself. For the most part, though, his fellow citizens had hunkered down to wait for the snow to melt.

What did normal people do on December 24? There would be no last-minute shopping today, that's for sure. Even Amazon couldn't fulfill impulsive wishes in the midst of a blizzard. Fortunately, Nathaniel had resources Amazon didn't possess. Early this morning, he had made a couple of phone calls and arranged to get a gift for Dani. She deserved at least that much for putting up with his bizarre situation.

The small neighborhood market shone like a beacon at the end of his journey, bringing cheer to the gray, icy day. In addition to the store's normal illumination, swags of colored lights festooned the entrance.

Inside, Nathaniel grabbed a shopping cart and stripped off his outer garments. Christmas music played from overhead speakers. Oddly, it didn't irritate him as it sometimes did. When he found himself humming along with a familiar tune, he frowned and concentrated on Dani's list.

The store was mostly empty. He was able to go as slowly as he wanted, one aisle at a time, until he was confident he had fulfilled his mission.

At the checkout stand, he began to have a few tiny doubts about getting all this stuff back to the condo. No matter. He'd told Dani it might take a while.

The store manager rang up the purchases. "You're a

brave man," he said. "Must have a woman at home ready to cook."

"Something like that."

When the last item was scanned, Nathaniel handed over his credit card and began loading the canvas duffel, putting the canned goods on the bottom. The manager looked to be in his late forties and bore a passing resemblance to Santa Claus. He was dressed in overalls and a red flannel shirt, probably not his usual work attire.

The older man began grouping smaller items and tying them into plastic bags to make them easier to stuff in the duffel. "You got a tree already?" he asked.

Nathaniel shook his head. "No. I don't usually decorate. It's a lot of trouble."

The Santa look-alike frowned. "Then you should take one of those small live trees. On the house. They'll be useless to me by Monday. For that matter, I'll throw in a stand and several strands of lights. Might as well. I'll be stuck with that whole display seventy-five percent off. I'd rather you and your lady friend enjoy them."

"Oh, but I—"

The manager interrupted, "I know, I know. You're walking. I get it. My son, Toby, is in the back unloading pallets. Do you know how hard it is for a seventeen-year-old boy to be snowed in the day before Christmas? The kid needs some exercise. He's driving me and his mom crazy. Let him walk back and carry the tree for you."

"It's a long way," Nathaniel protested.

"Won't matter." The man punched in a message on his cell phone. "He's on his way."

Moments later the kid appeared. Six foot four at least, with shoulders that told Nathaniel he probably played football. The teenager was visibly eager, chomping at the bit to get outside. "Happy to help, sir," he said, beaming at Nathaniel. "Which tree would you like?"

Nathaniel wanted to say *forget it*, but in his gut he knew Dani would love having a tree. "Any of them." Good grief.

The manager grimaced. "Sorry we don't have ornaments."

"Believe me," Nathaniel said, "it's okay."

The trip back to the condo was surprisingly entertaining. Nathaniel dragged the heavy duffel bag along behind him, occasionally changing arms when his shoulder protested. "So tell me, Toby, do you work at the store on a regular basis?"

"When I'm not practicing football or basketball or out with my girl."

Toby had the four-foot, live tree—in a plastic stand—balanced on one shoulder. In his other hand, he carried Dani's precious eggs, a loaf of bread and the strands of lights. The teenager wasn't even breathing hard, nor was he wearing gloves. Nathaniel, probably only fifteen years his senior, felt like an old man trying to keep up.

"Have you been dating this girl for a while?"

"A year and a half, sir. We have plans to go to college together and get married when we graduate."

"Your parents are okay with that?"

"Oh, yeah. They adore Kimberly. Her parents have been married almost as long as mine. Mom always told me to look at a girl's family. That way you know what's important to her, and you can decide if you're compatible."

The young man's casual confidence rattled Nathaniel. Was this what happened when you grew up with actual parental guidance? Surely this kid was far too young to know what he wanted out of life. Then again, Nathaniel wasn't qualified to weigh in on interpersonal relationships, not by a long shot.

Toby used the next twenty minutes to bend Nathaniel's ear about everything from his interest in NASCAR racing to his amazing girlfriend to the Central America trip he and his youth group were going to make during the summer.

Nathaniel listened with half an ear, wondering if he himself had ever been as passionate and excited about life as this young man. For Nathaniel, every goal had been about getting out on his own and proving himself *without* his parents. Yet here was an all-American kid who actually enjoyed his life.

Even Toby tired after the first half mile. When they stopped to catch their breath, Toby set the tree and his packages carefully on the ground and rolled his shoulders. He even put on a pair of gloves.

Nathaniel hid a grin. He did remember what it was like to be seventeen and driven by testosterone. Of course, with Dani in his home, those feelings were pretty much the same right now. He didn't feel the need to flex his muscles, but on the other hand, he *had* made a long trek through knee-deep ice and snow to bring home provisions. Maybe this was the twenty-first-century equivalent of slaying a wild animal and dragging it back to the cave.

Toby blew on his hands and bounced from one foot to the other. "What about you, Mr. Winston. Do you have any kids?"

For some reason, the question caught Nathaniel completely off guard. "Um, no…"

Toby grinned. "You don't sound too sure."

"I'm sure," Nathaniel said firmly. "Come on. Let's get going before we freeze to death."

At the condo, Dani buzzed them in and welcomed them at the door. The way her face lit up when she saw the scrawny little tree gave Nathaniel a warm fuzzy feeling that was scary as hell.

"This is Toby," Nathaniel said. "His dad manages the market. Toby got drafted to help me get back with all of this."

Dani beamed at the teenager, baby Peaches on her hip. "Thank you *so* much, Toby. Here, wait." She reached into her purse on the table in the foyer and pulled out a twenty-dollar bill. "Merry Christmas."

The boy's cheeks reddened even more than they had from the cold. Dani's smile could melt a snowman at fifty paces. "Merry Christmas, ma'am. Happy to do it."

"Will you stay long enough for me to make some hot chocolate?" Dani asked.

Toby grimaced. "Wish I could, but I'd better get back to the store. Your baby is cute." Peaches flirted with him unashamedly.

Dani blinked. "Oh, well, she's not mine, but thanks."

Toby shot Nathaniel a raised-eyebrow look. The baby wasn't Dani's, and Nathaniel had said he didn't have kids. No wonder the boy was confused.

Nathaniel decided to hurry the goodbyes along. "Too bad you can't stay. Thanks for your help. Tell your father thanks, too. Merry Christmas."

When the door closed behind the teenager, an awkward silence fell, one that weighed a thousand pounds. Nathaniel cleared his throat. "I got a tree," he said.

Dani nodded, eyes wide, cheeks flushed. "I see that."

"I thought you'd like it, it being Christmas Eve and all." He didn't tell her it wasn't his idea.

"I think it's wonderful," Dani said softly. She went up on tiptoe and kissed his cheek, so quickly he barely felt it. "Thank you, Nathaniel." She paused. "If you don't mind taking the baby, I'll start putting the groceries away. Would you like something warm to drink? I have a fresh pot of coffee brewing."

"Give me a minute first," he said gruffly. "I need a shower and different clothes."

Dani regretted the kiss as soon as she did it. She wasn't sure what had come over her except that she had been so darned touched by Nathaniel's effort. Toby had helped significantly, but still...

She suspected she had either shocked her boss or made him extremely uncomfortable or both. She came from a very affectionate family. For a moment, she had forgotten where she was. It was a mistake she wouldn't repeat. Nathaniel had disappeared so fast, he probably left a trail of steam.

Before Toby departed, the two men had hefted the full-to-the-brim canvas duffel onto the granite-topped kitchen island. Even with Peaches on one hip, Dani was able to begin putting cans and dry goods into the cupboard. She often enjoyed watching cooking shows on cable, but she didn't consider herself a pro. Something about Christmas Eve, though, gave her a tingling sense of anticipation for the dinner to come.

"Here's the thing," she whispered to Peaches. "It would be super helpful if you would take a nice long nap. Nathaniel needs one, too, and I have a ton of cooking to do." The little girl gazed up at her, fist in mouth. She didn't look at all sleepy.

"Okay, fine. Stay awake. But Santa doesn't visit cranky children, now does he?"

After half an hour, Nathaniel still hadn't appeared. Was he avoiding her? If they were to eat at a decent hour, she needed to get the roast in the oven and start on the pecan pie. For Christmas morning, she had planned a coffee cake with streusel topping and mimosas. Christmas lunch would consist of open-faced beef sandwiches with a cranberry salad.

Without the internet, she would have been lost. Her phone was her lifeline. It helped that Nathaniel kept a drawer full of extra charging cords. Impromptu travel with literally nothing except her purse was not the easiest thing in the world.

When four thirty rolled around, she decided to go in search of her missing boss. She found him facedown on his mattress, sound asleep. Poor man. She knew he wouldn't have left her to handle everything on purpose.

He was bare from the waist up, his tan evidence of holidays spent in tropical climates. His shoulders and back were smoothly muscled. The pair of navy knit pants he had pulled on rode low on his narrow hips.

This was what Nathaniel Winston would look like on lazy Saturday mornings before he climbed out of bed. *Or maybe he sleeps in the nude, Dani. He can't very well do that with his executive assistant and a baby in the house.*

Her cheeks hot, she debated her course of action. Peaches took it out of her hands. The little girl chortled loudly. Nathaniel shot straight up in bed, wild-eyed. "What's wrong?" He scraped his hands through his hair.

"Nothing," Dani said quickly. "Sorry to wake you. But I need to start dinner, and I can only do so much one-handed. I thought Peaches would be asleep by now, but she obviously knows it's Christmas Eve, and she's too excited to close her eyes."

Nathaniel didn't seem amused by her whimsy. "Let me have her. We'll play in the den and stay out of your way."

"How thoughtful," she said, deadpan.

His sharp look questioned her sincerity, and rightly so. It didn't take a genius to see that Nathaniel wanted to avoid

Dani as much as possible. Fine. She didn't need him in the kitchen getting underfoot anyway.

Fortunately, her ambitious Christmas Eve dinner menu consumed her attention for most of the subsequent hour. Once she had seared the roast and tucked it in a deep pan flanked with carrots and potatoes, she put the pie together and popped the sweet treat in the oven with the meat, very glad both dishes cooked at the same temperature.

The condo had a small dining room just off the kitchen. Inside a modern-looking buffet, Dani found navy placemats that matched the navy-and-cream stoneware in the kitchen cabinets. It frustrated her not to have the trappings of holiday colors or even a store-bought poinsettia. Even a couple of red candles would have been nice.

That was the problem with bachelors. They didn't know how to set a scene anywhere but in the bedroom.

Oops. Thinking about Nathaniel and bedrooms was bad mojo. She was already in trouble for her innocent thank-you kiss. Best not to let him see that she was curious enough and attracted enough to be fascinated by thoughts of his private life.

Which brought her directly back to Peaches and Ophelia. Damn Nathaniel's mystery woman. How had she found the chutzpah to pull off such an outrageous stunt?

Brooding over the baby's lack of a proper Christmas didn't help matters. Best to concentrate on what she could control. The only thing left was to put together a spinach-and-almond salad and prepare a light dressing. Serving pieces were ready. She and Nathaniel could take turns holding the baby during dinner, if necessary.

The roast and pecan pie had to cook for thirty more minutes. Plenty of time to put the Christmas tree in the den and decorate it. That meant running into Nathaniel again, but at least he had put on a shirt before he left his bedroom.

She knew that only because he had made a quick appearance in the kitchen earlier to grab coffee. Neither of them was dressed for a formal Christmas Eve meal. She supposed he had kept his appearance very casual in light of her predicament.

Wistfully, she imagined what it would be like if they were actually dating. She might find herself wearing a very special, sexy dress, knowing, or at least hoping, that Nathaniel would remove it at the end of the evening.

After her boss's chilly reception earlier, it took a measure of courage to intrude on his privacy. But the den was arguably the best place for the tree, and this designer condo needed a punch of color and light, tonight of all nights.

Nathaniel didn't look up when she entered the den dragging the tree along behind her. The fir had lost a significant percentage of its needles en route from the store, but it was still presentable. With the heavy plastic base already attached, all Dani would have to do was add some water tonight before going to bed. After all, the tree would stand guard beside the fireplace barely twenty-four hours before the lord of the manor tossed it out. She was pretty sure she knew Nathaniel that well.

Without speaking, she unboxed the tiny lights and began twining them around the tree, attaching one strand to the next. Still, Nathaniel didn't acknowledge her presence. Peaches sat on his knee, trying to get one of his shirt buttons in her mouth. Nathaniel held her firmly, but his attention was on the television. He flipped channels rapidly, presumably checking the football scores.

When she finished the tree and plugged it in, she expected at least a token comment. Her boss was mute. He had to have noticed the cheerful Christmas tree. It upped the cozy factor of the den tenfold. But maybe Nathaniel just didn't care. Stubborn, gorgeous man. She didn't know whether she wanted to kiss him or smack him.

Subdued and disappointed, she tweaked a branch and turned to walk out of the room. "Dinner in twenty minutes," she said over her shoulder.

"Wait, Dani," he said.

She turned around, bracing herself for criticism. "What?"

He lifted a shoulder and let it fall. "I don't mind the tree. But don't expect too much from me. This holiday stuff isn't my thing."

Five

A man knew when he was being an ass. Dani walked out on him without another word. Nathaniel was fully cognizant that he was exhibiting every characteristic of a bad host. The stupid Christmas tree was charming. And festive. Even Peaches cooed when she saw it. So why had he deliberately downplayed Dani's efforts?

Why were the aromas wafting from the kitchen both tantalizing and unsettling? He didn't want his condo to smell like Christmas. He didn't want a tree. He didn't want Dani.

What a liar you are. His libido was more honest than he.

In barely twenty-four hours, Dani had transformed Nathaniel's hideout from the world into a warm, holiday-scented, incredibly appealing home. How she had done it so quickly and so well, he couldn't exactly say. It was more than the groceries and the tree, though he couldn't put his finger on what was so different with her here.

Maybe it was the baby. Everyone knew that babies were precious and cute. Perhaps little Peaches was bachelor kryptonite. He sniffed her hair, wondering for the millionth time if he was her biological father. Shouldn't he be able to tell instinctively? Wasn't there some sort of parental bonding moment when all became clear?

If there was, he hadn't experienced it yet.

Dani didn't bother calling him to dinner. His phone dinged with a blunt, unemotional text. It's ready...

Standing up with a sigh, he took the baby to the tree. "Do you like it?" he asked softly. "It's supposed to have ornaments, but I don't have a single one."

The baby reached out to grab the lights. She'd probably chew the cord in two if he let her. Those bottom teeth had to be poking through soon. "No touching," he warned, nuzzling the top of her head with his chin. "We'd better go wash up for dinner before Dani loses patience with us."

The kitchen was filled with steam, delightful smells and a woman who resembled his efficient executive assistant, but in this setting looked more like a wife. The knot in his stomach grew.

Dani glared at him, clearly upset that he hadn't appreciated her efforts with the tree.

"Smells wonderful," he said, hoping to win a few points with genuine appreciation for her culinary efforts.

"We're eating in the dining room," she said, her tone frosty. "We may as well serve our plates in here. That way things won't get cold. I took the liberty of opening a bottle of wine. Let me have the baby. After you fix your plate, I'll do mine. There's plenty, but save room for dessert."

The solid meat-and-potatoes meal reminded him of something his grandmother might have prepared. His mother had grown up in her aunt's home, an orphan by the age of eight. But Nathaniel had substantial memories of his paternal grandmother. She had come over from Italy and spoke heavily accented English. Her cooking had been sublime.

He piled food onto his plate unapologetically. After his marathon trip in the snow today, a few extra calories were neither here nor there. Once he had set his plate in the dining room, he took the baby back. "Your turn, Madam Chef," he said lightly. To his surprise, Dani disappeared and came back lugging the Fraser fir—stand, lights and all.

"That's the advantage of a small tree," she said smugly. "They're sort of portable."

She plugged in the lights and sat down. At the last moment, she took her phone from her pocket and cued up Christmas music. Soon, they were eating in silence, save for the holiday tunes playing softly in the background.

With every bite Nathaniel took, his stomach tightened. The food was spectacular. The baby behaved. It was something else, something powerful and dangerous that stole his appetite and tightened his throat.

In this room, here and now, was everything he had never had, everything he told himself he didn't need. Family time. Cozy holidays. A beautiful, capable woman willing to work at his side to create a home.

He forced himself to clear his plate in deference to Dani's efforts on his behalf. Two glasses of wine didn't still his unease. They chatted lazily during the meal about the weather and the bowl games and whether the thaw would start Monday or wait until Tuesday.

Eventually, the baby fell asleep in Dani's arms. The two females were flushed and beautiful, Madonna and child.

"I feel terrible about this," Dani said suddenly, her expression troubled.

"About what?" There was no way she could have read his mind.

"About Peaches's first Christmas. She should have a stocking and leave cookies for Santa. That's how it's done, or so I'm told. Her mother's selfish behavior is robbing her of a special occasion."

Nathaniel shook his head. "As far as that baby's concerned, today might as well be April Fools'. The kid doesn't know the difference."

"*I* know," Dani said stubbornly.

"There's nothing we can do about it."

"If this was *Little House on the Prairie*, I'd make her a pinafore out of a flour sack, and you'd carve her a toy train with your pocketknife."

Even in the midst of his turmoil, he was amused. "I don't own a pocketknife."

"Well, I should have bought you one for Christmas."

An awkward silence fell. Nathaniel wished he was holding the baby. Peaches was a helpful decoy and a place to focus his attention.

In a few hours, it would be Christmas Day. If this was how Dani did Christmas Eve, what did she have up her sleeve for the following morning?

For the briefest of moments, he caught a flash of the two of them in bed, laughing, the baby between them. At the table eating breakfast. In front of the tree, opening presents. Panic shot through him with the force of an erupting geyser.

"This isn't real," he said, concealing his desperation beneath a veneer of calm.

Dani looked at him with a frown. "What's not real? The food? The baby? The tree? I'm confused."

He stood up to pace, tossing his napkin on the table. "We need to talk, Dani."

Her face went white, and she clutched the baby closer. "Go right ahead. Say what you have to say."

"*None* of this is real," he said doggedly. "We're not a family. This isn't a Norman Rockwell Christmas Eve. You and I are business associates. Peaches being with me is a big misunderstanding."

"I don't understand why you're so upset," Dani said quietly. She watched him with big blue eyes that saw far more than he wanted her to see.

Seeking to temper his anxiety and his distress, he sucked in a huge breath and turned his back for a moment on the sight of Dani and the baby sitting at his elegant mahogany table. The blizzard was to blame for all of this. All he had to do was remember that life would get back to normal soon.

He swung back around and sighed. "My father lost his company in his midfifties."

Dani blinked. "He did?"

Nathaniel nodded jerkily. "I told you my mother was not diagnosed until I was in high school. The episode that triggered her hospitalization was so severe she suffered a massive break from reality."

"That must have been terrifying for you and your dad."

"My father protected her as best he could all those years, but now she was institutionalized with little hope of returning home. It crushed him. He couldn't or wouldn't confide in me. Maybe he thought I was too young. The stress affected his health. Eventually, he found solace in the arms of a woman who worked for him. It didn't last long. Still, the damage was done. The employee filed a sexual harassment lawsuit, including charges for mental pain and anguish. A court awarded her a huge settlement, and my father had to liquidate the company to meet his obligations."

Nathaniel expected some response from Dani, any response. She stared at him blankly, as if nothing he had said made sense.

The silence grew—with it, the certainty he had ripped apart something fragile and wonderful. Dani's long-lashed blue eyes shone with tears. To her credit, she blinked them back successfully.

She bit her lip, her pallor marked. "Let me be sure I understand. This lecture you're giving me is because I cooked dinner and dared to acknowledge that tonight is Christmas Eve? Based on that, you're afraid I'm going to sue you and take away your livelihood? Have I got it, Nathaniel? Is that what you're telling me?"

"You're making me sound like a lunatic," he said sullenly.

Dani jumped to her feet, glaring at him, and headed for the door. Her chin wobbled ever so slightly. "No," she said, her voice tight with hurt. "You're doing a fine job of that all on your own. The thing is, Nathaniel, you're not a Scrooge at all. You're something far worse. Scrooge had a change of heart in his life. You don't have a heart at all. You're a machine. A cardboard figure of a man, a coward. I hope you choke on your pie."

If she had stormed out of the room, he might have found the energy to fight back. Instead, her icy, dignified departure warned him to let her go. It was Christmas Eve. The woman who had helped him with his baby crisis and done her best to create a bit of holiday joy in the midst of a snowstorm was insulted and pained beyond words, and it was his fault.

He should have handled things better. Nothing he said was a lie. But what he had failed to mention was how much it hurt to see what his life might have been like if he hadn't learned from his father's weakness.

Nathaniel didn't want to be weak. He didn't want the

responsibility of a spouse and children. His life had been rumbling along just fine. Why in the devil had he let himself fall prey to feelings that were nothing more than syrupy commercialism?

Holiday music and Christmas lights and good food were nothing more than a Band-Aid covering the world's ills. Come Monday, everyone's life would be as good or as bad as it ever was. Nathaniel was guided by reason and pragmatism. Those qualities in his leadership style had helped make New Century Tech prosper.

Doggedly, he ignored the sick lump of dread in his stomach. He went to the kitchen, cut a piece of the beautiful pecan pie, topped it with a swirl of whipped cream and returned to the dining room to eat his dessert in solitary splendor. After several minutes, he placed his fork on the empty plate and rested his elbows on the table, head in his hands.

Damn it, the pie was good. Downright amazing. The pecans had a crunchy glaze and the filling was sweet but not too sweet. If you wanted to know what happiness and love tasted like, this was it.

The condo was as quiet as a winter snowfall. Nathaniel had spent at least half a dozen December 24ths alone during his adult life, maybe a few more. But tonight—this very moment—was the first time he had ever *noticed* something was missing on Christmas Eve.

His outburst drained him. Dani's stricken response excoriated him. He felt raw, his emotions exposed for all the world to see. It wouldn't have mattered so much except that he valued Dani's good opinion.

Moving quietly, he cleared the table and set about cleaning up the kitchen. It was only fair. He hadn't helped with meal preparations. Truthfully, though, the reason for his efforts was more about delaying consequences than it was having a tidy home.

His brain whirred, jumping from thought to thought like a hound dog chasing butterflies in a meadow. What had he done? For that matter, what was he doing now? If Peaches were really his daughter, what did the future hold for him?

In forty-five minutes, every pot and pan and plate and bowl was out of sight. Countertops gleamed. It was easy enough to restore a kitchen to its original state. Unfortunately, the harsh words he had served Dani were far more difficult to put back in the box.

First things first. He picked up his phone and sent a text.

It's late. I'm coming to your room to get Peaches.

Dani's response was quick and terse.

No. She's asleep. You had her last night. My turn.

Nathaniel sent two more texts insisting that he be the one to deal with the baby, but there was no response at all. Either Dani had turned off her phone, or she was ignoring him. He couldn't bring himself to knock on her door. She deserved her privacy.

After half-heartedly watching TV for a couple of hours, he headed to his own room, intending to read. He'd bought the latest medical thriller by an author he admired. That should distract him from his jumbled thoughts.

Unfortunately, all he could focus on was the image of Dani. By now he had memorized everything about her. The low, husky music of her laugh. The way her blue eyes changed from light and sparkly to navy and mysterious. The graceful way she moved.

As the night waned, he dozed only in snatches. The silence in the house became oppressive. Was Dani okay? Was Peaches? Were both females sound asleep? He'd never experienced the wakefulness of being responsible for another human being.

Actually, that wasn't true. Long ago, during a time he tried to forget, this same stomach-curling worry had been his from time to time. Whenever his father had gone out of town on business, he always reminded Nathaniel to *keep an eye on your mother.*

Nathaniel had never really understood what he was watching out for. He only knew that his mother was not like his friends' moms. Those women baked cookies and sat on the bleachers at T-ball games. Nathaniel's mother mostly ignored him. When she did focus on his hapless self, her tendency was to smother him with adoration that held a marked tinge of frantic desperation and mania.

As much as he had craved her attention as a boy, he learned early on that it was better for the family dynamic when she didn't notice him.

His thoughts drifted back to Dani. She was warm and nurturing and so completely natural with Peaches. Not one echo of disapproval or reluctance marked the way she related to the baby. Even if she thought Nathaniel was a cold bastard for ignoring his own child up until now, she never voiced her concern. He had no idea if she believed him or not when he said the infant wasn't his.

What if he were wrong?

The mental struggles kept on coming. In the wee hours of Christmas morning, Nathaniel faced an unpalatable truth—the real reason he had created such an unfortunate scene at dinner.

For months now, he had been deeply attracted to his executive assistant. The only way he had been able to manage his unfortunate response to her was to pretend she was part of the office furnishings. Maintaining the status quo meant he was the boss and Dani an extremely valued employee.

The blizzard, along with Ophelia's dramatic stunt, had upset the balance in Nathaniel's life. At this point, he doubted whether the tide could be turned again. Dani was funny, compassionate…a *real*, breathing woman living beneath his roof. He liked her scent and the messy knot she fashioned to keep her hair out of her face. He loved the way her generous curves filled out his boring dress shirts.

Seeing her in his clothes was gut-level sexy. Like a film star in a magazine caught on camera in her own backyard, Dani was just Dani. No artifice. No mask to hide behind. No attempt to impress.

Nathaniel was very much afraid he was infatuated with her, maybe worse.

As he lay there in the dark, battling emotions he had kept locked away for so long, his chest ached and his eyes burned. Damn Ophelia. Damn the storm. If things hadn't gotten all jacked up, perhaps he could gradually have tested the waters with Dani.

Instead, here they were, thrust together in a faux environment. His sex hardened and his breathing grew ragged. What would it be like to take her here in his bed? Did she even have a boyfriend?

It stunned him to realize he didn't know the answer to that question. In the midst of his fantasies lay the grim realization he was probably the last person on the planet to whom Dani Meadows would turn for a relationship.

In little more than a week, they would both be back at New Century Tech, hard at work, each easing into familiar roles. Could he bear it? After having her here, just down the hall, would he be able to treat her like an employee again?

At 3:00 a.m., he climbed out of bed. He was only torturing himself by trying to sleep. In his sock feet, he tiptoed down the hall and listened at the guest room door. Not a sound emanated from within, though a tiny strip of light showed underneath the door.

He tapped quietly. "Dani. Are you awake?"

No answer. Any one of a number of possibilities came to mind. Dani might have fallen asleep exhausted and left a light on unintentionally. Or perhaps it was on so she could check the baby easily.

He shouldn't open the door. Every rule or law of hospitality expressly forbade it. Not to mention the fact that he and Dani had parted on angry terms.

Nathaniel turned the knob anyway.

The room was empty.

He stood there in the middle of the expensive plush carpet with his mouth agape. The bathroom door was open. No sense peering in there. Dani would have been talking to the baby if they were in residence. He liked how she communicated with the kid as if Peaches could understand every word.

Clearly, Dani had managed to slip quietly past Nathaniel's bedroom without him hearing a single thing.

Undaunted in his quest, he did an about-face and headed for the den. There he found a scene that gripped his heart and wouldn't let go.

Somehow, maybe while the baby slept, Dani had retrieved the small tree from the dining room and returned it to the place of honor beside the dancing orange and yellow flames. A simple cotton afghan was spread at the base of the tree. The baby slept peacefully on her tummy, one fist curled against her cheek.

Dani wasn't asleep at all. She sat on the stone hearth, elbows on her knees, fingers steepled beneath her chin. Wearing only his shirt that reached almost to her knees, she was barelegged and gorgeous. The misery on her face made his chest hurt.

He took the end of the sofa nearest the fireplace and leaned forward to face her. "I'm sorry," he said.

"No, you're not." Dani's cold certainty was worse than her anger. "You meant every word you said. The only reason you have any regrets now is because we're stuck with each other for at least another thirty-six hours, maybe more."

"Will you cut me some slack?" he pleaded.

"Why? Why should I?"

Who knew that blue eyes could freeze a man? He swallowed. "I don't know if I can explain."

"Try me." Perhaps she wasn't completely calm. She jumped to her feet and wrapped her arms around her waist, standing beside their small, fragrant Christmas tree and staring at it intently as if it had the power to provide answers to difficult questions.

She was so beautiful and yet so far away. *He* had put that emotional distance between them. Because he was scared. "Look at me, Dani." He stood as well, but he didn't pace. This was too important.

Slowly, she turned to face him. He couldn't read her expression. The woman who was usually open and without artifice had locked her emotions in a deep freeze. "You're the boss," she quipped, her tone deliberately inflammatory.

"This isn't easy for me," he said. The words felt like sand in his throat.

That chin wobble thing happened again. Dani's jaw worked as if she were trying not to cry. "Today is the worst Christmas I've ever had," she whispered. "And that's counting the one when my mom was in the hospital with pneumonia and my father burned the turkey. So don't talk to me about easy."

He bowed his head, tormented by guilt, wracked by indecision. No bolt of divine intervention came to save him. With a deep ragged breath, he managed to look at her straight on without flinching. "I'm becoming obsessed with you, Dani...and that scares the hell out of me. I don't know what to do."

"You probably ate too much," she taunted. "Indigestion passes. Grab an antacid. You'll be fine."

"Don't be flip," he growled. "I'm serious. All I can think about is kissing you to see where it takes us."

As it had earlier in the dining room, every scrap of color drained from Dani's face, leaving her pale. "You don't want to kiss me, not really. You think I'll ruin your life."

"Of course I want to kiss you, but that *won't* be the end of it. You're in my head, damn it. And in my gut. I can't sleep." He paused, his forehead damp and his hands clammy. In desperation, he said the one thing that a woman like Dani might respond to favorably. "I need you, Dani. Badly."

Almost in slow motion, he reached out and took her hand in his. She looked at him with an expression that was three parts fear and one part the same burning curiosity tearing him apart. If she had shown the slightest resistance, he would have stopped instantly.

Instead, she took a step toward him. "Nathaniel." The way she said his name, husky and sweet, was his undoing. He dragged her against his chest and held her so tightly she laughed softly.

"I have to breathe," she said.

Releasing her a millimeter, he sighed. "I'll breathe for both of us." He rested his chin on top of her head, feeling the silky, caramel-taffy waves tickle his middle-of-the-night beard. "Tell me to stop," he pleaded hoarsely.

"I won't." She licked the pulse beating at the base of his

throat. "But I won't be accused of seduction, though. If we do this, it's all on you, *Mr.* Winston. Maybe you should think long and hard before you do something you'll regret."

Her schoolmarmish admonishment only made him more desperate. How could she stand there and be so cool? "I'm already long and hard," he complained. "That's what I'm trying to tell you."

Dani felt ill. For months and months, she had wondered what it would be like to have Nathaniel look at her the way a man looks at a woman he desires. Well, now she knew. And it wasn't good.

Her boss didn't *want* to want her. Somehow that was a thousand times worse than the strict professionalism he showed her in their working relationship.

It took everything she had to pull away from him and back up when all she wanted to do was rip off his clothes. "I'm serious, Nathaniel. Do we have a physical spark— yes, but you're giving me mixed signals. Heaven knows that might be the understatement of the year. I'm a grown woman. I have needs, too. We're snowed in together with nothing to distract us. It stands to reason we might feel *something*. That doesn't mean we have to act on it."

"I said I was sorry for earlier." His gaze was stormy and hot with male intent.

"Sorry, maybe. But you spoke the truth. What could possibly induce me to do something so reckless and self-destructive?"

Reeling her in for a second time, he smoothed stray hairs from her cheek and tucked them behind her ear, his smile lopsided. The touch of his fingertips on her hot skin undid her. Like a foolish Victorian maiden made to swoon by pretty words and innocent caresses, she melted into his embrace.

As kisses went, it was world-class. Despite his professed conflicted emotions, Nathaniel was now totally in control, completely confident. He held her without a sign of awkwardness, as though the two of them had been intimate for weeks and months.

To his credit, he coaxed rather than insisted. The first kiss was soft and warm and exploratory. His taste was sinful and decadent. Dani's hands clung to his shoulders as if she were about to go down with the *Titanic*. Her heart beat so loudly in her ears, she wondered if he noticed.

One of his arms held her firmly against his chest. The other hand tangled in her hair and loosened the rubber band that was her only claim to style. Now her hair tumbled onto her shoulders. She had washed it at bedtime. It was still damp.

Nathaniel shuddered and buried his face in the curve of her neck. "You smell like apple pie," he muttered.

"It's the shampoo in your guest bathroom," she said primly. One part of her brain couldn't believe this was actually happening.

"Please tell me I'm not making a fool of myself, Dani."

She shook her head, finally brave enough to stroke the silky hair at the back of his neck. "You're a lot of things, Nathaniel Winston. But never a fool."

He pulled back and stared into her eyes. "Do you want me? Do you want this? Be honest, please."

Taking his face between her hands, she managed a smile. "I've never wanted anything more." She paused, biting her lip.

"What?" he asked sharply.

His frown alarmed her. "I'm on the Pill, but I need you to wear protection."

"Of course."

A dark red flush spread from his throat to his hairline.

She had either embarrassed him or angered him. "I'm not the kind of woman who takes chances," she said, "all evidence to the contrary."

"Of course not," he said. "But you need to believe me when I say I took no chances with Ophelia. It might have been a one-night stand, but I'm not suicidal. I used condoms. If Peaches is mine, it was conception that defied the odds."

The baby in question slept peacefully at their feet, the lights on the little tree casting colored shadows on her small body.

Dani sighed. "I believe you. Accidents happen, though."

He gripped her wrist, forcing her attention away from the child and back to him. "I'll get condoms," he said. "Don't move."

Nodding jerkily, she forced a smile. "Hurry."

When she was alone again, Dani blinked and sank to her knees on the rug. "Oh, Peaches. What have I done?"

Six

For one wild moment, Dani started to scoop up the baby. It wouldn't be hard to prevent herself from crossing a monumental line in the sand. All she had to do was pretend Peaches had awakened on her own. Babies did that all the time.

Her hand hovered over the downy head for what seemed like forever. Nerves sent her stomach into a free fall and then whooshed it back up again. *Oh, God, am I insane?* Nathaniel Winston was going to break her heart.

"Having second thoughts?"

The masculine voice startled her so badly, she lost her balance and sat down hard on her butt. "I didn't expect you back so soon."

He stared at her strangely. "My bedroom is two doors away. How long did you think it would take?"

"Oh." Suddenly, her nerves returned full force. Nathaniel was a sophisticated, highly sexual man. Dani was completely out of her depth. She swallowed hard. "When I fantasized about this, I was wearing my best panties and a sexy negligee."

His jaw dropped. "You fantasized about me?"

"Well, of course. You're you. Don't you ever look in a mirror?"

"That's ridiculous."

Against all odds, she had gained a temporary advantage. She stuck out her hand. "Help me up, please." When his hard, warm palm took hers, male fingers clasping smaller female ones, she exhaled shakily. "I didn't change my mind."

"Thank God."

Nathaniel scooped her up in his arms and carried her the few steps to the sofa. He deposited her on her back and began unbuttoning the borrowed shirt she wore. Dani had already rinsed out her only set of underwear in preparation for wearing it again the following day. Consequently, she was completely naked underneath.

When Nathaniel realized that pertinent fact, he froze for several seconds. Then he laid back the two sides of the shirt and studied her raptly. "Merry Christmas to me," he muttered, his eyes glazed with unmistakable hunger.

Dani had the strongest urge to reach for the afghan and cover herself. Her breasts were on the large side. Her tummy wasn't completely flat. The women in her family loved to cook and it showed. "Turn off the lamp," she begged. "We'll still have the tree."

Nathaniel shook his head slowly. "No. I want to see everything."

Reverently, he put a hand on one breast, cupping her fullness with his fingers.

Dani flinched instinctively. She wanted to dive into sex

without thinking, letting madness take control. Instead, Nathaniel seemed prepared to savor the moment.

She reached for the hem of his shirt, trying to lift it over his head. "We should hurry," she said. "Before the baby wakes up."

Nathaniel grabbed her wrist. "Not so fast. I want to look at you."

Apparently, he meant that quite literally. For the longest time, he simply stared. Beneath his intense regard, the tips of her breasts pebbled and ached. Gooseflesh broke out all over her body, though the room was plenty warm.

"Nathaniel…" She trailed off, not sure what she wanted to say.

His gaze met hers. "What?" His pupils were dilated.

"You're embarrassing me."

A tiny frown creased the real estate between his eyebrows. "Why? You're exquisite. A man could lose himself for hours doing nothing more than this." But at last, he released her breast and placed his hand, palm flat, on her abdomen. "I want to spend all night learning what you like…what you want."

"We don't have all night." It was true. They'd be lucky to have half an hour. Why was Nathaniel wasting time? She rested her fingertips on his taut thigh. "I want you naked. That's my Christmas wish right now. Come to me, Nathaniel."

Her urgent plea got through to him. With one rueful glance at the sleeping baby, he stood and ripped his shirt over his head.

The man was beautiful. There was no other way to describe it. Broad shoulders, a dusting of dark hair on his tautly muscled chest, bronzed skin. When he dragged the soft cotton pants down his legs and kicked them away, his erection sprang free, tall and thick and ready for action.

Oh, my.

He knelt beside the sofa and touched her upper thigh. "Let me pleasure you, sweet Dani. I want to hear you scream my name."

What followed next was an erotic assault on her senses. He caressed and teased and aroused her until she was half-mad with wanting him and completely blind to all the reasons she shouldn't. Dani had been with only two men. One was a long-term relationship in her early twenties, one that didn't work out. The second was a mistake born of loneliness and the conviction that life was passing her by.

Now here was Nathaniel. Not long-term. Definitely a mistake.

How could a woman leap into disaster and not even care? Turned out, it was easy. Too easy. All she had to do was close her eyes and pretend that Nathaniel was her happily-ever-after. That's what women did, right? Weave fantasies?

Unfortunately, Nathaniel wasn't in a mood to appease her fairy tales. At last, he stood again, this time coming down on top of her and moving between her thighs. "Open your eyes, Dani. This is me you're hiding from. I won't have it. Open your eyes."

Holding Nathaniel's gaze while he slid deep into her body shattered her. He witnessed every nuance of her reaction, including the slight wince when he pressed as far as he could go, thrust irrevocably at the mouth of her womb.

Dani shuddered and panted. It was too much and not enough. He filled her almost uncomfortably. She was tense and frightened—not of Nathaniel, but of her own wildly careening emotions.

She turned her head, watching the dancing flames that somehow had found their way into her body and were roasting her alive.

Her lover grasped her chin and turned her head to face him. His gaze was fierce. "If you wanted to change your mind, all you had to do was say so."

Shocked to the tips of her bare toes, she saw that she had hurt him. "Oh, Nathaniel, no. It's not that. I want you, I do." She linked her arms around his neck and canted her hips, allowing him to steal one more millimeter.

He kissed her roughly, his tongue tangling with hers. "Then why do you keep escaping in your head?" He nibbled the sensitive flesh below her ear and raked her collarbone with sharp teeth.

Dani moaned. "I'm scared. You make me crazy." She was afraid to come, terrified that she would shatter into a million jagged pieces and never be the same again.

His kisses gentled, even as his big frame shuddered. Much of his weight rested on his forearms, protecting her. But his lower body held her fast. "We're on even ground then, because I don't know what the hell we're doing. Don't be frightened of me, my brave, bighearted Dani. I won't let anything happen to you, I swear."

She kissed him then. Some might have called it a kiss of surrender. Dani knew it was more. It was taking what she wanted despite the inevitable consequences. "Make love to me, Nathaniel."

Whatever gentleness he had shown her in the beginning burned up in the fire of simple, undeniable, lustful pleasure. He pumped hard, rapidly. Her first climax hit sharp and sudden. She cried out and moaned as he carried her through it. But Nathaniel was far from done. They tumbled to the soft carpet with Dani on top. His fingers dug into her hips with bruising strength.

His chest heaved. His eyes blazed. "Ride me, honey. Find what you need. I can wait…maybe."

She took him at his word. It was exhilarating and frantic

and more wildly pleasurable than she had ever imagined. Twice more, she climaxed. With the last one, Nathaniel came as well, dragging her down to his chest and holding her in arms of steel as he groaned and thrust his way to the finish line.

When it was over, the only sound in the room was their labored breathing and the gentle hum of the gas logs.

Dani's bottom, exposed to the air, started to get cold. She dared not move. If she did, she would have to face Nathaniel. How could she do that? How would she ever again be able to look him in the eye and pretend they were nothing more than boss and assistant?

Thank God she had already been sending out résumés. Perhaps tonight was her subconscious way of making sure she followed through on her decision to leave New Century. Nothing about Nathaniel had changed. He'd warned her as much at the dinner table. Dani would have to be the one to make smart decisions.

But how? How was a woman supposed to resist a man who combed his fingers through her hair and seemed not to notice that she had the beginnings of muffin top? He made love to her like she was a pool of life-giving water, and he'd been lost in the Sahara. She'd felt his desperation. His whole body shook, and not just with orgasm, but as he caressed her breasts and kissed her so sweetly.

Doggedly, she told herself that Nathaniel was right. *None* of this was real. They were playacting. Making the best of a bad situation, or two bad situations, if you counted Peaches. The snow and the child. Blizzards and babies and boners, oh, my.

The irreverent thought made her giggle.

Nathaniel noticed, of course. He opened one eye and glared up at her. "I hope you're not laughing at me. I might point out you're in a very vulnerable position."

She sobered rapidly. "No, sir, boss." Brushing her lips across his stubbly jaw, she played the aggressor. "Merely wondering how long I have to wait for round two."

Disengaging their bodies, he scrambled to his feet and pulled her up with two hands. "I have a great shower. Lots of settings on the showerhead. You'll love it."

"Um…"

He lifted her chin. "Talk to me, little Christmas elf. I'm having the damnedest time reading you right now."

She shrugged, trying to pretend she wasn't naked. "Showers are kind of personal. I'm not exactly a *sharing* kind of person when it comes to personal hygiene."

Nathaniel's lips quirked. "It's a good thing you're cute."

"Why is that?"

He kissed her nose. "Because you're a lot of work."

"I am *not*," she said, affronted. "Have I complained once about being kidnapped and forced to be your nanny?"

"You've been a saint," he said gravely. "But I was talking about your emotional state. I've seen pictures of a sphinx who's less inscrutable than you are. Two days ago we were in the office doing the usual, and now you tell me you've been fantasizing about me. Who knew?" He sounded aggrieved.

It was too perfect an opening not to ask. She stroked one of his biceps, loving the way her caress made him shiver. "I'm curious. Did you ever fantasize about *me* when we were at the office?"

Doors slammed shut in Nathaniel's brain. *Danger, danger.* He drew in a ragged breath. "Hell, yes. But that was very unprofessional on my part." He backed away. "I think you're right about the shower. If you don't mind, I'll go first. If Peaches wakes up in the meantime, I'll give her a bottle so you can get some sleep."

He didn't remember how he got to his bedroom. He must have released Dani. He must have grabbed his shirt and pants, because they were clutched in his hands.

Swallowing back the taste of dread and panic, he showered quickly and changed into jeans and an old college sweatshirt. Despite the hot water, he was cold through to the bone.

The expression in Dani's eyes when she looked up at him hadn't been inscrutable at all. It encompassed vulnerability and shy affection and probably a million questions. Simple questions any woman had the right to ask when she had just surrendered her body to a man she should be able to trust. A man who had vowed to protect her.

For ten minutes, he paced the confines of his bedroom, formulating a game plan, deciding what to say. If he and Dani continued to have sex, she would expect things from him. Things he likely couldn't or wouldn't give. But if he came right out and said he was only playing around, he would leave himself open to her recriminations, maybe even reprisals.

She was a decent woman. With a kind heart. Still, he and she together had crossed a line. A line that made him as vulnerable as his father had been all those years ago.

Dani wouldn't sue him. He wouldn't lose his company. The chances of that happening were infinitesimal.

Without warning, a distant memory flashed, one he had forgotten in the mists of time. A woman in a professional, powder blue suit occupied the witness stand, her face hard and cold as she listed Nathaniel's father's transgressions, demanding vengeance. Nathaniel, almost eighteen by that time, had been sitting in the back row of the courtroom.

His mother was hospitalized. His father was a broken man, forced to appear before judge and jury and have his life's work torn to shreds. Nathaniel hadn't known how to help either of his parents.

A sound from outside the sanctuary of his bedroom jerked him back to the present. He had to go back to the den and face Dani. Squaring his shoulders, he told himself not to overreact. All he had to do was tread carefully. As soon as the snow melted and Ophelia retrieved the baby, life would go back to normal.

When he found his two female houseguests, they were ensconced on the sofa, wrapped in an afghan, Dani was wearing his shirt again. Her eyes were closed, her head resting against the back of the seat. Peaches was awake, noisily downing a bottle of formula. The lights were off. Only the flames from the fire illuminated the room.

Carefully, Nathaniel sat down beside woman and child. He put a hand on Dani's knee. She was sitting cross-legged with the baby in her lap. "You okay?" he asked softly. "Do you want me to take her?"

Dani opened her eyes and stared at him. He bore her scrutiny stoically. His assistant was a smart woman. She had to know something was wrong. Thankfully, she let it slide. "We're fine, Nathaniel. Why don't you go back to bed? You have no idea how long Peaches will be staying with you, and unfortunately, I won't be around to help much longer. You should get sleep while you can."

He inhaled sharply. Apparently they weren't going to discuss his earlier behavior. Instead, Dani let it be known very plainly she was not going to linger in his home waiting for scraps of his attention and affection. There was a quiet dignity about her that shamed him. The open, joyful response he'd seen in her after their intimate encounter was gone.

Moving his hand from her knee, he tried to breathe naturally. The gaping hole in his chest made that difficult.

Had he crushed the only person in his life who actually cared about him?

Dani lifted the baby onto her shoulder and patted her back. "How will you go about finding Ophelia?"

"I've contacted a private investigator. Needless to say, he's not eager to leave his family on Christmas. He's promised to get to work on the case first thing Monday. I'm confident Ophelia's still in the city. After all, how far could she get? If we're trapped, so is she."

"Good point." Dani stood, holding the baby carefully. Peaches had nodded off. "I think she'll sleep a few more hours now. We'll see you in the morning."

Nathaniel jumped to his feet. "Wait," he said hoarsely.

Dani turned back, but her posture was defensive, and she held the child as a shield. "What, Nathaniel? What do you want?"

On the surface, it was almost a rhetorical question. As if she knew he didn't know why he had stopped her. But then again, maybe she was demanding more. Explanations. Assurances. Unfortunately, he had none to give.

"It's December 25 already," he said, feeling foolish and desperate. "Merry Christmas, Dani."

Her smile was wistful, perhaps even sad. "Merry Christmas, Nathaniel."

After that, he let her go, because it was the right thing to do. He had no right to coax her into lingering so he would have someone to talk to. He liked being alone. He enjoyed his own company. It was only the snow and the holiday and the baby throwing him off balance.

He prowled the condo, unable to contemplate sleep. If he hadn't been such an ass, Dani might have been in his bed this very moment, her cuddly, warm body pressed against his as they dozed in between bouts of hot, satisfying sex.

What would it take to win a woman like Dani? For one

thing, he would have to change virtually everything about himself. Dani would expect open communication and an honest exchange of feelings and emotions. The thought made him shudder. He'd perfected the art of walling himself off from the world. It was too late to change now.

Walking alone was the only way he knew.

Dani cried herself to sleep. When she awoke four hours later, her head ached and she faced the inescapable conviction she was her own worse enemy. She *knew* what the boss was like, perhaps better than anyone else in his life. Why on earth had she asked him such a stupid question? *Did you ever fantasize about me when we were at the office?*

The raw honesty of his answer had revealed the extent of his conflicted emotions. Nathaniel was a man. Men were creatures of the moment. They compartmentalized things in their brains. Work, sex, food, sleep. The only reason she and Nathaniel ended up being intimate was the result of an unlikely set of circumstances.

As she changed a wet diaper and blew raspberries on a soft baby tummy, she fretted. She needed to get out of this condo. The sooner, the better. If she had sex with her boss a second time, she'd never convince herself to leave. Even worse, she might ignore all common sense and be put in the ignominious position of being *asked* to leave.

That wasn't going to happen. Ever. She might not be able to eradicate her feelings for the man down the hall, but he didn't have to know he was breaking her heart into jagged shards that would never properly fit back together.

Moving to the window, she twitched aside the sheers and looked out. The thaw was supposed to begin today, in theory. High of thirty-eight. Peeks of sunshine. So far, the skies were gray. The coating of ice on top of fifteen inches of snow meant the city was still obliterated. Only the most intrepid would venture out on Christmas Day.

When she closed the curtains and turned around, Nathaniel was standing in the doorway of the guest room. He held out a shopping bag with a quizzical smile on his face. "Your new friend, Reggie, the doorman, came through for us. He dropped off all these baby things a few minutes ago. I thanked him."

"And gave him a big fat Christmas tip, I hope."

"Of course."

"Too bad he has to work the holiday."

Nathaniel nodded. "At least he's only here until two. Several of them are dividing shifts today so no one gets stuck the whole time."

"I'm glad." Dani clutched Peaches like a lifeline. She had worried about imagining Nathaniel naked. The reality was much worse. He was fully dressed in khakis and a white button-front shirt with the sleeves rolled up. His tanned arms, lightly dusted with dark hair, were very masculine, as was the high-end gold watch on his left wrist. But that wasn't the bad part. What made her stomach do sickening flips and flops was this new awareness between them. She couldn't explain it, but it was *there*.

While she stood by the bed trying not to blush, Nathaniel upended the shopping bag and dumped a pile of baby clothes on the bed. "Good news, kid," he said with a chuckle. "You finally get to wear something new."

"Now, if only Reggie had access to my size," Dani joked. The fact that she was modeling another of Nathaniel's soft cotton dress shirts over the same gray thermal pants put her at a distinct disadvantage.

Nathaniel shot her a grin, his expression smug. "It's still early," he said. "I'm sure Santa hasn't forgotten you, Dani."

She had no clue what that meant. But she wasn't in the

mood for flirty repartee. Today was going to be Christmas without the feels.

To keep things on an impersonal track, she propped Peaches on her hip and began sorting through the clothing. Like most baby things, the rompers and sleepers and adorable dresses were mostly in mint condition. At this age, infants grew so fast, it was almost impossible to wear an outfit enough times to do any damage.

Nathaniel stood beside her, making her clumsy and nervous. He picked up a tiny green dress with candy canes appliqued at the hem. "I vote for this one," he said. "Perfect for Peaches's first Christmas Day."

Casually, Dani moved aside, putting a few feet between herself and temptation. "I agree. Why don't you do the honors?"

He blanched. "Me? I have big hands. This stuff looks like doll clothes. You'd better do it. If you don't mind."

Dani hesitated. "Well…"

"What's the problem?"

"I'm leaving when the snow melts, Nathaniel," she said bluntly. "You'll have to do all this yourself."

His expression gave new meaning to the term poker face. "I'll worry about that when the time comes. Besides, Peaches would rather have you dress her right now. She's more comfortable with you."

Dani laid the baby on the bed and quickly switched out the sleeper for the green dress. "Oh, my gosh. Look how cute she is. Hold her, Nathaniel. Let me take a picture." She grabbed her smartphone while Nathaniel made silly faces at Peaches and scooped up the little girl who might or might not be his daughter.

The sight of the big, macho man holding the small, smiling baby made her heart squeeze. They looked right together.

Moments later, Dani tucked the phone in her pocket and managed a casual smile. "If you two are okay for the moment, I'll put breakfast in the oven. Did I smell coffee brewing? Please say yes."

"Plenty for both of us," Nathaniel said. He rubbed noses with the baby. "This beauty and I will be in my office taking care of a little business. Come find us when it's ready."

She stared at him. Something in his voice gave her a little fillip of excitement. "Christmas secrets, Nathaniel?"

Seven

Nathaniel smiled, his expression deliberately bland. "Maybe yes, maybe no. I won't be long."

In his office, he spread a blanket on the floor. He'd grabbed it up from the pile on Dani's bed. "Play with your rattle, little one. I've got to wrap a package."

Reggie had proved to be quite accommodating when Nathaniel explained the situation. The overnight delivery had been signed for, and the doorman had sent up Christmas paper and tape. Unfortunately, turning out eye-catching packages was not in Nathaniel's skill set. He'd been a Boy Scout, but tying knots was a long way from handling thick, glossy paper and recalcitrant ribbon.

At last, he was satisfied. He held up the large rectangle and examined it. "What do you think, Peaches? I'm counting on this to win points with a certain prickly woman."

The baby gummed a pink-and-green teether from the drugstore enthusiastically, but didn't endorse Nathaniel's efforts. "I know," he said glumly. "It's probably too little, too late, but she deserves a merry Christmas, even if I *am* a Scrooge."

Since Peaches was in a mood to be cooperative, Nathaniel did a quick check of email, looking over his shoulder guiltily. There was more to life than work. He knew that. Trouble was, up until this particular odd Christmas, work was all he'd ever had on a day like today.

Half an hour later, Dani showed up, flushed and bright-eyed. "Everything's on the table," she said. "Come and eat."

Fortunately, he'd hidden the box behind a tall wooden file cabinet. Even when Dani crouched to pick up the baby, the gift was out of sight. Timing was everything.

In the kitchen, Dani had opted for casual, preparing two places at the granite counter island instead of in the dining room. The room smelled of cinnamon and yeast. "Wow," he said, inhaling with enjoyment. "You went to a lot of trouble." The mimosas were especially tempting, particularly since no one had to go anywhere.

On the other hand, he needed a clear head to negotiate a peace treaty with his beautiful houseguest. He took a stool and held out his hands. "I'll hold her while you eat."

Dani shook her head. "We can both eat. I think she'll be happy in her carrier for a little bit."

Either Dani was a gourmet cook or Nathaniel was starving or both. The streusel-topped coffee cake was warm and fragrant and tasted like heaven on a plate. He was on his third piece before he noticed Dani watching him with a grin.

He stopped dead, his fork halfway to his mouth. "Sorry," he mumbled. "I did leave some for you."

Her sunny smile was the first open, uncomplicated one he'd gotten from her since their encounter in the middle of the night. "It's quite all right. A cook likes to know her efforts are appreciated."

Deliberately finishing the last bite on his plate, he wiped the corner of his mouth with his napkin, drained his glass and reached across the small space separating them to stroke his thumb across her cheek. "I appreciate the hell out of you, my little Christmas elf."

Dani turned bright red and busied herself with the baby. "A simple thank-you will suffice," she muttered.

"What shall we do between now and lunch?" he asked in his most genial Christmas host voice. "When Peaches takes a nap, all sorts of things come to mind." He was treading a line between forcing Dani to remember the good parts of last night and hoping like hell she would overlook the bad ones.

"I really need to talk to my parents," she said, not taking the bait. "To see what the plans are for Tuesday. Perhaps you could entertain the baby while I do that. Afterward, I'll feed her and put her down."

"Of course."

To his disappointment and dismay, Dani handed off the kid and disappeared into her bedroom. Had Nathaniel spooked her, or was the excuse a genuine one?

He couldn't exactly listen at the door. Since he was too jumpy to sit down for any length of time, he cleared the breakfast dishes with one hand and loaded the dishwasher. Fortunately, there was no one around to reprimand him when he sneaked a few more bites of cake.

By the time Dani finally reappeared forty-five minutes later, the baby was getting fussy. Instead of handing her over, Nathaniel decided it was time for him to step up his game. "Let's go to the den," he said. "We don't want to waste that world-class tree. I'll feed the baby, and you can pick a movie. How's that?"

Dani seemed dubious, but she followed his lead. Nathaniel didn't bother with the sofa. He picked the recliner and got comfortable with Peaches in his lap. The baby, as always, guzzled her bottle and conked out.

Dani flipped through his Blu-ray collection and finally settled on one of the original Star Wars movies. He didn't have a single one of the romantic comedies that most women liked, so it was a good thing his guest seemed to share his taste in classic sci-fi/fantasy.

The opening credits had barely finished rolling before the second female in the room fell asleep. Nathaniel grinned wryly. So much for being a stimulating companion. He rubbed the baby's head. "Were you awake a lot during the night, little scamp? Or is Dani tired for another reason?"

His body tightened and his breath caught as lust roared in uninvited. His den was a far different place in the middle of the day than in the dark of night, but it was difficult not to remember holding a naked Dani in his arms and making love to her like a madman.

Hell. Why hadn't he stayed in the kitchen where the atmosphere was far less charged?

He watched the movie, but he'd seen it half a dozen times. It was far more satisfying to study the woman sleeping a few feet away. To a stranger, this scene would have seemed perfectly normal. Only Nathaniel and Dani knew how very abnormal it was.

She had made no bones about her plans to leave him. If memory served, Dani was using vacation days this week to spend time with her family. They certainly wouldn't understand if, at the last minute, New Century Tech demanded her attention.

No, work wasn't the answer. If he were going to keep Dani here, he'd have to try something risky. Maybe tell the truth. He didn't want to be alone this week. Not after he'd had a taste of what the holidays *could* be like.

In the meantime, he'd be content with the status quo.

Dani slept for half an hour and woke with a start. Her cheek was creased from the trim on the sofa arm, and her hair was mussed. "Sorry," she said, adorably flustered. "What did I miss?"

He laughed softly, careful not to wake Peaches. "Nothing you haven't seen before." He picked up the remote and hit Pause. He and Dani had known each other forever. They didn't need a movie for distraction, did they?

"Do you want me to take her?" Dani asked. "I've had a nap. It's your turn."

"I'm fine. Don't worry about me."

"If you say so."

An awkward silence fell. Maybe he was wrong about the movie.

He debated his options. The next move could make things better or worse. It surprised him that he couldn't predict the outcome. In a business negotiation, he would have known. But not now.

"Dani?"

"Hmm?" She stared at the fireplace, her expression pensive.

"Do you mind grabbing something from my office? I don't want to move and wake her."

"Of course." She hopped to her feet. "What am I looking for?"

"A large box on the far side of the wooden file cabinet."

"Got it. Back in a flash."

When she returned, she was carrying the package he had tried so hard to wrap artistically. The result looked even more amateurish now. "Thanks," he said.

"What did you do, Nathaniel? Buy her a four-foot teddy bear? This is heavy."

He shrugged. "It's for you. Merry Christmas, Dani."

She froze, her gaze panicked. "Oh, no. I have nothing for you. This is entirely inappropriate. I appreciate the gesture, but I can't accept."

"You don't even know what it is," he said, his tone mild. He knew if he pushed too hard, she might grow even more stubborn in her refusal.

Her hand smoothed the bright red paper, almost a caress. "It doesn't matter what it is," she said. "You gave me a Christmas bonus at the party Friday."

"It's not a present from your boss," he said, losing patience. "Open the box."

"So it's not from you?"

Was she deliberately misunderstanding him, or were they fighting some war he wasn't prepared to engage in? "Yes," he said, jaw clenched. "It *is* from me. To you. Man to woman. Not boss to assistant."

Dani set the box on the floor and curled her legs beneath her. "Did you get whatever this is before we had sex last night?"

"Well, of course, I did," he said unable to hide his irritation. "We've both been a little busy since then."

She studied his face, her expression earnest. What did she want from him?

"I don't think I can accept a present from you, Nathaniel." Her tone was apologetic. "It's a lovely thought, but under these circumstances, I think it would muddy the waters."

He counted to ten and then to fifteen. "Dani…"

"Yes?"

Why did she have to look at him like he was an ogre?

What did she think he was going to do to her? Lock her up in a harem?

"Open the damned box. Or you're fired."

"Fat chance," she muttered. "No one else would put up with you."

Apparently losing his temper had convinced her. Strange woman.

She picked at the paper like a Depression-era housewife planning to reuse every scrap of paper and tape and ribbon. The whole process was so slow, he wanted to bellow at her to hurry. It took a great deal of self-control to keep his mouth shut and let her finish.

When she finally removed the box lid and lifted the tissue, her mouth opened in a cute little O of surprise. "Nathaniel. What is all of this?"

Dani didn't know what she had expected. Truthfully, she had handled the gift with all the finesse of a bomb squad technician defusing a dangerous device. She didn't want gifts from Nathaniel. Not when their current situation was so remarkably out of control.

Once she had folded back the tissue, she simply stared at the contents, lifting one thing and the next in amazement. Nothing in the box raised any red flags. If anything, the individual items were extremely practical and thoughtful.

Nathaniel watched her, eagle-eyed, making her uneasy. "Well," he said gruffly. "What do you think? It's not the most exciting present in the world, but you strike me as a very practical woman. Who knows if you'll be able to get back to your apartment before you go to see your family. I tried to think of everything."

Everything was not an exaggeration. Inside the large, deep gift box was a collection of the most elegant clothing and toiletries Dani had ever owned. Dressy black pants in warm wool crepe. A red cashmere V-necked sweater. Two bras and several matching panties, more on the practical than sexy side, but very expensive.

Beneath that were designer jeans, casual tops, elegant sets of flats in black and taupe. Tennis shoes. Socks. A whisper-soft nightgown and matching robe in the palest ivory.

And then the cosmetics, glory be. Cleanser and lotion and mascara and everything else a woman might need to dress herself up for the holidays.

"How on earth did you manage this, Nathaniel?" She stared at him in amazement. "I know you work magic in the business world but this is incredible, even for you."

He shrugged, but she could tell her reaction pleased him. "I have a business associate whose wife works at Neiman Marcus. I called her first thing yesterday morning and told her what had happened with the blizzard and being stranded. I explained in general terms what I wanted to give you. She made it all happen."

"In the snow."

"Yep. I was very persuasive."

"This must have cost a fortune." She frowned slightly. "The snow was going to melt eventually. You know this wasn't necessary."

"It *was* necessary," he said forcefully. "Your holiday plans were wrecked. You've had to help care for a baby who is not yours. You've worked out grocery lists and prepared wonderful meals. This was the least I could do."

Dani set the heavy box aside and went to crouch beside his chair. "Thank you, Nathaniel," she whispered, her throat tight with emotion. Clearly he had gone to a great deal of trouble. The sizes were all correct, too. "For a man who bears a remarkable resemblance to Scrooge, you've done a lovely job with this Christmas surprise."

She kissed him softly on the cheek. "I don't know what to say. I'm touched."

He grumbled beneath his breath. "Babies sure as hell cramp a guy's style."

She grinned. "You were hoping my gratitude would translate to sex?"

"Nothing quite so crude." He winced. "But I did hope you wouldn't be mad at me anymore. I want you to be happy, Dani."

She noted that he didn't add the words *with me*. Maybe she was being too picky. "I am happy," she said quietly, brushing a lock of his hair from his forehead. He was holding the baby and couldn't respond physically, but his gaze seared her with its intensity. "Do you mind if I go take a shower and try on some of these things? I can't wait. Not that I don't appreciate the loan of your wardrobe," she said hastily.

He chuckled softly, caressing her visually, giving her goose bumps. "You look fine to me just like you are, but sure. Knock yourself out."

Dani practically danced down the hall. After two whole days of feeling grubby and unsophisticated, she was finally going to be able to meet Nathaniel on level ground. After a super quick shower during which she kept her hair dry, she put on the new undies and tried the red sweater and black pants. Everything fit perfectly.

Instead of twisting her hair up in a messy knot, she took the time to brush it over and over again until it swung thick and shiny at her shoulders. Too much makeup seemed like overkill at this point, but she used the mascara, and she added berry-red lip gloss to match her sweater. In the mirror, her reflection wasn't half-bad.

When she returned to the den, Peaches was awake and playing happily with a teething ring. Nathaniel's eyes widened when he saw Dani. "You look stunning," he said quietly. "Red is a great color on you."

"Nothing like new clothes to give a woman a boost. Thanks again."

"It was the least I could do."

"Are you getting hungry?"

"I could eat."

The stilted conversation was at odds with the almost palpable hunger coursing between them. Dani trembled. "I'll put Christmas dinner together. It will end up being a midafternoon meal, but we can snack later if we get hungry. Do you mind if I open a bottle of wine?"

"Mi casa es su casa," Nathaniel said. "Whatever you want." His words were warm, caressing.

In the kitchen, Dani was torn. Last night she had made use of the dining room for their dinner, and Nathaniel had freaked out. It didn't seem right, though, to have Christmas lunch at the kitchen counter. So no matter how skittish her boss was, she went right ahead with her holiday preparations the same way she would have if this were an ordinary situation.

She whisked together brown gravy. When it was warm and bubbling, she sliced the leftover roast beef in small pieces and added the meat to the pot. Peeling potatoes gave her too much time to think. Tonight the baby would fall asleep, and Dani would find herself alone with Nathaniel again. What was she going to do if he wanted sex? Could she hold him off? Did she want to say no?

Maybe she wanted to enjoy whatever time they had left in this odd and emotionally charged situation.

In less than an hour, she managed to put together a respectable meal—nothing too fancy, but far better than the peanut butter they had dined on the first night. Open-faced roast beef sandwiches on sourdough toast. Fluffy mashed potatoes. Cranberry salad and, of course, plenty of leftover pecan pie for dessert.

The end result was gratifying.

Nathaniel and Peaches appeared just as she was putting the finishing touches on the dinner table. Her boss frowned.

"What now?" Dani sighed. "I left the tree in the den. Nothing holidayish, I swear."

"It's not that," he said. "I just realized I'm going to owe you half a dozen fancy dinners at four-star restaurants to repay you for all you've done."

"Sit down and don't be ridiculous," she said. "I like eating as much as the next person. If I'd been at my parents' house, I would have worked even harder. My mom puts on quite a spread."

Nathaniel consumed most of his meal without speaking. It was impossible to read his mood. Once again, Dani was glad to have the baby as a diversion. Breaking bread together was actually a very intimate thing to do. This time, Nathaniel was the one holding the child and eating one-handed.

At last, Dani couldn't bear the silence any longer. "What are your plans for tomorrow?" she asked. "Assuming the weather does what they say it will."

He stood abruptly. "I'm going to grab some pie. You want yours now or later?"

"Later," she said. Was he in that much of a hurry for dessert, or did he not want to answer her question?

When Nathaniel returned, he held Peaches in one arm and a generous serving of gooey pie in the other hand.

Dani raised an eyebrow. "You'll make yourself sick," she warned.

His smile was wicked. "What a way to go."

While she appreciated the fact that her boss enjoyed her

cooking, bigger issues loomed on the horizon. Sex. The baby. Dani's imminent departure.

"I talked to my mom on speakerphone while I was cooking," she said.

Nathaniel swallowed a bite of pie. "Oh?"

"They thought about postponing our family Christmas until Wednesday, but my siblings can't be off work that day. So we're definitely celebrating Tuesday. I've promised to be there by ten in the morning."

"Sounds good."

Such a bullheaded, frustrating man. "Look at me, Nathaniel."

He lifted his head and eyed her with a deceptively mild expression. "What's wrong?"

"Nothing. Not exactly. But I'm worried about leaving you alone with the baby. Single parenting is hard for anybody."

"Especially a clueless male like me?"

"I didn't say that. Peaches is getting very comfortable with you and vice versa." She shook her head, wondering why she was obsessing about this. Peaches wasn't her problem. Still, it knotted her stomach to think about leaving man and baby to fend for themselves. "The trip from here to home is an hour and a half, give or take. Normally, I would simply drive up Tuesday morning. But first of all, we don't know how much snow and ice will melt tomorrow, and second of all, any standing water will probably refreeze tomorrow night."

"I'd say you're right."

"So I'll have to go tomorrow afternoon."

"Whatever you need to do."

"Do you even care that I'm leaving?" she cried.

He stood up abruptly, nearly knocking over his chair. Her statement echoed in the small dining room.

"This was never supposed to happen." He waved a hand. "I get it. You want to be with your family. I won't stand in your way. You have no obligation whatsoever to me or even to Peaches."

He was saying all the right words, but he was breaking her heart. He was so very much alone. Dani took a deep breath and gambled. "Come with me to visit my parents," she begged. "You and Peaches. I can't bear the thought of leaving you here alone."

Eight

Nathaniel blinked, feeling his anger and frustration winnow away to be replaced by something even more unsettling. He knew what it was like to have someone feel sorry for him, but it had been a very long time since he had been on the receiving end of that reaction. He didn't much care for it. There were any number of things he wanted from Dani. Pity wasn't one of them.

"I have to be at work on Tuesday," he said calmly, careful to reveal nothing of the confusion tearing him apart. "New Century Tech will be open for business. I have employees."

"What about the baby?"

Dani's dogged insistence on planning was commendable, but since he didn't have any of the answers she wanted, his only recourse was stonewalling. "I'll work something out. Besides, the baby will only be with me a day or two longer. I'm confident the investigator will find Ophelia quickly."

"I'm all in favor of positive thinking," Dani said wryly, "but that's not much of a strategy. Seriously, Nathaniel, come to Gainesville with me. It won't be odd if you show up. Mom and Dad often have stray guests at the dinner table, even at the holidays. We wouldn't sleep overnight at the house, of course. There are several nice hotels nearby."

"I appreciate what you're trying to do," he said, "but I'll be fine."

The combative subject was dropped by unspoken consent when Peaches decided she was hungry. Dani fed the baby while Nathaniel cleaned up the kitchen. Already, they had blown through most of the groceries he'd brought home on Saturday. Even the baby supplies were getting low.

When the kitchen was clean and the baby asleep on his bedroom floor, he realized he had to get out of the condo or risk making love to Dani. If they had sex again, she would make assumptions about the two of them. He wasn't ready for that.

The wonderful meal he had consumed sat like lead in his stomach. "I'm going to the store for round two," he said suddenly. "Make a list. I'll be back in a minute."

"Oh, but—"

He exited the warm, cozy kitchen before Dani could say anything else. When he had donned his parka and ski pants and gloves, he went back for the list. "Is it ready?" he asked, not looking at her. The cherry-red sweater he'd given her for Christmas clung to all the right places. Looking at her breasts was a bad idea.

"You can't go to the store, Nathaniel."

"Of course, I can."

"It's Christmas Day. I'm sure there might be some places open here and there, but probably not in walking distance. Quit worrying. I can stretch the food we have left until Monday afternoon. We can always do something simple tomorrow like bacon and eggs and pancakes."

He stripped off his outerwear a piece at a time, feeling ridiculous. "I keep forgetting it's Christmas," he muttered.

Dani shook her head in amusement. "First I've inundated you with too much Christmas, and now you say you forgot about it entirely. Make up your mind."

He shot her a glance, feeling his resolve wane. "I needed to get out of the house," he said bluntly. "Away from you. It wasn't really about the groceries."

"Oh." She looked stricken.

"I want you, Dani. Under the circumstances, it doesn't seem fair to you."

"Because?"

"Because you can't say no without causing tension between us." When she didn't say a word, he lifted his shoulders and rotated his neck. "Never mind. I'm going for a walk. Call me if there's an emergency."

Desperate to get away, he turned on his heel and strode out of the room. He made it to the front door before Dani intervened. The relief he experienced when he heard her voice call to him was overwhelming and inexplicable.

"Don't go out in the cold, Nathaniel. Stay with me."

He turned around slowly. She smiled faintly, but her eyes held secrets. Clearing his throat, he tossed his gloves on the console by the door and ran his hands through his hair. "If I stay, I'll make love to you. Sooner or later. You know that's true."

She swallowed visibly. "Yes."

"Things between us are complicated. You have to be sure."

Waiting for her answer was the longest five seconds of his life.

"I can't think of a better way to spend Christmas," she whispered.

The look on her face made him damned glad she had stopped him. "Now?" he asked hoarsely.

"Shouldn't we wait until tonight?" she said, her wide-eyed expression betrayed the struggle between madness and common sense.

"Maybe. But I can't." Deliberately, he began undressing, not only his cold-weather gear, but his socks and shoes and belt and everything down to his shirt and pants. Dani watched him intently, her cheeks flushed.

The door to his bedroom was open down the hall. They would hear the baby if she woke. "Say something," he demanded. "Tell me what you want."

"I'm not sure *what* I want," she said, wincing. He heard the truth in her words. "Maybe I just need you to know that *I* know."

His hands stilled on his shirt buttons. "Know what?"

"That we're taking a moment out of time. Period. That this ends when we walk out your front door tomorrow. I get it. You don't have to worry about me, Nathaniel. You're a sexy, interesting man. I want to be with you. But I won't make any uncomfortable demands. No awkward endings. You have my word."

Her ability to see right through to the deepest layers of his psyche alarmed him. The trouble was, he didn't have any pretty speeches to say in reply. Dani was one hundred percent correct. They had today and tonight and maybe tomorrow.

After that, the snow melted, the baby was reunited with her mother and Nathaniel went back to being top dog at New Century Tech. Business as usual.

He held out a hand. "Come here, little elf."

The choice on his part to remain still was deliberate.

He needed Dani's physical assurance that she wanted to take this step.

Instead of taking his hand, she flung herself at him, wrapped her arms around his neck and knocked the breath from his lungs. "Merry Christmas, Nathaniel."

He hugged her instinctively. Finding her mouth with his, he dove in for the taste that was his new addiction. "God, you're sweet."

She bit his neck, sharply enough to bruise. "I'm not particularly interested in *sweet* right now. Take me, Nathaniel. Show me the real you. I won't break, and I won't run away."

"God help us both," he muttered. He kissed her wildly, sliding his hands beneath her sweater and finding warm, soft breasts. "You didn't have to wear a bra," he complained.

"Your fault." Her voice was muffled against his collarbone. "New clothes. Didn't want to hurt your feelings."

Clumsily, he tugged the sweater over her head and unfastened the offending undergarment. When Dani was bare from the waist up, he put his hands on her hips and dragged her against him. "I'm too close to the edge," he groaned. "Embarrassingly so. Give me a minute."

Dani shook her head and leaned back to look up at him, her eyes bright with pleasure. "I like driving you mad," she said. "It gives me power."

She was joking. He knew that. He *knew* Dani. Still, the words sent a frisson of unease down his spine. Shaking off the sense of foreboding, he kissed her gently. "Take all the power you want, little elf. Tonight, you're mine."

Dani was under no illusions. She could only take what Nathaniel gave freely. There was a part of him that was off-limits to her, to everyone. She would have to be satisfied with the very appealing bits and pieces he offered. If the next twenty-four hours were to be their swan song, this unlikely pairing would be as special as she could make it.

Stuffing her doubts into a dark closet, she cupped his face in her hands. "You know how in movies the hero sometimes takes the heroine up against the front door, because he can't make it any farther before he has sex with her?"

Nathaniel rolled his eyes, but he grinned. "I get the general idea."

"Well..." She removed his shirt and pressed her naked breasts to his wonderfully hard, warm chest. "I was thinking we might try that."

He shuddered when she linked her arms around his waist and slid her fingertips inside his jeans, caressing his lower back. "I *could* use some exercise," he said soberly.

"Sex burns calories," she muttered. Perhaps they might just stand here like this all afternoon. She felt safe and warm, as if nothing bad would ever happen.

Nathaniel took her idea and ran with it. Before she blinked twice, he had her pants and undies down her legs. "Step out of them," he demanded.

There must have been a draft in the foyer. Goose-flesh broke out all over her body, and her nipples went on high alert. Stark naked, she wrapped her arms around her breasts. "Stop," she said hastily. "Your pants have to go, too."

He lifted an eyebrow, kneeling at her feet. "I've seen one or two of those movies. The guy keeps his pants on sometimes. You know...'cause he's in such a hurry."

She chuckled, despite her tendency to hyperventilate. "Now you're mocking me."

"A little bit." He stood and shucked his trousers and boxers casually, removing a couple of condoms from his pocket along the way. "If my back goes out from these shenanigans, you'll have to carry me to bed."

The humor didn't really compute. A naked Nathaniel Winston was even more powerful and intimidating than the one in the tailored suits and pristine white dress shirts. He was a male animal in his prime.

If she hadn't been breathless with longing and terrified the baby was going to wake up at the most inopportune moment, Dani might have taken the time to study her lover's body in detail. As it was, urgency overtook any desire to savor the moment.

"How do we do this?" she asked, the words embarrassingly weak and shaky.

Nathaniel's smile took all the starch out of her knees. "You let me worry about the logistics, honey. Right now I'm going to kiss you until you forget your name." With a nonchalance Dani could never have managed in a million years, he took care of the condom and tossed aside the packet.

Dani sighed when he folded her in his arms and held her loosely, brushing her forehead with a tender kiss.

"My lips are down here," she pointed out, trying to speed things along.

"I never noticed how bossy you are."

"I never noticed how slow you are."

Without warning, he scooped her up and palmed her bottom. She buried her face in the crook of his neck and wrapped her legs around his waist. His thick erection pressed against her. He shuddered and panted, his entire body rigid. "More foreplay later, I swear."

"I believe you."

The muscles in his arms corded and bunched as he lifted her slowly and carefully lowered her onto his sex. The feeling was indescribable. Despite their pretense that

Dani was calling the shots, this particular position put Nathaniel irrevocably in charge.

Gravity worked in his favor. The fit was tight, almost uncomfortable. Dani started to shake as nerves and arousal duked it out in her stomach.

Nathaniel cursed and groaned. "Too much?" he asked, jaw clenched, the words barely audible.

"No, no, no...but don't forget the door."

He staggered and laughed and stumbled forward until Dani's bottom made contact with cold, hard wood. "You asked for this, elf." With purchase now to aid his mission, Nathaniel thrust forcefully.

Dani held on, fingernails scoring his shoulders. Eyes closed, lungs starved for oxygen, she let him take her savagely, recklessly. It was too much in one second and not enough the next. Laughing, sobbing, she clung to him until she felt her orgasm rise up from the depths of her soul. It flashed and burst and consumed her.

A heartbeat later, Nathaniel pummeled his way to his own reward. "God, Dani. Hold on..." His words faded as he shuddered for what seemed like an eternity and finally slumped against her, pinning her to the door that had been the vehicle for her fantasy.

Afterward, she was never sure how long they stood there. Or rather, Nathaniel stood. Dani was limp and exhausted and completely at his mercy. She wouldn't have changed a thing.

In the aftermath of insanity, one thing was clear. She was in love with her boss. If she weren't mistaken, she had been for a very long time.

The blinders came off painfully. For months, she'd been telling herself she had to find new employment. Now she knew why. This was more than a simple crush. She was deeply, irrevocably in lust and love with this virile, complicated man.

She started to tremble and couldn't stop.

Nathaniel read her response as being cold. Without speaking or changing their positions, he carried her down the hall to his bedroom. They scooted past the baby and into the opulent master bathroom. Carefully, he lifted her and set her on her feet. "Was that everything you wanted it to be?"

His teasing smile—along with the smug satisfaction he radiated—made her blush.

"It was lovely," she said primly. "I'll check that off my bucket list."

He kissed her nose. "Something tells me I'd like to see your list if those are the kind of things on it."

"Private," she said airily. "Need-to-know basis, only." *And you don't need to know, Nathaniel Winston, because you won't be around to help me check them off.*

Refusing to ruin their romantic moment with her grief, she twisted her hair into a towel and turned on the water in the shower. "I don't want to get my hair wet. Peaches will be awake soon. Why don't I go first?"

Nathaniel shook his head, his expression brooking no argument. "I'll keep your hair dry, Dani, but you're not getting in *my* shower without me."

"Okay. It's your call." But the shower took a turn she hadn't expected. By the time she reached for the faucet and adjusted the water temperature, her boss-now-lover was hard again, impressively so.

Pretending not to notice, she backed into a corner of the marble enclosure. Grabbing a washcloth, she soaped it and prepared to execute the quickest cleanup on record.

Nathaniel took matters—and the washcloth—out of

her hands. "Don't be shy, Dani. Maybe this one is on *my* bucket list."

It was depressing to think he had probably enjoyed shower sex with any number of strange women. But when he gently washed her breasts and then moved lower, her eyes closed and her body went lax with pleasure. After he completed his mission, fore and aft, he used the detachable shower sprayer to rinse her completely. As he had promised, the towel protecting her hair stayed perfectly dry.

"Thank you," she muttered. She felt as if her entire body was covered in one big blush. She'd had sex with the man twice already. Yet still, his touch in this new context left her feeling vulnerable and uncertain.

"Will you do the honors?" He held out the washcloth with a challenging gleam in his eye. Not for the world would Dani let him see how very far out of her depth she was. Ocean deep. Wishing for a life raft. In imminent danger of drowning.

Nathaniel had been careful to point the showerhead away from her. Which meant that she could kneel at his feet and soap him up to her heart's content.

It was a dangerous game they played. Nathaniel clenched his fists, his eyes closed. His head fell back to rest against the wall. The length of him was fascinating—alive, powerful and so very sensitive to her touch.

For a man to allow a woman this level of intimate attention required a level of trust. In one brief moment, Nathaniel had chosen to yield his power for the sweet pleasure a lover's caress could bring. Dani held him in two hands, marveling at a creation that was at once so commonplace and yet so incredibly beautiful and life-giving.

The physical relationship between them was new and short-lived. Cleansing him was one thing. Other more intimate attentions were beyond her comfort level. She brushed a soft kiss across the head of his erection and rose to her feet. "Turn around, so I can finish."

His back was almost as compelling as other parts. Sleek muscles, male sinew and bone, all of it fascinated her. At last, she took the sprayer and removed every soapy bubble. "All done," she croaked.

Nathaniel spun around so quickly she gasped. He dragged her against him and kissed her hard, desperately. She felt the tang of blood in her mouth. "Dani," he groaned. "Dani, my sweet Dani." Maneuvering her like a rag doll, he turned her to the wall and placed her hands above her head, palms flat on the slick, wet surface. "Don't move."

One breathless heartbeat later she felt him enter her from behind. This time the theme was slow possession, so measured and deliberate she wanted to claw the wall. Her climax built in gentle swells and waves, one after the next. Nathaniel drew back and pushed in again, his size and force stimulating sensitive flesh already tender from their earlier lovemaking.

His big hands gripped her hips. "I won't let you forget this," he growled. "I'll take you again and again today until you beg me for more, and then we'll start all over again."

The provocative mental picture he painted sent her over the edge. She cried out and tried to stay still, but the end was too much for both of them, the shower floor too slick. Nathaniel scooped her up, took two steps out and deposited her on the thick, fluffy bathroom rug. He moved between her thighs with frantic haste. "Now," he moaned. "Come again, come with me."

Nathaniel slumped on top of Dani and tried to remember how to breathe. In the other room, the baby stirred. Damn it. How did couples with babies ever talk? No that he wanted to talk, not really. He was screwed and he knew it.

Dani would have to go to another division, another boss. The idea made his skin crawl. But he wasn't in denial. There was no way he could work with her now and not be constantly sidelined by lust. Already, he wanted her day and night.

The depth of that wanting scared him more than anything he had ever faced. No woman had ever mattered to him this way. He'd never allowed it. Now, though, he was torn between wanting to keep Dani at arm's length and being wildly jealous of any other man at NCT who might cross her path.

Incredulous that he had allowed himself to stray so far from his life's plan, he felt a lick of despair and panic.

He needed to think. He needed a plan. Unfortunately, this entire situation was spiraling madly out of control.

Dani shoved at his shoulders. "Let me go get her, please. She slept forever. I'm sure she's starving."

Rolling to one side, he slung an arm over his eyes and tried not to freak out. In his peripheral vision, he saw Dani take his terry robe from the back of the door and belt it twice around herself. The way her narrow waist flared into a curvy ass was an image he would never get out of his brain. His hands tingled with the need to touch her again.

He decided to let Dani tend to the kid for a few moments while he pulled himself together. Once he was dressed again, he felt marginally more normal. Unfortunately, he couldn't stay in the bathroom forever.

When he opened the door to the bedroom, woman and baby were gone. Made sense. The formula and bottles were in the kitchen. He found his missing houseguests there. Dani perched on a stool. Peaches was in her lap.

Dani didn't look at him, but she muttered a greeting. Her gaze was fixed on the baby. "I've seen how you look at her," she said. "You're already halfway in love with this baby. It's going to hurt like hell if she's not yours, isn't it?"

He poured himself a cup of coffee. "Sharing custody of a child with Ophelia would be a nightmare, so no."

"I wasn't talking about Ophelia. I was talking about you and Peaches. I've watched you with her. Deep down, you wouldn't be too upset if this baby carries your DNA."

"Quit trying to psychoanalyze me, Dani. I'm not a kid person. Never have been. Never will be. The baby is cute. I'll give you that. But believe me, I'll be happy to hand her back to her real parent. Hopefully sooner than later."

The inquisition should have bothered him far more than it did. But his body was relaxed and sated from really great sex, so it was almost impossible to get mad at Dani for weaving her naive theories.

"I do have a Christmas present for you after all," she said. Peaches finished the bottle. Dani put the baby on her shoulder and patted her back. "It's on my phone. Take a look."

The photograph Dani had captured at some point this weekend when he wasn't aware was beautiful. Even he had to admit that. He'd been in the den with the baby showing her the Christmas tree. The damned shot could have made the cover of a parenting magazine. *Man in Love with His New Child. Father Shares the Joys of Christmas with the Next Generation. Innocence and Trust. Daddy and Daughter.*

He clicked out of the photo app and laid the phone on the counter. "Thank you. Text it to me. It will be a good reminder to vet my future bed partners more carefully."

When Dani's face went blank, he cursed. "I'm sorry," he said stiffly. "That was a stupid thing to say. I'm sorry, Dani." He went to her and put his arms around her and the baby. "I'm not usually so clumsy. I was trying to be funny, but it wasn't funny at all. You're the only woman I want in my bed, I swear."

"For now. Not forever."

"I thought we both agreed this was a for-now kind of thing." Was she trying to make him feel guilty? It was working.

"We did. Of course." Dani wriggled free of his embrace and stood. "I think this would be a good time to finish that movie we started earlier."

Nathaniel released her reluctantly. Somehow they had segued from mind-blowing sex in his bedroom to acting like stilted strangers. He knew it was his fault. What he didn't know was how to fix it.

The remainder of Christmas Day passed slowly. Their snowed-in weekend was drawing to a close. Outside, a few of the main thoroughfares had been plowed and salted. Traffic was moving again, albeit slowly. The temperature had climbed above freezing for a few hours, but there was still plenty of snow cover. The side streets would be a mess.

Peaches was content to play on a blanket for long periods of time. She had napped a great deal of the day, so now she was awake and in a good mood.

Nathaniel was glad to have the child as a chaperone. Again and again, he revisited the invitation to accompany Dani to her parents' home. Was there a trap hidden in there, a trap he didn't see?

Dani was the least manipulative woman he knew. Then again, he had allowed her unprecedented access to his private life. Something had changed. Something more than the initiation of a physical relationship. He found himself wanting to lock the door and never let her leave. Here in his condo, he could control the outcome.

Once the real world intruded again, all bets were off.

Christmas supper was leftovers, but damned good leftovers. Afterward, Nathaniel entertained the baby while Dani spoke on the phone again to each of her siblings and her parents. It was clear to him that the Meadows clan was a tight-knit bunch. If Dani showed up with her boss and a baby in tow, wouldn't everyone think it was odd?

Again, he tried to sniff out danger. Finally, he asked Dani outright, "Won't your family think it strange if Peaches and I tag along with you?"

In her red sweater and black pants, Dani looked elegant and not nearly as approachable as the woman wearing his shirts. "Why? Are you thinking about changing your mind?"

"That's not an answer," he pointed out wryly.

Dani wrinkled her nose. "I'm the youngest. My parents have seen it all. Before my sister got married, she dated an insurance salesman with three boys under the age of seven. The man was looking for a built-in babysitter. Fortunately, Angie wised up before it was too late. He wasn't the only weirdo, though. There was a musician in an alternative rock band and a tax accountant turned street preacher."

"Wow."

"Yeah. Angie went through a rebellious stage before she settled down with my brother-in-law, who, by the way, is pretty much a saint."

Nathaniel grinned. "What about your brother?"

"He's not married yet. For the last couple of years, he's been dating a string of short-term partners. Nice women, but they haven't a clue what to do with Jared. He has an IQ in the hundred fifties. The man needs intellectual stimulation, even if he doesn't know it yet."

"I'm sure it will dawn on him eventually."

"We can only hope."

"I'm not sure where I fit in," Nathaniel drawled. "I'm

not a musician or much of a churchgoer. But I do temporarily have a baby to look after."

"I've been thinking about that," Dani said earnestly. "If you decide to come with me to Gainesville tomorrow, I'll simply introduce you as my boss. They know your name, of course, because I've spoken about you. I'll say you're caring for a friend's baby and that we got snowed in together. That's all they need to know."

"In their shoes, I might have a lot of questions."

"Even if that were true, they wouldn't make you uncomfortable. My parents are the consummate Southern hosts. They may feed you too much, and you might have to listen to my father's dumb jokes, but no one will put you on the spot."

"I'll think about it," he said.

Dani's pleased expression was its own reward.

At bedtime, they faced an awkward moment. Dani held Peaches, prepared to disappear into her room for the night. Nathaniel stopped her with a hand on her arm. He kissed her cheek. "Sleep in my bed tonight," he muttered.

"Are you sure?" Dani looked up at him searchingly as if she saw every one of his doubts.

"I'm sure."

Nine

An hour and a half later, he wasn't sure at all. Peaches was asleep in her little walled-off nest in the corner. Dani had chosen to get ready for bed in her own room and returned wearing the simple ivory silk gown and robe. She looked young and innocent and disturbingly bridal.

"I know I gave you those," he said gruffly. "But I'd rather have you naked."

Dani lifted an eyebrow. "Maybe if you dim the lights first?" she said, laughing.

"No. I don't think I will." He was counting on the fact that his feisty assistant never backed down from a challenge.

She shot him a glare promising retribution but seconds later stripped down to her bare skin, tossed the night clothes on the nearest chair and scuttled under the covers. "I'm cold," she complained.

The obvious ploy to reverse his command had no effect whatsoever. "I'll warm you up," he said.

Dani had the blanket pulled up to her chin. Her sultry smile promised all sorts of naughty delights.

With shaking hands, he unbuttoned his shirt and unfastened his pants. Having Dani watch him with rapt fascination did good things for a man's ego. When he was completely naked, he let her look her fill. His sex was rigid with anticipation, his body primed and hungry.

"Invite me to come to bed, little elf."

"It's your bed," she pointed out with inescapable logic. "I'm only visiting."

"You look good in there."

It was true. It had been a very long time since *any* woman had graced his condo with her presence. Now he had two females under his roof. No wonder he felt off balance.

Dani's dark, honey hair tumbled across the pillow. Her eyes were heavy-lidded with arousal. She couldn't hide from him. Not anymore.

"When I asked you to sleep with me tonight, I meant that literally," he confessed.

"I know." Her smile was equal parts wistful and wry. "But between the baby waking up at all hours and you waving *that* thing around, I can't imagine either of us will get much rest."

"It's called a penis," he chuckled, climbing underneath the covers and dragging her into his arms. She felt amazing tucked up against him. Feminine curves and soft, soft skin. "This was a very good idea."

"And you're so modest, too."

"Brat."

"Autocrat."

"Shrew."

She laughed softly, curling one arm around his neck and kissing his chin. "I like fighting with you."

"Is that what we're doing?" He rubbed his hands over her rounded butt, squeezing experimentally. "I thought we were negotiating."

She pulled back and stared at him, her expression wry. The lamp on the bedside table was still on, though the bulb was small and the light it cast not bright at all. "Everything I have is yours tonight, Nathaniel," she said softly. "No negotiating necessary. I'm here because I want to be."

Big blue eyes seemed to reflect the knowledge that he was incapable of giving her what she needed. He couldn't let this go too far. Not without risking his heart and his professional life. What did Dani expect from him?

His throat was so tight he had to swallow before he could speak. "I'm glad," he said gruffly.

Giving in to the greatest temptation he had ever known, he let himself wallow in her goodness, her welcome, her much-needed warmth. He had stocked the nearest drawer with a dozen condoms, and even that might not be enough. They came together in every way imaginable, hard and fast, lazy and slow. They dozed from time to time, and then he took her again.

He didn't know what love was. Surely not this desperate need to bind and irrevocably mark a woman. Love wasn't a sick feeling in the stomach, was it? Or the terrifying conviction that he had lost all control of his life? The notion that Dani was becoming *necessary* to him was scary as hell.

She was a decent woman and more honest than any other he had ever known. Her life was an open book. But if he told her even a fraction of what he was feeling, that would give her power over him, the power to destroy.

So he held his tongue, but he showed her with his body. Like a madman, he forced his way between smooth thighs and took her in an agony of longing, as if he would never get enough. As if filling her and finding release was the ultimate calling of his life.

Loving her gently was far easier when the first storm had passed. He stroked curves and valleys, feathering his fingertips across her most sensitive flesh and relishing her ragged cries when he gave her what she needed most.

Holding her afterward was almost as good. With her back pressed to his chest and her bottom cradled against his pelvis, he found peace. Burying his face in her hair, he inhaled her scent and tried to commit it to memory. Nothing this good could last. Nothing ever did.

In the middle of the night, Dani took a turn waking him. "Hold me," she whispered. "Make love to me again. Christmas is over, and I'm afraid of tomorrow."

He had no assurances to offer. They both knew the score. It added up to messy confusion and ultimately, change. A change he didn't want, but a change that was necessary. The best he could do right now was pretend.

Dani woke up just before 5:00 a.m. and went to the bathroom. Then, with her heart breaking, she stared into the mirror and tried to recognize the woman with the tousled hair and the tired eyes and the whisker burns on her neck.

How could they go forward from here? Nathaniel was never going to change. Dani had too much self-respect to settle for a relationship that was less than a hundred percent. She wanted a normal life.

Nathaniel Winston was not normal in any way. He was brilliant and driven. Generous, but at the same time distant. She knew he cared about her in an academic fashion. Just as he cared about Peaches. That wasn't enough. Dani wanted everything or nothing at all.

Maybe he felt something more for her than a primal, male need to possess. Maybe he could fall in love with her.

Was she willing to take that chance? Was she willing to wait for something that might never happen?

Yawning and desolate, she returned to the bedroom and climbed back under the covers. Nathaniel was dead asleep, but when she touched his chest, he mumbled and reached for her, dragging her against him. Dani closed her eyes and fell asleep, wrapped in the bittersweet comfort of ephemeral bliss.

The next time she awoke, the room was filled with light. Nathaniel lay on his side facing her, his head propped on his hand. He looked younger and happier than she had ever seen him. Peaches lay between them, contentedly gumming the edge of the sheet.

Dani rubbed her eyes with the heels of her hands and stretched with a yawn. "Sorry, I must have been out cold."

Nathaniel grinned. "You were indeed. I suppose someone kept you awake most of the night."

His smug, male satisfaction amused her despite the turmoil in her heart. She twirled one of the baby's curls around her finger. "Naughty baby."

"Very funny." He tangled his hand in Dani's hair and leaned over to kiss her. "I've decided to go to Gainesville with you. If the offer's still open."

"Of course it is. But what about work? What changed your mind?"

"NCT can do without me for one day. We've all three been cooped up since Friday. A road trip sounds like fun. You can tell your brother not to worry about picking you up."

"I hate to burst your bubble, but how exactly are we going to get there? Your Mercedes is in a drugstore parking lot under a mound of snow, and there's still the matter of the car seat."

"Out of curiosity, how did *you* envision us traveling when you first invited me to go with you?"

"Truthfully?" She grimaced. "I thought you would say no immediately, so it was a moot point."

Her answer bothered him. She could see it in his eyes, but he recovered quickly. "Well, I guess the joke is on you. I'm coming, and I've got the transportation problem solved. I've ordered a vehicle with a regulation car seat already installed."

"A car?"

"A vehicle."

"As in...?"

For a moment, he looked like a kid caught cheating on his homework. "I requested a Hummer. It will be delivered at four this afternoon."

Dani gaped. "A Hummer? Are you serious? Why would you do that?"

Nathaniel shrugged. "It's a virtually indestructible vehicle. Look out the window, woman. The melting has started, but it won't be gone in an hour. Nobody in Atlanta knows how to drive in the snow. It's dangerous to be out and about. Besides, all that water has to go somewhere, which means flooding. Peaches may not be mine, but I have a responsibility to keep her safe until the investigator gets some answers. I want to keep you safe, too."

"And you want to drive a Hummer."

His sheepish grin acknowledged the truth of her accusation. "Is that so bad?"

"My brother will go nuts. I hope you don't mind sharing. He'll have the two of you careening all over Hall County."

"There are worse ways to spend an afternoon."

"Good grief." She muttered the words beneath her breath as she got out of bed. At five this morning after visiting the bathroom, she had donned her nightgown before getting back under the covers. Her mental state required some kind of armor, even if it was flimsy silk and even if the silk had been purchased by the man on the other side of the bed. Now she added the robe and belted it. "Shall I fix us some breakfast?"

Every bit of humor left his face. His eyes darkened and his jaw tightened. "What I'd like is for Ophelia to reclaim her baby so I can spend a few more hours in bed with you. Last night was amazing."

"Hush," she said. "Not in front of Peaches."

He stared at her so intently her nipples beaded beneath two thin layers of silk. Nathaniel noticed, of course. "She doesn't understand a thing I'm saying. Nor does she know how badly I want her to take a long, morning nap."

"Stop it, please. You're embarrassing me." Her cheeks felt sunburned. Why did the man in the bed have to be so sexy, so charming, so funny, so *everything*?

"Fine," he said. "Go scramble a few eggs if it will make you happy. But don't expect me to forget about sex. Not after last night."

If Christmas Day had been long and lazy, Monday was anything but. Since the holiday fell on Sunday, most of Atlanta had Monday off, which meant traffic was lighter than usual on the interstates. That helped road crews who were trying desperately to restore order. Unfortunately, even that advantage was negated by the dozens of wrecks all over the city. Dani and Nathaniel took turns listening to the radio, scouring online news sites and occasionally catching breaking-news updates on TV.

Peaches was inconsolable for most of the day. She did, in fact, have one tiny tooth poking through on the bottom with a second one soon on the way. "No wonder she's cranky," Dani said after lunch. "Poor thing is miserable."

Since they didn't want to get out twice, Dani made a list

and Nathaniel placed a phone order to the same pharmacy/discount store where they had first gathered supplies for the baby. This time Dani included infant acetaminophen and a fluid-filled teething ring that could be frozen. They needed something to comfort the poor child.

While the grown-ups took turns packing overnight bags, the baby slept for no more than ten minutes at a time. Dani, frazzled and exhausted, began to wonder if this trip to Gainesville was a good idea after all. On the other hand, her parents would be crushed if she cancelled at this late date.

Nathaniel loaned her a small suitcase. She managed to get all of the gifts he had given her folded neatly inside. The family lunch would be extremely casual, and she had told Nathaniel as much. The jeans she chose to wear from her new mini wardrobe, however, were superchic, as was the long-sleeve top in shades of purple and mauve and silver. Never had she spent this much money on items that were essentially a knock-around wardrobe.

The outfit must have been flattering, because Nathaniel's eyes narrowed and his neck flushed when he saw her. "You almost ready?" he asked.

Dani nodded, tucking her hair behind her ears. "I think we're just waiting for the drugstore order and we're good to go."

Nathaniel handed her the baby. "I'm going downstairs to sign for the car. I'll load the delivery straight into the back."

"You won't need all that for one night."

"Doesn't matter. I've got plenty of room in the Hummer."

She laughed. "You love saying that, don't you?"

His wicked smile made her stomach flip. "I don't know *what* you're talking about."

When the front door slammed behind him, Dani nuzzled Peaches's soft cheeks and tried to remember everything she needed to pick up at her apartment. Thanks to Nathaniel's largesse, it was mostly only the presents for her family.

Thirty minutes later, they were on the road. Dani had worried about Peaches's safety, but the car seat was top-of-the-line and installed correctly. The baby settled down once they were in the ridiculously large and noticeable vehicle, perhaps from the novelty of being outside.

The huge amounts of melting snow did indeed create a nightmare. Not only that, but Nathaniel was forced to dodge vehicles that had been abandoned Friday night. The side trip to Dani's apartment took far longer than it should have. She shared the top floor of an old Victorian house in the Piedmont Park area.

"This is nice," Nathaniel said, surveying the tree-lined streets and charming architecture.

"I won't be long at all."

"Don't you need help?"

"No. I'll be fine." She didn't want Nathaniel inside her home, even briefly. It was going to be hard enough to root him out of her life without the memory of his presence inside the one place that was her peaceful sanctuary at the end of a long day.

She was gone fifteen minutes, maybe twenty. "Sorry," she said as she carefully placed the sack of gifts in the back and climbed into the front of the vehicle. "I had to water a couple of plants."

"No worries."

As Nathaniel negotiated the newly created obstacle course to get out of town, Dani texted back and forth with her mother. Finally, she shut off her phone and tossed it in her purse. "I hope we make it to Gainesville and the hotel in one piece."

He shifted into a lower gear to tackle an icy hill. "We'll make it," he said. "And we'll celebrate in bed, little elf. Frankly, it's all I'm thinking about at the moment. That and trying not to smash up this tank I'm driving."

"I thought it wasn't smashable," she quipped, goading him for no good reason.

He scowled as the driver to their right ran a stop sign. "True. It would be more correct to say I'm worried about smashing up all the *other* vehicles on the road. Do me a favor and quit talking for now. I need to concentrate."

Normally the drive from Atlanta to Gainesville—northeast of the city—took an hour to an hour and half, depending upon time of day. Today, the traffic crawled. All lanes of the interstate were clear, but stranded vehicles on the side of the road created hazards. Not only that, but the people who hadn't been able to travel Saturday and Sunday were out in full force, clogging the roads.

When they finally made it to the outskirts of Dani's hometown, she had a tension headache and an empty stomach. Peaches had slept the first hour and cried on and off the rest of the trip. Nathaniel pointed out a popular steak house. "Do you want to stop for dinner before we check in?"

The thought of juggling a cranky baby was daunting. "Would you mind if we ordered pizza and had it delivered to the room?"

"Not at all. I should have thought of that."

The all-suite hotel Dani had chosen was part of a chain, but a nice one. A friendly bellman helped them wrangle all their stuff upstairs and beamed when Nathaniel tipped him generously. The young man wanted to linger and discuss the Hummer's unique features. Dani eased him out the door. "We need to feed the baby. Thanks again for all your help."

Nathaniel collapsed in an armchair and rubbed his temples. "I *never* want to make that drive again."

"Me, either," Dani said, feeling guilty. "I had no idea it would be so bad. I'm sorry I dragged you into this."

He gave her a tired smile that still had enough wattage to curl her toes. "I came along of my own free will. Besides, this may be the only time in my life I can justify the Hummer."

"Was it worth the price?"

"Every penny." He kicked off his shoes. "Let me have the baby, and you order our pizza. I'll eat anything but anchovies. And onions."

"Sounds good."

Often, when Nathaniel decided to work through lunch at NCT, Dani was the one who ordered meals brought in. It wasn't unusual for the two of them to sit together in Nathaniel's office and eat while he kept working and she took notes or sent emails at his request.

Never once in those situations had she ever felt self-conscious or weird. Tonight, every moment felt like new territory.

Fortunately, the local pizza place was close by. Delivery was prompt and efficient. While Dani handled the meal order, Nathaniel gave Peaches a bottle. He was an old pro at it already. Soon, Peaches was asleep. They spread a blanket on the rug near them and put the baby on her tummy. She scrunched her cute little face and drew her knees under her, her bottom tilted upward in her favorite sleep position.

While they consumed the hot, extra cheesy ham-and-pineapple pizza, silence reigned. Dani knew she should come right out and tell Nathaniel she was looking for another job. He would probably be pleased. It would be impossible for things to go back to the way they were at the office. After this bizarre Christmas weekend that was both wonderful and challenging in equal parts, life was going to be very different.

Dani wasn't scheduled to go back to work until January 3. She'd banked the last of her vacation time to give herself a nice, long holiday at the end of the year. Her plans for the remainder of this week were modest: clean out her closet, see a couple of movies she had missed and stock up on groceries to cook healthy, yummy meals for January.

She didn't always make New Year's resolutions, but this time around was different. In the spirit of being proactive, she would schedule herself an appointment on Nathaniel's calendar for that first day back, sit down with him and quit her job face-to-face.

Just thinking of it made her hands clammy and her stomach queasy. The boss was a holy terror when he was mad. Woe to the person who became the focus of his icy cold displeasure. Still, only a coward ended a job *or* a relationship with a note, online or otherwise.

Nathaniel tapped the edge of the box. "You want to share the last piece?"

"It's all yours," she said.

If Nathaniel had even once offered a single shred of evidence that he was thinking about a future for the two of them, she might have found the courage to tell him she loved him. After all, nothing dictated that the man had to be first to lay his heart on the line.

Unfortunately, Nathaniel had done nothing to indicate a desire for permanence.

Which meant that tonight and tomorrow were it.

Without saying a word, he gathered up the empty pizza box and the paper plates and napkins, and carried them out to the trash chute in the hall. When he returned, he lifted an eyebrow. "What's wrong, Christmas elf? I've never seen you bite your fingernails."

She jerked her hand away from her mouth. "Nothing's wrong," she lied. "I might be a tiny bit nervous about tomorrow, that's all."

They had been sitting on the floor with their backs against the sofa. He dropped down beside her and put a hand on her knee. "Peaches and I can always stay here. Your brother could pick you up and bring you back."

"I want you to come," she said slowly. "I just don't want anybody getting stupid ideas about you and me."

It was the perfect opening for him to make a suggestive remark, or even admit he wouldn't think that was a terrible idea if it happened.

Nathaniel did neither.

Instead, he picked up his phone and began looking at emails. "I thought I would hear something from the investigator by now."

Dani swallowed her disappointment and hurt. It wasn't Nathaniel's fault she'd been weaving fantasies. She stood and crossed the room to put some distance between them. "Did he say how he would start his search?"

"I imagine he'll follow the credit card trail. That seems to be the easiest route."

"Except if Ophelia got stuck in one place like we were, there might be no credit card activity to find."

"True. But even if that were so, I'm betting today is different. As soon as transactions start popping up, he'll find her."

"I hope so." She crouched beside the baby, already half in love with Peaches herself. "She's so sweet and good-natured. I hope that means Ophelia is a good mother most of the time."

Nathaniel's expression darkened. "I didn't have much of a mother at all, but I turned out okay, didn't I?"

"Of course," Dani said lightly. *If you don't count the fact that you're distrustful of women in general and emotionally closed off to a clinical degree.* "I think there are a couple of bowl games on. If you want to watch them, I'll read for a while. I grabbed a book when I ran up to the apartment."

"You don't mind?"

"Not at all."

The tension between them was impossible to ignore. Big emotions were at stake, but Nathaniel *wouldn't* talk about them, and Dani couldn't. The result was an uneasy truce.

Peaches woke up after an hour. The atmosphere in the hotel room eased after that. The baby provided not only a center point for conversation, but plenty of hands-on work to keep them busy.

At almost ten, Nathaniel's cell phone dinged. His expression was triumphant as he read the text. He looked up at Dani with a grim smile. "She bought gas and groceries in Decatur."

"That's good, then—right? She's still in town?"

"Unless she's headed north to run away."

"Don't think like that," Dani said. "Being the mother of an infant is stressful and emotionally draining. I'll bet Ophelia had a freak-out moment for some reason, and she brought the baby to you. Once she gets her head on straight, she'll want Peaches back again."

"Let's hope so."

Their little charge went out for the night not long after that. Dani showered and put on the ivory gown and robe. The king-size bed in the center of the room was an invitation for romantic sex, or so it seemed to Dani's heated longings.

As if he had read her mind, Nathaniel crossed the space

separating them and moved behind her, linking his arms around her waist. He rested his chin on top of her head. "I *am* ready for bed," he said.

"I *am* pretty tired."

He spun her around to face him and bent to stare into her eyes. "Please tell me that was a joke. I should get stars in my crown for keeping my hands off you all day."

"You were too busy with the traffic to notice me."

"Don't fish for compliments, elf. I'm obsessed with you, and it's damned uncomfortable."

Ten

Nathaniel had never meant to be so honest. But his moments with Dani were slipping away. He couldn't afford to waste a single one.

Tonight seemed like an ending—bittersweet and momentous at the same time. He was damned tempted not to let her go. Her openness and caring were the antithesis of the way he lived his life. Keeping her would be not only dangerous, but selfish. He couldn't imagine a future without her, but he *knew* he wasn't equipped to be the man she needed.

He undressed her carefully and then removed the athletic pants he had donned after his shower. They climbed into bed without speaking. He pulled her to the center of the mattress and wrapped his arms around her. "I don't want to hurt you, Dani."

Dani went rigid in his embrace. "I can take care of myself," she said, the words tart. "Maybe you should worry about *me* hurting you."

He smiled in the darkness. She was reminding him that their relationship was a two-way street. What she couldn't know was that he had gone years without letting women get close enough to penetrate the walls around his heart. If anyone had the power, it would have been Dani. But he was in no danger. He held all the cards.

As long as he remained in control, everything would go according to plan. He could assign Dani to a new division and gradually wean himself from her allure.

He hadn't allowed himself to fall in love with her. That was how he knew everything was going to be okay.

For the next hour, he lost himself in the pleasure of her body. The sex was as good as it had ever been, but something was a little off. His Christmas elf wasn't as open with him as before. She held something back. Put up a few no-trespassing signs.

Her reticence might have been infuriating if he hadn't been balls deep in making love to her. Not *loving* her. There was a difference.

Each time he made her come, he was jubilant. She might have other lovers after him, but he was determined she wouldn't be able to erase the memories of tonight.

Beyond that testosterone-fueled goal lingered a strange mixture of elation and terror. His body was sated, lax with bone-deep pleasure. He held Dani close and buried his face in her hair.

It was only sex, he told himself desperately. Only sex…

Morning came far too soon. Peaches had given them a good six-hour stretch, taken a bottle and then gone right back to sleep until almost eight o'clock. Even so, Nathaniel wanted to spend the morning in bed. With Dani.

As they took turns getting ready, his lover was quiet.

It was just as well. He had nothing witty to say, no funny quips about melting snow or holiday blues or poopy diapers.

Dani's mother was preparing Christmas lunch for the midday meal. Dani and Nathaniel were instructed to arrive no later than eleven in order to have time for opening presents and taking official family photos.

The Meadows family owned fifteen acres of land outside of town. Their property ran alongside a rich river bottom and up the side of a small hill. Dani had told him stories about running barefoot through fields of cotton and catching fireflies on hot summer nights.

He was charmed in spite of himself. Such rustic, simple pleasures were a million miles away from his own upbringing. Oftentimes as a kid, he'd spent hours at the kitchen table, figuring out homework on his own and listening to the ticking of the mantel clock as it echoed in their elegant, lonely home.

Shaking off the maudlin thoughts, he concentrated on maneuvering the Hummer around Gainesville. "Nice town," he said.

"It was a fun place to grow up. I love Atlanta, though. I'm a big-city girl at heart. I even thought about moving to New York at one time."

"But?"

"It's expensive. And I would miss my family. Atlanta is home."

At a red light, he braked and glanced in the rearview mirror. "Is she doing okay?"

"Almost asleep. I wish we could drive around long enough for her get a good nap. Mom expects promptness, though. My siblings and I learned that the hard way. If we came in late from a date or a party, we'd be grounded for two weeks. It was effective punishment."

"Don't take this wrong, but it sounds like the Meadowses are a typical American family. It's nice."

Dani shrugged. "You could say that. Still, even typical American families have problems, Nathaniel. Normalcy doesn't exempt anyone from pain and tragedy."

He mulled over her odd answer as they drove ever closer to Dani's childhood home. Was she trying to tell him something, or was he reading too much into her words?

When they finally made it to the other side of town and out into the country, Nathaniel thought they were home free. The sky was gray and the trees bare, but it was warm—fifty degrees already. He hadn't counted on the scenic creek that ran through the Meadowses' property.

To ascend the drive that led to the house, it was necessary to cross the creek on a narrow concrete bridge. Today, the creek was a raging river...and rising rapidly.

Dani's hands gripped the dash and the door, white-knuckle. "I don't like this, Nathaniel."

"Hummers were meant for situations like today," he said. "There's barely any water over the bridge yet, so I'll take it slow and we'll be fine."

They inched their way forward. The water was still rising, but certainly not fast enough to sweep the Hummer off the bridge. For a brief moment, it occurred to him he might be getting stuck with Dani in another weather-related situation, but he ignored the thought. He tightened his grip on the wheel and pressed the gas pedal carefully.

The vehicle kept a gratifying grip on the road surface. "See," he said. "You were worried about nothing."

In the next second, he saw a large section of creek bank in front of them crumble into the muddy water. With a loud, groaning *crack*, a corner of the concrete bridge gave in to forces it was never meant to withstand.

"Hold on," Nathaniel yelled. They were six feet from

safety. More of the concrete could give way at any moment. He gunned the engine, floored the gas pedal and made the unwieldy vehicle lurch forward like an elephant released from a slingshot.

Everything happened in slow motion. Dani screamed. Another chunk of the bridge sheared off. But the Hummer came through for him. They landed on firm ground, inches away from the disaster they had so narrowly missed.

He shifted into Park with a shaky hand and reached for Dani. "God, I'm sorry. Are you okay?" They glanced at the back seat in unison, reassuring themselves that the baby had slept through it all.

Dani nodded, her face milk white. "I'm fine. It wasn't your fault."

It was, and he would kick himself for that later, but now all he wanted to do was reassure himself they were alive. He cupped Dani's head in two hands and turned her face up to his for a frantic kiss. His heart still beat in sickening thuds. "Your parents will shoot me," he said hoarsely.

Dani's arms were wrapped so tightly around his neck she threatened to strangle him. It didn't matter. The fragrance of her skin and the tremors that shook her body were killing him bit by bit with guilt. She might have been hurt. He could have lost her.

"We're fine," she insisted, though it was clear she couldn't stop shaking. "You saved us, Nathaniel. If we'd been on that bridge and it collapsed, we could have ended up nose first in the water. I don't even want to think about it."

"Me, either," he said. He rested his forehead against hers. "Damn it, little elf, I nearly ruined your storybook Christmas."

She laughed softly, her fingertips caressing the hair at his nape and making him shiver. "There was never anything storybook about this holiday. I suppose today is more of the same. Come on. Let's go get some lunch. Adrenaline makes me hungry."

Dani moved through the next hours in a dream. She'd done her best to reassure Nathaniel that their near disaster wasn't his fault. The experience shook her to the core. Personal danger wasn't at the heart of it. What if Peaches had come to harm? Or Nathaniel?

The terrifying moments on the bridge replayed in slow motion in her brain, even as she greeted her family and introduced Nathaniel and Peaches all around. It had been a long time since the Meadows clan had an infant in the house, so the baby helped defuse any awkwardness about Nathaniel's presence.

Nathaniel himself rolled out a generous helping of charm, complimenting Dani's parents on their home and their view. Lunch was delayed when the men decided they needed to check the status of the rising creek. The four males donned rain boots—some borrowed—and trudged down to the bottom of the hill while Dani and her mom and sister put the finishing touches on the meal.

Dani held the baby and snitched a piece of ham. "This looks amazing, Mom. You must have been up since dawn."

"Angie helped a lot. Why don't we go hang out in the den until the boys get back? No sense standing when we can sit."

Dani knew what was coming next. Jared hadn't brought a date. With only her mother and sister in the room, the confrontation to come was a given.

Angie played leadoff. "So tell me, little sis. Since when are you and the head of NCT so chummy?"

"I explained that already. It was a weird situation. He

was going to drive me to the train station, but the snow got too bad too fast."

"And that's when you found the baby." Angie rolled her eyes. "Give me a break. This sounds like an episode of a really bad soap opera."

Dani's mother intervened. "Don't be rude to your sister, Angie." She pinned Dani with the kind of look parents perfect when their kids are still toddlers. "Are you sleeping with him?"

"Mom!" Mortification flooded Dani's face with heat.

"That's not an answer."

"He's my boss," Dani said, desperately wishing she had never initiated the idea of Nathaniel coming with her. "That would be entirely inappropriate."

"Danielle..." Her mother's voice went up an octave.

Dani clutched Peaches and straightened her spine. "There's nothing going on between us. Nathaniel doesn't trust women. He's a confirmed bachelor."

Angie pointed across the room, sympathy on her face. "Too late, kid. Give it up. Mom was worried about the creek. She and Dad have been scouring the valley all morning."

Dani looked over at the cushioned seat in the bay window. There were the high-end binoculars she had bought her dad last Christmas. For bird-watching. "Oh?"

Her sister put an arm around her waist and leaned in to whisper in her ear. "They saw the kiss, Dani. Every passionate second. You're busted."

"I can explain. We were scared. It was adrenaline."

Her mother frowned. "Is this serious, Dani?"

"No," she cried. "I swear it's not. Please don't make a big deal about nothing."

Fortunately, the men returned before her mother could continue the inquisition. Dani was temporarily saved from further embarrassment. Everyone was hungry, so presents had to wait.

Over lunch, the adults teased each other with old stories about Christmases past. The year Jared opened all his presents in the middle of the night and tried to rewrap them before morning. The time Angie cried when she didn't get a doll she had actually forgotten to ask Santa for. And then Dani's most embarrassing Christmas. The one when her high-school boyfriend gave her a kitten because he didn't know she was allergic.

Jared finished the tale. "Oh, man, Nathaniel, you should have seen Dani. She was covered in red welts from head to toe. It was the quickest breakup in the history of teenage dating."

Nathaniel grinned. "It's hard to imagine. The Dani I know at work never gets flustered by anything."

"Okay," Dani said. "Enough family stories. Pass the sweet potatoes, please. Mom, why don't you and Dad tell Nathaniel about your trip to Hong Kong last summer."

Nathaniel was actually having fun. He had expected to sit back as a spectator while Dani enjoyed holiday rituals with her family. Instead, he had been pulled into the fray with a vengeance. The Meadows clan swapped jokes and debated blockbuster movies and argued politics passionately, including Nathaniel at every turn.

The only subject completely off-limits was Peaches. He knew Dani had explained the bare bones of the situation. Dani's siblings and parents handled the baby's presence with sensitivity. They didn't ignore her, but they also didn't say or do anything to make Nathaniel feel uncomfortable.

In the unlikely situation in which he found himself, his hosts' kindness and generosity were extraordinary. "May I propose a toast?" he asked as Mrs. Meadows brought out a ten-layer apple stack cake and a bowl of freshly whipped cream.

"Of course," Jared said. "But do it quick—before we all fall asleep. The tryptophan in the turkey is doing a number on me."

Nathaniel raised his glass of wine. "To snowstorms and spontaneity and hospitable families. Thanks for including me."

"Hear, hear," Dani's father said. "Now, about that Hummer…"

As Jared and his father argued over who would get first turn behind the wheel, Nathaniel followed Dani into the den where a mound of beautifully wrapped presents was piled beneath a real Fraser fir Christmas tree. The room smelled amazing, a cross between Alpine ski weekends and the comfort of home.

For a moment, Nathaniel felt a keen sense of loss for something he had never known in the first place. Shaking off the odd feeling, he took the baby from Dani. "You've been holding her forever. My turn, I think."

It was eye-opening to watch how the siblings and Dani's parents related to her. At New Century Tech, Nathaniel knew Dani as sharp and capable and goal oriented. In this setting, she was the "baby" of the crew. They petted her and teased her. Perhaps it was so ingrained in the family dynamic they didn't realize how much they underestimated her.

Nathaniel had done nearly the same on a more personal level. At work, he kept such rigid boundaries he never allowed himself to fully appreciate Dani's qualities as a woman, though the physical awareness had been there all along. It had taken a massive snowstorm to make him see what he was missing.

Dani was funny and warm and sexy. Brains and beauty in one appealing package.

Not for the world would he have embarrassed her in front of her family. Despite his hunger to be with her, he kept his distance physically, never touching her arm or tucking her hair behind her ear. He and Dani played the role of business associates perfectly. No one would ever guess they had spent the weekend making love at every turn.

He was touched and surprised to know that Dani's mother had somehow found a couple of things to wrap for *him*. He opened a navy-and-burgundy silk tie and a pair of sterling silver cuff links.

In the midst of the pandemonium of wrapping paper and boxes and bows, Nathaniel found himself trying to imagine what it would be like if he were a real member of this family. Heart pounding in his chest, he looked across the room at Dani and found her gaze on him. Her beautiful blue eyes shone bright with happiness.

The truth hit him without warning. A tsunami of feelings tightened his throat and glazed his eyes with moisture. He loved her. He was in love with his executive assistant.

This was a hell of a time for a personal epiphany. His head spun. The conversation swirled around him. He must have participated in appropriate ways, but he felt clumsy, his faculties impaired.

"Excuse me," he said, when he could form the words. "Peaches wants her bottle. I'll be right back."

He fled the family celebration. In the kitchen, he clutched the baby and searched for the premixed bottles of formula Dani had ordered, the same kind they had used that first night. With shaking hands, he uncapped and heated and tested. The routine was not so intimidating now. Against all odds, he was learning how to deal with a baby.

Once the bottle was ready, he went in search of a quiet bedroom. The house was very nice, but not all that large. Even with the door closed, he could hear echoes of the festivities from down the hall. He sat on the edge of the bed and cradled the little girl in his arms. She smiled up at him as she gripped the bottle.

Damn it. Dani was right. He didn't want the complicated situation, but it was going to break his heart if she weren't his flesh and blood.

Females were trouble. That was the truth. How was he going to let either one of them go?

Immediately after the formula was gone, Peaches fell sound asleep. He tugged the bottle from her hands and set it aside. Carefully, he lifted the small, limp body onto his shoulder.

He wanted to be alone. He needed time and space to process everything that was happening to him. Unfortunately, he was smack-dab in the middle of a good old-fashioned family Christmas.

When he made it back to the den, Jared cornered him. "It's not going to be safe to get across that bridge. At least not until the water goes down and Dad and I can see how much damage was done. There's an alternate route off the back side of the property, but it will add almost an hour to your trip."

Dani's mother joined them. "I know we're crowded, but I would feel better if you stayed the night, Nathaniel. I don't want you taking my daughter and the baby across the bridge today, Hummer or no Hummer. And that other road is terrible. We have all sorts of blankets and sleeping bags, more than enough to make comfy pallets here in front of the fire. I thought about kicking Jared out of his room, but his is a twin bed, so not much help."

Nathaniel swallowed his misgivings. "Dani can have the sofa. I'd be happy to stay, Mrs. Meadows, but I definitely will have to get on the road first thing in the morning to make it back to work."

"Of course," Dani's mother said. She turned around and looked at her daughter. "You don't mind camping out for just one night, do you, sweetheart?"

Dani had a deer-in-the-headlights look. "It's okay with me, Mama, if Nathaniel agrees."

Mrs. Meadows beamed. "Then it's settled."

For Nathaniel, the torture was only beginning. His plan had been to leave around four in the afternoon and hightail it back to Atlanta. He would drop Dani off at her apartment, and he and Peaches would go to his condo to wait for Ophelia.

Now he was going to spend another night with the woman he wanted more than his next breath. In her parents' house. With a baby as chaperone. God help him. It was everything he feared and everything he couldn't have.

The warm, loving family, the precious baby, the woman who tempted him beyond reason. How could he keep a rein on his hunger if the two of them were trapped in this house?

Despite his inner turmoil, the day passed quickly. As Dani had warned, the men were eager to try out the Hummer. Even Angie's husband went along for the excursion across snow-covered fields.

Nathaniel enjoyed the outing far more than he expected. Angie's husband possessed a dry wit. Dani's father turned out to be a good old country boy at heart and Jared was, as Dani had told him, brilliant. The four men took turns behind the wheel, tackling hills and whooping it up when the Hummer conquered all obstacles.

Before returning home, they went as close as they dared to the raging creek and assessed the conditions. According to the National Weather Service, the rising waters had finally peaked. With no rain in the forecast and only the melting snow to feed the torrent, the outlook was good. By morning it was possible that the usually placid brook might be near normal levels.

Back at the house, the women had whipped up another batch of mouthwatering food for dinner. Nathaniel was amazed the whole family managed to stay fit and trim. Maybe they burned it off because no one ever sat still.

The evening was devoted to charades and card games. Nathaniel cleaned up at poker but was lousy at charades. Even Angie's husband, the other outsider, was better at guessing clues than Nathaniel. They all teased him, but it was good-natured.

How could he tell them his focus was shot to hell because he was fixated on the prospect of another night with Dani?

At long last, the day drew to a close. One by one, family members disappeared to shower and get ready for bed. Dani's father dragged out all the extra bedding and helped make a comfortable sleeping spot for Nathaniel and Peaches. Dani tucked a sheet around the sofa cushions and added a blanket.

"We'll be fine, Dad. Thanks for everything."

Nathaniel nodded. "Thank you, sir. It was a great day."

Was it his imagination, or did Dani's father give him the stink eye before walking out of the room? Then it dawned on Nathaniel. The den had no door. A double doorway, yes. But no way to secure privacy with lock and key. *Hell's bells.*

Dani didn't bother with the nightwear he had bought for her. She was wearing borrowed sweatpants from her sister, topped with an Atlanta Braves T-shirt. With her hair up in a ponytail, she could have passed for a teenager.

Nathaniel excused himself for a turn in the bathroom. He opted for soft athletic pants and a thin cotton shirt, leaving it unbuttoned in deference to the fact that the fire made the den *very* toasty. They wouldn't have to worry about Peaches getting cold.

When he returned, Dani had turned out all the lights. She was tucked into her temporary bed on the sofa with the covers pulled up to her chin. She had taken the rubber band out of her hair, and now the thick, caramel tresses fanned out across her pillow in an appealing tumble. Her eyes were closed, but he'd bet a thousand dollars she was wide awake.

Peaches was asleep in her usual position.

He sat down on the end of the sofa and put Dani's feet in his lap.

She opened one eye. "I just got comfortable," she complained. "Shouldn't we get some sleep if we're getting up early?"

"It's ten thirty," he pointed out. "You and I are usually good for another several hours at this point. You know, when things get cranked up."

Her gaze was wild. "Nathaniel! Hush! Are you out of your mind? Somebody could be standing outside in the hall listening to us."

"They're not. I checked." He slipped his hand under the covers and played with her ankle bone. "I've barely touched you all day."

Eleven

Dani moaned. With Nathaniel's thumb pressing into the arch of her foot, her whole body turned to honey. "We can't," she muttered. "Somebody might come in."

"You don't think they'll give us privacy?"

"Yes. No. I don't know." He ran his hand up her calf but stopped at her knee. She wanted him so badly she was shaking. But this situation was fraught with impossibility.

Nathaniel nodded soberly. In the firelight, she could swear his eyes danced with mischief. "I understand. You think this is a bad idea. No worries. I'll read a book on my iPad and let you sleep."

When he started to stand up, Dani grabbed his wrist. "We'll have to be very quiet," she said, caving in to the yearning that made her abandon caution in favor of gratification.

Nathaniel looked shocked. "You're serious? I was kidding, Dani. I assumed fooling around was out of the question. You know, under the circumstances."

She sat up and raked the hair away from her face. "I need you," she said, searching his face to see if he felt even a fraction of the urgency that tore her apart. Need and want and every nuanced shading in between. She loved him. Greedily, she would snatch every possible opportunity to be with him.

"I won't say no to you, elf. How could I?"

He dragged her into his arms and kissed her softly, his fingers winnowing through her tangled hair. His breathing was not quite steady. That reassured Dani on some level. She didn't want to be the only one flying blind—jumping without a net—indulging without weighing the consequences.

Carefully, tenderly, he eased her down onto the carpet and slid both his hands under her shirt. When he cupped her breasts and thumbed her nipples, she had to bite down hard on her lower lip to keep from crying out.

The need for silence was frustrating, but it lent a titillating touch of danger. She cupped his face in her hands. He hadn't shaved. His jaw was covered in masculine stubble. "I'm glad you're here," she whispered.

"Me, too."

After that, there was not much need for words. The fire popped and crackled. Occasionally the baby made tiny noises in her sleep. Nathaniel slid Dani's pants and panties down her legs and removed them. With her shirt rucked up to her armpits, she was essentially naked. He stared her as if he had never seen her before, or maybe he had never seen a *woman* before. That's how wild and reckless and incredulous he seemed.

He freed his sex and found a condom. Seconds later he spread her thighs and thrust roughly, pinning her wrists above her head with one big hand. "I don't know what to do about you, elf. Tell me. Can anything this good last?"

When she didn't answer, his jaw hardened. What did he expect? What did he want from her? It was a rhetorical question as far as Dani could tell.

Nathaniel's big body was warm and hard against hers. He took her forcefully at first and then tauntingly slow in the next minute. Dani unraveled rapidly. With her hands bound, she felt helpless. At his mercy. His masculine scent surrounded her, making her crazy.

"Ah, damn," he groaned. His entire body went rigid. His chest radiated heat. His hips pinned her to the floor. He kissed her with bruising demand.

Rolling onto his side and moving her with him, he took advantage of the new position and touched her sex intimately. Heartbeats later, Dani came.

He covered her mouth with one large hand to smother her cry. Then he shoved her onto her back again and pummeled wildly until he buried his face in her neck and came for long, stormy seconds.

Dani dozed in Nathaniel's embrace until she found the strength to drag herself back to reality. Her body was relaxed and sated, but her heart ached with a throb that frightened her. She didn't want to love Nathaniel like this. She hated feeling so vulnerable. Most of all, she was terrified that sooner rather than later she was going to have to live through the end of whatever this thing was between them.

Affair. Fling. Momentary insanity. Any description she chose sounded temporary and ultimately painful.

Nathaniel roused finally and yawned. "Damn, elf. You're killing me."

She managed a smile. "I don't see you complaining."

"Probably because I'm not an idiot. If a man has to die, there are worse ways to go."

Their lighthearted teasing was a cover for deeper, darker emotions. Nathaniel had to know the end was in sight. She'd told him flat out she wouldn't expect more.

At any point in the past few days he'd had ample opportunity to declare his undying love and beg her to marry him. *That* hadn't happened. He'd done nothing that could be construed as leading her on. Their sexual romp was on her and her alone. She'd made a choice. Now she had to live with the consequences.

"We should get dressed," she said.

"Yeah." His yawn cracked his jaw.

"I hope the creek will be down far enough in the morning. I know you don't want to miss work."

"Doesn't matter," he said. "I called and arranged for a helicopter to pick us up. Jared has offered to return the Hummer to Atlanta for me. If you're afraid to fly, Peaches and I will go without you and you can come with your brother in a day or two."

Was that what he wanted? A clean break?

She swallowed hard. "I don't mind flying. I've never been in a helicopter, though." Men like Nathaniel Winston did things like that. Private jets. Corporate choppers. Once again, the vast gulf between their worlds mocked her.

"You'll like it, I think. Once you catch your breath."

"Sounds fun."

She eluded his embrace and pulled on her clothes. "I need to go to the bathroom."

When she returned, Nathaniel was standing in front of the fire, his back to her. One hand rested on the mantel. The other was shoved in his back pocket. What was he thinking? Poor man. He didn't celebrate Christmas, and yet here he was, neck deep in a Meadows family holiday.

She touched him on the shoulder. "Good night."

He whirled around as if she had startled him, as if

he had been lost in thought. He nodded, his expression hooded. "Sleep well, elf." He kissed her gently on the lips.

Dani held back stupid tears. "You, too."

Surprisingly, the night passed without incident. Peaches didn't wake up at all, perhaps worn out from all the extra attention. When the baby finally roused at seven, Dani and Nathaniel were already dressed.

Her mom and dad were early risers. Angie and her husband were still asleep. Jared wouldn't surface until ten at least. He took his days off seriously. It was only the four other adults in the kitchen drinking coffee as the baby took her bottle.

Dani's mom held out her arms. "May I hold her? It's been far too long since we've had a baby in the house. I thought I would have grandchildren by now."

Nathaniel ignored the verbal bait. Dani flushed. Her father sipped his coffee and smiled placidly.

They dined well on apple cake and hot, crispy bacon with fluffy scrambled eggs. Eventually, Nathaniel dabbed his lips with his napkin and glanced at his watch. "We'd better make sure the bags are ready. Won't be long now. Thank you both, for everything."

Dani's mother smiled. "We're so glad you could visit, Nathaniel. I was very sorry to hear Dani will be leaving NCT. I know she has learned so much from you."

The split second of silence was like the sizzle of ozone in the wake of a lightning strike. Nathaniel flinched, his expression blank with shock.

Perhaps Dani was the only one who noticed. He recovered so rapidly, she was stunned. When he looked at her, his gaze was bleak. "Dani has many talents, Mrs. Meadows. I'm sure she'll land on her feet."

He strode out of the room.

Dani followed on his heels, grabbed his arm in the hallway and tried to halt his progress. She might as well have attempted to hold back the ocean. He jerked free, his big, masculine frame rigid.

"I was going to tell you," she said. The explanation sounded weak even to her own ears. "After the holidays. When things settled down."

He seized her wrist in a bruising grasp and dragged her into the hall bathroom, the only place they could be sure of a private moment. When the door was locked behind them, he dropped her hand abruptly as if he couldn't bear to touch her.

"Tell me now," he said coldly. "Tell me the pay was unfair. Tell me I worked you too hard. Tell me I was a sucky boss."

"That's not why," she said, trying to swallow against the giant lump in her throat. "You know it was none of those things. It was this." She cupped his cheek with her hand. "I couldn't stay, because I knew sooner or later you would realize I wanted you. I never dreamed we would end up in bed together," she whispered, willing him to understand.

He stepped backward, forcing her hand to fall, and wrapped his arms around his chest, staring at her with an inscrutable expression. "Do other people at NCT know?"

"Of course not. I thought about telling you this weekend, but I didn't want to ruin things. It was Christmas, not the time to talk about business."

His tight smile made her stomach hurt. "You forget, Dani. I *am* my business." Then he waved a hand sharply as if consigning her to the trash bin. "No matter. I'll make this easy for you. I accept your resignation. I'll have someone pack up the personal items in your desk and deliver them to you next week."

"Nathaniel." She said his name softly—desperately—

searching for the right words. "I didn't do anything wrong. You're overreacting. I'm sorry I didn't talk to you sooner. But honestly, this was going to happen anyway. You know I can't work for you anymore." She sucked in a ragged breath. "I care about you."

"Do you? Do you really?" His sarcasm was drenched in ice. "Or is this a female ploy to bring me to my knees?"

"That's not fair." Tears clogged her throat.

With a careless grasp, he took her chin and tipped it upward so they were eye to eye. What destroyed her most was the bleak misery beneath his supercilious glare. Against all odds, she had hurt him deeply, it seemed. "Life's not fair, elf. I learned that a long time ago."

She made the mistake of trying one more time. "I'll go back on the chopper with you. We can talk later today. You need my help with the baby, surely."

Every human emotion inside him shut down as if someone had flipped a switch. His smile chilled her. "On the contrary, Dani. I think I can manage just fine on my own."

Stepping around her, he unlocked the door and walked away.

Watching Nathaniel take Peaches and climb into a fragile-looking helicopter was the worst moment of Dani's life. The rotors hummed with a high-pitched shriek. Wild air currents stirred up leaves and other debris. Moments later, the chopper lifted straight into the air and headed south.

Dani couldn't break down. Not in front of her family. "I'm going for a walk," she muttered. "I'll be back for lunch."

Before either of her parents could say a word of protest, she took off for the hill at the back of the house. The chopper had landed on the only flat spot just behind her father's work shed. Now Dani hurtled down the incline, slipping and stumbling, falling to her knees more than once but getting up again and running. Running.

The pain in her chest was unbearable. She couldn't breathe. She couldn't think.

Why hadn't she talked to him about leaving? Surely he would have understood her decision if he hadn't been blindsided. Hell, he probably would have applauded it. Nathaniel Winston didn't want any messy personal situations to derail his perfectly ordered life.

At last, she came to the copse of trees where she'd passed many a childhood afternoon. On balmy summer nights, she and her siblings had occasionally been allowed to sleep out under the stars in rope hammocks—with their father close at hand, of course.

Today, all the tree limbs were barren, the ground below soggy and muddy from the melting snow. Barely conscious of what she was doing, she jumped for a familiar branch and hauled herself up to sit with her legs dangling. Propping her back against the tree trunk, she put her hands to her face and sobbed.

There was no one around to hear. A hawk soared high above on wind currents. The sun's weak rays provided little warmth. She cried forever it seemed, unconsciously scanning the sky between her fingers, hoping to see the helicopter's return.

Everything was ruined. Even if she found the courage now to tell Nathaniel she loved him, he would question her motives. Distrust and cynicism were deeply ingrained in his personality. She understood why, but understanding didn't make it any easier.

Adding to her distress was the knowledge she would never see the baby again, either. She had hoped to be a support for Nathaniel when everything with Ophelia began to shake out. Either way—father or not the father—Nathaniel would need help sorting through his feelings.

Eventually, she became so cold she knew she had to go inside or risk serious consequences. Her fingers were stiff and numb. She lost her grip getting down from the tree and fell on her face, knocking the wind out of her chest and scratching her chin.

Somehow, the pain seemed appropriate.

The uphill return trip to the house was far longer and more difficult than the flight down. With her head bowed and her eyes wet with tears, she concentrated on not throwing up the breakfast she had eaten earlier.

Jared met her halfway back. She never even saw him coming until he was right in front of her.

He took off his coat and wrapped it around her. "You okay, sis?"

She must have looked dreadful, because her brother's gaze was a mix of concern and alarm. "I will be." It was a promise to herself as well as the answer to his question, but a vow she had no idea how to keep.

Jared put an arm around her waist as they climbed. "I'm gonna go out on a limb here and guess that Nathaniel Winston is more than your boss. Am I right?"

She wiped her nose with the back of her hand. "Yes." Then the truth hit her. "No. Not anymore." The tears came again and with them the certainty that she had derailed her life completely. "I didn't want to fall in love with him, so I began sending out résumés, looking for another job. I was going to tell him soon…about the résumés, not the love thing, but then Mom let the cat out of the bag and now he's furious."

Stumbling to a halt, barely able to catch her breath at the crest of the steep incline, she shivered uncontrollably.

Jared took her by the shoulders and gave her a little

shake. "You can't go into the house like this. Mom will freak out. Stay in the shed while I see if the coast is clear."

"Okay."

He was back in under two minutes. "The rest of them are playing cards in the den. If we're quiet, we can slip in the back door and make it to my room. I already grabbed your suitcase."

"Thank you," she whispered.

Jared hesitated. "What are you going to do, Dani?"

She sniffed, wrapping her arms around her waist to keep from flying apart. "I want to go back to Atlanta—right now. I need to talk to him. Will you take me?"

"If we can get the Hummer across the bridge, yes."

"Mom and Dad must be wondering why I didn't get on the helicopter."

"They're smart people. I'm pretty sure they've figured it out by now. Mom feels awful, by the way."

"It wasn't her fault. I never said the job search was a secret."

"Are you positive it wouldn't be better to let this be the end? When only one person is in love, things can get ugly."

"You should know." She managed a teasing tone though she had never felt less like laughing. "Nathaniel doesn't love me. It's true. He won't let himself love anyone. But I *have* been important to him, and I hurt him, I think. I need to apologize. I need closure. So I can move on."

"What if he won't see you?"

She hadn't thought of that. "He will," she said. "I won't give up."

After a restorative hot shower and wearing another set of the clothing Nathaniel had bought for her, Dani found a measure of calm. The conversation with her parents was awkward, but necessary. Though she never mentioned the affair in so many words, it was clear they understood what she had done. They didn't ask questions. It couldn't be easy for a father to think about his daughter having sex.

She spoke with Angie separately and a bit more honestly.

Angie hugged her. "I've had my share of screwups, baby sister. You'll survive this, I swear. Call me day or night. I'll even come to Atlanta if you need me."

"Thank you, Angie. I appreciate it."

After that, it was goodbyes all around, and then time to go. While Dani and Angie were having their heart-to-heart, the men had been down to the creek and decided it was safe to traverse the bridge. Though two small sections of concrete were missing, the rest of the structure was sound.

Dani's mom was worried, but Jared kissed her cheek. "I won't do anything stupid, I swear. We'll be fine."

In the end, crossing the bridge was anticlimactic.

Once they negotiated the streets of Gainesville and made it to the other side of town, Jared turned on the radio. The two of them didn't talk, but the lack of conversation was comfortable. He was her brother. He was on her side.

The trip went smoothly. When Jared finally parked the Hummer in front of the building that housed her apartment, he rested an arm on the steering wheel, and turned to face her. "You want me to come in?"

"Not necessary. Thanks for the ride and thanks for returning the Hummer."

His broad grin was cheeky. "I might take it for a little spin before I swing by the car place."

"Jared," she warned, frowning at him.

"Unlimited mileage. I read the contract. As long as I have it there by five o'clock, it's all good."

"You're impossible."

"But you love me."

"Yes, I do." She leaned over and kissed his cheek. "Thanks for everything."

"Do you mind a word of advice?"

"When has that ever stopped you?" It was a rhetorical question.

Jared grimaced. "I'm a guy, Dani. I know how guys think. Sometimes we have to process things. I think you'd be wise to give Winston a few days to cool off. He'll calm down. He'll realize you weren't keeping him in the dark on purpose. If you try to have a confrontation today, things might get even worse."

"I'll think about it," she promised, jumping down from her seat and retrieving her things. She stood on the sidewalk long enough to watch him drive away. The she picked up her suitcase and trudged up the flagstone path to the house.

Twelve

Nathaniel had woefully underestimated how difficult it was going to be to have Peaches at work with him, even for a little while. To make matters worse, Dani's empty office mocked him at every turn. He'd called a temp agency to hire a nanny for the day, but they had no one available except a college student with no real experience in childcare.

Because he was desperate, he told them to send her over. The girl, Wendy, was fine with the baby, careful and attentive to Nathaniel's instructions, but Wendy was a talker. By midafternoon, Nathaniel's patience was shot.

He desperately needed two files Dani had been working on before the holidays. Both were spreadsheets containing customer information. He found the emails where Dani had sent him an original draft, but the contact info he needed was more recent. Unfortunately, he didn't know the passwords for his executive assistant's computer.

A tension headache wrapped his skull in pain. *Get over*

it, Nathaniel. This is your new reality. No Dani. No smooth days at work. No hot, erotic nights at home. He was alone everywhere he turned.

That was the way he liked it. That was the way he had crafted his life.

At least he had the baby.

Taking Jared's advice was virtually impossible. Dani tried, she really did. She checked off all the items on her vacation-days to-do list one by one. But eventually, her apartment was spotless. Her closets were an efficiency expert's dream, and she had made it through not one but two blockbuster movies at the theater and couldn't have done a recap if she'd been under oath. The hours crawled by.

Friday morning, she caved. With trembling fingers, she picked up her cell phone and called the main line at New Century Tech. When the receptionist answered, Dani cleared her throat. "May I speak to Nathaniel Winston, please?"

The woman's voice was perky. "I'm so sorry, ma'am. Mr. Winston won't be in today. May I give you his voice mail?"

"No, thanks. It will keep till next week."

She hung up and gnawed the edge of her fingernail. Nathaniel Workaholic Winston had taken a day off? It didn't compute. Quickly, she ran through all the scenarios. Maybe he had the flu. Maybe the baby was sick. Maybe Ophelia had eluded investigators.

Or perhaps the baby had been returned to her mother, and Nathaniel was now headed for the Caribbean and a much-needed diving trip to unwind.

In the absence of hard facts, Dani didn't know what to do. In her mind, she had seen herself marching into New Century Tech armed with righteous indignation and confronting the wretched man on familiar ground. She definitely didn't want to go to the one place where she had first been intimate with him.

Memories of Christmas weekend made her shiver with a combination of yearning and dread. For those three days, she had lived in a dream world where Nathaniel needed and wanted her. But it had been a charade. A pleasant fiction.

Today was reality. The only choice left was to venture into enemy territory.

She had laundered the clothes Nathaniel bought for her and tucked them in a corner of her closet where she wouldn't have to think about him. Instead of couture items, today she chose from her own carefully curated wardrobe.

Appearance was important. She wanted to look confidant and poised. If there was any hope of convincing Nathaniel to give their relationship a fair hearing, she had to maintain control of her emotions *and* the confrontation.

He owed her an apology. Beyond that, she desperately hoped he owed her some kind of admission that he wanted more from her. More from them. Despite what he had told her about his childhood and adolescence, she refused to believe his heart was as impenetrable as he pretended.

She had watched him with Peaches. Seen the tenderness. The protectiveness. Nathaniel had a deep capacity for caring, even if he didn't recognize it. There was more to him than the hard-edged businessman who refused to be manipulated.

At least she hoped so. Hope was all she had left at this point.

In the end, she chose a work outfit. Black pencil skirt, royal blue sleeveless silk top and a matching waist-length jacket. The temps had remained balmy since the thaw, so she omitted tights and added her favorite pair of black flats. Her hair was cooperating for once. She brushed it vigorously and left it down.

The snow was completely gone by now, though the ground remained damp and mushy. Spring came early to Atlanta. It wouldn't be many weeks before daffodils began popping up. When she slid behind the wheel of her little car, it was impossible not to compare it to Nathaniel's Mercedes or the Hummer or even the helicopter.

None of those things were requirements for her happiness. As nice as it was to be pampered with fancy clothes and pricey transportation and a luxurious condo, they meant nothing in the end. It was the man she wanted, the man she needed. Even if he lost everything he had built from the ground up, just as his father had, the man at the helm of NCT would be more than enough for Dani.

She found a parking space on the street and fed the meter. Nathaniel's building was not someplace she could simply sashay into and catch a ride upstairs. Fortunately for her, Reggie was on duty.

He gave her a broad smile. "Hey there, Ms. Meadows. How was your holiday with the family?"

"Wonderful. And your clan?"

"Can't complain."

She gave him a conspiratorial smile. "I was hoping to surprise Mr. Winston. Do you mind letting me go up without telling him I'm on the way?"

His smile faded. "Mr. Winston's a tough customer, ma'am. He goes by the book. I can't afford to lose my job."

Squashing her panicky, guilty feelings, she nodded. "I understand. But you have my solemn word that if anything were to happen, I'd vouch for you. I'd tell him I slipped past you when you weren't looking." She stopped and decided to be honest. "We had an argument. A bad one. He's being bullheaded. Please. If he slams the door in my face, I'll leave and won't come back, I swear."

The man shifted from one foot to the other. "Let me call him first."

Damn it. She knew what the answer would be. "Never mind," she said dully. "I'll catch him at work next week." With the one tiny bit of hope she had amassed crushed into nothingness, she turned and headed for the street.

"Wait." Reggie called out to her, but not before her hand was on the glass door.

She turned around. "Yes?"

"I'll do it. I'll let you go up. I've seen how that man looks at you."

"You will? You have?"

The too-overweight-to-run security guard in his navy serge uniform and wrinkled white shirt nodded glumly. "Women. Y'all are pretty to look at, but sometimes you twist a man in knots. No offense, ma'am."

"None taken." She beamed at him. "Thank you. Thank you."

He grimaced. "Don't thank me yet. I've seen that gentleman angry. I hope you know what you're doing."

She didn't. Not at all. In the elevator, she trained her gaze on the neon-lit strip above the doors and watched the numbers increase. At last, the elevator swished to a smooth stop, a distant bell dinged and the doors opened.

Unfortunately, she'd left her stomach behind somewhere, several floors below.

Smoothing her damp palms on her skirt, she hitched the narrow strap of her modest purse higher on her shoulder and said a little prayer. Then she pressed the buzzer and waited.

Long moments later, the door swung open. Nathaniel stood there staring at her with narrowed eyes, naked from the waist up. He wore dress pants and socks and shoes, but his broad, tanned, really spectacular chest was bare.

"What do you want, Dani? I'm busy."

His expression could have frozen the sun.

She refused to take a step backward. "I need to talk to you. It's important."

"I'm not giving you your job back." Now his glare held a lick of heat.

"I'm not here about the job."

A sound from the other room drew his attention. "Fifteen minutes," he said. He strode away, leaving her to follow him in confusion.

In the den, she found Peaches, happily sitting in a wide-based contraption with music knobs and chew toys and other brightly colored amusements. The baby chortled as if she recognized Dani. Dani crouched and tickled the little girl's cheeks. "Hey, honey bunch. Did you miss me?"

Nathaniel stood in silence, frowning, his arms crossed over his chest.

She noticed several things at once—number one, a pale blue dress shirt tossed over the arm of the sofa. It was covered in infant cereal, presumably from the bowl of congealing goo on the coffee table. No fire burned in the grate. The small Christmas tree was gone.

Rising to her feet, she eyed him calmly. "I take it they haven't found Ophelia?"

"That's not really your concern, Dani. Say what you have to say and get out."

He wasn't making this easy. Hostility. Impatience. Barely disguised anger.

When her chin started to tremble, she locked her knees, clasped her hands at her waist and bit down hard on her bottom lip. The pain made her focus. "The reason I was sending out résumés is because I was attracted to you. I knew we couldn't work together under those conditions."

Not by even the flicker of an eyelash did he betray a response.

"Did you hear what I said?"

He shrugged. "It's a nice story."

"You owe me an apology," she said firmly.

Dark eyes glowed with heat. "The hell you say. I wasn't the one sneaking around."

"Don't use that snotty tone with me," she shot back. "You're hardly a saint."

"I'll give you that one. But at least I've been honest with you. Which is more than you can say in return."

She inhaled sharply, taking the biggest gamble of her life. "No," she said bluntly. "You haven't been honest with me at all."

His jaw dropped. "Of course I have."

"You have feelings for me. You might even love me. But you're too scared to let me get close. The reason you freaked out when you heard I was looking for another job was that I hurt your feelings. And maybe you thought I was abandoning you. But I wasn't. I'm not."

"Don't flatter yourself, Dani. Women come and women go. You're no different from the rest."

"Nice speech. Have you been practicing?"

The lightning flash of fury in his gaze told her she might have gone too far.

Peaches played happily between them, her innocent baby noises a bizarre backdrop to the gravity of the moment.

Nathaniel ran a hand through his hair, a gesture indicating he was perhaps no calmer than she was. "Did you know NCT will be having a VP opening in the spring? McCaffrey is moving to the West Coast to care for his ailing parents. I had decided to recommend you for the spot. I'm sure with your new degree and your depth of experience at NCT, the board would have agreed."

"*Had* decided?" she asked faintly.

"Definitely past tense. You're the one who chose to leave." He picked up the baby who had begun to fuss. "It's time for her nap. Feel free to let yourself out."

When he returned several minutes later, Dani glared at him. "You're an ass, you know that?" Frustration clogged her throat.

"And you're an opportunist."

"Let me get this straight," she said tightly. "I produced a blizzard, planted a baby carrier on your car and arranged for myself to become indispensable to you so you would fall for my charms and I wouldn't have to leave?"

"I have no idea what goes through your mind. All I can say for sure is that you tried to manipulate me, but it won't happen. I won't let it, Dani. You can take your stories about *falling in love*—and peddle them elsewhere."

He was goading her. Trying to hurt her. And it was working. But the bitter ridicule was his defense mechanism. No one in his personal life had ever put him first. Through no fault of their own, his parents had abandoned him emotionally. Seeing his father's downfall after cheating with a coworker had cemented the idea that women—and lovers in particular—couldn't be trusted.

And then came Ophelia's manipulations. Poor Nathaniel. Beset at every turn.

Dani refused to back down or look away. In that intense moment, she saw the truth. He *was* feeling something. And it looked a lot like despair and yearning. Could it be true?

Clinging to the hope that what they had shared in this very room was more than lust and opportunity, she went to him and placed both hands, palms flat on his chest. The soft, springy hair beneath her fingertips was like silk. His flesh was hot and smooth.

He sucked in a startled breath when she touched him and then went rigid. "Get out," he said, the words hoarse, barely audible.

Dani shook her head. "I can't," she said softly. "Everything I need is right here. Maybe you don't believe me today. And maybe not tomorrow or the next day or the next. It doesn't matter. I'll keep telling you again and again as long as it takes."

She went up on her tiptoes, cradled his face in her hands and kissed him. "I love you, Nathaniel Winston. You're hard and stubborn and suspicious, but you're also intelligent and decent, and you have a deep capacity for love even if you don't know it. How many men would take in a baby who's probably not even his and care for her despite the havoc she wreaks in his life?"

She kissed him one more time. For a moment, she thought she had won. His hand cupped the back of her head, pulling her close and holding her as he responded to her kiss with bruising desperation.

But it didn't last. He jerked free and wiped his mouth with the back of his hand. "What would you say if I told you Peaches really is mine after all? That her real name is Lila, and that her mother doesn't want her…that Ophelia has signed away her rights because she's leaving the country with a man who doesn't tolerate children. What then, Dani? What if I said I'd marry you, but only with an ironclad prenup that puts everything in trust for the child?"

Stumbling backward in shock, she sank onto the sofa. She looked at the baby and back at Nathaniel. "It's true? She's yours?"

He didn't say a word. He simply stared at her with an expression she couldn't read.

Well, here was her choice. Nathaniel needed a mother for his new daughter. Apparently, he was willing to spin the game to his advantage. Dani swallowed hard. "I'm very happy for you," she whispered. "I know you'll be a wonderful father."

Tears clogged her throat. She couldn't do it. She couldn't marry him knowing he didn't want her the same way she wanted him. It would destroy her.

Before coming here today, she had hoped to look into his eyes and see the truth about what he felt for her. She had told herself even a little flicker of love could grow.

If there was nothing in his feelings for Dani but lust, she was better off without him. She had to clear her throat twice before she could speak. "I'd take that deal in a heartbeat if you loved me. But you don't, do you?"

She stood on shaky legs and composed her expression. "I won't bother you again, Nathaniel. I wish you and Peaches all the best."

Rapidly, she walked out of the room, her heart beating in her chest so wildly she felt sick. Yanking open the door in the foyer that led to the hallway, she wiped her eyes, intending to flee, but Nathaniel was right on her heels.

"That's it?" he shouted. "You lose your shot at the money, and you're gone?"

"No," she said raggedly, turning to face him, tears spilling over and wetting her face. "I didn't lose. The truth is, I had a narrow escape. I don't want your money or your sterile condo or your stupidly expensive vehicles. I wanted a man who would love me. That's all. Now, forgive me for being slow, but I've finally figured out that man isn't you. You're going to live alone and die alone. I feel sorry for you, actually."

"I don't need your pity," he snarled.

She reached blindly for the doorknob, desperate to escape. A hard masculine hand came down on her shoulder, spinning her around. Nathaniel's face was white, his eyes glittering like coals.

"Let me go," she cried.

He got up in her face, his breath warm on her cheeks, his grip on her shoulders viselike. "What makes you think you can save me from myself?"

And then she saw it. Buried beneath the layers of fury and condemnation was a pained uncertainty. Nathaniel Winston thought he was unlovable.

Her whole body went limp. She could fight his pigheadedness but not such aching vulnerability from a man who prided himself on icy control. She could barely breathe.

"I was hoping we could save each other," she whispered. The time for self-preservation was gone. She would give him complete honesty or nothing at all. "The world is a scary place, Nathaniel. But when I'm with you, everything seems possible. I didn't want to fall in love. That's why I was leaving NCT. But I waited too long and the snow came, and now I can't imagine waking up every morning and not seeing your face."

Thirteen

Nathaniel still reeled from the shock of finding out he was a father, and now Dani expected him to believe the two of them had a chance?

He shoved her away and paced the confines of the foyer, feeling sick. "Love makes a man stupid," he muttered. "Did you see all that baby stuff I bought? I'm a sucker."

Dani stood watching him with pity in her eyes, her arms wrapped around her waist. He didn't need that, not from her. She looked beautiful and professional and exactly like the woman who had worked with him for almost two years. But things had changed.

She lifted her shoulders and let them fall. "You'll be a better parent than either your father *or* your mother was if you put your mind to it. I'm sorry Ophelia abandoned her daughter."

Rage filled his chest. "People shouldn't have babies if they can't follow through. It's criminal."

His ragged shout echoed in the small foyer. Dani stared at him, her blue eyes awash in tears. "I can't make up for what you lost, Nathaniel. I wish to God it was possible. But we could do it right this time. Peaches doesn't have to be the only one. Families are wonderful."

He blinked, not sure what he was hearing. After every cruel, heartless thing he had said to her? He cleared his throat, his head spinning. "Are you offering to give me a baby?"

Her chin wobbled. "No. I'm saying I want to *make* a baby with you. When the time is right." She tried to smile, but the failed attempt broke his heart. "I love you. Even though you're acting like a jackass and trying to shove me out the door, I won't stop loving you. I'll sign a legal document if you need a tangible reason to trust me."

Fear like he had never known clutched him from every angle. Spending time with Dani's parents and siblings had shown him what normal family life could look like. The yearning had hit him hard, reminding of everything his mother's illness had cost him.

"I lied to you, Dani," he muttered, stung by the enormity of his sins.

She frowned. "About what?"

"You asked me if I had ever fantasized about you at the office."

She paled. "You told me you *had*."

"That was an understatement," he said flatly. "The truth was too damning."

"I don't understand."

"Six months after you first started working with me, I began dreaming about you. Every night. In vivid Technicolor."

Her eyes widened. "Oh."

He shrugged. "It scared the hell out of me. I'd watched

my father go down that road and be ripped apart financially and emotionally. For years, I told myself I would never get involved with an employee. But there you were, so bright and funny and damned good at the job. I was stuck. Every day you and I worked together like the proverbial well-oiled machine, and every night I undressed you a thousand times and a thousand ways in my mind."

"So it wasn't just me…" Her eyes were round.

He shuddered, wanting her desperately and yet afraid to touch her. "No."

"Are you in love with me, Nathaniel?"

The words were barely audible. Maybe she was scared, but she didn't show it. The stupid woman didn't know how to protect herself. "Men like fucking," he said. "We don't wrap it up in pretty ribbons."

He was testing her. Pushing her. Trying to drive her away.

Dani inhaled sharply and fell back a step as if his deliberate profanity were a physical blow. "So you would rather have a temporary affair?"

"Are you available?" He stared at his nemesis, stone-faced. Every emotion he felt for her hammered in his chest like a wild swarm of butterflies trying desperately to break free.

In the hushed silence, he witnessed the moment Dani saw past his facade. Her expression softened.

"For one night," she said softly, her face aglow as if she heard something amazing in his crude offer. She was young but wise. Sure of herself and maybe of him, as well. "And the next and the next and all the ones after that."

"Fine," he said. His hands trembled, so he jammed them in his pockets. "Don't most women want a man down on one knee? The pricey ring. The pretty speeches? I'm surprised you're selling yourself short."

"Shut up, Nathaniel." Her wry smile warmed him from the inside out. "Shut up and prove to me I'm not making the biggest mistake of my life." She wrapped her arms around his waist and laid her cheek exactly over the spot where his heart pounded madly.

His hands tangled in her hair. He couldn't stop shaking. It was a mostly unmanly thing to do, but Dani didn't seem to mind. He clutched her tightly. "I don't know how to do forever."

She went up on her tiptoes and pressed her lips to his. "We'll figure it out together," she said. "It won't be so bad, Nathaniel, I promise."

The walls came down, every brick, every fragment of mortar. He inhaled her scent, his mind a blank. "I need you, my sweet Christmas elf."

"I know," Dani whispered. "I know…"

Epilogue

Thirty-six hours later, New Year's Eve

Nathaniel flung open the door to his condo and dropped a pile of packages on the chair in the foyer. "I'm home," he yelled.

Dani appeared, her radiant smile catching him unawares and wiping every coherent thought from his brain. "What took you so long?" she said.

He scooped her up and twirled her in dizzying circles until her hair fanned out from her head and they both laughed breathlessly. "It's not easy finding a Christmas tree on December 31." He released her and grabbed up the largest bag. "What do you think?"

The tree was prelit, but that was its only claim to fame. Twelve inches high and already shedding artificial needles, it was a tree only a mother could love…or a man bent on setting the stage for romance.

"I adore it," Dani said, her eyes dancing with amusement.

"Help me carry everything." he said. He headed straight for the den and began setting out his bounty. Carryout containers from Dani's favorite restaurant. An eighty-dollar bottle of champagne. Tulips and roses from a ridiculously expensive Buckhead florist.

Dani plugged in the tiny tree and set it on the hearth, then stood back and watched, her expression caught somewhere between excitement and apprehension. The two of them had spent the majority of yesterday afternoon and evening making love. Nathaniel had slept the entire night with her in his arms. This morning they had made French toast together.

Now came the hard part.

When he was finished with the accoutrements, he examined his handiwork. He'd never tried to impress a woman before, not really. Tonight, it was vital that Dani understand what was happening.

He took her hand. "We need to talk." Fortunately, Peaches was asleep at the moment.

Dani blinked. "Ouch. Barely a day and a half and we already need to *talk*?"

Drawing her over to the sofa, he sat down and pointed to the opposite end. "You, there," he said. He had important things to say. His self-control was tenuous at best, so he wasn't taking any chances.

She cooperated obediently, leaning back into the corner embrace of his expensive leather sofa and crisscrossing her legs like a child. Her hair was clean and damp and shiny. He knew she had showered while he was gone, because he smelled the soap his housekeeper put in the bathrooms.

They had stopped by Dani's apartment late yesterday, so now she had her own wardrobe to choose from. Tonight she was wearing gray leggings and an off-the-shoulder, cotton-candy-pink sweater. Her feet were bare. There was a good chance she wasn't wearing a bra. He didn't look too closely, because if she weren't, he might forget his speech.

Dani held out her hands, palms up. "The food is getting cold, Nathaniel. Say whatever you have to say."

Her lips smiled, but her gaze was wary. That expression in her eyes crucified him. How long would it take before she ceased expecting the worst from him?

He jumped to his feet and paced. For the past hour, he'd rehearsed what he wanted to say. Now, suddenly, his brain fogged. "You were right to say I owed you an apology. Looking for other employment was a very professional thing for you to do. But the prospect of you not being in the office every day caught me off guard. I never wanted you to resign, not really. I was angry, and I lashed out." His stomach cramped. "You have an incredible brain and the ability to connect with all kinds of people. I would hate to see you leave NCT. You deserve the chance to prove what you can do for the company."

"I see."

"You already said that once," he muttered.

"True." Dani gnawed her bottom lip. "Is what I do at NCT more important to you than talking about us?"

"I didn't say that."

"I'm confused. Now that we're practicing détente, I assumed our personal life was going to take precedence over work."

"It does. It will." He stopped and cleared his throat. "Maybe this will help." He reached inside the pocket of his jacket and pulled out a folded sheaf of papers. "Happy New Year, Dani. I may be the world's most stubborn man, but I believe in second chances, and I hope you do, too. That's not a prenup, by the way," he said hastily.

She unfolded the papers and stared at them, turning one

page at a time slowly. Nathaniel had paid his expensive legal team a fat bonus to put the wheels in motion on his grand gesture before the clock struck midnight.

Dani throat worked. She refolded the document he had worked so hard to procure and handed it back to him. "No. No, Nathaniel. I won't take it."

He had signed over half his company to her. A partnership holding in NCT. It was a small enough price to pay for her willingness to forgive him and promise him a future.

His face heated. "I don't know what you want from me, damn it. How many ways do I have to say it?"

Dani jumped to her feet and scowled. "You haven't even said it once, you big blockhead. I never wanted your life's work. All I want is to hear you tell me the truth."

Ah, hell. The shakes came back. "You know how I feel about you," he said gruffly.

She shook her head slowly. "Not good enough, Winston. Try again."

"Marry me," he blurted.

"Why?"

His throat closed up. Sweat broke out on his forehead. "I can't explain. It won't make sense."

"Try me," she said gently.

He fell to his knees on the thick, plush carpet and wrapped his arms around her hips, resting his cheek against her belly. "I want to feel him here," he said. "Our son, or maybe another daughter, kicking and making herself known. I want her to know she is loved from the moment she takes her first breath."

Dani's hands tangled in his hair. "Is that all?"

He shook his head, his throat tight. "No. I want her to know how much I love her mother."

Dani knelt as well and kissed him softly. "That wasn't so difficult, was it? You're going to have to practice," she whispered, tears streaming down her face. "I'm not going to drag it out of you every time I need to hear it."

He rested his forehead against hers. "I adore you. I want you. I'll love you for a hundred years. I was afraid of this. Afraid of you..."

"And now?"

"Now you're my heart, my home," he said simply. "Everything I ever wanted and more. I'm never letting go..."

* * * * *

TWELVE NIGHTS
OF TEMPTATION

BARBARA DUNLOP

For Jane Porter

One

A banging on Tasha Lowell's bedroom door jarred her awake. It was midnight in the Whiskey Bay Marina staff quarters, and she'd been asleep for less than an hour.

"Tasha?" Marina owner Matt Emerson's voice was a further jolt to her system, since she'd been dreaming about him.

"What is it?" she called out, then realized he'd never hear her sleep-croaky voice. "What?" she called louder as she forced herself from beneath the covers.

It might be unseasonably warm on the Pacific Northwest coast, but it was still December, the holiday season, and the eight-unit staff quarters building had been around since the '70s.

"*Orca's Run* broke down off Tyree, Oregon."

"What happened?" she asked reflexively as she crossed the cold wooden floor on her bare feet. Even as she said the words, she knew it was a foolish question. Wealthy, urbane Matt Emerson wouldn't know an injector pump from an alternator.

She swung the door open, coming face-to-face with the object of what she suddenly remembered had been a very R-rated dream.

"The engine quit. Captain Johansson says they're anchored in the bay."

This was very bad news. Tasha had been chief mechanic at Whiskey Bay Marina for less than two weeks, and she knew Matt had hesitated in giving her the promotion. He'd be right to hold her responsible for not noticing a problem with *Orca's Run*'s engine or not anticipating some kind of wear and tear.

"I serviced it right before they left." She knew how important this particular charter was to the company.

Orca's Run was a ninety-foot yacht, the second largest in the fleet. It had been chartered by Hans Reinstead, an influential businessman out of Munich. Matt had recently spent considerable effort and money getting a toehold in the European market, and Hans was one of his first major clients. The last thing Whiskey Bay Marina needed was for the Reinstead family to have a disappointing trip.

Tasha grabbed the red plaid button-down shirt she'd discarded on a chair and put it on over her T-shirt. Then she stepped into a pair of heavy cargo pants, zipping them over her flannel shorts.

Matt watched her progress as she popped a cap on top of her braided hair. Socks and work boots took her about thirty seconds, and she was ready.

"That's it?" he asked.

"What?" She didn't understand the question.

"You're ready to go?"

She glanced down at herself, then looked back into the dim bedroom. "I'm ready." The necessities that most women carried in a purse were in the zipped pockets of her pants.

For some reason, he gave a crooked smile. "Then let's go."

"What's funny?" she asked as she fell into step beside him.

"Nothing."

They started down the wooden walkway that led to the Whiskey Bay Marina pier.

"You're laughing," she said.

"I'm not."

"You're laughing at me." Did she look that bad rolling straight out of bed? She rubbed her eyes, lifted her cap to smooth her hair and tried to shake some more sense into her brain.

"I'm smiling. It's not the same thing."

"I've amused you." Tasha hated to be amusing. She

wanted people, especially men, *especially* her employer, to take her seriously.

"You impressed me."

"By getting dressed?"

"By being efficient."

She didn't know what to say to that. It wasn't quite sexist…maybe…

She let it drop.

They went single file down the ramp with him in the lead.

"What are we taking?" she asked.

"Monty's Pride."

The answer surprised her. *Monty's Pride* was the biggest yacht in the fleet, a 115-footer, refurbished last year to an impeccably high standard. It was obvious what Matt intended to do.

"Do you think we'll need to replace *Orca's Run*?" She'd prefer to be optimistic and take the repair boat instead. *Monty's Pride* would burn an enormous amount of fuel getting to Tyree. "There's a good chance I can fix whatever's gone wrong."

"And if you can't?"

"What did the captain say happened?" She wasn't ready to admit defeat before they'd even left the marina.

"That it quit."

It was a pathetic amount of information.

"Did it stop all of a sudden?" she asked. "Did it slow? Was there any particular sound, a smell? Was there smoke?"

"I didn't ask."

"You should have asked."

Matt shot her a look of impatience, and she realized she'd stepped over the line. He was her boss after all.

"I'm just thinking that taking *Monty's Pride* is a whole lot of fuel to waste," she elaborated on her thinking. "We can save the money if I can do a quick repair."

"We're not even going to try a quick repair. I'll move the

passengers and crew over to *Monty's Pride* while you fix whatever's gone wrong."

Tasha hated that her possible negligence would cost the company so much money. "Maybe if I talk to the captain on the radio."

"I don't want to mess around, Tasha." Matt punched in the combination for the pier's chain-link gate and swung it open.

"I'm not asking you to mess around. I'm suggesting we explore our options. *Monty's Pride* burns a hundred gallons an hour."

"My priority is customer service."

"This is expensive customer service."

"Yes, it is."

His tone was flat, and she couldn't tell if he was angry or not.

She wished she was back in her dream. Matt had been so nice in her dream. They'd been warm, cocooned together, and he'd been joking, stroking her hair, kissing her mouth. *Wait. No.* That was bad. That wasn't what she wanted at all.

"I want Hans Reinstead to go back to Germany a happy man," Matt continued. "I want him to rave to his friends and business associates about the over-the-top service he received, even when there was a problem. Whether we fix it in five minutes or five hours is irrelevant. They had a breakdown, and we upgraded them. People love an upgrade. So much so, that they're generally willing to gloss over the reason for getting it."

Tasha had to admit it was logical. It was expensive, but it was also logical.

Matt might be willing to take the financial hit in the name of customer service, but if it turned out to be something she'd missed, it would be a black mark against her.

They approached the slip where *Monty's Pride* was moored. A crew member was on deck while another was on the wharf, ready to cast off.

"Fuel?" Matt asked the young man on deck.

"Three thousand gallons."

"That'll do," Matt said as he crossed the gangway to the stern of the main deck.

Tasha followed. *Monty's Pride*'s twin diesel engines rumbled beneath them.

"Is my toolbox on board?" she asked.

"We put it in storage."

"Thanks." While they crossed the deck, she reviewed *Orca's Run*'s engine service in her mind. Had she missed something, a belt or a hose? She thought she'd checked them all. But nobody's memory was infallible.

"It could be as simple as a belt," she said to Matt.

"That will be good news." He made his way to the bridge, and she followed close behind.

She had to give it one last shot, so as soon as they were inside, she went for the radio, dialing in the company frequency. "*Orca's Run*, this is *Monty's Pride*. Captain, are you there?"

While she did that, he slid open the side window and called out to the hand to cast off.

She keyed the mike again. "Come in, *Orca's Run*."

Matt brought up the revs and pulled away from the pier.

Matt knew he had taken a gamble by using *Monty's Pride* instead of the repair boat, but so far it looked like it had been the right call. Two hours into the trip down the coast, even Tasha had been forced to admit a quick fix wasn't likely. She'd had Captain Johansson walk her through a second-by-second rehash of the engine failure over the radio, asking him about sounds, smells and warning lights. Then she had him send a deckhand back and forth from the engine room for a visual inspection and to relay details.

He'd been impressed by her thorough, methodical approach. But in the end, she concluded that she needed to check the engine herself. There was nothing to do for the next three hours but make their way to Tyree.

It was obvious she was ready to blame herself.

But even if the breakdown turned out to be her fault, it wasn't the end of the world. And they didn't even know what had happened. It was way too early to start pointing fingers.

"You should lie down for a while," he told her.

She looked tired, and there was no point in both of them staying up all night.

"I'm fine." She lifted her chin, gazing out the windshield into the starry night.

There were clusters of lights along the shore, only a few other ships in the distance, and his GPS and charts were top-notch. It was an easy chore to pilot the boat single-handed.

"You don't have to keep me company."

"And you don't have to coddle me."

"You have absolutely nothing to prove, Tasha." He knew she took pride in her work, and he knew she was determined to do a good job after her promotion. But sleep deprivation wasn't a job requirement.

"I'm not trying to prove anything. Did you get any sleep at all? Do you want to lie down?"

"I'm fine." He knew she was perfectly capable of piloting the boat, but he'd feel guilty leaving all the work to her.

"No need for us both to stay awake," she said.

"My date ended early. I slept a little."

Since his divorce had been finalized, Matt and his friend TJ Bauer had hit the Olympia social circuit. They were pushing each other to get out and meet new people. They met a few women, most were nice, but he hadn't felt a spark with any of them, including the one he'd taken out tonight. He'd come home early, done a little Christmas shopping online for his nieces and nephews and dozed off on the sofa.

"You don't need to tell me about your dates," Tasha said.

"There's nothing to tell."

"Well, that's too bad." Her tone was lighter. It sounded like she was joking. "It might help pass the time."

"Sorry," he said lightly in return. "I wish I could be more entertaining. What about you?" he asked.

As he voiced the question, he found himself curious about Tasha's love life. Did she have a boyfriend? Did she date? She was always such a no-nonsense fixture at the marina, he didn't think of her beyond being a valued employee.

"What about me?" she asked.

"Do you ever go out?"

"Out where?"

"Out, out. On-a-date out. Dinner, dancing…"

She scoffed out a laugh.

"Is that a no?"

"That's a no."

"Why not?" Now he was really curious. She might dress in plain T-shirts and cargo pants, but underneath what struck him now as a disguise, she was a lovely woman. "Don't you like to dress up? Do you ever dress up?"

He tried to remember if he'd ever seen her in anything stylish. He couldn't, and he was pretty sure he'd remember.

She shifted on the swivel chair, angling toward him. "Why the third degree?"

"Since stories of my dates won't distract us, I thought maybe yours could." He found himself scrutinizing her face from an objective point of view.

She had startling green eyes, the vivid color of emeralds or a glacial, deep-water pond. They were framed in thick lashes. Her cheekbones were high. Her chin was the perfect angle. Her nose was narrow, almost delicate. And her lips were deep coral, the bottom slightly fuller than the top.

He wanted to kiss them.

"Nothing to tell," she said. Her voice jolted him back to reality, and he turned to the windshield, rewinding the conversation.

"You must dress up sometimes."

"I prefer to focus on work."

"Why?"

"Because it's satisfying." Her answer didn't ring true.

He owned the company, and he still found time for a social life. "I dress up. I date. I still find time to work."

She made a motion with her hand, indicating up and down his body. "Of course you date. A guy like you is definitely going to date."

He had no idea what she meant. "A guy like me?"

"Good-looking. Rich. Eligible."

"Good-looking?" He was surprised that she thought so, even more surprised that she'd said so.

She rolled her eyes. "It's not me, Matt. The world thinks you're good-looking. Don't pretend you've never noticed."

He'd never given it much thought. Looks were so much a matter of taste. He was fairly average. He'd never thought there was anything wrong with being average.

"I'm eligible now," he said.

The rich part was also debatable. He hadn't had enough money to satisfy his ex-wife. And now that they'd divorced, he had even less. He'd borrowed money to pay her out, and he was going to have to work hard over the next year or two to get back to a comfortable financial position.

"And so are you," he said to Tasha. "You're intelligent, hardworking and pretty. You should definitely be out there dating."

He couldn't help but compare her with the women he'd met lately. The truth was, they couldn't hold a candle to her. There was so much about her that was compelling. Funny that he'd never noticed before.

"Dazzle them with your intelligence and hard work."

"Can we not do this?" she asked.

"Make conversation?"

"I'm a licensed marine mechanic. And I want people to take me seriously as that."

"You can't do both?"

"Not in my experience." She slipped down from the high white leather chair.

"What are you doing?" he asked. He didn't want her to leave.

"I'm going to take your advice."

"What advice is that?"

"I'm going to lie down and rest." She glanced at her watch. "You think two hours?"

"I didn't mean to chase you away."

"You didn't."

"We don't have to talk about dating." But then he took in her pursed lips and realized he still wanted to kiss them. Where was this impulse coming from?

"I have work to do when we get there."

He realized he'd be selfish to stop her. "You're right. You should get some sleep."

As she walked away, he considered the implications of being attracted to an employee. He couldn't act on it. He shouldn't act on it.

Then he laughed at himself. It wasn't like she'd given him any encouragement. Well, other than saying he was good-looking.

She thought he was good-looking.

As he piloted his way along the dark coastline, he couldn't help but smile.

Tasha's problem wasn't dating in general. Her problem was the thought of dating Matt. He wasn't her type. There was no way he was her type. She knew that for an absolute fact.

She'd dated guys like him before—capable, confident, secure in the knowledge that the world rolled itself out at their feet. She knew all that. Still, she couldn't seem to stop herself from dreaming about him.

They'd arrived off Tyree and boarded *Orca's Run* shortly

after dawn. Tall and confident, he'd greeted the clients like he owned the place—which he did, of course.

Tasha had kept to the background, making sure her toolbox was moved discreetly on board, while Matt had charmed the family, apologizing for the delay in the trip, offering *Monty's Pride* as a replacement, explaining that the larger, faster yacht would easily make up the time they'd lost overnight.

It was obvious the client was delighted with the solution, and Tasha had turned her attention to the diesel engine. It took her over an hour to discover the water separator was the problem. In an unlikely coincidence, the water-in-fuel indicator light bulb had also broken. Otherwise, it would have alerted her to the fact that the water separator was full, starving the engine of fuel.

The two things happening together were surprising. They were more than surprising. They were downright strange.

From their anchorage in Tyree, Matt had taken the launch and run for parts in the small town. And by noon, she'd replaced the water separator. While she'd worked, she'd cataloged who'd had access to *Orca's Run*. Virtually all the staff of Whiskey Bay Marina had access. But most of them didn't know anything about engines.

There were a couple of contract mechanics who did repairs from time to time. And there were countless customers who had been on the property. She found her brain going in fantastical directions, imagining someone might have purposely damaged the engine.

But who? And why? And was she being ridiculously paranoid?

She had no idea.

While she'd worked, diesel fuel had sprayed her clothes and soaked into her hair, so she'd used the staff shower to clean up and commandeered a steward's uniform from the supply closet.

After cleaning up, her mind still pinging from possibility to possibility, she made her way up the stairs to the main cabin. There she was surprised to realize the yacht wasn't yet under way.

"Did something else go wrong?" she asked Matt, immediately worried they had another problem.

He was in the galley instead of piloting the yacht. The deckhand had stayed with *Monty's Pride*, since the bigger ship needed an extra crew member. Matt and Tasha were fully capable of returning *Orca's Run* to Whiskey Bay.

"It's all good," Matt said.

"We're not under power?" Her hair was still damp, and she tucked it behind her ears as she approached the countertop that separated the galley from the main living area.

"Are you hungry?" he asked, placing a pan on the stove.

She was starving. "Sure. But I can eat something on the way."

"Coffee?"

"Sure."

He extracted two cups from a cupboard and poured. "*Monty's Pride* is headed south. Everyone seems happy."

"You were right," she admitted as she rounded the counter. "Bringing *Monty's Pride* was a good idea. I can cook if you want to get going."

He gave a thoughtful nod. "This charter matters."

"Because it's a German client?"

"It's the first significant booking out of the fall trade show. He's a prominent businessman with loads of connections."

"I'm sorry I argued with you." She realized her stance had been about her pride, not about the good of the company.

"You should always say what you think."

"I should listen, too."

"You don't listen?"

"Sometimes I get fixated on my own ideas." She couldn't help but revisit her theory about someone tampering with the engine.

Matt gave a smile. "You have conviction. That's not a bad thing. Besides, it keeps the conversation interesting."

He handed her a cup of coffee.

She took a sip, welcoming the hit of caffeine.

He seemed to ponder her for a moment. "You definitely keep things interesting."

She didn't know how to respond.

His blue eyes were dark but soft, and he had an incredibly handsome face. His chin was square, unshaven and slightly shadowed, but that only made him look more rugged. His nose was straight, his jaw angular and his lips were full, dark pink, completely kissable.

Warm waves of energy seemed to stream from him to cradle her. It was disconcerting, and she shifted to put some more space between them. "The engine was interesting."

Mug to his lips, he lifted his brow.

"The odds of the water separator filling and the indicator light going at the same time are very low."

His brow furrowed then, and he lowered the mug. "And?"

"Recognizing that this is my first idea, and that I can sometimes get fixated on those, it seems wrong to me. I mean, it seems odd to me."

"Are you saying someone broke something on purpose?"

"No, I'm not saying that." Out loud, it sounded even less plausible than it had inside her head. "I'm saying it was a bizarre coincidence, and I must be having a run of bad luck."

"You fixed it, so that's good luck."

"Glass half-full?"

"You did a good job, Tasha."

"It wasn't that complicated."

A teasing glint came into his eyes. "You mean, you're that skilled?"

"The cause was peculiar." She could have sworn she'd just serviced the water separator. "The repair was easy."

Their gazes held, and they fell silent again. Raindrops clattered against the window, while the temperature seemed to inch up around her. Her dream came back once again, Matt cradling her, kissing her. Heat rose in her cheeks.

She forced herself back to the present, trying to keep her mind on an even keel. "It could have been excess water in the fuel, maybe a loose cap. I did check it. At least I think I checked it. I always check it." She paused. "I hope I checked it."

He set down his mug. "Don't."

She didn't understand.

He took a step forward. "Don't second-guess yourself."

"Okay." It seemed like the easiest answer, since she was losing track of the conversation.

He took another step, and then another.

Inside her head, she shouted for him to stop. But she didn't make a sound.

She didn't want him to stop. She could almost feel his arms around her.

He was right there.

Thunder suddenly cracked through the sky above them. A wave surged beneath them, and she grabbed for the counter. She missed, stumbling into his chest.

In a split second, his arms were around her, steadying her.

She fought the desire that fogged her brain. "Sorry."

"Weather's coming up," he said, his deep voice rumbling in her ear and vibrating her chest, which was pressed tight against his.

"We won't be—" Words failed her as she looked into his blue eyes, so close, so compelling.

He stilled, the sapphire of his eyes softening to summer sky.

"Tasha." Her name was barely a breath on his lips.

She softened against him.

He lowered his lips, closer and closer. They brushed lightly against hers, then they firmed, then they parted, and the kiss sent bolts of pleasure ricocheting through her.

She gripped his shoulders to steady herself. A rational part of her brain told her to stop. But she was beyond stopping.

She was beyond caring about anything but the cataclysmic kiss between them.

It was Matt who finally pulled back.

He looked as dazed as she felt, and he blew out a breath. "I'm…" He gave his head a little shake. "I don't know what to say."

She forced herself to step back. "Don't." She had no idea what to say either. "Don't try. It was just…something…that happened."

"It was something," he said.

"It was a mistake."

He raked a hand through his short hair. "It sure wasn't on purpose."

"We should get going," she said, anxious to focus on something else.

The last thing she wanted to do was dissect their kiss. The last thing she wanted to do was admit how it impacted her. The last thing she wanted her boss to know was that she saw him as a man, more than a boss.

She couldn't do that. She had to stop doing it. In this relationship, she was a mechanic, not a woman.

"We're not going anywhere." He looked pointedly out the window where the rain was driving down.

Tasha took note of the pitching floor beneath her.

It was Matt who reached for the marine radio and turned the dial to get a weather report.

"We might as well grab something to eat," he said. "This could last awhile."

Two

Waiting out the storm, Matt had fallen asleep in the living area. He awoke four hours later to find Tasha gone, and he went looking.

The yacht was rocking up and down on six-foot swells, and rain clattered against the windows. He couldn't find her on the upper decks, so he took the narrow staircase, making his way to the engine and mechanical rooms. Sure enough, he found her there. She'd removed the front panel of the generator and was elbow deep in the mechanics.

"What are you doing?" he asked.

She tensed at the sound of his voice. She was obviously remembering their kiss. Well, he remembered it, too, and it sure made him tense up. Partly because he was her boss and he felt guilty for letting things get out of hand. But partly because it had been such an amazing kiss and he desperately wanted to do it again.

"Maintenance," she answered him without turning.

He settled his shoulder against the doorjamb. "Can you elaborate?"

"I inspected the electric and serviced the batteries. Some of the battery connections needed cleaning. Hoses and belts all look good in here. But it was worth changing the oil filter."

"I thought you would sleep."

This was above and beyond the call of duty for anyone. He'd known Tasha was a dedicated employee, but this trip was teaching him she was one in a million.

She finally turned to face him. "I did sleep. Then I woke up."

She'd found a pair of coveralls somewhere. They were miles too big, but she'd rolled up the sleeves and the pant legs. A woman shouldn't look sexy with a wrench in her hand, a smudge of oil on her cheek, swimming in a shapeless steel gray sack.

But this one did. And he wanted to do a whole lot more than kiss her. He mentally shook away the feelings.

"If it was me—" he tried to lighten the mood and put her at ease "—I think I might have inspected the liquor cabinet."

She smiled for the briefest of seconds. "Lucky your employees aren't like you."

The smile warmed him. It turned him on, but it also made him happy.

"True enough," he said. "But there is a nice cognac in there. Perfect to have on a rainy afternoon." He could picture them doing just that.

Instead of answering, she returned to work.

He watched for a few minutes, struggling with his feelings, knowing he had to put their relationship back on an even keel.

Work—he needed to say something about work instead of sharing a cozy drink.

"Are you trying to impress me?" he asked.

She didn't pause. "Yes."

"I'm impressed."

"Good."

"You should stop working."

"I'm not finished."

"You're making me feel guilty."

She looked his way and rolled her eyes. "I'm not trying to make you feel guilty."

"Then what?"

"The maintenance needed doing. I was here. There was an opportunity."

He fought an urge to close the space between them. "Are you always like this?"

"Like what?"

"I don't know, überindustrious?"

"You say that like it's a bad thing."

He did move closer. He shouldn't, couldn't, *wouldn't* bring up their kiss. But he desperately wanted to bring it up, discuss it, dissect it, relive it. How did she feel about it now? Was she angry? Was there a chance in the world she wanted to do it again?

"It's an unnerving thing," he said.

"Then, you're very easily unnerved."

He couldn't help but smile at her comeback. "I'm trying to figure you out."

"Well, that's a waste of time."

"I realize I don't know you well."

"You don't need to know me well. Just sign my paycheck."

Well, that was a crystal clear signal. He was her boss, nothing more. He swallowed his disappointment.

Then again, if he was her boss, he was her boss. He reached forward to take the wrench from her hand. "It's after five and it's a Saturday and you're done."

Their fingers touched. Stupid mistake. He felt a current run up the center of his arm.

Her grip tightened on the wrench as she tried to tug it from his grasp. "Let it go."

"It's time to clock out."

"Seriously, Matt. I'm not done yet."

His hand wrapped around hers, and his feet took him closer still.

"Matt." There was a warning in her voice, but then their gazes caught and held.

Her eyes turned moss green, deep and yielding. She was feeling something. She had to be feeling something.

She used her free hand to grasp his arm. Her grip was strong, stronger than he'd imagined. He liked that.

"We can't do this, Matt."

"I know."

She swallowed, and her voice seemed strained. "So let go."

"I want to kiss you again."

"It's a bad idea."

"You're right." His disappointment was acute. "It is."

She didn't step back, and her lips parted as she drew in a breath. "We need to keep it simple, straightforward."

"Why?"

"The signature on my paycheck."

"Is that the only reason?" It was valid. But he was curious. He was intensely curious.

"I'm not that kind of girl."

He knew she didn't mean to be funny, but he couldn't help but joke. "The kind that kisses men?"

"The kind that randomly kisses my boss—or any coworker for that matter—while I'm working, in an engine room, covered in grease."

"That's fair."

"You bet, it's fair. Not that I need your approval. Now, let go of my hand."

He glanced down, realizing they were still touching. The last thing he wanted to do was let her go. But he had no choice.

She set down the wrench, replacing it with a screwdriver. Then she lifted the generator panel and put it in place.

He moved away and braced a hand on a crossbeam above his head. "The storm's letting up."

"Good." The word sounded final. Matt didn't want it to be final.

He was her boss, sure. He understood that was a complication. But did it have to be a deal breaker? But he wanted to get to know her. He'd barely scratched the surface, and he liked her a lot.

They'd brought *Orca's Run* back to the marina, arriving late in the evening.

Tasha had spent the night and half of today attempting to purge Matt's kiss from her mind. It wasn't working. She kept reliving the pleasure, then asking herself what it all meant.

She didn't even know how she felt, never mind how Matt felt. He was a smooth-talking, great-looking man who, from everything she'd seen, could have any woman in the world. What could possibly be his interest in her?

Okay, maybe if she'd taken her mother's advice, maybe if she'd acted like a woman, dressed like a woman and got a different job, maybe then it would make sense for Matt to be interested. Matt reminded her so much of the guys she'd known in Boston, the ones who'd dated her sisters and attended all the parties.

They'd all wanted women who were super feminine. They'd been amused by Tasha. She wasn't a buddy and she wasn't, in their minds, a woman worth pursuing. She hadn't fit in anywhere. It was the reason she'd left. And now Matt was confusing her. She hated being confused.

So, right now, this afternoon, she had a new focus.

Since she'd been promoted, she had to replace herself. Matt employed several general dock laborers who also worked as mechanical assistants, and they pulled in mechanical specialists when necessary. But one staff mechanic couldn't keep up with the workload at Whiskey Bay. Matt owned twenty-four boats in all, ranging from *Monty's Pride* right down to a seventeen-foot runabout they used in the bay. Some were workboats, but most were pleasure craft available for rental.

Cash flow was a definite issue, especially after Matt's divorce. It was more important than ever that the yachts stay in good working order to maximize rentals.

Tasha was using a vacant office in the main marina building at the edge of the company pier. The place was a sprawling, utilitarian building, first constructed in 1970, with major additions built in 2000 and 2010. Its clay-colored steel siding protected against the wind and salt water.

Inside, the client area was nicely decorated, as were Matt's and the sales manager's offices. But down the hall, where the offices connected to the utility areas and eventually to the boat garage and the small dry dock, the finishing was more Spartan. Even still, she felt pretentious sitting behind a wooden desk with a guest chair in front.

She'd been through four applicants so far. One and two were nonstarters. They were handymen rather than certified marine mechanics. The third one had his certification, but something about him made Tasha cautious. He was a little too eager to list his accomplishments. He was beyond self-confident, bordering on arrogant. She didn't see him fitting in at Whiskey Bay.

The fourth applicant had been five minutes late. Not a promising start.

But then a woman appeared in the doorway. "My apologies," she said in a rush as she entered.

Tasha stood. "Alex Dumont?"

"Yes." The woman smiled broadly as she moved forward, holding out her hand.

Tasha shook it, laughing at herself for having made the assumption that Alex was a man.

"Alexandria," the woman elaborated, her eyes sparkling with humor.

"Of all people, I shouldn't make gender assumptions."

"It happens so often, I don't even think about it."

"I hear you," Tasha said. "Please, sit down."

"At least with the name Tasha nobody makes that mistake." Alex settled into the chair. "Though I have to imagine you've been written off a few times before they even met you."

"I'm not sure which is worse," Tasha said.

"I prefer the surprise value. That's why I shortened my name. I have to say this is the first time I've been interviewed by a woman."

Alex was tall, probably about five foot eight. She had wispy, wheat-blond hair, a few freckles and a pretty smile. If Tasha hadn't seen her résumé, she would have guessed she was younger than twenty-five.

"You're moving from Chicago?" Tasha asked, flipping through the three pages of Alex's résumé.

"I've already moved, three weeks ago."

"Any particular reason?" Tasha was hoping for someone who would stay in Whiskey Bay for the long term.

"I've always loved the West Coast. But mostly, it was time to make a break from the family."

Tasha could relate to that. "They didn't support your career choice?" she guessed.

"No." Alex gave a little laugh. "Quite the opposite. My father and two brothers are mechanics. They wouldn't leave me alone."

"Did you work with them?"

"At first. Then I got a job with another company. It didn't help. They still interrogated me every night and gave me advice on whatever repair I was undertaking."

"You lived with them?"

"Not anymore."

Tasha couldn't help contrasting their experiences. "I grew up in Boston. My parents wanted me to find a nice doctor or lawyer and become a wife instead of a mechanic. Though they probably would have settled for me being a landscape painter or a dancer."

"Any brothers and sisters?"

"Two sisters. Both married to lawyers." Tasha didn't like to dwell on her family. It had been a long time since she'd spoken to them. She stopped herself now, and went back to Alex's résumé. "At Schneider Marine, you worked on both gas and diesel engines?"

"Yes. Gas, anywhere from 120-horse outboards and up, and diesel, up to 550."

"Any experience on Broadmores?"

"Oh, yeah. Finicky buggers, those."

"We have two of them."

"Well, I've got their number."

Tasha couldn't help but smile. This was the kind of confidence she liked. "And you went to Riverside Tech?"

"I did. I finished my apprenticeship four years ago. I can get you a copy of my transcript if you need it."

Tasha shook her head. "I'm more interested in your recent experience. How much time on gasoline engines versus diesel?"

"More diesel, maybe seventy-five/twenty-five. Lots of service, plenty of rebuilds."

"Diagnostics?"

"I was their youngest mechanic, so I wasn't afraid of the new scan tools."

"You dive right in?" Tasha was liking Alex more and more as the interview went on.

"I dive right in."

"When can you start?"

Alex grinned. "Can you give me a few days to unpack?"

"Absolutely."

Both women came to their feet.

"Then, I'm in," Alex said.

Tasha shook her hand, excited at the prospect of another female mechanic in the company. "Welcome aboard."

Alex left, but a few minutes later, Tasha was still smiling when Matt came through the door.

"What?" he asked.

"What?" she returned, forcibly dampening her exhilaration at the sight of him.

She couldn't do this. She *wouldn't* do this. They had an employer-employee relationship, not a man-woman relationship.

"You're smiling," he said.

"I'm happy."

"About what?"

"I love my job."

"Is that all?"

"You don't think I love my job?" She did love it. And she had a feeling she'd love it even more with Alex around.

"I was hoping you were happy to see me."

"Matt." She put a warning in her voice.

"Are we going to just ignore it?"

She quickly closed the door to make sure nobody could overhear. "Yes, we're going to ignore it."

"By *it*, I mean our kiss."

She folded her arms over her chest and gave him a glare. "I know what you mean."

"Just checking," he said, looking dejected.

"Stop." She wasn't going to be emotionally manipulated.

"I'm not going to pretend. I miss you."

"There's nothing to miss. I'm right here."

"Prepared to talk work and only work."

"Yes."

He was silent for a moment. "Fine. Okay. I'll take it."

"Good." She knew with absolute certainty that it was for the best.

He squared his shoulders. "Who was that leaving?"

"That was Alex Dumont. She's our new mechanic."

Matt's brows went up. "We have a new mechanic?"

"You knew I was hiring one."

"But…"

Tasha couldn't help an inward sigh. She'd seen this reaction before. "But…she's a woman."

"That's not what I was going to say. I was surprised, is all."

"That she was light on testosterone?"

"You keep putting words in my mouth."

"Well, you keep putting expressions in your eyes."

He opened his mouth, but then he seemed to think better of whatever he'd planned to say.

"What?" she asked before she could stop herself.

"Nothing." He took a backward step. "I'm backing off. This is me backing off."

"From who I hire?"

Matt focused in on her eyes. His eyes smoldered, and she felt desire arc between them.

"I can feel it from here," he said, as if he was reading her mind.

Her brain stumbled. "There's…uh… I'm…"

"You can't quite spit out the lie, can you?"

She couldn't. Lying wouldn't help. "We have to ignore it."

"Why?"

"We do. We do, Matt."

There was a long beat of silence.

"I have a date Saturday night," he said.

A pain crossed her chest, but she steeled herself. "No kidding."

"I don't date that much."

"I don't pay any attention."

It was a lie. From the staff quarters, she'd seen him leave his house on the hill on many occasions, dressed to the nines. She'd often wondered where he'd gone, whom he'd been with, how late he'd come home.

And she'd watched him bring women to his house. They often dined on the deck. Caterers would set up candles and white linens, and then Matt and his date would chat and laugh the evening away.

She'd paid attention all right. But wild horses wouldn't drag the admission out of her.

So Saturday night, Matt had picked up the tall, willowy, expensively coiffed Emilie and brought her home for arctic char and risotto, catered by a local chef. They were dining in his glass-walled living room to candlelight and a full moon. The wine was from the Napa Valley, and the chocolate truffles were handcrafted with Belgian chocolate.

It should have been perfect. Emilie was a real estate company manager, intelligent, gracious, even a little bit funny. She was friendly and flirtatious, and made no secret of the fact that she expected a very romantic conclusion to the evening.

But Matt's gaze kept straying to the pier below, to the yachts, the office building and the repair shop. Finally, Tasha appeared. She strode briskly beneath the overhead lights, through the security gate and up the stairway that led to the staff quarters. Some of his staff members had families and houses in town. The younger, single crew members, especially those who had moved to Whiskey Bay to work at the marina, seemed to appreciate the free rent, even if the staff units were small and basic. He was happy at the moment that Tasha was one of them.

He reflexively glanced at his watch. It was nearly ten o'clock. Even for Tasha, this was late.

"Matt?" Emilie said.

"Yes?" He quickly returned his attention to her.

She gave a very pretty smile. "I asked if they were all yours?"

"All what?"

"The boats. Do you really own that many boats?"

"I do," he said. He'd told this story a hundred times. "I started with three about a decade ago. Business was good, so I gradually added to the fleet."

He glanced back to the pier, but Tasha had disappeared from view. He told himself not to be disappointed. He'd see her again soon. It had been a few days now since they'd run into each other. He'd tried not to miss her, but he did. He'd find a reason to talk to her tomorrow.

Emilie pointed toward the window. "That one is *huge*."

"*Monty's Pride* is our largest vessel."

"Could I see the inside?" she asked, eyes alight. "Would you give me a tour?"

Before Matt could answer, there was a pounding on his door.

"Expecting someone?" she asked, looking a little bit frustrated by the interruption.

His friends and neighbors, Caleb Watford and TJ Bauer, were the only people who routinely dropped by. But neither of them would knock. At most, they'd call out from the entryway if they thought they might walk in on something.

Matt rose. "I'll be right back."

"Sure." Emilie helped herself to another truffle. "I'll wait here."

The date had been going pretty well so far. But Matt couldn't say he was thrilled with the touch of sarcasm he'd just heard in Emilie's voice.

The knock came again as he got to the front entry. He swung open the door.

Tasha stood on his porch, her work jacket wrinkled, a blue baseball cap snug on her head and her work boots sturdy against the cool weather.

His immediate reaction was delight. He wanted to drag her inside and make her stay for a while.

"What's up?" he asked instead, remembering the promise he'd made, holding himself firmly at a respectful distance.

"Something's going on," she said.

"Between us?" he asked before he could stop himself, resisting the urge to glance back and be sure Emilie was still out of sight.

Tasha frowned. "*No.* With *Pacific Wind.*" She named the single-engine twenty-eight-footer. "It's just a feeling. But I'm worried."

He stepped back and gestured for her to come inside.

She glanced down at her boots.

"Don't worry about it," he said. "I have a cleaning service."

"A cable broke on the steering system," she said.

"Is that a major problem?"

He didn't particularly care why she'd decided to come up and tell him in person. He was just glad she had.

It was the first time she'd been inside his house. He couldn't help but wonder if she liked the modern styling, the way it jutted out from the hillside, the clean lines, glass walls and unobstructed view. He really wanted to find out. He hadn't been interested in Emilie's opinion, but he was curious about Tasha's.

"It's not a big problem," she said. "I fixed it. It's fixed."

"That's good." He dared to hope all over again that this was a personal visit disguised as business.

"Matt?" came Emilie's voice.

He realized he'd forgotten all about her.

"I'll just be a minute," he called back to her.

"You're busy," Tasha said, looking instantly regretful. "Of course you're busy. I didn't think." She glanced at her watch. "This is Saturday, isn't it?"

"You forgot the day of the week?"

"Matt, honey." Emilie came up behind him.

Honey? Seriously? After a single date?

Not even a single date, really. The date hadn't concluded yet.

"Who's this?" Emilie asked.

There was a dismissive edge to her voice and judgment in her expression as she gave Tasha the once-over, clearly finding her lacking.

The superior attitude annoyed Matt. "This is Tasha."

"I'm the mechanic," Tasha said, not seeming remotely bothered by Emilie's condescension.

"Hmph," Emilie said, wrinkling her perfect nose. She wrapped her arm possessively through Matt's. "Is this an emergency?"

Tasha took a step back, opening her mouth to speak.

"Yes," Matt said. "It's an emergency. I'm afraid I'm going to have to cut our date short."

He wasn't sure who looked more surprised by his words, Emilie or Tasha.

"I'll call you a ride." He took out his phone.

It took Emilie a moment to find her voice. "What *kind* of emergency?"

"The mechanical kind," he said flatly, suddenly tired of her company.

He typed in the request. He definitely didn't want Tasha to leave.

"But—" Emilie began.

"The ride will be here in three minutes," he said. "I'll get your coat."

He did a quick check of Tasha's expression, steeling himself for the possibility that she'd speak up and out him as a liar.

She didn't.

He quickly retrieved Emilie's coat and purse.

"I don't mind waiting," Emilie said, a plaintive whine in her voice.

"I couldn't ask you to do that." He held up the coat.

"How long do you think—"

"Could be a long time. It could be a very long time. It's complicated."

"Matt, I can—" Tasha began.

"No. Nope." He gave a definitive shake to his head. "It's business. It's important." It might not be critical, but Tasha had never sought him out after hours before, so there had to be something going on.

"You're a *mechanic*?" Emilie asked Tasha.

"A marine mechanic."

"So you get all greasy and stuff?"

"Sometimes."

"That must be awful." Emilie gave a little shudder.

"Emilie." Matt put a warning tone in his voice.

She crooked her head back to look at him. "What? It's weird."

"It's not weird."

"It's unusual," Tasha said. "But women are up to nearly fifteen percent in the mechanical trades, higher when you look at statistics for those of us under thirty-five."

Emilie didn't seem to know what to say in response.

Matt's phone pinged.

"Your ride's here," he told Emilie, ushering her toward the door.

Tasha stood to one side, and he watched until Emilie got into the car.

"You didn't have to do that," Tasha said as he closed the door.

"It wasn't going well."

"In that case, I'm happy to be your wingman."

Matt zeroed in on her expression to see if she was joking. She looked serious, and he didn't like the sound of that.

"I don't need a wingman."

"Tell me what's going on." He gestured through the archway to the living room.

She crouched down to untie her boots.

"You don't have to—"

"Your carpet is white," she said.

"I suppose."

Most of the women he brought home wore delicate shoes, stiletto heels and such.

Tasha peeled off her boots, revealing thick wool socks. For some reason, the sight made him smile.

She rose, looking all business.

"Care for a drink?" he asked, gesturing her forward.

She moved, shooting him an expression of disbelief on the way past. "No, I don't want a drink."

"I opened a great bottle of pinot noir. I'm not going to finish it myself."

"This isn't a social visit," she said, glancing around the room at the pale white leather furniture and long, narrow gas fireplace.

She was obviously hesitant to sit down in her work clothes.

"Here," he suggested, pointing to the formal dining room. The chairs were dark oak, likely less intimidating if she was worried about leaving dirt on anything.

While she sat down, he retrieved the pinot from the glass porch and brought two fresh glasses.

He sat down cornerwise to her and set down the wine.

She gave him an exaggerated sigh. "I'm not drinking while I work."

"It's ten o'clock on a Saturday night."

"Your point?"

"My point is you're officially off the clock."

"So, you're not paying me?"

"I'll pay you anything you want." He poured them each some of the rich, dark wine. "Aren't you on salary?"

"I am."

"You work an awful lot of overtime."

"A good deal for you."

"I'm giving you a raise." He held one of the glasses out for her.

"Ha ha," she mocked.

"Take it," he said.

She did, but set it down on the table in front of her.

"Twenty percent," he told her.

"You can't do that."

"I absolutely can." He raised his glass. "Let's toast your raise."

"I came here to tell you I might have made a big mistake."

Three

Tasha reluctantly took a sip of the wine, noting right away that it was a fantastic vintage. She looked at the bottle, recognizing the Palmer Valley label as one of her parents' favorites, and the Crispin Pinot Noir as one of their higher-end brands.

"You have good taste in wine," she said.

"I'm glad you like it."

His smile was warm, and she felt an unwelcome glow in the pit of her stomach.

To distract herself, she tipped the bottle to check the year.

"You know the label?" he asked, sounding surprised.

"Mechanics can't appreciate fine wine?"

He paused to take in her expression. "Clearly, they can."

It was annoying how his deep voice strummed along her nervous system. She seemed to have no defenses against him.

She set down her glass and straightened in her chair, reminding herself this was business.

"What did I say?" he asked.

"I came here to tell you—"

"I just said something wrong," he persisted. "What was it?"

"You didn't say anything wrong." It was her problem, not his. "*Pacific Wind* broke down near Granite Point."

"Another breakdown?"

"Like I said, a cable was broken."

"But you fixed it." He slid the wineglass a little closer to her. "Good job. Well done, you."

"It shouldn't have happened. I serviced it just last week. I must have missed a weak point."

His lips tightened in what looked like frustration. "Why

are you so quick to blame yourself? It obviously broke *after* you did your work."

"The sequence of events isn't logical. It shouldn't have broken all of a sudden. Wear and tear should have been obvious when I was working on it." She'd been mulling over the possibilities for hours now. "It could have been a faulty part, weak material in the cable maybe, something that wasn't visible that would leave it prone to breaking."

"There you go."

"Or…" She hesitated to even voice her speculation.

"Or?" he prompted.

"Somebody wanted it to break. It's far-fetched. I get that. And on the surface, it seems like I'm making excuses for my own incompetence—coming up with some grand scheme of sabotage to explain it all away. But the thing is, I checked with the fuel supply company right after we got back from Tyree. We were the only customer that had a water problem. And none of our other yachts were affected, only *Orca's Run*. How does that work? How does water only get into one fuel system?" She gave in and took another drink of the wine.

"Tasha?" Matt asked.

"Yeah?" She set down her glass, oddly relieved at having said it out loud. Now they could discuss it and dismiss it.

"Can you parse that out a little more for me?"

She nodded, happy to delve into her theory and find the flaws. "It's far from definitive. It's only possible. It's possible that someone put water in the fuel and damaged the pump. And it's possible someone partially cut the cable."

"The question is, why?"

She agreed. "Do you have any enemies?"

"None that I know about."

"A competitor, maybe?"

He sat back in his chair. "Wow."

"*Wow* that somebody could be secretly working against you?"

"No. I was just thinking that after-dinner conversation with you is *so* much more interesting than with Emilie."

"So you think my theory is too far-fetched." She was inclined to agree.

"That's not what I said at all. I'm thinking you could be right. And we should investigate. And that's kind of exciting."

"You think it's exciting? That someone might be damaging your boats and undermining your company's reputation?"

He topped up both of their glasses. "I think it could be exciting to investigate. It's not like anything was seriously or permanently damaged. It seems like more mischief than anything. And haven't you ever wanted to be an amateur sleuth?"

"No." She could honestly say it had never crossed her mind.

"Come on. You investigate, diagnose and fix problems all the time."

"There are no bad guys lurking inside engines."

"The bad guy only adds a new dimension to the problem."

She couldn't understand his jovial attitude. There wasn't a positive side to this. "There's something wrong with you, Matt."

"Will you help me?" he asked, his eyes alight in a way that trapped and held her gaze. His eyes were vivid blue right now, the color of the bay at a summer sunrise.

"It's my job." She fought an inappropriate thrill at the prospect of working closely with him. She should be staying away from him. That's what she should be doing.

"We need to start with a list of suspects. Who has access to the engines and steering systems?"

"I do, and the contract mechanics from Dean's Repairs and Corner Service. And Alex now. But she wasn't even here when we had the *Orca's Run* problem."

"Was she in Whiskey Bay?"

"Yes but… You're not suggesting she's a mole."

"I'm not suggesting anything yet. I'm only laying out the facts."

Tasha didn't want to suspect Alex, but she couldn't disagree with Matt's approach. They had to start with everyone who had access, especially those with mechanical skills. Whoever did this understood boats and engines well enough to at least attempt to cover their tracks.

"At least we can rule you out," Matt said with a smirk.

"And you," she returned.

"And me. What about the rest of the staff? Who can we rule out?"

"Can we get a list of everyone's hours for the past couple of weeks?"

"Easily."

"What about your competitors?" It seemed to Tasha that Matt's competitors would have motive to see him fail.

"They'd have a financial motive, I suppose. But I know most of the ones in the area, and I can't imagine any of them doing something underhanded."

"Maybe they didn't," she said, realizing the enormity of her accusations. Never mind the enormity, what about the likelihood that somebody was out to harm Matt's business?

She was reevaluating this whole thing. "Maybe it was just my making a mistake."

He paused and seemed to consider. "Do you believe that's what happened?"

"Nobody's perfect." She knew her negligence could account for the cable.

Then again, the water in the fuel of *Orca's Run* was something else. It was a lot less likely she'd been responsible for that.

He watched her closely, his gaze penetrating. "Tasha, I can tell by your expression you know it wasn't you."

"I can't be one hundred percent certain."

He took her hand in both of his. "I am."

Their gazes met and held, and the air temperature in the room seemed to rise. Subtle sounds magnified: the wind, the surf, the hiss of the fireplace. Heat rushed up her arm, blooming into desire in her chest.

Like the first rumblings of an earthquake, she could feel it starting all over again.

"I have to go." She jumped to her feet.

He stood with her, still holding her hand. His gaze moved to her lips.

They tingled.

She knew she should move. She needed to move *right now*.

She did move. But it was to step forward, not backward.

She brought her free hand up to his. He interlaced their fingers.

"Tasha," he whispered.

She should run. Leave. But instead she let her eyes drift closed. She leaned in, crossing the last few inches between them. She tipped her chin, tilted her head. She might not have a lot of experience with romance, but she knew she was asking for his kiss.

He didn't disappoint.

With a swift, indrawn breath, he brought his lips to hers.

The kiss was tender, soft and tentative. But it sent waves through her body, heat and energy. It was she who pressed harder, she who parted her lips and she who disentangled her hands to wrap her arms around his neck.

He gave a small groan, and he embraced her, his solid forearms against her back, pressing her curves against the length of his body, thigh to thigh, chest to chest. Her nipples peaked at his touch, the heat of his skin. She desperately wanted to feel his skin against hers. But she'd retained just enough sanity to stop herself.

The kiss was as far as it could go.

She reluctantly drew back. She wished she could look away and pretend it hadn't happened. But she didn't. She wouldn't. She faced him head-on.

His eyes were opaque, and there was a ghost of a smile on his face.

"You're amazing," he said.

"We can't do that." Regret was pouring in, along with a healthy dose of self-recrimination.

"But, we do."

"You know what I mean."

"You mean *shouldn't*." His closeness was still clouding her mind.

"Yes, shouldn't. No, can't. You have to help me here, Matt." She stepped away, putting some space between them.

He gave an exaggerated sigh. "You're asking a lot."

She wanted to be honest, and she wanted both of them to be realistic. "I like it here."

He glanced around his living room that jutted out from the cliff, affording incredible views of the bay. He was clearly proud of the design, proud of his home. "I'm glad to hear that."

"Not the house," she quickly corrected him.

"You don't like my house?"

"That's not what I mean. I do like your house." The house was stunningly gorgeous; anyone would love it. "I mean I like working at Whiskey Bay. I don't want to have to quit."

His expression turned to incredulity. "You're making some pretty huge leaps in logic."

She knew that was true, and she backpedaled. "I'm not assuming you want a fling."

"That's not what I—"

"It's hard for a woman to be taken seriously as a mechanic."

"So you've said."

"I want to keep my personal life and my professional life separate."

"Everybody does. Until something happens that makes them want something else."

Now she just wanted out of this conversation. "I'm afraid I've given you the wrong idea."

"The only idea you've given me is that you're attracted to me."

She wanted to protest, but she wasn't going to lie.

He continued. "That and the fact that you believe my company is the target of sabotage."

She quickly latched onto the alternative subject. "I do. At least, it's a possibility that we should consider."

"And I trust your judgment, so we're going to investigate."

Tasha drew a breath of relief. They were back on solid ground. All work with Matt, no play. That was her mission going forward.

Matt couldn't concentrate on work. He kept reliving his kiss with Tasha over and over again.

He was with TJ and Caleb on the top deck of his marina building, standing around the propane fireplace as the sun sank into the Pacific. The other men's voices were more a drone of noise than a conversation.

"Why would anyone sabotage your engines?" TJ broke through Matt's daydreaming.

"What?" he asked, shaking himself back to the present.

"Why would they do it?"

"Competition is my guess." Matt hadn't been able to come up with another reason.

Caleb levered into one of the padded deck chairs. It was a cool evening, but the men still sipped on chilled beers.

"What about your surveillance cameras?" Caleb asked.

"Not enough of them to provide full coverage. They're pretty easy to avoid if that's your intention."

"You should get more."

"I've ordered more." It was one of the first moves Matt had made. He took a chair himself.

"Did you call the police?" TJ asked, sitting down.

"Not yet. I can't imagine it would be a priority for them. And I want to make sure we're right before I waste anybody's time."

"So, Tasha is wrong?"

Matt found himself bristling at what was only the slightest of criticisms of Tasha. "No, she's not wrong."

"I'm just asking," TJ said, obviously catching the tone in Matt's voice.

"And I'm just answering. She's not one hundred percent convinced yet either. So, we'll wait."

"Until it happens again?" Caleb asked. "What if it's more serious this time? What if whoever it is targets more than the marina?"

"Are you worried about the Crab Shack?" Matt hadn't thought about the other businesses in the area, including the Crab Shack restaurant run by Caleb's new wife, Jules, who was five months pregnant with twins.

"Not yet." Caleb seemed to further contemplate the question. "I might ask Noah to spend a little more time over there."

"Nobody's going to mess with Noah," TJ said.

"He's scrappy," Caleb agreed.

Caleb's sister-in-law's boyfriend had spent a short time in jail after a fistfight in self-defense. He was tough and no-nonsense, and he'd protect Jules and her sister, Melissa, against anything and anyone.

"What about your security cameras at the Crab Shack?" TJ asked Caleb. "Would any of them reach this far?"

"I'll check," Caleb said. "But I doubt the resolution is high enough to be of any help."

"I'd appreciate that," Matt said to Caleb.

It hadn't occurred to him to worry about Tasha's or anyone else's safety. But maybe Caleb was onto something. Maybe Matt should take a few precautions. So far, the incidents had been minor, and nobody had come close to being hurt. But that wasn't to say it couldn't happen. The incidents could escalate.

"Matt?" It was Tasha's voice coming from the pier below, and he felt the timbre radiate through his chest.

He swiftly rose and crossed to the rail, where he could see her. "Are you okay?"

She seemed puzzled by his concern. "I'm fine."

"Good."

"*Never Fear* and *Crystal Zone* are both ready to go in the morning. I'm heading into town for a few hours."

"What for?" The question was out of Matt's mouth before he realized it was none of his business. It was after five, and Tasha was free to do anything she wanted.

"Meeting some guys."

Guys? What did she mean *guys*? He wanted to ask if it was one particular guy, or if it was a group of guys. Were they all just friends?

"Hey, Tasha." TJ appeared at the rail beside him.

"Hi, TJ." Her greeting was casual, and her attention went back to Matt. "Alex will fill the fuel tanks first thing. The clients are expected at ten."

"Got it," Matt said, wishing he could ask more questions about her evening. Or better still, invite her to join them, where they could talk and laugh together.

Not that they were in the habit of friendly conversation. Mostly, they debated. But he'd be happy to engage her in a rollicking debate about pretty much any subject.

As she walked away, TJ spoke up. "I may just take another shot."

"Another shot at what?" Matt asked.

"At your mechanic."

"*What?*" Matt turned.

"I like her."

"What do you mean *another* shot?" Matt was surprised by the level of his anger. "You took a shot at her already?"

TJ was obviously taken aback by Matt's reaction. "I asked you back in the summer. You told me to go for it."

"That was months ago."

"That's when I asked her out. I suggested dinner and dancing. That might have been my mistake."

Matt took a drink of his beer to keep himself from saying anything more. He didn't like the thought of Tasha with any guy, never mind TJ. TJ was the epitome of rich, good-looking and eligible. Matt had seen the way a lot of women reacted to him. Not that Tasha was an ordinary woman. Still, she was a woman.

TJ kept talking, half to himself. "Maybe a monster truck rally? She is a mechanic."

Caleb joined them at the rail.

TJ tried again. "Maybe an auto show. There's one coming up in Seattle."

"You can't ask her out," Matt said.

The protest caught Caleb's attention. "Why can't he ask her out?"

"Because she's already turned him down."

"I could be persistent," TJ said.

"I really don't think dinner and dancing or persistence was the problem," Matt said.

"How would you know that?" TJ asked.

Caleb's expression took a speculative turn. "You have a problem with TJ asking Tasha out?"

"No," Matt responded to Caleb. Then he reconsidered his answer. "Yes."

TJ leaned an elbow on the rail, a grin forming on his face. "Oh, this is interesting."

"It's not interesting," Matt said.

"Is something going on between you two?" Caleb asked.

"No. Nothing is going on."

"But you like her." TJ's grin was full-on now.

"I kissed her. She kissed me. We kissed." Matt wasn't proud that it sounded like he was bragging. "She's a nice woman. And I like her. But nothing has happened."

"Are you telling me to back off?" TJ asked.

"That's pretty loud and clear," Caleb said.

TJ held up his hands in mock surrender. "Backing off."

"She said she was meeting a guy tonight?" Caleb raised a brow.

Matt narrowed his gaze. "She said *guys*, plural. They're probably just friends of hers."

"Probably," said TJ with exaggerated skepticism, still clearly amused at Matt's expense.

"It took you long enough," Caleb said.

"There is no *it*," Matt responded. It had taken him too long to notice her. He'd own that.

"Have you asked her out?"

"We're a little busy at the moment. You know, distracted by criminal activity."

"That's a no," TJ said. "At least I took the plunge."

"You got shot down," Caleb reminded TJ.

"No risk, no reward."

"She's gun-shy," Matt said. He didn't know what made her that way, but it was obvious she was wary of dating.

"So, what are you going to do?" Caleb asked.

"Nothing."

"That's a mistake."

"I'm not going to force anything." The last thing Matt wanted to do was make Tasha feel uncomfortable working at the marina.

He wanted her to stay. For all kinds of different reasons, both personal and professional, but he definitely wanted her to stay.

The Edge Bar and Grill in the town of Whiskey Bay was a popular hangout for the marina staff. It also drew in the working class from the local service and supply businesses. The artsy crowd preferred the Blue Badger on Third Avenue. While those who were looking for something high-end and refined could choose the Ocean View Lounge across the highway. While the Crab Shack was becoming popular, drawing people from the surrounding towns and even as far away as Olympia.

Tasha liked the Edge. The decor was particularly attractive tonight, decked out for the season with a tree, lights and miles of evergreen garlands. A huge wreath over the bar was covered in gold balls and poinsettia flowers.

As was usual, the music had a rock-and-country flare. The menu was unpretentious. They had good beer on tap, and soda refills were free. She was driving her and Alex home tonight, so she'd gone with cola.

"Have you heard of anybody having any unexpected engine problems lately?" she asked Henry Schneider, who was sitting across the table.

Henry was a marine mechanic at Shutters Corner ten miles down the highway near the public wharf.

"Unexpected how?" he asked.

"We had some water in the fuel with no apparent cause."

"Loose cap?"

"Checked that, along with the fuel source. The water separator was full."

"There's your problem."

"I swapped it out, but I couldn't figure out how it got that way."

Henry gave a shrug. "It happens."

Alex returned from the small dance floor with another mechanic, James Hamilton, in tow.

"So, no reports of anything strange?" Tasha asked Henry.

"Strange?" James asked, helping Alex onto the high stool.

"Unexplained mechanical failures in the area."

"There's always an explanation," James said. "Sometimes you just have to keep looking."

"You want to dance?" Alex asked Henry.

"Who says I was through dancing?" James asked her.

"Dance with Tasha." Alex motioned for Henry to come with her.

He swallowed the remainder of his beer and rose from his chair.

James held out his hand to Tasha.

She gave up talking shop and accepted the invitation.

James was younger than Henry, likely in his late twenties. He was from Idaho and had a fresh-faced openness about him that Tasha liked. He was tall and lanky. His hair was red, and his complexion was fair. She didn't think she'd ever seen him in a bad mood.

It wasn't the first time they'd ever danced together, and he was good at it. He'd once told her barn dancing was a popular pastime in the small town where he'd grown up. She knew he'd left his high school sweetheart behind, and she got the feeling he'd one day return to her, even if he did prefer the West Coast to rural Idaho.

As the song ended, a figure appeared behind James. It took only a split second for Tasha to recognize Matt.

"What are you doing here?" she asked him, her guard immediately going up. She assumed this was too simple, too low-key to be his kind of place. "Is something wrong?"

"Dance?" he asked instead of answering.

James backed away. "Catch you later."

Matt stepped in front of her as a Bruce Springsteen song came up.

He took her hand.

"Did something happen?" she asked. "Was there another breakdown?"

"Nothing happened. Can't a guy go out for the evening?"

She struggled to ignore his light touch on her back and the heat where his hand joined hers. It was a lost cause. "This isn't your typical hangout."

"Sure it is."

"I can tell when you're lying."

He hesitated. "I was worried about you."

"Why?"

"There's a criminal out there."

She almost laughed. "If there is, he's focused on your company. It has nothing to do with me."

"We don't know that."

"We do."

He drew her closer as they danced, even though she knew getting more intimate with Matt was a big mistake.

But the words didn't come. Instead of speaking, she followed his lead. It was the path of least resistance, since their bodies moved seamlessly together. He was tall and solid and a smooth, skilled dancer.

She told herself she could handle it. They were in public after all. It's not like they would get carried away.

"I know you like to be independent," he said.

"I am independent."

"The truth is, people are less likely to harass you if you're with me."

His words were confusing.

"Nobody's been harassing me. Nobody's going to harass me."

Matt glanced around the room with apparent skepticism, as if he was expecting a gang of criminals to be lurking next to the dance floor.

"See that guy in the red shirt?" She pointed. "He worked at Shutters Corner. And the guy talking to Alex? He's Henry's coworker. They're local guys, Matt. They're mechanics. There are a lot of local mechanics here. And I'm talking to them all."

Matt's hold on her tightened. "Are you dancing with them all?"

She tipped her chin to look up at him, seeing his lips were thin and his jaw was tight.

He looked jealous. The last thing she wanted him to be was jealous. But her heart involuntarily lifted at the idea.

"No." The sharp retort was as much for her as it was for him. "I'm here asking questions. I'm gathering evidence, if you must know."

"Oh," he drawled with immediate understanding.

"Yes, *oh*. If anybody's having the same problems as us, these guys are going to know about it."

"That's a really good idea."

She put a note of sarcasm into her tone. "Why, thank you."

"I'm not crazy about the dancing part."

"*You* asked *me*," she pointed out.

"What? No, not with me." He canted his head. "With them."

She wanted to point out that he was dating other women. But she quickly stopped herself. Matt's romantic life was none of her business. And hers was none of his. The more women he dated, the better.

His voice lowered. "You can dance with me all you want."

"We're not going there, Matt."

"Okay." His agreement was easy, but his hold still felt intimate.

"You say okay, but we're still dancing." She knew she could pull away herself. She knew she should do exactly that, but he felt so good in her arms, she wanted to hang on just a little bit longer.

"The song will be over soon." He went silent for a moment. "How are you getting home?"

"Driving."

"You came alone?"

"I drove with Alex. Matt, I've been going out at night on my own for the past six years."

"Not while my boats were being sabotaged all around you."

"We don't know that they are being sabotaged. Honestly, I'm beginning to regret sharing my suspicions with you." The last thing she'd expected was for him to go all bodyguard on her.

"We don't know that they're not. And don't you dare hold anything back."

She stopped dancing. "Matt."

His hand contracted around her shoulder. "I didn't mean for that to sound like an order."

"Is there something you're not telling me?"

Had there been some development? Was there a danger she didn't know about?

"I heard TJ ask you out."

The statement took her completely by surprise. "That was a long time ago. You can't possibly suspect TJ."

Sure, she'd turned TJ down. But he and Matt were good friends. He wouldn't take out his anger with her by harming Matt. Plus, he hadn't even seemed to care that much. He was still friendly to her.

"I *don't* suspect TJ."

The song changed to a Christmas tune. It wasn't the best dance music in the world, but Matt kept leading, so she followed.

"Then why are we talking about him?"

Matt seemed to be reviewing their conversation so far. "It was Caleb."

"You suspect Caleb?" That was even more outlandish than suspecting TJ.

"Caleb's the one who got me worried about the sabotage. He's worried about Jules, which got me to thinking about you. And then TJ mentioned that he'd asked you out."

"Caleb worries too much. And TJ was months ago."

"So, you're not interested in him?"

Tasha was more than confused here. "Did he ask you to ask me?"

One minute, she thought Matt was romancing her, and she braced herself to shut him down. And then he seemed to be TJ's wingman. Their kisses notwithstanding, maybe she was reading his interest all wrong.

Before Matt could respond, she jumped back in. "TJ's not my type."

Alex appeared beside Tasha on the dance floor.

She took Tasha's arm and leaned into her ear. "James offered me a ride home."

Tasha pulled back to look at her friend. "Is that a good thing?"

Alex's eyes were alight. "You bet."

Since Alex had a done a whole lot more dancing than drinking, Tasha wasn't worried about her. And Tasha had known James for months. He seemed like a very upstanding guy.

"Do you mind if I bail on you?" Alex asked.

"Not at all. I'll see you later."

Alex grinned. "Thanks." Her walk was light as she moved away.

"So, you're driving home alone," Matt said. "I'll follow you."

Tasha rolled her eyes at him.

"I'm serious."

"Thanks for the dance," she said and pulled back from his arms.

She was going to have another drink. She was going to chat with Henry and the other mechanics. She didn't need a bodyguard.

Four

Matt hung back as Tasha approached her compact car in the Edge's parking lot. It was in a dark corner, and he moved out of the building's lights so his eyes could adjust.

It was obvious she knew he was there, knew he'd waited for her to leave for home. She'd shot him a look of frustration as she'd headed for the front door and he'd risen from his seat at the bar.

Now, she shook her head with exaggerated resignation and gave him a mocking wave as she slipped into the driver's seat.

He didn't really care how she felt. Caleb had him worried about safety. He headed for his own car at the opposite side of the parking lot. The bar was only half-full at ten o'clock. But even on a weeknight, the crowd here would keep going until midnight, when the place shut down.

Tasha's engine cranked. Then it cranked again. But it didn't catch and start. A third crank was followed by silence.

Matt turned back.

She was out of the car and opening the hood.

"Need some help?" he asked as he approached.

She laughed. "You *have* read my résumé, right?"

"I'm not questioning your technical skills. And it's obviously a dead battery."

Her annoyance seemed to fade. "That's exactly what it is."

As they gazed at the cold engine, a thought struck him. "Could this be sabotage?"

"No." Her answer was definitive.

"How can you be sure?"

"Because it's related to my having an old battery. I've been limping it along for a while now. Do you have cables?"

"In my BMW?"

"BMWs run the same way as any other car."

"My battery's under warranty. And I have roadside assistance. You don't have cables?"

Tasha was a be-prepared kind of woman. Jumper cables seemed like the kind of thing she would carry.

She looked embarrassed. "I do. Usually. I took them out of my trunk to help Alex move her stuff."

"Come on," he said, motioning to his car.

"I'll call a tow truck and get a jump."

"There's no need." He wasn't about to leave her standing in a dark parking lot waiting for a tow truck. "I'll bring you back tomorrow with your jumper cables."

"I can take care of it."

His frustration mounted. "Why are you arguing?"

She squared her shoulders and lifted her chin but didn't answer.

"Well?" he prompted.

"I don't know."

He couldn't help but grin. "Pride?"

"Maybe. I don't like to be rescued."

"But you'll accept help from a random tow truck driver."

She dropped the hood down, and the sound echoed. "He's paid to help me. But you're right. I'm wrong. I'd appreciate the ride home."

"Did you just say I was right?"

She locked the driver's door and started walking. "I did."

He fell into step beside her. "It's fun being right."

"Calm down. It's not that exciting."

He hit the remote to unlock the doors. "You're positive somebody wasn't messing with your battery?"

"I'm positive. It's unrelated. And if we try to link it in, we'll set ourselves off in the wrong direction."

Matt thought about her logic for a moment. "Okay. Now you're the one who's right."

She cracked a smile. "Thank goodness I'm evening things up."

He opened the driver's door while she did the same on the passenger side.

"But I'm not wrong," he pointed out.

"Maybe a little bit."

"Maybe not at all. I just asked a question. Postulating something is not the same as being incorrect about it."

"You're right," she said and plunked into the seat.

He leaned down to look through his open door. "That's two for me."

She was smiling as she buckled her seat belt.

He started the engine, turned down the music and pulled out of the parking lot.

The temperature was in the fifties, but the interior heated up quickly, and Tasha unzipped her fitted gray leather jacket. She wore a purple tank top beneath it over a boxy pair of faded blue jeans and brown Western-style boots. Her hair was pulled into a high ponytail. It was mostly brunette, but it flashed with amber highlights as they drove.

She looked casual and comfortable, sexy at the same time. He liked it. He liked it a lot.

"Nobody I talked to knew anything," she said. "Nothing weird going on out there in the broader Whiskey Bay mechanical world."

"So the marina is the target."

"That would be my guess. Or it's a couple of coincidences. It could still be that."

He didn't disagree. He hoped it was a couple of coincidences. "I'm going to check out my competition."

"How?"

"'Tis the season. There are a lot of gatherings and parties coming up. The business community likes to celebrate together."

"I remember."

"Were you here last year?"

She'd been working at the marina only since March.

"I was talking about the business community anywhere. It was the same while I was growing up."

"You went to corporate Christmas parties?" He tried to picture it.

"I read about them," she continued, quickly. "They sounded…posh and snooty and boring."

He laughed at how she wrinkled her nose. "They're not bad. They are fancy. But some of the people are interesting."

She gave a derisive scoff.

"Hey, I'm one of those people. Am I that bad?"

"In some ways, yes."

"What ways?" He tried not to let her opinion get to him.

"The way you dress. The way you talk."

"What's wrong with the way I talk?"

She seemed to think about that. "It's clear and precise, with very little slang. You have a wide vocabulary."

"I'm not seeing the problem."

"It sounds posh."

"What about you?"

She was easily as articulate as him.

"I'm perfectly ordinary."

She wasn't. But he wasn't going to get into that argument right now.

"And so are the people at the corporate parties. You shouldn't be biased against them." He slowed the car and turned from the highway down his long driveway that wound through the woods.

"I can't stand those frilly, frothy dresses, those pretentious caviar and foie gras canapés, and the ceaseless conversation about who's making partner and the who's marrying who."

He wasn't about to admit she'd nailed it—at least when it came to some of the guests at those parties.

"You shouldn't knock it until you've tried it," he said instead.

"You're right."

He chuckled. "And I've hit the trifecta."

Then the headlights caught his house. He blinked to check his vision on what he thought he saw there. His stomach curled. It couldn't be.

"Who's that?" Tasha asked as the car came to a stop.

Matt shut off the engine. "My ex-wife."

Tasha gazed through the windshield. "So that's her."

"I take it you haven't met her?"

"I only saw her from a distance. She didn't seem to be around much."

Those last few months, his ex had used any excuse to travel.

"She liked France," he said. "She still likes France. There's a man there."

"Oh," Tasha said with obvious understanding.

"Yeah." Matt released his seat belt. "I can't even imagine what she's doing back here."

He and Tasha both stepped out of the car.

"Hello, Dianne," he said as he approached the lit porch.

Her dark hair was pulled back from her face with some kind of headband, the ends of her hair brushing her shoulders. She wore a black wool jacket with leather trim, a pair of black slacks and very high heels. Her makeup was perfect, as always. Her mouth was tight. Her eyes narrowed.

"Where have you been?" she asked. Then her gaze swept Tasha.

"This is Tasha." He didn't like the dismissive expression on Dianne's face. "She and I have been dancing."

He felt Tasha's look of surprise but ignored it.

"What are you doing here?" he asked Dianne.

"I need to speak with you."

Her nostrils flared with an indrawn breath. "It's a private matter."

"Well, I'm not about to end my evening early to listen to you."

Whatever Dianne had to say to him—and he couldn't imagine what that might be—it could wait until morning.

"You can call me tomorrow, Dianne." He started for the door, gesturing for Tasha to go ahead of him.

"It's about François," Dianne blurted out.

Matt kept walking.

Whatever was going on between Dianne and her new husband was completely their business. Matt couldn't stay far enough away.

"He left me."

Matt paused. "I'm sorry, Dianne. It's none of my business."

"He stole my money."

"Matt?" Tasha said with a little tug against his hand.

"*All* of my money," Dianne said.

"It'll still wait until morning." Matt punched in the key code to his front door. "Do you need me to call you a ride?"

"Matt," Dianne practically wailed.

"We're divorced, Dianne. As I recall, your settlement was more than generous."

Matt had only wanted it to be over. Although his lawyer had argued with him, he'd given her everything she'd asked for. It had meant significant refinancing of the marina, but if he worked hard, he'd be back on solid footing within two or three years.

He retrieved his phone and pulled up his ride app, requesting a car. "Call me tomorrow. I assume you still have my number?"

"I'm in trouble, Matt," Dianne said. "Deep trouble."

"Then I suggest you call a lawyer."

Her voice rose. "I didn't commit a crime."

"I'm glad to hear that. Your car will be here in a couple of minutes."

He opened the door and Tasha went inside.

"How can you be so cruel?" Dianne called out from behind him.

He turned. "How can you have the nerve to ask me to drop everything and deal with your problems? You cheated

on me, left me and put my business at risk through your un-
bridled greed."

A pair of headlights flashed through the trees.

"Your ride is here, Dianne." He stepped through the open
door, closing it to then face Tasha.

Matt leaned back against his front door as if he expected
his ex-wife to try to break it down.

"Sorry about that," he said.

Tasha wasn't sure how she should feel about the exchange.
She knew divorces could be acrimonious, and Matt was
within his rights to stay at arm's length from his ex-wife,
but Dianne had seemed genuinely upset.

"It sounds like she could use a friend," Tasha said.

"Truthfully, it's hard to know for sure. She's a drama
queen. Her reaction to a fire or a flood is the same as her reaction to a broken fingernail."

Tasha tried not to smile. It didn't seem like there was anything funny in the situation.

Matt pushed away from the door. "She was supposed to
be in France. She was supposed to stay in France. I'd really
hoped she'd stay in France forever. I need a drink. Do you
want a drink?"

He started down the short staircase to the glass-walled
living room. On the way, he seemed to absently hit a wall
switch, and the long fireplace came to life. Fed by gas, it was
glassed in on all sides and stretched the length of the living
room, separating a kitchen area from a lounge area where
white leather armchairs faced a pair of matching sofas.

Tasha knew she should head home. But she found herself
curious about Matt, about Dianne, and she'd been sipping on
sodas all night long. A real drink sounded appealing.

"I'm thinking tequila," Matt said as he passed one end of
the fireplace into the kitchen.

Tasha threw caution to the wind. "I love margaritas."

"Margaritas it is." He opened a double-doored stainless steel refrigerator. "We have limes." He held them up. "Glasses are above the long counter. Pick whatever looks good."

Feeling happier than she had any right to feel about sharing a drink with Matt, Tasha moved to the opposite end of the kitchen. Near the glass wraparound wall, she opened an upper cupboard, finding a selection of crystal glasses. She chose a pair with deep bowls and sturdy-looking bases.

"Frozen or on the rocks?" he asked.

"Frozen."

He was cutting limes on an acrylic board. "There should be some coarse salt in the pantry. Through that door." He pointed with the tip of his knife.

Tasha crossed behind him to the back of the kitchen.

The walk-in pantry was impressive. It was large and lined with shelves of staples and exotic treats.

"Do you like to cook?" she called out to him.

"It's a hobby."

She located the coarse salt and reemerged. "I wouldn't have guessed that."

"Why?" He seemed puzzled.

"Good question."

"Thanks."

"You seem—" she struggled to put it into words "—like the kind of guy who would have a housekeeper."

"I do."

"Aha!"

"She's not a cook. I decided a long time ago that I couldn't do everything around here and run a business, too, so I chose to do the things I like the best and give up the things I didn't enjoy."

"What is it you like best?" Tasha helped herself to one of the limes. She'd spotted some small glass bowls in the cupboard and retrieved one for the salt.

"Cooking, working, the gym."

"Dating?" she asked.

"That's recent."

"But you like it. You do it quite a lot now."

"I do, and I do." He stilled then and seemed to think more about his answer.

"What?" she prompted.

"Nothing. That about sums it up."

"What about friends?"

"Caleb and TJ? Sure. I hang with them whenever I can. With them being so close, we don't really plan anything, we just drop by. It's kind of like background noise."

"Like family," Tasha mused as she cut the lime in half.

She'd observed the relationship between the three men. It was as if they were brothers. She'd like to have close relationships like that. But she had absolutely nothing in common with her two sisters.

"Like family," Matt agreed. "They're going to flip when they find out Dianne's back."

"Do you expect her to stick around?"

It was none of Tasha's business. And she wasn't entitled to have an opinion one way or the other. But she liked that Matt was single. After all, a fantasy was fun only if it had an outside chance of coming true.

The knife slipped, and she cut her finger.

"Ouch!"

"What happened?" He was by her side in an instant.

"I wasn't paying attention."

"Is it bad?" He gently took her hand. "You're bleeding."

"Just a little. Don't let me ruin the drinks."

He seemed amused by her priority as he reached for a tissue from a box on the counter. "Let's get you a bandage."

"I bet it'll stop on its own." She pressed the tissue against the cut.

"This way." He took her elbow. "We can't have you bleeding into the salt."

He led her up the steps toward the entry hall, but then veered right, taking her down a long hallway with plush silver-gray carpet. Some of the doors were open, and she saw an office and what looked like a comfortable sunroom.

"This is nice," she said.

They entered one room, and it took her only a second to realize it had to be the master bedroom. She hesitated and stumbled.

"Careful," he said.

"This is…"

He paused and glanced around at the king-size bed with taupe accents, two leather and polished metal easy chairs, twin white bedside tables and a polished oak floor with geometric-patterned throw rugs. Here, too, there were walls of windows looking across the bay and over the forest.

"What?" he prompted.

"Big." She settled on the word. She wanted to say *intimidating*, maybe even *arousing*. She was inside Matt's bedroom. How had that happened?

"I know there are bandages in here." He gestured toward the open door to an en suite.

She struggled to even her breathing as she entered the bathroom. "This is big, too."

"I like my space. And I didn't need too many bedrooms, so it was easy to go for something big for the master."

She moved with him to the sink.

"Do you want kids?" She had no idea where that question came from.

He shrugged. "Dianne didn't want them. I'm easy. I could go either way." Then he gave a chuckle as he opened the upper cabinet.

Tasha averted her eyes. Seeing what was in his medicine cabinet seemed far too personal.

"I figure once I meet Caleb's twins," Matt continued, "it'll either make me want some of my own, or cure me of that idea forever."

He set a small bandage on the counter, shut the cabinet and gently removed the tissue from her cut finger.

"I can do this myself," she said, feeling the effects of his closeness.

She liked his smell. She liked his voice. His touch was gentle.

"Two hands are better than one." He turned on the water, waited a moment then tested the temperature.

Tasha could feel her heart tap against her rib cage. Her gaze was caught on his face. He looked inordinately sexy, and amazingly handsome.

"What about you?" he asked, his attention on her finger as he held it under the warm flow of water.

"Huh?" She gave herself a mental shake and shifted her gaze.

"Do you want kids?"

"Sure. I suppose so. Maybe."

"You haven't thought about it?"

She really hadn't. Her focus had been on her career and making it to the top of her profession. "I guess I'm not in any rush."

"Fair enough." He wrapped the small bandage around the end of her finger and secured it in place. "Good as new."

"Thank you." She made the mistake of looking into his eyes.

His twinkled, and he smiled at her.

For a moment, she thought he was going to kiss her. But instead, he brushed a playful finger across the tip of her nose and stepped back.

"Our ice is melting," he said. "We better blend those drinks."

Sitting across from Dianne at a window table in the Crab Shack, Matt had asked for a water. Now he wished he'd ordered something stronger.

He hadn't wanted to meet her at his house. He was steadily working to move forward with his life; he didn't want to go backward.

"You gave him control of your *entire* portfolio?" Matt couldn't believe what he was hearing.

"He had a mansion," Dianne said, a whine in her tone. "He had a yacht and a jet and memberships at these exclusive clubs. He didn't even want a prenup. Why wouldn't I trust him?"

"Because he was a con artist?"

She gave a pout. "How was I supposed to know that?"

"You weren't," Matt acknowledged. "What you were supposed to do was keep control of your own assets." He was appalled that she would be so blindly trusting of anyone.

"It was all in French," she said. "I couldn't understand it. It only made sense for him to take over the details."

It sounded like the man had taken over a whole lot more than just the details of her assets. He'd obviously taken complete charge of her money. But Matt wasn't about to lengthen the debate. He'd agreed to meet Dianne today, but he had no intention of stepping back into her life, no matter what kind of mess she'd made of it. And by the sounds of it, she'd made a pretty big mess.

Her exotic French husband had taken her money and disappeared, leaving a trail of debts and charges of fraud behind him.

"So, what are you going to do?" he asked her.

She opened her eyes wide, and let her lower lip go soft. "I miss you, Matt."

"Oh, no you don't." He wasn't going there. He so wasn't going there. "What are you going to do, Dianne? *You*, not me. You alone."

Her eyes narrowed, and he stared straight back at her.

Then what looked like fear came over her expression. "I don't know *what* to do."

"Get a job?" he suggested.

The Crab Shack waitress arrived with their lunches, lobster salad for Dianne, a platter of hand-cut halibut and fries for Matt. He had developed a serious fondness for the Crab Shack's signature sauces.

Dianne waited for the waitress to leave. Then she leaned forward, her tone a hiss. "You want me to work? I don't know how to work."

"I don't *want* you to do anything."

"I can't do it, Matt," she said with conviction.

"I'm not going to solve this for you, Dianne." He popped a crispy fry into his mouth.

"You've got loads of money."

"No, I don't. I had to refinance everything to pay your settlement. And even if I did have money, you have no call on it."

"That's my home." She gazed out the window at the cliff side where his house jutted out over the ocean.

"It *was* your home. Temporarily. I paid for the house. Then I paid you half its value in the divorce. Then you sucked out every nickel of my business profits."

"But—"

"Enjoy your lunch, Dianne. Because it's the last thing I'll ever buy for you."

Her mouth worked, but no sounds came out.

"Matt?" Caleb's wife, Jules, arrived to greet him, her tone tentative. She'd obviously caught the expression on his face and Dianne's and knew something was wrong.

He neutralized his own expression. "Jules. How are you?"

Her stomach was well rounded from the twins she was carrying.

"Doing great." She rested a hand on her belly. Then she turned to Dianne, obviously waiting for an introduction.

"Jules, this is my ex-wife, Dianne."

Jules's eyes widened. "Oh."

"She's in town for a short visit."

"I see." It was pretty clear Jules didn't see. As far as Caleb or anybody else knew—including Matt—Dianne had planned to spend the rest of her life in France. "It's nice to meet you, Dianne. Welcome to the Crab Shack."

Dianne didn't respond, her face still tight with obvious anger.

"Are you coming to the chamber of commerce gala?" Matt asked Jules, ignoring Dianne's angry silence.

Jules was coming up on six months pregnant, and her doctor had advised her to keep her feet up as much as possible.

"I'll definitely be there. I'm good for a couple of hours between rests."

"You look fantastic."

Dianne shifted restlessly in her seat, drawing Jules's brief glance.

"You'll be there?" Jules asked Matt.

"I agreed to speak."

"Oh, good. You'll be so much more entertaining than the mayor, and that Neil Himmelsbach they had on Labor Day. I should let you two finish lunch."

Matt rose to give her a quick hug and a kiss on the cheek. "Nice to see you, Jules."

She patted his shoulder. "Better go." Her attention moved to the front entrance, where a customer had just entered the restaurant.

Matt did a double take when he saw it was Tasha. He paused, watching, wondering what she was doing at the Crab Shack.

"Sit *down*," Dianne said to him.

Matt didn't want to sit down. He was waiting to see if Tasha would notice him and react in some way, maybe a wave, maybe a hello, maybe to come over and talk to him.

But she didn't.

"I'll be right back," he said to Dianne, taking matters into his own hands.

"But you—"

He didn't hear the rest.

"Hey, Tasha," he said as he came up to her.

She looked at him in obvious surprise.

"Lunch break?" he asked.

He couldn't help but notice she was dressed in clean jeans and wearing a silky top and her leather jacket. She didn't dress like that for work.

"I started early this morning." It was obviously an explanation for her boss.

"You don't need to punch a time clock with me. Take as long a lunch as you want."

"I'm having lunch with Jules."

"Really?" The revelation surprised Matt. He hadn't realized she and Jules were getting to know each other.

"She invited me," Tasha said.

"That's nice. That's good."

Tasha's gaze strayed past him, and he could tell the moment she spotted Dianne.

"This is going to sound weird," he said, moving in closer and lowering his voice.

"That would be a first."

"Can I kiss you on the cheek? Maybe give you a hug? Just a little one."

Tasha stared up at him. "Are you drunk?"

"No. It's Dianne. It would help me if she thought you and I were… You know…"

"I take it she wants to rekindle something?"

"She wants money above anything else. If she believes I'm with you, it'll stop her from thinking romancing me to get it is an option."

Tasha glanced around the crowded restaurant. It was clear she was checking to see if they knew anyone else here.

"Jules will understand the score," he assured her, assuming she didn't want anyone to get the wrong impression. "I'm sure Caleb's told her all about Dianne."

"I'm not worried about Jules."

"Then what?"

Something was making her hesitate. He dared to hope she

was remembering those brief moments in his bathroom when he'd felt a connection to her. Could she be worried about developing feelings for him?

But then her answer was brisk. "Nothing. I'm not worried about anything. Kiss on the cheek. Quick hug. No problem."

Though he was disappointed, Matt smiled his appreciation. "You're the best."

"You gave me a twenty percent raise. It's the least I can do."

So much for his musings about her feelings for him.

"This is above and beyond," he whispered as he moved in for the cheek kiss.

She smelled amazing. She tasted fantastic. It was brutal for him to have to pull back.

"You know it is," she said with a thread of laughter.

He gave her an equally quick hug. "I owe you."

He squeezed her hands, wishing with all his heart the crowd would disappear from around them and he could be alone with her.

Then he turned away, heading back across the restaurant to where Dianne was glaring at him.

Five

As always, Tasha was impressed with the Crab Shack. During lunch, it was bright and airy, with wooden tables, a casual ambiance and sweeping views of the ocean and cliffs. Then for dinner, they set out white tablecloths, candles and linen, bringing up the outdoor lighting, making it both elegant and cozy. It was no surprise that its popularity was growing fast.

Back in Boston, expensive restaurants had been the norm for her on weekends. She'd been forced to stop whatever it was she was doing far too early in the afternoon, clean up, dress up and go on parade to impress her parents' associates with their three perfect daughters.

She had wasted so much valuable time primping and engaging in inconsequential conversation. To top it off, the food had been absurdly fancy, not at all filling. There were many nights that she'd gone home and made herself a sandwich after dining at a five-star restaurant.

But the Crab Shack wasn't like that. The food was good and the atmosphere comfortable. It was refreshing to be in a place that was high quality without the pretention.

"It's this way," Jules told her, leading a weaving pattern through the tables.

Tasha gave in to temptation and took a final glance at Matt's handsome profile before following.

Jules led her into an office next to the kitchen. "It's a bit crowded in here," she apologized.

"Not a problem."

The square room held a desk with a computer and stacks of papers, a small meeting table with three chairs, and a couple of filing cabinets. It wasn't as bright as the restaurant, but there was a window that faced toward the marina and Caleb's partially built Neo restaurant.

Jules gestured to the table. "I hope you don't mind, I ordered us a bunch of appetizers."

"That sounds great." Tasha wasn't fussy.

"I do better with small things." Jules gave a self-conscious laugh. "That sounds silly. What I mean, is I tend to graze my way through the day rather than attempting a big meal."

"I can imagine your stomach is a bit crowded in there."

Jules was glowing with pregnancy.

"Between the three of us, we do fight for space," Jules said.

Tasha smiled.

Jules opened a laptop on the table. "We have security video files going back three weeks."

"I really appreciate this," Tasha said.

"Caleb has ordered more security cameras, better security cameras with higher resolution. The ones we have now don't show a lot of detail at a distance."

"Anything will help."

Jules moved the mouse and opened the first file.

To say it was boring was an understatement. They set it on a fast speed and sat back to watch.

"Matt's not normally an affectionate guy," Jules mentioned in an overly casual tone.

The observation took Tasha by surprise. It also put her on edge.

"He hugged you," Jules continued, turning her attention from the screen to Tasha. "And he kissed you."

"On the cheek," Tasha said, keeping her own attention on the view of the marina.

The camera angle showed the gate, part of the path and the first thirty feet of the pier. The yachts rocked in fast motion, while people zipped back and forth along the pier and the sun moved toward the horizon.

"It's still odd for him."

"It was for Dianne's benefit," Tasha said. "He wants her to think we're dating."

"They're divorced."

Tasha gave a shrug. "It could be ego, I suppose."

"That doesn't sound like Matt."

Tasha agreed. "Dianne seems to need money. Matt's worried she'll try to latch back onto him."

"Now, *that* sounds like the Dianne I've heard about."

On the video, the lights came up as the sun sank away.

That had been Tasha's impression, as well. "I only met her briefly last night, but—"

"Last night?" The interest in Jules's tone perked up.

"We were coming back from the Edge, and she was waiting for him."

"A date?"

"No." Tasha was careful not to protest too strongly. "A coincidence. I was there talking to the mechanics in the area. I wanted to know if anyone else was having weird engine failures."

"That's a good idea."

"I thought so. Wait, what's that?" Tasha pointed at the screen. The picture was dark and shadowy, but it looked like someone was scaling the fence. She checked the date and time stamp. "That's the night before *Orca's Run* went out."

"So, it was sabotage."

"Maybe."

They watched the figure move along the pier. It went out of the frame before coming to the slip for *Orca's Run*.

"That has to be it," Jules said.

Tasha wasn't as ready to draw a concrete conclusion. "It didn't look like he was carrying anything, no fuel, no water."

"But he broke in. Whoever it was, was up to no good."

"It's evidence of that," Tasha agreed. She'd hate to assume something and potentially be led in the wrong direction. "We should watch the rest of the video. I can do it myself if you're busy."

"No way. This is the most interesting thing I've done lately. And I'm supposed to sit down every couple of hours." Jules made a show of putting her feet up on the third chair.

There was a light rap on the door, and a waitress pushed it open, arriving with a tray of appetizers and two icy soft drinks.

"I hope you're hungry," Jules said as the server set everything down on the table.

"I'm starving."

"Make sure you try the crab puffs. They're my secret recipe."

"I'm in." Tasha spread a napkin in her lap and helped herself to a crab puff.

"I've been going nuts over smoked salmon," Jules said, going for a decorative morsel on a flat pastry shell. "I don't know why, but my taste buds are big into salt."

Tasha took a bite of the crab puff. It was heavenly. "Mmm," she said around the bite.

Jules's eyes lit up. "See what I mean?"

"You're a genius."

"They're the most popular item on the menu. Caleb wants to steal them for Neo, but I won't let him."

"Stick to your guns," Tasha said before popping the second half of the crab puff into her mouth.

"Oh, I will. We're each half owner of the other's restaurant now, but it's still a competition."

"I hope you're winning. Wait. Take a look." Tasha drew Jules's attention to the laptop screen.

The figure returned to the gate and seemed to toss something over the fence beside it. The two women watched as he climbed the fence, then appeared to look for the object. But then something seemed to startle him, and he ducked away, out of camera range.

"He was up to something," Jules said.

"That was definitely odd," Tasha said. "It could have been tools. I wish we had a better view."

The video got boring again, nothing but yachts bobbing on the midnight tide. Jules took a drink and went for another crab puff.

The office door opened and Caleb appeared.

"How's it going in here?" he asked.

Jules stretched her back as she spoke. "We saw a guy climb over the fence onto the pier and sneak back out again."

Caleb moved past Tasha. He stood behind Jules's chair and began rubbing her shoulders.

"What did he do?" Caleb asked.

"He threw something over the fence," Jules said. "Tasha thinks it might have been tools."

"We couldn't tell for sure," Tasha put in, not wanting to jump to conclusions. "And the frame's not wide enough to see what he did while he was on the pier. It could have been nothing."

The door opened again, and Matt joined them.

"I'll bet it was something," Jules said.

"You'll bet what was something?" Matt asked, glancing around at all three of them.

Tasha couldn't stop herself from reacting to his presence. She imagined his hands on her shoulders, the way Caleb was rubbing Jules's.

"There was a guy," Jules said.

"It might have been something," Tasha jumped in, shaking off the fantasy. "A guy climbing the fence and leaving again. But we couldn't see enough to be sure. There's a lot more video to watch."

"Dianne gone?" Jules asked Matt.

"Hopefully."

"What happened?" Caleb asked. "I didn't expect to see her back in Whiskey Bay…well, ever."

"Neither did I," Matt said. "It turns out her French finance tycoon wasn't all he claimed to be."

"Uh-oh," Caleb said.

"All that money she got in the divorce…"

"No way," Caleb said.

Tasha kept her attention fixed on the screen and away from Matt.

"All gone," he said.

"How is that possible?" Jules asked. "You gave her a fortune."

"The court gave her a fortune," Matt said.

"You didn't fight it."

"I wanted my freedom."

"And she's back anyway," Caleb said. "That didn't work out so well."

"You're not giving her any more money," Jules said.

Tasha wanted to echo the advice, but she didn't feel that it was her business to jump in. Matt and Caleb had been good friends for years. She knew Matt thought of him as a brother.

"I told her to get a job."

"Good advice."

"Let's see if she takes it." Matt didn't sound convinced she would.

Then his hand did come down on Tasha's shoulder. The warmth of his palm surged into her, leaving a tingle behind.

"Anything else going on?"

It was daylight on the video now and people were moving back and forth along the pier: crew, customers, delivery companies and Matt. She watched Matt stride confidently through the frame, and her chest tightened.

She had to struggle to find her voice. "Nothing out of the ordinary. It would be nice to have a wider view."

"You've looked through your own footage?" Caleb asked Matt.

"We have," Matt answered. "But the camera showing the main part of the pier had malfunctioned."

"Malfunctioned?" The skepticism was clear in Caleb's tone.

"We had a technician look at it. The case was cracked.

Salt spray got in and caused corrosion. It might be wear and tear, but it could have been pried open on purpose."

"Who would do that?" Caleb asked. "Why would they do that?"

"I wish I knew," Matt said. "I hate to suspect staff, but there are a couple of new hires on the dock. We're checking into their histories."

"Why would staff have to climb the fence?" Caleb asked.

"Not everyone has the combination," Tasha answered. "Not everyone needs it."

"I don't hand it out to the new hires," Matt said.

Tasha knew the footage narrowed the list of suspects—at least of possible staff members as suspects.

"A little to the left," Jules said on a moan.

Caleb smiled down at his wife.

Matt's hand tightened around Tasha's shoulder.

Arousal washed through her with the force of a riptide.

She ordered herself to concentrate. She refocused on the screen, desperately hoping something would happen on the pier to distract her from his touch.

Matt was happy to speak at the chamber of commerce's annual Christmas gala. He knew the chamber did important work. He'd benefited from its programs in the past. Without its loan guarantees, he never could have purchased Whiskey Bay Marina, never mind grown it to the size it was today, or recovered from the financial hit of his divorce for that matter.

He'd started life out in South Boston. There, his father ran a small residential construction company, while his mother did home care for the elderly. His parents had raised six children. Matt was the youngest and easily the most ambitious. His older siblings all still lived in the South Boston area, most working for his father, all raising families of their own.

They seemed content with barbecues and baseball games. But Matt had wanted more. He'd always wanted more out of life. He'd worked construction long enough to put himself through college and set aside a nest egg. Then he'd bought a few fixer-upper houses, sold them for a profit and finally ended up on the West Coast taking what was probably a ridiculous risk on the Whiskey Bay Marina. But it had turned out well.

It seemed people found it an inspiring story.

Finished with his cuff links and his bow tie, he shrugged into his tux jacket. It was custom fitted and made him feel good, confident, like he'd arrived. It was a self-indulgent moment, dressing in an expensive suit for a fine dinner. And he'd admit to enjoying it.

Tonight he had an additional mission. The owners of the three other marinas in the area would be at the gala. A competitor would have a motive for sabotage. Matt had never trusted Stuart Moorlag. He seemed secretive, and Matt had heard stories of him cutting corners on maintenance and overbilling clients. He could have financial troubles.

There was a knock on the front door, and Matt made his way past the living room to the entry hall. He'd ordered a car for the evening to keep from having to drive home after the party.

But it wasn't the driver standing on his porch. It was Tasha.

"We have a problem," she said without preamble, walking into the entry hall.

"Okay."

Then she stopped and looked him up and down. "Wow."

"It's the gala tonight," he said.

"Still. Wow."

"Is *wow* a good thing?"

"You look pretentious."

"So, not good." He told himself he wasn't disappointed. He'd have been surprised if she had liked him in a tux. He wished she did. But wishing didn't seem to help him when it came to Tasha.

"Good if pretentious was your goal."

"Well, that was a dig."

"I'm sorry. I didn't mean it to sound like that. What I meant was, you'll impress all the people at what I'm guessing is a very fancy event tonight."

"Thanks. I think." It wasn't quite an insult anymore, but it wasn't quite a compliment either. He decided to move on.

He gave a glance to his watch. He had a few minutes, but not long. "What's the problem?"

"The sabotage is escalating."

That got his instant and full attention. Tasha definitely wasn't one to exaggerate.

"How?" he asked.

"I found a peeled wire in the electric system of *Salty Sea*. It seemed suspicious, so I checked further and found a fuel leak."

He didn't understand the significance. "And?"

"Together, they would likely have started a fire."

"Are you *kidding* me?" He couldn't believe what he was hearing.

"I wish I was."

"People could have been *hurt*?"

A fire on a boat was incredibly serious, especially in December. If they had to jump into the water, hypothermia was the likely result.

"Badly," she said.

He didn't want to leave her to attend the gala. He wanted to explore what she'd found, talk this out. He wanted to plan their next move.

"I have to go to the gala," he said, thinking maybe they could meet later. "I'm speaking at it. And the other marina owners will be there. I was going to use it as an excuse to feel them out."

She didn't hesitate. "I want to come."

The statement took him completely by surprise. He couldn't help but take in her outfit of cargo pants, jersey top and a work jacket.

"Not like this," she said, frowning at him.

"Do you have something to wear?"

Her hands went to her hips, shoulders squaring. "You don't think I can clean up, right?"

Registering the determination in her expression—although he had his doubts—he wasn't about to argue that particular point. He looked at his watch again. "I don't have a lot of time. My car will be here in a few minutes."

Her lips pursed in obvious thought. "I don't have a ball gown in my room. But did Dianne leave anything behind? A dress or something?"

"You want to wear my ex-wife's clothes?" Matt was no expert, but that didn't sound like something an ordinary woman would volunteer to do.

"What've you got?"

"You're serious?"

"You don't think I look serious?" she asked.

"You look very serious."

"So?"

He gave up, even though he had major reservations about how this was going to turn out. "There are some things left in the basement. This way." He led her around the corner to the basement stairs.

He flipped the switch as they started down. "She was a shopaholic. Didn't even bother to take all of it with her. Some of the stuff has probably never been worn."

They went past the pool table and entered a cluttered storage room. The dresses were in plastic film, hanging on a rack, jackets and slacks beside them, shoes in boxes beneath. "I hadn't had the time to get rid of it yet."

"I'll be quick," Tasha said, marching up to the rack and searching her way through.

After a few minutes, she chose something red with sparkles.

"Wow," he said.

"You don't think I can pull off red?"

"It's very bold."

"Trust me. I want them to notice." She hunted through the shoe boxes. "I don't suppose you know what size shoe your ex wore?"

"I have no idea."

Tasha held up a black pump, turning it to various angles. Then she straightened, stripped off her boot and fuzzy sock and wiggled her foot into it.

"It'll do," she said.

"Seriously? Just like that?" He'd seen Dianne spend two hours choosing an outfit.

"You said you were in a hurry." Tasha brushed by him.

"Yes, but…"

"Then, let's do this."

He followed behind, shutting off the lights as they went. "You're a strange woman."

"If by *strange*, you mean *efficient*, then thank you."

By *strange*, he meant *unique*. She was like nobody he'd ever met. Not that it was a bad thing. It was a good thing. At the very least, it was an entertaining thing.

"Yes," he said. "I meant efficient."

"Can I borrow your bathroom?"

"Be my guest."

There was another knock on the front door. This time it was sure to be the driver.

"I have to speak at eight," he called to Tasha's back as she scooted down the hall, clothes bundled in her arms, wearing one work boot and one bare foot.

She waved away his warning, and he turned to answer the door.

Ten minutes later, or maybe it was only five, she emerged from the hallway looking ravishing.

Matt blinked, thinking it had to be an optical illusion. No woman could go from regular Tasha to this screaming ten of a bombshell in five minutes. It wasn't possible.

Her hair was swooped in a wispy updo. The straps of the

dress clung to her slim, creamy shoulders. It sparkled with rhinestones as she walked, the full red skirt swishing above her knees. Her green eyes sparkled, the dark lashes framing their beauty. Her lips were deep red, her cheeks flushed, and her limbs were long, toned and graceful.

He couldn't speak.

"Will I do?" she asked, giving him a graceful twirl. Her tone was softer than normal, her words slower and more measured.

He opened his mouth. "Uh…"

"Don't get all fussy on me, Matt. It was a rush job."

"You look terrific."

She glanced down at herself. "Good enough."

"No, not just good enough. Jaw dropping. How did you do that?" How had this gorgeous, feminine creature stayed hidden beneath the baggy clothes and grease all this time?

"I took off my other clothes and put these ones on."

There was more to it than that. "Your hair?"

"Takes about thirty seconds. Are you ready?"

"I'm ready." He was more than ready. He was *so* ready to go on a date with Tasha.

Okay, so they were investigating more than they were dating. And the new information she'd just brought him was unsettling. They'd have to talk more about that in the car.

But she was more ravishingly beautiful than he could have possibly imagined, and she was his partner for the gala. He felt fantastic, far better than he had merely putting on the fine tux, maybe better than he'd felt in his whole life.

At the ballroom in downtown Olympia, Tasha felt like she was stepping into her own past. She'd been to this party dozens of times, the chamber orchestra, the high-end hors d'oeuvres, the glittering women and stiffly dressed men. And, in this case, the rich Christmas decorations, floral arrangements, garlands of holly and evergreen, thousands of white lights, swirls of spun-glass snow and a huge Christmas tree on the back wall, covered in oversize blue and white ornaments and twinkling lights.

"You going to be okay in all this?" Matt asked as they walked through the grand entry.

"I'll be fine." She could do this in her sleep.

"We'll have to sit down near the front. They want me close by for my presentation."

"No problem." She was used to her parents being VIPs at events in Boston. From the time she was seven or eight, she'd learned to sit still through interminable speeches and to respond politely to small talk from her parents' friends and business connections. "Shall we mingle our way down?"

He looked surprised by the suggestion. "Sure."

"Can you point out the other marina owners?"

They began walking as Matt gazed around the room.

"Hello there, Matt." A fiftysomething man approached, clasping Matt's hand in a hearty shake.

"Hugh," Matt responded. "Good to see you again." He immediately turned to Tasha. "This is Tasha Lowell. Tasha, Hugh Mercer owns Mercer Manufacturing, headquartered here in Olympia."

Tasha offered her hand and gave Hugh Mercer a warm smile. "It's a pleasure to meet you, sir." She quickly moved her attention on to the woman standing next to Hugh.

Hugh cleared his throat. "This is my wife, Rebecca."

"Hello, Rebecca," Tasha said, moving close to the woman, half turning away from Hugh and Matt. If she'd learned anything over the years, it was to keep her attention firmly off any man, no matter his age, who had a date by his side. "I *love* that necklace," she said to Rebecca. "A Nischelle?"

Rebecca returned Tasha's smile. "Why, yes. A gift from Hugh for our anniversary."

"How many years?" Tasha asked.

"Twenty-five."

"Congratulations on that. Was it a winter wedding?"

"Spring," Rebecca said. "We were married in New York. My parents lived there at the time."

"I love New York in the spring." Tasha put some enthusiasm in her voice. "Tell me it was a grand affair."

"We held it at Blair Club in the Hamptons."

"Were the cherry blossoms out?" Tasha had been to the Blair Club on a number of occasions. Their gardens were legendary.

"They were."

"It sounds like a dream." Tasha looped her arm through Matt's, taking advantage of a brief lull in the men's conversation. "Darling, I'm really looking forward to some champagne."

He covered her hand. "Of course. Nice to see you, Hugh. Rebecca, you look fantastic."

"Enjoy the party," Hugh said.

Tasha gave a cheery little wave as they moved away.

"*What* was that?" Matt whispered in her ear. "Cherry blossoms? You made it sound like you'd been there."

She didn't want to reveal her past to Matt. She wanted it kept firmly there—in the past.

"Cherry blossoms seemed like a safe bet in the spring. You don't mind my pulling us away from the Mercers, do you? They're not our target."

Too late, it occurred to her that Matt might have some kind of reason for chatting Hugh up. She hoped she hadn't spoiled his plans.

"You were right. They're not our targets." He put a hand on the small of her back. "There. Two o'clock. The man with the burgundy patterned tie."

Ignoring the distraction of Matt's touch, Tasha looked in that direction. "Tall, short brown hair, long nose?"

"Yes. That's Ralph Moretti. He owns Waterside Charters. They're smaller than Whiskey Bay, but they're closest to us geographically."

"Is he married?"

Matt's hand flexed against her waist. "Why?"

"So I know how to play this."

"Play this?"

"If he's up to something, he'll be a lot more likely to give information away based on my giggling, ingenuous questions than if you start grilling him. But if he has a wife who's likely to show up halfway through the conversation, it going to throw us off the game."

"You're going to flirt with him?" Matt did not sound pleased.

"I wouldn't call it flirting."

"What would you call it?"

"Disarming." She sized up Ralph Moretti as they drew closer.

"There's a distinction?" Matt asked.

"Absolutely."

They'd run out of room. Ralph was right there in front of them.

"Moretti," Matt greeted with a handshake.

"Emerson," Ralph responded.

Ralph's guarded tone immediately piqued Tasha's interest.

It took about half a second for his gaze to move to her and stop.

"Tasha Lowell." She offered him her hand.

"Call me Ralph," he told her, lightly shaking. He was gentlemanly enough not to squeeze.

"Ralph," she said with a bright smile. "Matt tells me you have a marina."

"I do indeed."

"I have a thing for boats."

The pressure of Matt's hand increased against her back.

"Really?" Ralph asked, with the barest of gazes at Matt. "What do you like about them?"

"Everything," she said. "The lines of the craft, the motion of the waves, the way they can take you on adventures."

"A woman of good taste," he said.

"How far do you go?" she asked.

Matt coughed.

"Excuse me?" Ralph asked.

Tasha leaned in just a little bit. "Your charters. Oregon? California? Do you go up to Canada?"

"Washington and Oregon mostly," he said.

"Are you looking to expand?"

Ralph's gaze flicked to Matt. Was it a look of guilt?

"Maybe in the future," Ralph said, bringing his attention back to Tasha.

"What about markets?" she asked.

His expression turned confused, maybe slightly suspicious.

"Do you get a lot of women clients?" She breezed past the topic she'd intended to broach. "Party boats. Me and my friends like to have fun."

"Ah," he said, obviously relaxing again. "Yes. Waterside can party it up with the best of them."

"Whiskey Bay—" she touched Matt lightly on the arm "—seems to go for an older crowd."

He stiffened beside her.

She ignored the reaction and carried on. "I don't know if I've seen your advertising. Do you have a website?"

"We're upgrading it," Ralph said.

"Expanding your reach? There is a Midwest full of clients right next door. Spring break would be an awesome time to get their attention."

"Do you have a job?" Ralph asked her.

She laughed. "Are you offering?"

"You'd make one heck of an ambassador."

She held up her palms. "*That's* what I keep telling Matt."

"You're missing the boat on this, Matt." There was an edge of humor to Ralph's tone, but he kept his gaze on Tasha this time.

Matt spoke up. "She can have any job she wants at Whiskey Bay for as long as she wants it."

Ralph quickly glanced up. Whatever he saw on Matt's expression caused him to take a step back.

"It was nice to meet you, Tasha," Ralph said.

"Moretti," Matt said by way of goodbye. Then he steered Tasha away.

"Well, that was interesting," Tasha said.

"Is *that* what you call it?"

"Yes. He wants to expand his business. And something about you put him on edge."

"Because he was trying to steal my date."

"Nah." She didn't buy that. "He reacted when I asked if he was expanding. And he's revamping his website. He's looking to make a move on your customers."

"He's looking to make a move on you."

"Don't be so paranoid."

A wave of mottled mauve silk moved in front of them.

"Hello, Matt."

Tasha was astonished to come face-to-face with Dianne.

"Dianne," Matt said evenly. "What are you doing here?"

"Enjoying the season." She eyed Tasha up and down, a delicate sneer coming over her face as she looked down her nose.

Tasha had seen that expression a thousand times, from women and girls who were certain they were a cut above a plain-looking mechanic and not the least bit hesitant to try to put Tasha in her place.

Still, Tasha felt like she should muster up some sympathy. Dianne was in a tough spot.

"Merry Christmas," she said to Dianne in her most polite voice.

"I see you got out of those oily rags," Dianne returned. "Is that last year's frock?"

"I like to think Bareese is timeless," Tasha said with an air of indifference.

Dianne wrinkled her nose.

Tasha took in Dianne's opulent gown. "Your Moreau must

be worth a fortune." She blinked her eyes in mock innocence. "You could auction it after the party. For the funds, I mean."

Matt stifled a laugh.

Dianne's complexion went a shade darker. "Why, you little—"

"Time for us to take our seats," Matt said, taking Tasha's hand. "What is up with you?" he asked as they moved away.

Tasha winced. "I'm sorry. I shouldn't have said that."

"That's not what I meant."

"It was really rude."

The lights blinked, and the MC made his way onto the stage.

"Dianne was the one who was rude. And I'm grateful," Matt continued, picking up the pace. "You keep it up, and she's going to leave town in a hurry. Besides, she deserves a little of her own medicine for once."

Matt's odd compliment warmed Tasha. She wasn't particularly proud of going mean-girl debutante on Dianne. But Matt's life would be better if Dianne left. And Tasha found she wanted that, too.

Six

Matt's speech had gone well. People had laughed in the right spots and clapped in the right spots. He was happy to have been entertaining. But he was happier still to watch Tasha's face in the front row. Every time she'd smiled, he'd felt a physical jolt.

He couldn't believe how feminine, how beautiful, how downright elegant she'd looked surrounded by the splendor of the ballroom. And now, swaying in his arms, she was graceful and light. The transformation was astonishing. Cinderella had nothing on Tasha.

"You've done this before," he guessed as he guided her into a slow spin.

"Danced? Yes, I have."

"Been the belle of a ball."

She smiled at that as she came back into his arms. "I'm far from the belle of any ball."

The dance floor was nicely filled. The music was superb, and beautiful women floated past on the arms of their partners. None could hold a candle to Tasha.

"You are to me," he said.

"You're flirting?"

"No. I'm disarming."

She gave a short laugh. "It's not going to work."

He supposed not. "You have definitely done this before."

"I've been to a few balls in my time."

"I never would have guessed. I mean before tonight I never would have guessed. You sure don't let on that there's an elegant lifestyle in your past."

"I don't spend much time dwelling on it."

"You're very good at this." He'd been stunned at her ability to make small talk, to get the other marina owners to relax and be chatty. They hadn't come up with any solid leads or suspects, but they'd learned Waterside Charters was expanding and Rose and Company was taking delivery of a new seventy-five-foot yacht in the spring. Both would be competing head-to-head with Whiskey Bay Marina.

"You don't have to like something to be good at it."

"Do you like dancing?" he asked, wanting to hear that she did, hoping to hear that she liked dancing with him.

"Yes. But not necessarily in these shoes."

He glanced down. "Do they hurt?"

"You've never worn high heels before, have you?"

"That would be a no."

"Yes, they hurt. They don't fit all that well."

"Should we stop?"

"I'll survive."

He debated finding them a place to sit down. But he liked having her in his arms. So he settled for slowing the pace, inching even closer to her. It was a good decision.

"So where did you attend these formative balls?"

"Boston, mostly. Some in New York. Once in DC when I was around seventeen."

"You're a fellow Bostonian?" He was surprised by the idea.

She drew back to look at him. "You, too?"

"Southie."

"And you left?" She seemed to be the one surprised now.

"I did. The rest of my family stayed in the neighborhood, though."

The song ended, and another started. He danced them right through the change.

"Brothers and sisters?" she asked.

"Three brothers, two sisters. I'm the youngest. What about you?"

"Wow. Six kids?"

"Yep."

"Your parents must have been busy."

"It was busy and crowded. I had absolutely no desire to live like that. Where did you grow up?"

Since she'd talked about balls and flying off to New York and Washington for parties, he was guessing she wasn't a Southie.

It took her a minute to answer. "Beacon Hill."

So, she had lived posh.

"It's nice up there," he said.

"It's snooty up there. At least the people I knew, and especially my parents' friends and associates. I couldn't wait to get away from their judgment."

"Spread your wings?" he asked.

"Something like that. Yes, very much like that."

He found the insight quite fascinating. "Does your family still live there?" For some reason, learning she was from Boston made their connection seem stronger.

"Absolutely."

"Brothers and sisters?" he asked when she didn't offer details.

"Two sisters. Youngest here, too," she said with an almost guilty smile.

"Makes it easy to get away with things," he said.

"Made it easy to slip town."

"Are you close to them?"

He'd never heard her talk about her family. Then again, they hadn't had a whole lot of in-depth conversations about either of their backgrounds. Mostly he liked to leave his alone.

"We don't have a lot in common." There was something in her tone, not regret exactly, but acceptance of some kind.

"I hear you," he said, recognizing the emotion.

He and his family seemed to operate in different dimensions. He saw value in financial success. He'd worked hard to get here, and he had no problem enjoying it. The rest of his family held financial success in suspicion. He'd tried to get his mind around it, but at the end of the day he just couldn't agree.

Dianne had understood. It was one of the things that first drew him to her. She liked the finer things, and was unapologetic about her ambition. That trait might have turned on her now. But the theory was still sound. He was still going after success.

"My family..." he began, wondering how to frame it. "They're content to pay the bills, throw potlucks on Sundays, take their kids to community center dance lessons and cheer for the Red Sox at tailgate parties."

"Oh, the horror," she mocked.

"I want more," he said.

"Why?"

"Why not?" He looked around the ballroom. "This is nice. This is great. And who wouldn't want the freedom to take any trip, eat at any restaurant, accept any party invitation."

"Are you free, Matt? Really?"

"I'm pretty damn free."

His choice of lifestyle had allowed him to work hard, to focus on his business, to succeed in a way that was satisfying to him. If he'd strapped on a tool belt in Southie, met a nice woman and had a few kids, it would have meant being dishonest about himself.

It was Tasha's turn to look around the room. "This all doesn't feel like a straitjacket to you?"

"Not at all." He didn't understand her attitude. She seemed to be having a good time. "And I'm here by choice."

"These people don't seem disingenuous to you?"

"Maybe the ones that are sabotaging my boats. But we're not even sure they're here. It's just as likely they're at the Edge."

"What's wrong with the Edge?"

"Nothing. Did I say there was something wrong with the Edge?"

"You used it as a negative comparator to this party."

"It's a whole lot different than this party. Like Beacon Hill and Southie. Do you honestly think people prefer Southie?"

"They might."

Matt wasn't buying the argument. "Sure. People from Southie are proud. I get that. Believe me, I've lived that. But you give them a real and serious choice, they'd be in Beacon Hill in a heartbeat."

Tasha's steps slowed. "It's kind of sad that you believe that."

"It's not sad. And I don't just believe that. It's true."

She stopped. "Thanks for the dance, Matt."

"You can't honestly be annoyed with me." It wasn't reasonable.

"I'm going to rest my feet."

"I'll take you—"

"No." She put her hand on his chest and moved back. "Go mingle. I'll see you later on."

"Tasha." He couldn't believe she was walking away.

Tasha wasn't angry with Matt. She felt more sad than anything.

Sure, he'd made some money in his life. But up to now he'd struck her as being mostly down-to-earth. She'd thought the money was incidental to him, running a business that he loved. It was disappointing to discover that his goal had been wealth.

Seeing him tonight, she realized her initial instincts were right. He was exactly the kind of man she'd left behind. Ironically, he was the kind of man her parents would love.

If this were a Boston party, her parents would be throwing her into his arms. The Lowells were an old Bostonian family, but her parents wouldn't hold Matt's Southie roots against him, not like her grandparents or great-grandparents would have.

In this day and age, money was money. Her father in particular respected men who pulled themselves up from nothing. It was a darn good thing they weren't back in Boston right now.

She crossed the relative quiet of the foyer, following the signs to the ladies' room. She needed to freshen up. Then she really was going to find a place to sit down and rest her feet. The shoes might be slightly large, but they were also slightly narrow for her feet, and she had developed stinging blisters on both of her baby toes.

As she passed an alcove, she caught sight of Dianne's unmistakable mauve dress. Dianne was sitting on a small bench, gazing out a bay window at the city lights. Her shoulders were hunched, and they were shaking.

Tasha felt like a heel. One of the reasons she avoided these upper-crust events was that they brought out the worst in her. She seemed too easily influenced by the snobbery and spitefulness.

The last thing in the world she wanted to do was comfort Matt's ex-wife. But it was partly her fault that Dianne was upset. She'd been insufferably rude in suggesting she auction off her dress.

Tasha took a turn and crossed the alcove, coming up beside Dianne.

Dianne looked up in what appeared to be horror. She quickly swiped her hand beneath her eyes. But the action did nothing to hide the red puffiness.

"Are you okay?" Tasha asked.

"I'm fine." Dianne gave a jerky nod. "Fine."

It was patently obvious it was a lie.

Tasha gave an inward sigh and sat down on the other end of the padded French provincial bench. "You don't look fine."

"I got something in my eyes. Or maybe it was the perfume. Allergies, you know."

Tasha told herself to accept the explanation and walk away. She didn't know Dianne. Given the circumstances, fake though her relationship with Matt was, she was likely the last person Dianne wanted to talk to. But it would be heartless to simply leave her there.

"You're obviously upset," Tasha said.

"Aren't *you* the observant one."

"Don't."

"Why? What do you want? To rub my nose in it? Again?"

"No. I want to apologize. I was nasty to you earlier. I'm really sorry about that. I thought you were…" Tasha struggled for the right words. "Stronger. I thought you were tough. I didn't mean to upset you."

Dianne's tone changed. "It's not you. It's…" She closed her eyes for a long second. A couple of more tears leaked out. "I can't," she said.

Tasha moved closer. She put a hand on Dianne's arm. "Will talking to me make it any worse?"

Dianne drew in a shuddering breath. She opened her eyes and gazed at Tasha for a long time.

"I've made such a mess of it," she finally said.

"You mean losing the money?"

Dianne nodded. "François was charming, attentive, affectionate. Matt was working all the time. He never wanted to travel with me. I thought… I thought our life together would be different. But it wasn't any fun. It was all work, work, work. And then I met François. It wasn't on purpose. I'm not a bad person."

"I don't think you're a bad person." Tasha was being honest about that.

Dianne might not be the right person for Matt, and maybe she had a selfish streak, but right now she just seemed sad and defeated. Tasha would have to be made of stone not to feel sympathy.

Dianne gave a brittle laugh. "I thought François not wanting a prenup was the perfect sign, the proof that he loved me for me. He seemed to have so much more money than I did. And he'd invested so successfully, that I thought I couldn't lose…but I did lose. And I'd hoped Matt…"

"What exactly do you want from Matt?" Tasha might be sympathetic, but she knew sympathy alone wouldn't help Dianne.

Dianne shrugged. "At first… At first I thought there might still be a chance for us. I was the one who left him, not the other way around. I thought he might still…" She shook her head. "But then I met you, and I realized he'd moved on."

A part of Tasha wanted to confess. But she knew Matt wouldn't consider a reconciliation with Dianne. And telling Dianne she and Matt weren't dating would be a betrayal of him. She couldn't do it.

"So, now what?" Tasha asked.

"I don't know." Dianne's tears welled up again. "I honestly don't know."

"You need to know," Tasha said as gently as she could. "You need a plan. You need to take care of yourself."

"I can't."

"You can. Everyone can. It's a matter of finding your strengths."

"My strength is marrying rich men."

"That's not true. It's not your only strength. And even if it was your only strength, it's a bad strength, not one you want to depend on. Look what happened last time."

"I have no money," Dianne said, looking truly terrified. "I've nearly maxed out my credit cards. I've missed payments. They're going to cancel them. I really will be selling my clothes on the street corner."

"Okay, now you're being melodramatic."

"I'm not," she moaned.

"What about your family? Could you stay with family?" Dianne gave a choppy shake of her head. "There's no one."

"No one at all?"

"My dad died. My stepmother sent me to boarding school. She couldn't wait to get me out of the house."

"Are they in Washington State?"

"Boston."

Tasha was surprised. "You, too?"

Dianne stilled. "You're from Boston?"

"I am."

Dianne searched Tasha's face. "You're a Lowell. *The* Lowells?"

Tasha was embarrassed. "I don't know if there are any 'the' Lowells."

"The Vincent Lowell Library?"

"My grandfather," Tasha admitted.

"Does Matt know?" Before Tasha could respond, Dianne continued on a slightly shrill laugh. "Of course he knows. Why didn't I see that before? You're his dream match."

Tasha was confident Matt didn't know. And there wasn't much to know anyway. The Lowells might be an old Boston family. But there were plenty of those around. It wasn't all that noteworthy.

"Do you want to go back to Boston?" Tasha asked, turning the subject back to Dianne.

"No. Never. That's not in the cards."

"Do you want to stay here?" Tasha was trying to find a starting point, any starting point for Dianne.

Dianne lifted her head and looked around. "There's nothing left for me here either." Her voice cracked again. "Not without Matt."

"You really need to think about a job. You're young. Get started on a career. Did you go to college?"

"Only for a year. I took fine arts. I didn't pass much."

"What would you like to do? What are you good at?"

Dianne looked Tasha in the eyes. "Why are you doing this?"

"I want to help," Tasha answered honestly.

"Why? I'm nothing to you."

"You're a fellow human being, a fellow Bostonian, part of the sisterhood."

Dianne gave a hollow laugh. "There's no sisterhood. Are you a do-gooder? Am I a charitable thing for you?"

"No." Tasha gave it some thought. "I don't know, really." It was as honest as she could be.

"I gave parties," Dianne said in a tired, self-mocking voice. "I can make small talk and order hors d'oeuvres."

The germ of an idea came to Tasha.

Caleb had fancy restaurants all over the country. Perhaps Jules, Tasha knew her better than she did Caleb, might be willing to help Dianne.

"I'm going to ask around," Tasha said.

"Matt won't like that."

"Doesn't matter." Tasha wasn't sure if Matt would care or not. But surely he'd be in favor of anything that put Dianne back on her feet, helped her to take care of herself.

She didn't have to make a big deal with Jules. And if Matt did find out, he'd see the logic and reason, she assured herself. He was a very reasonable man.

On the drive home, Tasha seemed lost in thought. Either that, or she was still annoyed with Matt for appreciating financial security. He'd wanted to talk about it some more, maybe help her understand his motivations. But he didn't want to rekindle their argument. He liked it better when they were on the same side of something.

"Could we really have had a fire?" he asked her.

She turned from where she'd been gazing out the window into the darkness. "What?"

"On *Salty Sea*. Would there have been a fire?"

"Yes. Almost certainly. The fuel from the fuel line leak would have sprayed across the spark from the electric short, and *bam*, it would have ignited."

"It looks odd," he said. "You talking about the inner workings of an engine while you're dressed like that."

"That's why I don't dress like this."

"You look terrific."

"I feel like a fraud. I can't wait to get out of this getup." She reached down and peeled off the black pumps.

The action was sexy, very sexy. He immediately imagined her shrugging down the straps of the dress. He shifted in his seat.

"Feet sore?" he asked.

"And how. Steel-toed boots might be clunky, but they're built for wearing, not for show."

"They wouldn't go with the dress."

"Ha ha."

"And it would be hard to dance in them."

Tasha curled her legs up on the seat, a hand going to one foot to rub it. "I'd be willing to give it a shot."

Matt curled his hands to keep them still. "The new cameras are being installed tomorrow."

"We need them. I'm doubling up on my inspections. Alex and I are going to check every boat the morning before it leaves port."

"Won't that be a lot of work?"

"I couldn't do everything I'd like, not without hiring three more mechanics. But we can cover the basics."

"Do you need to hire someone else?"

She switched her self-massage to the other foot. "I'll call in all the contract mechanics. But I have to believe this is temporary. The next time that guy tries something, we're going to catch him on camera and have him arrested."

Matt gave in to temptation and reached across the back seat for one of her feet.

"Don't." She jumped at his touch.

He looked meaningfully at the driver. "It's just a foot."

"That's not a good idea."

He ignored her, settling her foot in his lap and pressing his thumb into the arch.

She gave a small moan.

"Those blisters look awful," he said.

Her baby toes and the backs of her heels were swollen and red.

"They'll heal."

"Why didn't you say something?"

"I did."

"You didn't tell me how bad it was." He massaged carefully around the swollen skin.

"That feels good," she said.

"Do you need to take the day off tomorrow?"

"You're funny."

"I'm serious. It's Sunday. Don't work."

"And let Alex do it all?"

He didn't have a comeback for that. He had to admire Tasha's work ethic. Still, he couldn't let her burn herself out. And her feet were going to be painful tomorrow.

"As long as I don't put on the same shoes," she said. "I'll use bandages and wear thick socks. I'll be fine."

"You're a trouper," he said with honest admiration.

The driver slowed as Matt's driveway came up on the right.

"You're easily impressed," she said.

"Not really."

They were silent as the car cruised through the trees to the house. While they did, Matt continued his massage. His image of her strong and sturdy on the job faded to how she was now…soft, smooth, almost delicate.

When the car came to a stop, he reached to the floor and collected her shoes.

"What are you doing?" she asked.

"Wait right there." He exited from his side and tipped the driver.

Then he went around to her, opening the door and reaching in to lift her from the seat.

"Oh, no you don't," she protested.

"Oh, yes I do. You can't put these shoes back on. You'll burst the blisters and bleed all over the place."

"Then I'll walk barefoot."

"Over the rocks and through the mud? Hang on."

"Put me down."

But even as she protested, he hoisted her easily into the air, and her arms went around his shoulders. He pushed the sedan door shut with his shoulder and started to the stairs that led to the staff quarters.

"This is ridiculous," she said. "Nobody better see us."

"It's dark."

"There are lights on the porch."

"It's after midnight. Everyone will be asleep."

"They better be."

He couldn't help but smile to himself. He'd learned by now that Tasha hated anything that made her look remotely weak.

"Blisters are nothing to be ashamed of," he said.

"I'm not ashamed of having blisters." She paused. "I'm ashamed of having some Neanderthal carry my apparently feeble self to my room."

"I'm wearing a tux."

"So?"

"I'm just saying, your average Neanderthal probably didn't wear a tux."

The joke got him a bop in the shoulder.

"Not much of a comeback," he said.

"We're here. You can put me down now."

"Not yet." He mounted the stairs for the second floor.

She squirmed in his arms. "I can walk on wooden stairs in my bare feet."

"Splinters."

"I'm not going to get splinters."

"We're here. Where's your key?"

"You can put me down on the mat."

"I like holding you." He did. He was in absolutely no hurry to put her down. "You're light. You're soft. Your hair smells like vanilla."

"It's not locked," she said.

"Are you kidding me?" he barked. "With all that's been going on?" He couldn't believe she would be so cavalier about her own safety.

He reached for the doorknob and opened the door. He set her down on the floor inside and immediately turned on the light switch, checking all the corners of the room, the small sitting area, the kitchenette, the double bed. Then he crossed to the bathroom and opened up the door.

"Matt, this is silly."

He was annoyed with her. No, he was downright angry. Somebody was targeting them for unknown reasons, and so far it had more to do with her than with anybody else at Whiskey Bay, and she was leaving her door unlocked?

He turned back. "Please tell me you lock it at night."

She looked decidedly guilty. "I can start."

He took the paces that brought him in front of her. "You bet your life you're going to start. You're going to start tonight, now, right away."

"You don't need to get upset," she said.

"You're scaring me." His gaze fell on her gorgeous green eyes. "I'm afraid for you." He took in her flushed cheeks. "I want to protect you. I…"

Their gazes meshed, and the sound of the surf filled the silence. She just stood there in the shadows looking like his fondest dream come true.

She looked delicate and enticing. Her hair was mussed. One strap had fallen down, leaving her shoulder bare. He wanted to kiss her shoulder. He wanted to taste that shoulder more than he'd ever wanted anything in his life.

He gave in.

He leaned forward, gently wrapping his hands around her upper arms. He placed a light kiss on her shoulder. Then he tasted her skin with the tip of his tongue. He kissed her again, made his way to her neck.

She tipped her head sideways, giving him better access.

He brushed her hair back, kissing his way to her ear, her temple, her closed eyes and finally her mouth.

She kissed him back, and he spread his fingers into her hair.

She stepped into his arms, an enchanting, elegant, utterly feminine woman pressing against his hard, heated body.

He reached out and pushed the door shut behind her.

He deepened their kiss.

He began to unzip her dress, paused, running his hands over the smooth skin of her back.

"Don't stop," she gasped. "Don't, don't stop."

Seven

Everything flooded from Tasha's mind, everything except the taste of Matt's lips, the feel of his hands and the sound of his voice. His heart beat against her chest where they pressed together. She wanted this. No, she needed this. Whatever it was that had been building between them for days on end was bursting out, and there was no stopping it.

She pushed off his tux jacket, and he tossed it on the chair. She tugged his bow tie loose, and it dangled around his neck. She kissed his square chin, struggled with the buttons of his shirt, while his hands roamed her back.

His hands were warm, the fingertips calloused. As she peeled away his tuxedo, the urbane facade seemed to melt away along with it. He was tough underneath, muscular and masculine. A small scar marred his chest, another across his shoulder.

She kissed the shoulder and traced a fingertip along his chest. "What happened?"

"Working," he answered, his breathing deep. "Winch handle and a rogue wave."

"You should be more careful."

"I will."

She couldn't help but smile at his easy capitulation.

His hands went to her dress straps. He eased them down, baring her breasts in the cool air.

"Gorgeous," he said stopping to stare.

It had been a long time since a man had seen her naked, never if you didn't count an eighteen-year-old freshman. She was glad it was Matt, glad he seemed pleased, happy to bask in the heat of his gaze.

He slowly reached out, brushing his thumb across her

nipple. She sucked in a breath, a shudder running through to her core. She closed her eyes, waiting for him to do it again.

"Oh, Tasha," he whispered, his hand closing over her breasts.

She tipped her head for his kiss, and her dress slithered to the floor.

His palms slipped to her rear, covering her satin panties. His lips found hers again, his kiss deep and delicious. His shirt separated, and they were skin to skin.

"You're so soft." His hand continued its exploration of her breast.

Rockets of sensation streamed from her hard nipples to the apex of her thighs.

Impatient, she reached for his belt, looping it free, popping the button of his pants and dragging down the zipper.

He groaned as her knuckles grazed him.

Then he scooped her back into his arms and carried her to the double bed, stripping back the blankets to lay her on the cool sheets. He was beside her in a moment, shucking his pants.

He came to his knees, hooking his thumbs in the waist of her panties, drawing them slowly down, to her thighs, to her knees and over her ankles.

He kissed her ankle, then her knee, then her thigh and her hip bone, making his way to her breasts, kissing them both, making her heartbeat echo all through her.

She raked her fingers into his hair. A buzzing started within her, making her twitch with need.

"You have a condom?" she asked breathlessly. She was woefully unprepared.

"I've got it," he said. "Don't worry."

He rose up and kissed her mouth. Then his hands went on a glorious exploration, touching her everywhere, discovering secrets, making her writhe with impatience and need.

"Please, Matt," she finally whimpered.

"Oh, yes," he said, levering above her, stroking her thighs. She watched him closely as he pressed slowly, steadily inside.

She rocked her hips upward, closing her legs around him.

He moved, pulling out, pushing in, grasping her to him as he kissed her deeper and deeper. She met his tongue thrust for thrust, and her hands gripped his back. She needed an anchor as gravity gave way.

The room grew hotter. The waves sounded louder on the rocks below. Matt's body moved faster, and she arched to meet him, the rhythm increasing.

Fulfillment started as a deep glow, burning hotter, moving outward, taking over her belly, then her breasts, then her legs and her arms. It tingled in her toes and in the roots of her hair. She cried out as sensation lifted her. Then she flew and then floated.

"Tasha," Matt cried, his body shuddering against her.

She absorbed every tremor, his body slick, his heartbeat steady. Her waves of pleasure were unending, until she finally fell still, exhausted, unable to move beneath his comfortable weight on top of her.

She didn't know what she'd done.

Okay, she knew what she'd done. She knew exactly what she'd done. She also knew she shouldn't have done it.

"Stop," he muttered in her ear.

"Stop what?"

He rose up on an elbow. "I can feel you second-guessing yourself."

"We can't undo that," she said.

"Who wants to undo it?"

"We do. We should. That wasn't part of the plan."

"There was a plan?"

"Quit laughing at me."

He enveloped her in a warm hug.

It shouldn't have felt so great. It couldn't feel this great.

"Oh, Tasha. We made love. People do it all the time. The world will keep spinning, I promise."

"Maybe *you* do it all the time."

"I didn't mean that the way it sounded." He eased back to look at her again. He smoothed the hair from her eyes. "I don't do it all the time. My marriage was on the rocks for quite a while. And since then… Well, I've only just started dating again."

Tasha shouldn't have cared whom Matt had been with before her. But she found herself glad that he hadn't had an active sex life. She didn't want it to matter, but it did.

"I'm—" She stopped short, realizing she was going to sound hopelessly unsophisticated.

His eyes widened, and he drew sharply back. "You weren't…"

"A virgin? No. I would have said something."

"Thank goodness."

"I did have a boyfriend," she said. "Right after high school."

"One?" Matt asked. "Singular?"

"I couldn't date anyone in trade school. There were three women in a class of thirty-six. We were way too smart to get involved with anyone. It could have killed our chances of being treated as peers."

"I suppose," Matt said. Then he touched a finger to the bottom of her chin. "So, you're saying one then? Just the one guy?"

"Just the one," she admitted, feeling a bit foolish. She should have kept her mouth shut.

"Tasha Lowell." His kissed her tenderly on the mouth. "I am honored."

"Oh, that didn't sound outmoded at all."

He grinned. "You could be honored back at me."

"Okay," she said, fighting a smile. "Matt Emerson, I am honored. And I'm embarrassed. And I'm certainly soon to be regretful."

"But not yet?" he asked on an exaggerated note of hope-fulness.

"I can feel it coming."

"You have nothing to regret."

She wriggled to relieve the pressure on her hip, and he eased off to one side.

"You said that about our kiss," she said, sitting up and pulling a sheet over her breasts.

"Did you?" He traced a line along her knuckles.

"I don't know." Things had changed so fundamentally between them. Was that single kiss to blame?

She didn't want to talk about it right now. She didn't want to dissect this.

"I could stay," he offered in a soft voice.

She jumped an inch off the bed and her voice rose an octave. "What?"

"I don't have to rush off."

"Yes, you do." She looked around for her clothes, realizing she needed to get out of the bed right now. "You can't stay here. It's the staff quarters. You need to get out while it's still dark, before anybody starts work."

He didn't look happy. But he also seemed to understand. "I know. This isn't exactly discreet. But I don't want to leave you." He reached for her.

She evaded his grasp. "If you don't. If somebody sees you, then it's trade school all over again. Only this time I had a one-night stand with the teacher."

His brow went up. "How am I the teacher?"

"You know what I mean. You're in a position of authority. It's worse than sleeping with a peer. I lose any and all credibility. Everybody's reminded that I'm not one of the guys."

"They respect you, Tasha. And who says this is a one-night stand?"

"Who says it's not? So far that's exactly what it is."

"But—"

"But nothing, Matt. The mathematical odds that this leads to something, I mean something besides a fling based on chemistry alone, are, I don't know, maybe five, six percent.

The mathematical odds of this leading to the dismantling of my credibility and reputation are around ninety. What would you do if you were me?"

"Where did you come up with five or six percent?"

"I did a quick calculation in my head."

"That's insane." He reached for her again, and she backed to an ever safer distance.

She didn't want him to leave. But he had to leave. He had to leave now before she weakened.

"Please, Matt," she said.

He hardened his jaw. "Of course." He threw back the covers and came to his feet.

She didn't want to watch him walk naked across the room. But she couldn't help herself. He was magnificent, and the sight of him brought back instant memories of their lovemaking.

Her skin flushed. Then goose bumps formed. But she had to be strong. She would force herself to let him leave.

With Noah Glover's electric expertise to guide them, Matt, Caleb and TJ had spent the day installing the new security cameras. Now as a thank-you, Matt was hosting dinner for Caleb and Jules, TJ and Jules's sister, Melissa, along with Noah.

Watching Caleb with Jules, and Noah with Melissa, Matt couldn't help thinking about Tasha. She'd made herself scarce all day, while he'd spent most of it watching for her. He couldn't stop thinking about her. He'd lain awake half the night thinking about her, wishing he could have slept with her. After their mind-blowing lovemaking, his arms felt completely empty without her.

"I hope the extra cameras do the trick," TJ said as he joined Matt by the dining table.

Matt was setting out plates and glasses, since Jules had all but kicked him out of the kitchen.

"I don't care what it takes," Matt responded. "I'm catching this guy and throwing him in jail. His last stunt could have caused a fire. People could have been seriously hurt, or worse."

"Your competition?" TJ asked, gazing through the glass wall to the marina below.

"I talked to all of them at the gala last night. Waterside Charters is expanding, and Rose and Company bought a new seventy-five-footer. Both would be happy to steal business from me. But I don't see them doing it this way."

"Then what?" TJ asked.

"If I have my way, we'll find out soon." Matt took in the overview of the marina, his gaze settling on the staff quarters. Tasha was there.

Giving up fighting with himself, he extracted his cell phone. "I'll just be a minute," he said to TJ, then moved down the hall.

He typed into his phone: Dinner with Caleb and Jules at my place. Talking about the new cameras. Can you come?

He hit Send and waited. It was a stretch of an excuse, but he didn't care. He wanted her here with him.

Jules and Melissa were laughing in the kitchen. TJ's voice blended with Caleb's and Noah's. Everybody sounded happy. It had been a good day's work. It was a good night with friends. Matt should have felt terrific.

His phone pinged with Tasha's response. Just leaving. Meeting some people for drinks.

Disappointment thudded hard in his stomach. He wanted to ask who. He wanted to ask where. Mostly, he wanted to ask why she'd choose them over him.

"Hey, Matt?" Noah appeared and moved down the hall toward him.

"Hi. Thanks again for your help today."

"Sure." Noah looked nervous.

"What's up?" Matt asked.

Noah glanced down the hall behind him. "You mind if I hijack dessert tonight?"

"You brought dessert?"

"No, no. I brought a bottle of champagne."

Matt waited for the explanation.

"And this," Noah said, producing a small velvet box.

There was no mistaking the shape of the box.

"Are you serious?" Matt asked, surprised.

Noah flipped it open to reveal a diamond solitaire. "Dead serious."

"Are you sure?" Matt lowered his voice. "I mean, not are you sure you want to propose, Melissa is amazing. Are you sure you want to do it in front of us?"

Noah gave a self-conscious grin. "You've all been fantastic. You're all family. I really think she'd want to share the moment."

"That's a bold move. But you know her better than the rest of us. Well, maybe not better than Jules. Does Jules know?"

"Nobody knows."

"Okay." Matt couldn't help but grin. He had to admire Noah for this one. "Dessert's all yours."

Noah snapped the ring box shut and tucked it back in his pocket.

Matt slapped him on the shoulder as they turned for the living room. "I thought you looked a little overdressed tonight."

It was rare for Noah to wear a pressed shirt, jacket and slacks. He was more a blue jeans kind of guy.

"Everything's ready," Jules called out from the kitchen.

"Let's get this show on the road," Melissa added.

Matt and TJ took the ends of the rectangular table, with Caleb and Jules along the glass wall, and Noah and Melissa facing the view.

Matt lit the candles and Caleb poured the wine. Caleb had the best-stocked cellar, and he always brought along a few bottles. Matt had long since given up trying to compete.

"Why haven't you decorated for the holidays?" Jules asked Matt, gazing around the room. "No tinsel? No tree?"

Caleb gave a grin as he held the baked salmon platter for Jules. "Our place looks like Rockefeller Square attacked the North Pole."

"You don't even have a string of lights," Melissa said, helping herself to a roll.

"There's not a lot of point." Matt wasn't about to put up the decorations he'd shared with Dianne. And he didn't care enough to go shopping for more.

"Is it depressing?" Jules asked him, looking worried. "Being here on your own for Christmas?"

Depressed was the last thing Matt was feeling. Relieved was more like it. The last Christmas with Dianne had been painful.

"I'm fine," he told Jules. "I'm just not feeling it this year."

"Well, I can't stand it," Melissa said. "We need to do something. You do have decorations, right?"

"Whoa," Noah said. "That's up to Matt."

"No big deal," Matt was quick to put in. The last thing he wanted was for Noah and Melissa to get into an argument tonight.

"He needs new stuff," TJ said. "That's what I did. Well, I waited one Christmas." He sobered as he added some salad to his plate.

The table went silent, remembering the loss of TJ's wife.

He looked up at the quiet table. "Oh, no you don't. It's been two years. I'm all right, and I'm looking forward to Christmas this year."

"You'll come to our place," Jules said. "You'll *all* come to our place."

"We can figure it out closer to the day." Matt didn't want to hold her to the impulsive invitation.

It was her first Christmas with Caleb. And Noah and

Melissa would be engaged. The two sisters were working through a rocky, although improving, relationship with their father. They might not need a big crowd around them.

Matt's thoughts went back to Tasha. He wondered to what she'd done last year for Christmas. Had she gone home for a few days? Had she celebrated here with friends? He didn't know. He was definitely going to ask.

Conversation went on, and it was easy for him to coast. He laughed in the right places, made the odd comment, but his mind wasn't there. It was with Tasha, where she'd gone, what she was doing, whom she was doing it with.

As they finished eating, Matt cleared away the plates while Jules cut into the chocolate hazelnut layer cake. He couldn't take any credit for it. A local bakery, Persichetti, had delivered it earlier in the day.

"I love Persichetti cake," Melissa said with a grin. "Do you have whipped cream?" she asked Matt.

"Coming up." He had it ready.

"A man after my own heart."

Matt couldn't help but glance at Noah. But Noah just grinned and rolled his eyes. He was clearly confident in his relationship. Matt couldn't help but feel a stab of jealousy. He couldn't remember ever being that content.

When Matt sat down, Noah rose.

"Before we start," Noah said.

"No." Melissa gave a mock whine.

"Hold tight," he said to her, giving her a squeeze on the shoulder.

Then he went to the refrigerator and produced the bottle of champagne he'd squirreled away.

"We need the right beverage for this." Noah presented the bottle.

"Oh, my favorite," Melissa said, clearly mollified by the offer of champagne.

Matt quickly moved to get six flutes from his cupboard.

"Nice," Caleb said. "What's the occasion?"

"Good friends," Noah said as he popped the cork. "Good family." He filled the flutes and Matt passed them around.

Then Matt sat down again.

Noah took Melissa's hand. He raised it and gave it a gentle kiss.

Something in his expression made her go still, and everyone went quiet along with her.

"You accepted me from minute one," he said to her. "All of you." He looked around at the group. "Every one of you welcomed me in, without judging, without suspicion."

"I judged a little," Caleb said.

Jules reached out to squeeze her husband's hand.

"You were protecting Jules," Noah said. "And you were protecting Melissa. And you were smart to do that with my history."

"You proved me wrong," Caleb said.

"I did. And now, I think, I hope…" Noah drew a deep breath. "Melissa, darling." His hand went to his pocket and extracted the ring box.

When she saw it, Melissa's eyes went round, and a flush came up on her cheeks.

Matt quickly reached for his phone, hitting the camera button.

Noah popped open the box. "Marry me?"

Melissa gasped. Jules squealed. And Matt got a fantastic picture of the moment.

Melissa's gaze went to the ring, and she leaned closer in. "It is absolutely gorgeous."

"Not as gorgeous as you."

She looked back to Noah. "Yes," she said. "Yes, yes, yes!"

His grin nearly split his face. Everyone cheered.

Her hand trembled as he slipped the ring on her finger. Then he drew her to her feet and kissed her, enveloping her in a sheltering hug. He looked like he'd never let her go.

Matt took one more shot, finding his chest tight, his

thoughts going back to Tasha. He'd held her that tight and more last night. And, in the moment, he'd never wanted to let her go.

Tasha had to get away from Matt for a while. She needed to do something ordinary and find some perspective. Their lovemaking last night had tilted her universe, and she was desperate to get it back on an even keel.

She and Alex had taken a cab to the Edge tonight. They'd started with a couple of tequila shots and danced with a bunch of different guys. Then James Hamilton showed up and commandeered Alex for several dances in a row.

Tasha moved from partner to partner, and by the time she and Alex reconnected at the table, she was sweaty and on a second margarita. The drinks were bringing back memories of Matt, but she'd stopped caring.

James was talking to a couple of his friends across the room, leaving Alex alone with Tasha.

"So, are the two of you an item?" she asked Alex.

Alex shrugged. "I don't know. I like him. He seems to want to hang out a lot. Why?"

"Does it worry you?" Tasha asked. "Dating a mechanic. Do you think you'll lose your credibility? I always worried about dating someone in the business."

"It's a risk," Alex agreed, sipping some ice water through a straw. "But so far all we're doing is dancing."

"Oh." Tasha was surprised by that.

"You thought I was sleeping with James?"

"You left together the other night."

Alex laughed. "I wonder if that's what everybody thinks. And if it is…" She waggled her brows. "What's holding me back?"

Tasha felt terrible for making the assumption, worse for saying it out loud. "I didn't mean to judge, or to push you in any particular direction."

"You're not. You won't. You need to stop worrying so much. We're here to have fun."

"That's right. We are." Tasha lifted her drink in a toast.

As she clinked glasses with Alex, a man at the front door caught her attention. It was Matt. He walked in, and his gaze zeroed in on her with laser precision.

"No," she whispered under her breath.

"What?" Alex asked, leaning in to scrutinize her expression.

"Nothing. Do you mind if I dance with James?"

"Why would I mind? Go for it. I can use the rest."

Tasha slipped from the high stool at their compact round table. As Matt made his way toward her, she went off on an opposite tangent, heading straight for James.

"Dance?" she asked him brightly.

He looked a little surprised, but recovered quickly. "You bet." He took her hand.

The dance floor was crowded and vibrating, and she quickly lost sight of Matt, throwing herself into the beat of the music.

The song ended too soon, and Matt cut in. James happily gave way.

"No," Tasha said to Matt as he tried to take her hand.

"No, what?"

"No, I don't want to do this."

The music was coming up, and she had to dance or look conspicuous out on the floor. She started to move, but kept a distance between them.

He closed the gap, enunciating above the music. "We're going to have to talk sometime."

She raised her voice to be heard. "What's the rush?"

"You'd rather let things build?"

"I was hoping they'd fade."

"My feelings aren't fading."

She glanced around, worried that people might overhear. The crowd was close, so she headed for the edge of the floor.

Matt followed.

When they got to a quieter corner, she spoke again. "Give it some time. We both need some space."

"Can you honestly say your feelings are fading?"

Her feelings weren't fading. They were intensifying.

"If nothing else, we work together," he said. "We have to interact to get our jobs done. And besides, beyond anything else, I'm worried about you."

"There's nothing to worry about." She paused. "Okay, but that thing is *you*."

"Very funny. I'm watching for anything unusual."

"So am I." She'd been working on the sabotage problem all night.

"What I'm seeing is a guy."

Her interest perked up. "At the pier?"

"Not there. Don't look right away, but he's over by the bar. He's been staring at you. And it looks odd. I mean, suspicious."

"What's that got to do with your yachts?"

"I don't know. Maybe nothing."

"Probably nothing. Almost certainly nothing."

"Turn slowly, pretend you're looking at the bottle display behind the bar, maybe picking out a brand. Then glance at the guy in the blue shirt with the black baseball cap. He's slouched at the second seat from the end."

"That sounds needlessly elaborate." She felt like she was in a spy movie.

"I want you to know what he looks like. In case he shows up somewhere else."

"This is silly."

"Humor me."

"Fine." She did as Matt suggested, focusing on the bottles, then doing a quick sweep of the guy Matt had described.

He looked like a perfectly normal fiftysomething, probably a little shy and nerdy sitting alone having a drink. He wasn't staring. He was likely people watching and just happened on Tasha when Matt walked in.

She turned back to Matt. "Okay, I saw him."

"Good. You need a drink?"

"I have a drink."

Matt looked at her hands.

The truth was Tasha didn't normally leave her drinks alone. She'd done it now because Matt had thrown her when he walked in. She hadn't been expecting him, and she'd taken the first opportunity to get out of his way. She might be in a low-risk environment, but it wasn't a risk she normally took.

"I'll get myself a new drink." She started for the bar, hoping he'd stay behind. She'd come here to clear her head, avoid the memories of Matt's lovemaking. She had to focus, wanting to figure out whether the marina was in trouble…or maybe Matt was? The last thing she needed was to be distracted by his quick smile, broad chest and shoulders, his handsome face…

A tune blasted from the turntable, while voices of the crowd ebbed and flowed, laughter all around them under the festive lights. He fell into step beside her.

"I thought you were having dinner with Caleb and Jules," she said.

"Dinner ended early. Noah and Melissa got engaged."

Tasha was getting to know Melissa, and she'd met Noah a few times. "Noah proposed in front of everyone?"

"It was a daring move on Noah's part." Matt's gaze swept the room, obviously checking on the guy at the end of the bar. "I expect it left everybody feeling romantic, so they wanted to head home. Bit of a bummer for TJ. He fights it, but he's lonely. He liked being married."

"How did his wife die?" Tasha liked TJ. Her heart went out to him over the loss.

"Breast cancer."

"That's really sad."

"Yeah." Matt's voice was gruff. "It's been a tough haul. Let me get you that drink."

"I'm going to take off." She wanted to stay, but she needed to go. Clearing her head with Matt in front of her was impossible.

"We need to talk eventually."

"Later."

"I don't want you to be upset."

"I'm not. Actually, I'm not sure what I am."

He hesitated. "Okay. Fine. I don't want to push."

Relieved, she texted for a cab and let Alex know she was leaving. She knew it was the right thing to do, but she couldn't shake a hollow feeling as she headed for the parking lot.

Eight

When Tasha left the bar, the stranger left, too.

Matt followed him as far as the door, watching to be sure he didn't harass her in the parking lot. But she got immediately into a cab and left.

The stranger drove off a few minutes later in the opposite direction.

Back inside, Matt returned to the table to where Alex was now sitting.

"Hey, boss," she greeted with a smile.

"Having a good time?" he asked.

"You bet. Have you met James Hamilton?"

Matt shook the man's hand. "Good to meet you, James."

James nodded. "You, too."

Matt returned his attention to Alex. "Did you happen to notice if anyone was paying particular attention to Tasha tonight?"

Alex looked puzzled, but then shook her head. "She was dancing with lots of guys, but nobody in particular. A lot of them she knows from the area."

"Do you mean the old dude in the black cap?" James asked.

"Yes," Matt answered. "He was watching her the whole time I was here."

"Yeah. I noticed it most of the night. I don't know what his deal was. He never talked to her."

Alex looked to James. "Somebody was watching Tasha?"

"She's pretty hot," James said. "I just thought it was a bit of a creep factor. You know, because the guy was old. But he seemed harmless enough."

"He left when she left," Matt said.

James's gaze flicked to the door. "Did he give her any trouble?"

"No. I watched her get into a cab."

James gave a thoughtful nod.

"With everything that's going on at the marina…" Matt ventured.

"I know what you mean," Alex said. "It's happening more and more."

"What do you mean more and more?" Matt asked.

"Little things," Alex said. "Stupid things."

"Was there something besides the fuel leak and the electric short?"

"None worth getting excited about on their own. And we've checked the cameras. Nobody climbed the fence again."

"So a staff member? While you were open during the day?"

"It's possible. But I hear you've done at least ten background checks and didn't find anything."

Matt knew that was true.

"What's weird to me," Alex continued, "is that they're always on jobs done by Tasha."

Matt felt a prickle along his spine. "Are you sure about that?"

"Positive. We fix them. It doesn't take long."

"Why hasn't she said anything to me?" He'd hate to think the change in their personal relationship had made her reluctant to share information.

"She's starting to question her own memory. Any of them could have been mistakes. But any of them could have been on purpose, too."

"There's nothing wrong with her memory."

Tasha was smart, capable and thorough.

"I'm still wondering if it could be an inside job. I don't want to think that about any of my employees, but… As you're new to the team, has anyone struck you as suspicious?"

A hand clapped down on Matt's shoulder.

He turned quickly, ready for anything. But it was TJ.

"Didn't know you were headed out, too," TJ said.

"I didn't know you hung out here," Matt responded, surprised to see his friend.

"I spotted your car in the lot. I was too restless to sleep. Hey, Alex." Then TJ turned his attention to James, holding out a hand. "TJ Bauer."

"I know who you are," James said.

"Really?"

"My mom's on the hospital auxiliary. I hear all about your generous donations."

Matt looked to TJ. He knew TJ's financial company made a number of charitable contributions. He hadn't realized they were noteworthy.

TJ waved the statement away. "It's a corporate thing. Most companies have a charitable arm."

"They were very excited to get the new CT scanner. So on behalf of my mom and the hospital, thank you."

"I better buy you a drink," Matt said to TJ.

"You'd better," TJ returned. "So, what's going on?"

"Some guy was watching Tasha all night long."

"Tasha's here?" TJ gazed around.

Matt couldn't seem to forget that TJ had been attracted to Tasha. Sure, it was mostly from afar, and sure, he'd promised to back off. Still, Matt couldn't help but be jealous.

"She left," he said.

"Too bad." Then TJ gave an unabashed grin and jostled Matt with his elbow.

Alex watched the exchange with obvious interest.

Matt braced himself, wishing he could shut TJ up.

But TJ was done. He drummed his hands against the wooden tabletop. "Is there a waiter or waitress around here?"

"I can go to the bar," James quickly offered.

"I'll come with," Alex said, sliding off the high stool.

"Whatever they have on tap," TJ said.

"Same for me," Matt said, sliding James a fifty. "Get yourselves something, too."

"Best boss in the world." Alex grinned.

"You know how to keep employees happy," TJ said as the pair walked away.

"I wish I knew how to keep one particular employee safe."

"You've got the new cameras now."

"Alex just told me there've been a couple of other minor incidents that looked like tampering. Tasha didn't say anything to me about them." Matt was definitely going to bring that up with her. He wished he could do it now. He didn't want to wait until morning.

"She probably didn't want you going all white knight on her."

"I don't do that."

"You like her, bro."

Matt wasn't about to deny it.

"And you worry about her. And she strikes me as the self-sufficient type."

"She is that," Matt agreed. "But she knows we're all looking to find this guy. Why would she withhold information?"

"Ask her."

"I will. The other thing Alex said was the weird things only happened after Tasha had done a repair, not when it was Alex or anyone else. And this guy watching her tonight? That makes me even more curious." Matt hated to think Tasha might be some kind of target in all this.

"It seems unlikely tonight's guy is related to the sabotage," TJ said.

"He followed her out."

"Probably working up his nerve to ask her on a date."

Matt scoffed at that. "He was twice her age."

"Some guys still think they have a shot. And he doesn't know he'd have to go through you to get to her."

Matt didn't respond. He didn't usually keep things from

his friend, but he had no intention of telling TJ how far things had gone with Tasha. "I'm worried about her."

"Worry away. Just don't do anything outrageous."

Like sleeping with her? "Like what?"

"Like locking her up in a tower."

Despite his worry, Matt couldn't help but smile at that. "My place does have a great security system."

TJ chuckled. "Now *that* would be an example of what not to do."

"I won't." But there were a dozen reasons why Matt would love to lock her away in his house and keep her all to himself.

As the sun rose in the early morning, Tasha made her way up from the compact engine room into the bridge and living quarters of the yacht *Crystal Zone*. Between reliving her lovemaking with Matt and worrying about the sabotage, she'd barely been able to sleep. After tossing and turning most of the night, an early start had seemed like the most productive solution.

Now, she came to the top of the stairs in the yacht's main living area, and a sixth sense made her scalp tingle. She froze. She looked around, but nothing seemed out of place. She listened, hearing only the lapping of the waves and the creak of the ship against the pier.

Still, she couldn't shake the unsettling feeling. She wrinkled her nose and realized it was a scent. There was an odd scent in the room. It seemed familiar, yet out of place. She tried to make herself move, but she couldn't get her legs to cooperate.

She ordered herself to quit freaking out. Everything was fine with the engine. It was in better shape than ever, since she kept fussing with it. The door to the rear deck was closed. Dawn had broken, and she could see through the window that nobody was outside.

Nobody was watching her.

She forced herself to take a step forward, walking on the

cardboard stripping that covered the polished floor to protect it from grease and oil. *Crystal Zone* was going out today on a six-day run.

Then she heard a sound.

She stopped dead.

It came again.

Somebody was on the forward deck. The outer door creaked open. She grabbed for the biggest wrench in her tool belt, sliding it out. If this was someone up to no good, they were going to have a fight on their hands.

She gripped the wrench tightly, moving stealthily forward.

"Matt?" a man's voice called out.

It was Caleb.

Her knees nearly gave way with relief. Nobody had broken in. Caleb had the gate code and was obviously looking for Matt.

She swallowed, reclaiming her voice. "It's Tasha. I'm in here."

"Tasha?" Caleb appeared on the bridge. "Is Matt with you?"

"He's not here."

"I saw the light was on. Why are you starting so early?" Caleb glanced at his watch.

"Couldn't sleep," she said, her stomach relaxing. She slid the wrench back into the loop.

"Way too much going on," he said with understanding.

"I heard Melissa and Noah got engaged."

"They did. It was pretty great." Caleb moved farther into the living area. "Did Matt tell you Melissa and Jules are determined to decorate his place for the holidays?"

"I'm sure he appreciates it."

Caleb chuckled. "I'm sure he doesn't. Dianne was big on decorating."

"Oh."

"I heard you met her." Caleb seemed to be fishing for something.

"I did."

"How did it go?"

Tasha couldn't help remembering her last conversation with Dianne. "I'm not sure. She seems...sad."

The answer obviously surprised Caleb. "Sad? Dianne?"

Tasha weighed the wisdom of taking this chance to ask Caleb directly about a job. She didn't want to put him on the spot.

Then again, she didn't know him very well, so he could easily turn her down without hurting her feelings.

"Can I ask you something?" she asked.

He looked curious. "Fire away."

"I know you have Neo restaurant locations all over the country."

"We have a few."

"Dianne is in pretty dire straits. She's lost everything."

Caleb's expression hardened a shade, but Tasha forced herself to go on.

"She has no money. And she needs a job. I think she's pretty desperate."

"She snowed you," Caleb said, tone flat.

"That doesn't seem true. She didn't know I was there. And she was pretty obviously distraught. Also, she doesn't strike me as somebody whose first plan of attack would be to seek employment."

"You've got that right. She likely hasn't worked a day in her life."

"She admits she doesn't have a lot of marketable skills. But she said she can host parties. She's attractive, articulate, refined."

"What are you getting at?"

"Maybe a hostess position or special events planner somewhere...not here, maybe on the eastern seaboard?"

"Ah." A look of comprehension came over Caleb's face. "Get her out of Matt's hair."

"Well, that, and give her a chance at building a life. If she's telling the truth, and she definitely seemed sincere, she has absolutely nothing left and nowhere to turn."

"It's her own fault," Caleb said.

"No argument from me. But everybody makes mistakes."

He paused, seeming to consider the point. "I know I've made enough of them." He seemed to be speaking half to himself.

"Will you think about it?" Tasha dared to press.

"I'll see what I can do. I suppose it's the season to do the right thing."

"It is."

Light rain drizzled down from the gray clouds above, the temperature hovering in the fifties. It hadn't snowed this year. Snow was always a rare event in this pocket of the coast, and the last white Christmas had been ten years back.

"If you come across Matt, will you tell him I'm looking for him?" Caleb was probably regretting his decision to check inside *Crystal Zone*.

"Anything I can help you with?" she asked.

"Nope. I just want to warn him that Jules and Melissa are going shopping today for holiday decorations. He better brace himself to look festive."

Tasha couldn't stop a smile. "I'll tell him."

"Thanks."

"No, thank you. Seriously, Caleb, thank you for helping Dianne."

"I haven't done anything yet."

"But you're going to try."

He turned to leave, but then braced a hand on the stairway, turning back. "You do know this isn't your problem."

"I know. But it's hard when you don't have a family. People to support you."

He hesitated. "You don't have a family?"

"Estranged. It's lonely at times."

"Same with me," he said. "But my wife, Jules, Melissa,

Noah, TJ, they're good people, I've found a family here. I bet you have, too."

"Soon you'll have two more members in your new family."

Caleb broke into a wide smile. "You got that right. See you, Tasha."

"Goodbye, Caleb."

The sun was now up, and Tasha's feeling of uneasiness had completely faded. She was glad she'd asked Caleb about the job directly. It was better than dragging Jules into the middle of it.

Tasha gathered up the rest of her tools, turned off the lights and secured the doors. She'd head to the main building and get cleaned up before she started on the next job. Alex would probably be in by now, and they could plan the details of their day.

Out on the pier, she shifted the toolbox to her right hand and started to make her way to shore. Almost immediately she saw Matt coming the other way.

His shoulders were square, his stride determined and his chin was held high. She wondered if he'd found some information on the saboteur.

"Morning," she called out as she grew closer.

He didn't smile.

"Did something happen?" She reflexively checked out the remaining row of yachts. She didn't see anything out of place.

"I just talked to Caleb."

"Oh, good. He was looking for you." She struggled to figure out why Matt was frowning.

"You asked him about Dianne." The anger in Matt's tone was clear.

"I…" She'd known it was a risk. She shouldn't be surprised by his anger. "I only asked if he could help."

"Without even *telling* me, you asked my best friend to give my ex-wife a job?"

When he put it that way, it didn't sound very good.

"Only if he didn't mind," she said.

"You don't think that was unfair to him? What if he doesn't want to hire her? Heck, I'm not sure I'd want to hire her."

"Then he can say no. It was a question. He has a choice."

"You put him in an impossible situation."

"Matt, I know it was a bad divorce. Dianne might not be the greatest person in the world. But she is a person. And she is in trouble."

"She got herself into it."

"She made a mistake. She knows that."

Tasha set down the toolbox. It was growing heavy. "You can give her a break, Matt. Everybody deserves a break at some point."

"There's such a thing as justice."

"It seems she's experienced justice and then some."

"You don't know her."

"She can't be all bad. You married her. You must have loved her at some point, right?"

The question seemed to give him pause. The wind whipped his short hair, and the salt spray misted over them.

"I'm not sure I ever did," he finally said.

"What?" Tasha couldn't imagine marrying anyone she didn't love. She would never marry someone she didn't love.

"I didn't see her clearly at first. It seemed like we wanted the same things out of life."

The admission shouldn't have taken her by surprise. Matt had never made a secret of the fact that he wanted wealth, status and luxury.

"Don't be like them," she said.

He looked confused. "Like Dianne? I'm not like Dianne. I've worked hard for everything I've earned, and I appreciate it and don't take it for granted."

"I know." She did. "What I mean is, don't turn into one of those callous elites, forgetting about the day-to-day struggles of ordinary people."

"Except that Dianne is calculating."

"She needs a job."

"She does. But all she's ever aspired to is a free ride."

"Desperation is a powerful motivator. And Caleb can always fire her."

Matt clamped his jaw. "You shouldn't have interfered."

"Maybe not." She couldn't entirely disagree. "I felt sorry for her."

"Because you're too trusting."

Tasha didn't think that was true, but she wasn't going to argue anymore. She'd done what she'd done, and he had every right to be upset. "I have to meet Alex now."

"Right." He looked like he wanted to say more. "I'll catch you later."

"Sure." At this point, she had her doubts that he'd try.

Matt entered the Crab Shack after the lunch rush to find Caleb at the bar talking with his sister-in-law, Melissa.

He knew he couldn't let this morning's argument sit. He had to address it right away.

He stopped in front of Caleb, bracing himself. "I didn't mean to jump down your throat this morning."

"Not a problem," Caleb easily replied.

From behind the bar, Melissa poured them each an ice water and excused herself.

"I was shocked is all," Matt said. "Tasha put you in an awkward situation. I should have made it clear right then that I didn't want you to do it."

"It's already done."

"What?"

Caleb stirred the ice water with the straw. "Dianne has a job at the Phoenix Neo and a plane ticket to get there."

"You didn't. Why would you do that? We didn't even finish our conversation."

"I didn't do it for you, Matt. I did it for Dianne. I did it for everyone."

"She probably won't work out."

"Maybe, maybe not."

"She needs to face the results of her own actions. It's not up to you to rescue her."

"I didn't rescue her. I gave her a shot. She's lost her fortune. She's lost you. She's lost that guy she thought was going to be her Prince Charming. It's not up to me, you're right. It's up to her. She'll make it at Neo or she won't, just like any other employee we've ever hired."

Matt hated to admit it, but Caleb was making good points. Dianne was on her own now. And she'd have to work if she wanted to succeed. There was justice in that.

"And she's in Phoenix," Caleb finished. "She's not here."

"I suppose I should thank you for that," Matt said. He took a big swallow of the water. Not having to see Dianne, frankly, was a huge relief.

"You bet you should thank me for that. And that's what friends do, by the way."

"There's a fire!" Melissa suddenly cried from the opposite side of the restaurant. "Oh, Matt, it looks like one of your boats!"

Matt dropped his glass on the bar and rushed across the room. Smoke billowed up from the far end of the pier. He couldn't tell which yacht was on fire, but all he could think of was Tasha. Where was Tasha?

"Call 911," he yelled to Melissa as he sprinted for the door.

He jumped into his car. Caleb clambered in beside him. Caleb barely got the door shut, and Matt was peeling from the parking lot.

"Can you tell what's on fire?" he asked Caleb as they sped along the spit of land that housed the Crab Shack.

"It has to be a boat. *Orca's Run* is blocking the view. But I don't think it's the one on fire."

"How the hell did he do it?" Matt gripped the steering wheel, sliding around the corner at the shoreline, heading for the pier. "If it's a stranger, how did he get to another one? Everyone's been on the lookout."

"I can see flames," Caleb said. "It's bad."

"Can you see people? Tasha?"

"There are people running down the pier. I can't tell who is who."

It felt like an eternity before Matt hit the parking lot. He slammed on the brakes, but it was still a run to get to the pier. The gate was open, and he sprinted through. "Grab the hoses," he called to the deckhands and maintenance crews. Could it be one of them? Was it possible that someone on the inside had actually set a boat on fire? "Start the pumps!"

The staff drilled for fires. At full deployment, their equipment could pump over a hundred gallons a minute from the ocean.

It was the fifty-foot *Crystal Zone* that was on fire. The entire cabin was engulfed in flames, and they were threatening the smaller craft, *Never Fear*, that was moored directly behind on a floater jutting out from the pier.

He looked behind him to see three crew members lugging lengths of fire hose. Caleb was helping them. But Matt didn't see Tasha. Where was Tasha?

And then he saw her. She was climbing onto the deck of *Salty Sea*, which was in the berth next to *Crystal Zone*. It was barely ten feet away from the flames. There were clients on that boat, two families due to leave port in a couple of hours. The smoke was thick, and she quickly disappeared into it.

Matt increased his speed, running up the gangway to the deck of *Salty Sea*.

"Tasha!" His lungs filled with smoke, and he quickly ducked to breathe cleaner air.

And then he saw her. She was shepherding a mother and two children toward the gangway.

"Five more," she called out harshly as she passed him.

He wanted to grab her. He wanted to hug her. He wanted to reassure himself that she was okay. But he knew it would have to wait. The passengers needed his help.

Eyes watering, he pressed on toward the cabin.

There he met one of the dads, the other mother and the remaining two children.

"Follow me," he rasped, picking up the smallest child.

They made it quickly to the gangway, where the air was clear.

"We're missing one," Tasha said, starting back.

"Stay here!" he told her.

She ignored him, pushing back into the smoke.

Together, they found the last man. He was on the top deck, and Matt guided him to a ladder. They quickly got him to the gangway, and he made his way down.

Matt took a second to survey the disastrous scene.

Neither he nor Tasha said a word.

Caleb and the workers were connecting the lengths of hose.

Alex was preparing the pump.

His gaze went to *Crystal Zone*. She was a complete loss, and *Never Fear* was next. It was too far away from the pier. The spray wouldn't reach it.

Then Matt heard it or smelled it or felt it.

"Get down!" he shouted, grabbing Tasha and throwing her to the deck, covering her body with his and closing his eyes tight.

Never Fear's gasoline tanks exploded. The boom echoing in his ears, the shock wave and heat rushed over him. People on the dock roared in fear.

While debris rained down on him and Tasha, and his ears rang from the boom, Matt gave a frantic look to the people on the pier.

Some had been knocked down, but *Crystal Zone* had blocked most of the blast. He and Tasha had taken the brunt.

"We're good," Caleb called out to him, rushing from person to person. "We're all good."

Matt watched a moment longer before looking to Tasha beneath him.

"Are you hurt?" he asked her.

She shook her head. Then she coughed. When she spoke, her voice was strangled. "I'm fine." She paused. "Oh, Matt."

"I know," he said.

"I don't understand. Who would do this? People could have been killed."

"Yeah," he agreed, coughing himself. He eased off her. "Can you move?"

"Yes." She came to her knees.

He did the same.

She looked around. "You've lost two boats."

"Maybe three." *Salty Sea* was also damaged, its windows blown out from the blast.

Sirens sounded in the distance as the fire department made its way down the cliff road.

Matt took Tasha's hand. "We need to get off here. It's going to catch, too."

She came shakily to her feet.

Caleb met them at the bottom of the gangway.

Alex had the pumps running, and the crew was spraying water on the flames.

The fire engine stopped in the parking lot, and the firefighters geared up, heading down the pier on foot.

Matt turned Tasha to face him, taking in every inch of her. "Are you sure you're all right?"

"You're hurt," she said, pointing to his shoulder.

"You're bleeding," Caleb told him.

"It feels fine." Matt didn't feel a thing.

"You'll need stitches," she said.

"There'll be a medic here in a few minutes. They can bandage me up."

Looking around, it seemed Matt's was the only injury. He'd have plenty of attention. And his shoulder didn't hurt yet.

"Thank you." Tasha's low voice was shaking.

He wrapped an arm around her shoulders. "You probably

saved their lives." If she hadn't got everyone out of the cabin, they would have been caught in the blast.

"You, too."

He drew a deep breath and coughed some more.

"The media is here," Caleb said.

Matt realized publicity was inevitable. "I'll talk to them in a minute."

"Are you going to tell them about the sabotage?" Tasha asked.

"No. It's better that we keep that quiet for now."

"I checked *Crystal Zone* this morning. There was no reason in the world for it to catch fire." A funny expression came over her face.

"What is it?"

Her eyes narrowed.

"Tasha?"

"You're going to think I'm nuts."

"Whatever it is, tell me."

"When I came up from the engine room, I got this creepy feeling, a sixth-sense thing. It felt like somebody was watching me. But then Caleb showed up, and I thought he was the reason."

Fear flashed through Matt. "Somebody else was on the boat with you? Did you see who?"

"I didn't. I mean, besides Caleb. But now…"

"Mr. Emerson?" A reporter shoved a microphone in front of him.

Someone else snapped a picture.

He nudged Tasha to leave. She didn't need to face this.

He'd get it over with, answer their questions, get the fire out and then sit down and figure out what on earth was going on.

Nine

For the first time, Tasha wished her room in the staff quarters had a bathtub. She was usually content with a quick shower. Getting clean was her objective, not soaking in foamy or scented water.

But tonight, she'd have given a lot for the huge soaker tub from her old bathroom in Boston. She shampooed her hair a second time, trying to remove the smoke smell. She scrubbed her skin, finding bumps and bruises. And when she started to shake, she reminded herself that she was fine, Matt was fine, everybody was thankfully fine.

The police were getting involved now, so surely they'd get to the bottom of the inexplicable sabotage. Matt had said, and she agreed, this went far beyond what any of his competitors would do to gain a business advantage. So unless something had gone catastrophically wrong in an unplanned way today, they were looking for a much more sinister motive.

The firefighters had said the blaze had started in the engine room, identifying it as the source of the fire. They expected to know more specifics in the next few days.

She shut off the taps, wrapped a towel around her hair, dried her skin and shrugged into her terry-cloth robe. It was only eight in the evening, but she was going to bed. Maybe she'd read a while to calm her mind. But she was exhausted. And tomorrow was going to be another overwhelming day.

A knock sounded on her door, startling her. Adrenaline rushed her system, and her heart thudded in her chest. It was silly to be frightened. She was not going to be frightened.

"Tasha?" It was Matt.

"Yes?"

He waited a moment. "Can you open the door?"

She almost said she wasn't dressed. But the man had already seen her naked. The bathrobe, by comparison, was overdressed. She tightened the sash and unlocked the door, pulling it open.

"Hey," he said, his blue eyes gentle.

She fought an urge to walk into his arms. "Hi."

"How are you feeling?"

"I'll be fine."

"I didn't ask what you'd be. I asked how you are." He looked solid and strong, like a hug from him would be exactly the reassurance she needed right now.

But she had to be strong herself. "Sore." It was a truthful answer without going into her state of mind. "You?"

"Yeah. Pretty sore." He gestured into the room.

She stepped aside. It felt reassuring to have him here. It was good to have his company.

He closed the door and leaned back against it. "I don't think you're safe."

She was jumpy. But she knew it was a natural reaction to being so close to an explosion. She'd be fine after a good night's sleep.

"I'm okay," she said.

He eased a little closer. "We agree this wasn't a competitor. And if it's not Whiskey Bay Marina—and it's likely *not* Whiskey Bay Marina—then the next logical guess is you."

"That doesn't make sense." She couldn't wrap her mind around someone, *anyone*, targeting her.

"I'm afraid for you, Tasha."

"We don't know—"

He moved closer still. "I don't care what we know and don't know."

"Matt."

He took her hands in his. "Listen to me."

"This is wild speculation."

She tried to ignore his touch. But it felt good. It felt right. It felt more comforting than made sense. She prided herself on her independence, and here she was wishing she could lean on Matt.

"Somebody's targeted you," he said. "Somebody who's willing to commit arson and harm people."

"Why would they do that to me? Who would do that to me?"

"I don't know. All I do know is that it's happening, and you need protection. I want to do that, Tasha. I want to protect you." He squeezed her hands. "I couldn't live with myself if anything happened to you."

"You're blowing this out of proportion, Matt."

He crossed the last inches between them, and his arms brushed hers. "They set a boat on fire."

She didn't have a response for that.

"I want you to stay at the main house."

"You mean your house." That was a dangerous idea. It was a frightening idea. Just standing so close to him now, her emotions were swinging off-kilter.

"I have an alarm system. I have good locks on my doors. And I'm there. I'm *there* if anything goes wrong."

"It's nice of you to offer," she said, her logical self at odds with the roller coaster of her emotions.

She couldn't stay under the same roof as Matt, not with her feelings about him so confused, not with her attraction to him so strong, and certainly not right out there in front of the entire staff and crew of the marina.

"I am your boss, and as a condition of your employment, you need to stay safe, Tasha."

"You *know* what people will think." She grasped at a perfectly logical argument. No way, no how was she going to admit she didn't trust herself with him.

"I couldn't care less what people will think."

"I do. I care."

"Do you want a chaperone? Should we ask someone to come stay there with us?"

"That would make it look even worse."

He drew back a little and gently let her hands go, seeming to give her some space.

"I have a guest room. This is about security and nothing more. Everybody here knows you. If you don't make a big deal about the arrangement, neither will they. The police are involved. There's a serious criminal out there, and it has something to do with you."

She closed her eyes for a long second, steeling herself, telling herself she could handle it. She had control of her emotions.

He was right, and she needed to make the best of it. She'd go stay behind his locks and his alarm system. She'd be practical. She could keep her distance. And she'd keep it light.

"Do you have a soaker tub?" she joked, wincing at her sore muscles.

He gave a ghost of a smile. "Yes, I do. Get your things."

She moved to the closet where she had a gym bag, feeling every muscle involved. "I feel like I've been in a bar fight."

"Have you been in many bar fights?"

"Have you?" she countered.

"A couple. And, yeah, this is pretty much what it feels like."

Having accepted the inevitable, Tasha tossed some necessities into her gym bag, changed in the bathroom and was ready in a few minutes.

"You're frighteningly fast at that," Matt noted as they stepped onto the porch.

"I'm leaving my ball gowns behind."

"Are you going to lock it?" he asked, looking pointedly at the door.

"There's not much inside."

"With all that's going on?" He raised his brow.

"Fine. You're right. It's the smart thing to do." She dug into the pocket of her pants, found the key and turned it in the lock.

He lifted her bag from her hand. She would have protested, but it seemed like too much trouble. It was only a five-minute climb to the front door of his house. She couldn't bring herself to worry about which one of them carried her bag.

Inside Matt's house, boxes and bags littered the entryway. There were more of them in the living room, stacked on the coffee table and on the sofa and chairs.

"You did a little shopping?" she asked, relieved to have something to be amused about.

"Jules and Melissa. They were going to decorate tonight. But, well…maybe tomorrow."

"Maybe," Tasha echoed.

It was less than two weeks until Christmas, but she couldn't imagine Matt was feeling very much like celebrating the season.

He set her bag down at the end of the hall. "Thirsty?"

"Yes." She found a vacant spot on the sofa and sat down.

If Matt wanted to bring her a drink, she wasn't about to argue. He went into the kitchen, opening cupboards and sliding drawers.

Curious, she leaned forward to look inside one of the shopping bags. Wrapped in tissue paper were three porcelain snowmen with smiling faces, checkerboard scarves and top hats. They were adorable.

She spied a long, narrow white shelf suspended above the fireplace. It was sparsely decorated, so she set the snowmen up at one end.

"There's no way to stop this, is there?" Matt gazed in resignation at the snowmen.

"You don't like them?" She was disappointed.

"No. They're cute. They're different. Different is good." He had a glass of amber liquid in each hand. It was obvious from their balloon shape that he'd poured some kind of brandy.

"This is your first Christmas since the divorce." It wasn't a question. It was an observation.

"It is." He handed her one of the glasses. "Caleb gave Dianne a job in Phoenix thanks to you."

Tasha wasn't sure how to respond. She couldn't tell from Matt's tone if he was still angry. "We aren't going to fight again, are we?"

"No. I hope not. Too much else has happened."

She returned to the sofa and took a sip of the brandy.

"This is delicious," she said.

He took the only vacant armchair. "A gift from Caleb. He's more of a connoisseur than I am."

"He has good taste."

Matt raised his glass. "To Caleb's good taste."

She lifted her own. "Thank you, Caleb."

Matt sighed, leaned back in the soft chair and closed his eyes.

Tasha felt self-conscious, as if she'd intruded on his life.

She gazed at his handsome face for a few more minutes. Then her attention drifted to the glass walls, to the extraordinary view of the bay and the marina. The Neo restaurant was well under way. The job site was lit at night, a few people still working. She could see the flash of a welder and the outline of a crane against the steel frame of the building.

The yachts bobbed on the tides, a gaping black hole where the fire had burned. *Crystal Zone* hadn't been the finest in the fleet, but it was a favorite of Tasha's. She was going to miss working on it.

"You're going to have to help me," Matt said.

"Help you with what?"

He opened his eyes. "Buy a new boat. Make that two new boats."

"You'll be able to repair *Salty Sea*?"

"I think so. We'll have to strip it down, but it's not a total write-off. *Never Fear* is mostly debris at the bottom of the bay."

"Ironic that," she said.

"In what way?"

"We should have feared her."

Matt smiled. Then he took another sip of his brandy.

She set down her glass and looked into another of the shopping bags. This one contained cylindrical glass containers, stubby candles, glass beads and a bag of cranberries.

"I know exactly what to do with these," she said.

"Here we go." He sat up straighter.

She opened the bag of glass beads, slowly pouring a layer into each of the two containers. "Do you mind if I put this together?"

"Please do."

She set the candles inside, positioning them straight. Then she poured a layer of cranberries around them, finishing off with more glass beads.

While she worked, Matt rose and removed the bags from the coffee table, the sofa and elsewhere, and gathered them off to the side of the room. He positioned her finished creations in the center of the table and retrieved a long butane lighter from above the fireplace.

"You're not going to save them for Christmas?"

"I'm sure we can get more candles." He touched the lighter's flame to each wick. Lastly, he dimmed the lights. "This is nice."

When he moved past her, his shoulder touching hers, her nerve endings came to attention. He paused, and the warmth of his body seemed to permeate her skin.

She drew a deep breath, inhaling his scent. A part of her acknowledged that this was exactly what she'd feared and reminded herself she needed to fight it. Another part of her wanted the moment to go on forever.

"I'm glad you're here," he said in a soft tone.

It took a second to find her voice. She forced herself to keep it light. "Because you need help decorating?"

He didn't answer right away. When he did, he sounded disappointed. "Right. That's the reason."

She gave herself an extra couple of seconds, and then she eased away.

He seemed to take the hint and moved back to his chair.

She shook her emotions back to some semblance of normal. "So that's it?" She looked pointedly at the rest of the bags. "We're giving up on the decorating?"

"We're resting." He sounded normal again. "It's been a long day."

"Well, I'm curious now." It felt like there were unopened presents just waiting for her to dig in.

He gave a helpless shrug and a smile. "Go for it."

Tasha dug into a few more bags. She put silver stylized trees on the end tables, a basket of pinecones and red balls next to the candles. She hung two silver and snowflake-printed stockings above the fire, and wrestled a bent willow reindeer out of its box to set it up on the floor beside the fireplace.

When she discovered the components of an artificial tree, Matt gave up watching and rose to help.

"I knew you'd cave," she told him with a teasing smile.

"It says on the box that it's ten feet high. You'll never get it up by yourself."

"Oh, ye of little faith."

"Oh, ye of little height."

She laughed, amazed that she could do that at the end of such a trying day.

Together, they read the directions and fit the various pieces together, eventually ending up with a ten-foot balsam fir standing majestically in the center of the front window.

They both stood back to admire their work.

"Is that enough for tonight?" he asked.

"It's enough for tonight."

She felt an overwhelming urge to hug him. She wanted to thank him for helping with the tree. She wanted to thank him for saving her from the explosion.

More than that, she wanted to kiss him and make love to

him and spend the night in his arms. Her feelings were dangerous. She had to control them.

Steeling herself, she stepped away. "Okay to finish my brandy in the tub?"

His gaze sizzled on her for a moment.

"Alone," she said.

"I know."

She forced her feet to move.

Matt shouldn't have been surprised to find Tasha gone when he went into the kitchen for breakfast. She'd probably left early, hoping nobody would notice she hadn't slept in the staff quarters.

He wanted to text her to make sure she was all right. But he settled for staring out the window as he sipped his coffee, waiting until he spotted her on the pier with Alex. Only then did he pop a bagel in the toaster and check the news.

As expected, the fire was front and center in the local and state news. But he was surprised to see the article displayed prominently on a national site. He supposed the combination of fire, high-end yachts and an explosion, especially when there were pictures, was pretty hard to resist. They showed a shot of him and Tasha coming off *Salty Sea* after the explosion, side by side with a still photo of the crews fighting the flames.

He had planned to work at home this morning, as he normally did. But he was going down to the office instead. He wanted to be close to Tasha in case anything more happened.

Before he could leave, Jules and Melissa came by, calling out from the entryway.

"In the kitchen," he called back.

Jules spoke up. "We came to see how you were doing." She paused before coming down the four steps into the main living area. "And to see how you liked the decorations." She continued into the living room and gestured around. "Hey, you really got into the spirit."

"I did."

"Nice work." Melissa gazed around approvingly.

He knew he should credit Tasha. And he knew it wouldn't stay secret that she was sleeping here. But he wasn't in a rush to share the information. There was enough going on today.

"The insurance adjustors will be here at noon," he said instead.

"That's fast."

"I need to get things under way." If he was going to replace the boats before the spring season, he had no time to lose.

"Good thing it's the off-season," Melissa said, obviously following his train of thought.

"If there's anything to be grateful for, that's it. And that nobody got hurt." He was grateful for both things, but he wasn't going to relax until the perpetrator was caught and put in jail.

TJ was next through the door.

"How're you doing?" he asked Matt, giving Jules and Melissa each a nod.

"Fine." Matt thought about his conversation with Tasha last night, and he couldn't help but smile. "A bit like I've been in a bar fight."

TJ grinned back. "My guess is that two of the yachts are write-offs?"

"I'll confirm that today. But, I can't see how we save either of them."

"If you need interim financing, just let me know."

It was on the tip of Matt's tongue to refuse. He hated to take advantage of his friends. And he was already one favor down because of Caleb hiring Dianne.

But he had to be practical. TJ had access to almost unlimited funds. Matt would cover any interest payments. And having TJ write a check, instead of explaining the situation to a banker, would definitely speed things up.

"I might," he said to TJ. "I'm going to track down replacements just as soon as I can make some appointments."

"New yachts," Melissa said with a grin. "Now, *that's* what I call a Christmas gift."

"You can help me test them out," Matt offered.

"I'm your girl," she said.

Matt retrieved his cup and took the final swallow of his coffee. "Thanks for checking on me, guys. But I have to get to work."

"We'll get out of your way," Jules said.

"Nice job with the decorating," Melissa said as they turned to leave.

"I thought we were going to have to do it all," Jules said to her sister as they headed through the foyer.

As the door closed behind Jules and Melissa, TJ looked pointedly around the room. "What is with all this?"

"Tasha helped," Matt said.

"Last night?" TJ asked, his interest obviously perking up.

"I wanted her safely surrounded by an alarm system."

"So, it wasn't…"

"She slept in the guest room."

"Too bad."

"Seriously? She was nearly blown up yesterday. So were we."

"And you couldn't find it in your heart to comfort her?"

Matt knew it was a joke. TJ was absolutely not the kind of guy who would take advantage of a woman's emotional state.

"Is she staying again tonight?" TJ asked.

"Until we catch the jerk that did this. Yes, she's staying right here. I wish I hadn't committed to the mayor's party this evening."

"I could hang out with her."

Since TJ had once asked Tasha on a date, Matt wasn't crazy about that idea.

TJ put on an affronted expression. "You honestly think I'd make a move on her?"

"Of course not."

"Take her with you," TJ suggested.

"She hates those kinds of parties." It was too bad. Matt would happily keep her by his side.

"Everybody hates those kinds of parties."

"I don't."

"Then there's something wrong with you."

Matt didn't think there was anything wrong with him. There were a lot of positives to his hard work, and socializing was one of them. He employed nearly fifty people. He brought economic activity to Whiskey Bay, a town he loved.

And he liked the people of Whiskey Bay. He liked discussing issues with them. He liked strategizing with the other business owners, and he sure didn't mind doing it in a gracious setting.

"The food's good. The drinks are good. I like the music, and the company is usually pleasant. Plus tonight. Tonight everyone will want to talk about the fire. And I can use that as a way to pump them all for information. You never know what people might have seen or heard around town."

"Tell that to Tasha," TJ said.

Matt paused to think about that. He had to admit it was a good idea. "She was willing to come along last time when it was part of the investigation."

"Keeps her with you."

"She's a pretty skilled interrogator. You know, for somebody who hates those kinds of parties, she handles them beautifully. Did you know she grew up in Boston? Beacon Hill. She can hobnob with the best of them. And she's totally disarming. She's pretty, smart and funny. Easy to talk to. Trustworthy. People will tell her anything. It's perfect."

Matt stopped talking to find TJ staring quizzically at him.

"You do get what's going on here, right?" TJ asked.

"No." Did TJ know something about the saboteur? "Did you hear something? Did you see something? Why didn't you *say* something?"

"You're falling in love with Tasha."

Matt shook his head to get the astonishment out. "I thought you were talking about the fire."

"Mark my words."

"You're about a thousand steps ahead of yourself."

Being attracted to a woman didn't equate to happily-ever-after. Sure, he was incredibly attracted to Tasha. And he'd admit to himself that it wasn't simply physical. Although mostly what they did was argue. And they'd slept together exactly *one* time. TJ didn't even know about that.

Matt was miles away from thinking about love.

"I can read the signs," TJ said.

"Well, you're getting a false reading. And I'm going to work now." Matt started for his front door.

TJ trailed behind. "Better brace yourself, buddy. Because I *can* read the signs."

Officially, Tasha agreed to attend the mayor's party because she could talk to people, see if anybody knew anything. If the price for that was dancing with Matt, so be it.

Anticipation brought a smile to her face as she got ready for the evening.

Tasha quickly found a dress she liked in Matt's basement. Sleeveless, with a short, full skirt, it was made of shimmering champagne tulle. The outer dress was trimmed and decorated with hand-stitched lace, and the underdress was soft satin. Altogether, it was made for dancing.

A pair of shoes and the small clutch purse in a box below had obviously been bought to match the dress. The shoes were definitely not made for dancing, but Tasha was going to wear them anyway. Her more practical side protested the frivolous decision. But she wanted to look beautiful tonight.

She wanted to look beautiful for Matt.

She paused for a moment to let the thought sink in.

She had at first chosen a basic black dress from the rack. There was nothing wrong with it. It was understated but perfectly acceptable. Black wasn't exactly her color. But it was a safe choice.

"Tasha?" Matt called from the hallway.

"Yes?" she called back.

"We've got about twenty minutes, and then we should get going."

"No problem." But then she'd spotted a champagne-colored gown and it had held her attention. She'd left with both dresses, and she glanced from one to the other now. Letting out a deep breath, she plucked the champagne-colored one from the hanger. She couldn't help feeling like one of her sisters, primping for a fancy party in the hopes of impressing a rich man.

She'd never understood it before, and she didn't want to understand it now. But she did. She couldn't help herself. She wanted Matt to see her as beautiful.

She set the dress on the bed and shoes on the floor. The guest bathroom was spacious and opulent. Her few toiletries took up only a tiny corner of the vanity.

She stripped off her clothes, noting small bruises on her elbow and her shoulder. She was feeling a lot better than yesterday, but she was still sore. Her gaze strayed to the huge soaker tub next to the walk-in shower. She promised herself she'd take advantage of it later.

For now, she twisted her hair into a braided updo, brushed her teeth, put on some makeup and shimmied into the dress. She didn't have much in the way of jewelry, but she did have a little pair of emerald-and-diamond studs that her parents had given her for her eighteenth birthday.

The last thing she put on was the shoes. They weren't a perfect fit, but they did look terrific. She popped her phone and a credit card into the purse, and headed out to meet Matt.

His bedroom door was open, and the room was empty, as was the living room. Then she heard movement at the front door. Feeling guilty for having kept him waiting, she headed that way.

When she rounded the corner, he stopped still and his eyes went wide.

"What?" She glanced down at herself. Had she missed removing a tag?

"You look fantastic."

She relaxed and couldn't help but smile. The compliment warmed her straight through.

He moved closer. "I shouldn't be so shocked when you dress up like this."

He took her hands. "Seriously, Tasha. You're a knockout. It's a crying shame that you hide under baseball caps and boxy clothes."

His compliment warmed her, and she didn't know how to respond. She knew how she should respond—with annoyance at him for being shallow and disappointment in herself for succumbing to vanity. But that wasn't what she was feeling. She was feeling happy, excited, aroused. She'd dressed up for him, and he liked it.

"You're not so bad yourself," she said, her voice coming out husky.

He wore a tux better than anyone in the world.

"I don't want to share you," he said, drawing her closer.

"You think I'm yours to share?" She put a teasing lilt in her voice.

"You should be. You should be mine. Why aren't you mine, Tasha?" He searched her expression for a split second, and then his mouth came down on hers.

She knew there were all kinds of reasons that this was a bad idea. But she didn't have it in her. She wanted it as much as he did, maybe more. She wrapped her arms around his neck and returned his kiss.

She pressed her body against his. The arm at her waist held her tight. His free hand moved across her cheek, into her hair, cradling her face as he deepened the kiss. His leg nudged between hers, sending tendrils of desire along her inner thighs. Her nipples hardened against him, and a small pulse throbbed at her core.

He kissed her neck, nibbled her ear, his palm stroked up her spine, coming to the bare skin at the top of her back, slipping under the dress to caress her shoulder.

"Forget this," he muttered.

Then he scooped her into his arms and carried her farther into the house, down the hallway to his bedroom.

He dropped to the bed, bringing her with him, stretching her out in his arms, never stopping the path of his kisses.

"Matt?" she gasped, even as she inhaled his scent, gripped tight to his strong shoulders and marveled at how the world was spinning in a whole new direction. "The party."

Her body was on fire. Her skin craved his touch. Her lips couldn't get enough of his taste.

"Forget the party," he growled. "I need you, Tasha. I've imagined you in my bed so many, many times."

"I need you, too," she answered honestly.

It might have been the emotion of the past two days. Maybe it was the way he'd saved her. Maybe it was the intimacy of decorating for Christmas. Or maybe it was just hormones, chemistry. Matt wasn't like anyone she'd ever met.

He stripped off her dress and tossed his tux aside piece by piece.

When they were naked, they rolled together, wrapped in each other's arms.

She ended up on top. And she sat up, straddling him, smiling down.

"I have dreamed of this," he whispered, stroking his hands up her sides, moving to settle on her breasts.

"This might be a dream." She'd dreamed of him too, too many times to count. If this was another, she didn't want to wake up.

"You might be a dream," he said. "But this isn't a dream. This is so real."

"It feels real to me." Unwilling to wait, she guided him

inside, gasping as sensations threatened to overwhelm her. "Very, very, very real."

"Oh, Tasha," he groaned and pulled her close to kiss her.

She moved her hips, pleasure spiraling through her.

"Don't stop," he said, matching her motion.

"No way," she answered against his mouth.

She wanted to say more, but words failed her. Her brain had shut down. All she could do was kiss and caress him, drink in every touch and motion he made.

The world contracted to his room, to his bed, to Matt, beautiful, wonderful Matt.

She sat up to gaze at his gorgeous face. His eyes were opaque. His lips were dark red. His jaw was clenched tight. She captured his hand, lifted it to her face and drew one of his fingers into her mouth. Even his hands tasted amazing.

His other hand clasped her hips. He thrust harder, arching off the bed, creating sparks that turned to colors that turned to sounds. Lights flashed in her brain and a roar came up in her ears. Matt called her name over and over as she cata-pulted into an abyss.

Then she melted forward, and his strong arms went around her, holding her close, rocking her in his arms.

"That was…" he whispered in her ear.

"Unbelievable," she finished on a gasping voice.

"How did we do that? What's your magic?"

She smiled. "I thought it was yours."

"It's ours," he said.

Moments slipped by while they both caught their breaths.

"Are we still going to the party?" she asked.

"I'm not willing to share." He trailed his fingertips along her bare back.

She knew she should call him out for those words. But she was too happy, too content. She wasn't going to do any-thing to break the spell.

Ten

Matt resented real life. He wanted to lock himself away with Tasha and never come out. He'd held her in his arms all night long, waking to her smile, laughing with her over breakfast.

But she had insisted on going to work, and now he had a fire investigator sitting across from him in his office.

"Who was the last person to work on the engine before the fire?" Clayton Ludlow asked.

"My chief mechanic, Tasha Lowell. She's on her way here, but I can guarantee you she didn't make a mistake."

"I'm not suggesting she did. But I need to establish who had access to the engine room."

"After Tasha, I have no idea."

"You have security cameras?"

"I do."

"You reviewed the footage?" Clayton made some notes on a small pad of paper.

"Of course."

"Did anyone else board *Crystal Zone* the rest of the day?"

"Not that we could see. But Tasha thought..." Matt hesitated.

"Thought what?"

"She had a feeling someone was on board at the same time as her."

"Did she see someone?"

"No. It was just a feeling." And at this point, it was worrying Matt more than ever.

"There's nothing I can do with the *feeling* of another potential suspect."

"Tasha's not a suspect." Matt wanted the investigator to be clear on that.

Clayton's tone became brisk. "Are there blind spots left by the security cameras?"

"No."

Clayton's arched expression told Matt he was jumping to conclusions about Tasha.

"You know we've suspected sabotage," Matt said.

"I know. And we also know what started the fire."

Matt's interest ramped up. "How did he do it?"

"He *or she* left some oily rags in a pile. They ignited."

There was a knock on the door and Tasha pushed it open.

Matt waved her inside, and she took the vinyl guest chair next to Clayton.

Matt got straight to the point. "There were some oily rags left in the engine room. Any chance they were yours?"

He didn't believe for a minute they were, but he didn't want Clayton to think he was covering for Tasha. Not that he would need to. There was absolutely no way she was the saboteur.

"No," she said. "Never. Not a chance."

Matt looked to Clayton.

"How many boats do you work on in an average day?"

"One to six."

"So, you're busy."

"I'm busy," she said. "But I didn't forget something like that."

"How many boats did you work on the day of the fire?"

"Three." She paused. "No, four."

"This is a waste of time," Matt said.

Clayton ignored him. "The other problems Whiskey Bay has been having. I understand you were the last person to work on each of the engines."

"I was also the one to discover the wire short and the fuel leak that prevented the last fire." She slid a glance to Matt. It was obvious her patience was wearing.

Clayton made some more notes.

"Are you planning to charge me with something?" Tasha asked.

Her voice had gone higher, and her posture had grown stiff in the chair. Matt would have given anything to spirit her back to his house.

"Are you expecting to be charged with something?"

"No." She was emphatic.

Clayton didn't answer. He just nodded.

"We're wasting time," Matt said. "The real criminal is out there, and we're wasting time."

"Let me do my job," Clayton said.

"That's all we want." Matt nodded.

"It wasn't me," Tasha said.

"Noted. And now I have to finish my report." Clayton came to his feet.

Tasha stood, as well. "And I have engines to inspect. Think what you want about me," she said to Clayton. "But whoever is trying to hurt Matt's business is still trying to hurt Matt's business. If you don't want another disaster on your hands, help us find them."

She turned and left the office.

"Is she always so emotional?" Clayton asked.

"She's never emotional. And she's not emotional now. But I'm getting there." Matt rose. "Fill out your report. But if you pursue Tasha as a suspect or accomplice, you'll only be wasting valuable time."

Tasha paced her way down the pier, past the burned boats to *Monty's Pride*, which, thankfully, hadn't been damaged at all. She knew the inspector was only doing his job. But it was frustrating to have them spend so much time on her instead of looking for the real culprit. She had no doubt she'd be exonerated, no matter what people might believe right now. But she hated to think about the damage that could potentially be done in the meantime.

She heard the echoing sound of an open boat moving toward her. From the sound, she figured it was a small cartopper with a 150-horse outboard. Alex had chased a couple of reporters and a dozen lookie-loos away from the docks already this morning.

The red open boat was piloted by a man in a steel gray hoodie. He wasn't even wearing a life jacket.

"Jerk," she muttered under her breath, climbing down to the floater where it was obvious he was planning to dock.

"This is private property," she called out to him, waving him away.

He kept coming.

He didn't have a camera out yet; at least that was something.

She moved to the edge of the floater. "I said, this is private property."

He put a hand up to cup his ear.

He looked to be in his late fifties. He could be hard of hearing. Or it could simply be the noise of the outboard motor.

It was odd that he was wearing a hoodie. She associated them with teenagers, not older adults.

The boat touched broadside on the tire bumpers.

Tasha crouched to grasp the gunwale. "Is there something I can help you with?"

The man seemed oddly familiar.

"Have we met?" she asked, puzzled.

Maybe she'd been too quick to try to send him away. His business could be legitimate.

He shifted in his seat, coming closer to her.

And then she smelled it, the cologne or aftershave that she'd smelled the morning of the *Crystal Zone* fire.

"Only once," he said, raising an arm.

She jerked back, but she was too late.

Her world went dark.

* * *

It could have been minutes or hours later when she pushed her way to consciousness. She felt disoriented, and pain pulsed at her temples. Her first thought was to reach for Matt. She'd fallen asleep in his arms last night, and she wanted to wake up the same way.

She reached out, but instead of finding Matt, her hand hit a wall. No, it wasn't a wall. It was fabric. It was springy. It felt like the back of a sofa, and it had a musty smell.

She forced her eyes open, blinking in dim light.

The light was from a window up high in the room.

Her head throbbed harder, and she reached up to find a lump at her temple.

Then it all came back to her, the boat, the man, the smell. He'd hit her on the head. He'd knocked her out.

She sat up straight, pain ricocheting through her skull.

"You should have come home, Tasha." The voice was low and gravelly.

She looked rapidly around, trying to locate the source.

"Your mother misses you," he said.

She squinted at a shadowy figure in a kitchen chair across the room. "Who are you? Where am I? What do you want?"

"You're safe," he said.

She gave a hollow laugh. "I have a hard time believing that."

She gazed around the big room. It was more like a shed or a garage. She could make out a workbench of some kind. There were yard tools stacked against one wall, some sheers and a weed trimmer hanging on hooks.

"Where am I?" She put her feet on the floor, finding it was concrete.

The garage wasn't heated, and she was chilly.

"It's not important." He waved a dismissive hand. "We won't be here long."

"Where are we going?" Her mind was scrambling.

He'd pulled down his hoodie, but her vision was poor in

the dim light. She'd thought she recognized him, but she couldn't place him. And she found herself wondering if she'd been mistaken.

But the cologne smell was familiar. It was… It was…

Her father's!

"Where's my dad?" she asked, sitting forward, debating her odds of overpowering the man.

He was older, but she was woozy, and her pounding headache was making her dizzy.

"He's in Boston. As always. Why would he be anywhere else?"

She wasn't going to give away that she'd made the cologne connection. It might give her some kind of advantage.

"No reason."

The man rose to his feet. "Tasha, Tasha, Tasha. You have proved so difficult."

She wished she knew how long she'd been here. Would Matt have noticed her missing yet? There'd be no tracks, nothing on the security cameras. The man had used a boat. That's how he'd got onto *Crystal Zone* without being seen yesterday morning. He'd come by water.

"You were the one who lit the oily rags," she said.

She couldn't tell for sure, but it looked as if he'd smiled.

"Used a candle as a wick," he said with a certain amount of pride in his voice, taking a few paces in front of her. "The wax just disappears." He fluttered his fingers. "For all anyone knows, they spontaneously combusted. Didn't anyone teach you the dangers of oily rags?"

"Of course they did. Nobody's going to believe I'd make a mistake like that."

"Well, it wouldn't have come to that—" now he sounded angry "—if you hadn't spent so much time cozying up to Matt Emerson. Otherwise you would have been fired days ago. I didn't see that one coming."

Tasha was speechless. Who was this man? How long had he been watching her? And what had he seen between her and Matt? As quickly as the thought formed, she realized that some stranger knowing she'd slept with Matt was the least of her worries.

She was in serious trouble here. She had no idea what this man intended to do with her.

Cold fear gripped the pit of her stomach.

"Have you seen Tasha?" Matt had found Alex on the pier next to *Orca's Run*, moving a wheeled toolbox.

"Not since this morning. Didn't she talk to the investigator?"

"That was three hours ago." Matt was starting to worry.

"Maybe she took a long lunch."

"Without saying anything?"

Alex gave him an odd look, and he realized his relationship with Tasha was far different from what everyone believed.

"Have you tried the Crab Shack?" Alex asked.

"That's a good idea."

Tasha had been getting to know Jules and Melissa recently. Matt liked that. He liked that she fit in with his circle of friends.

"Thanks," he said to Alex, waving as he strode down the pier. At the same time, he called Jules's cell phone, too impatient to wait until he got there.

"I don't know," Jules said when he asked the question. "I'm at home, feet up. They're really swollen today."

"Sorry to hear that."

"It's the price you pay." She sounded cheerful.

"Is Melissa at the restaurant?"

"I expect so. Is something wrong, Matt? You sound worried."

"I'm looking for Tasha."

Jules's tone changed. "Did something happen?"

"I don't know. She's not around. I can't find her on the

pier or in the main building. I checked the staff quarters and nothing."

"Maybe she went into town?"

"Not without telling me."

There was a silent pause. "Because of the fire?"

It was on the tip of his tongue to tell Jules he thought Tasha was the target. He might not have any proof, but his instincts were telling him somebody was out to discredit her. Heck, they already had the fire department thinking she was the culprit. But he didn't want to upset Jules. Her focus needed to be on her and the babies. She needed to stay relaxed.

"It's probably nothing." He forced a note of cheer into his voice. "I'll walk over to the Crab Shack myself. Or maybe she did go into town. She might have needed parts."

"I'll let you know if I hear from her," Jules said.

"Thanks. You relax. Take care of those babies."

Matt signed off.

He'd been walking fast, and he headed down the stairs to the parking lot.

"Matt!" It was Caleb, exiting his own car.

Matt trotted the rest of the way, hoping Caleb had news about Tasha.

Caleb was accompanied by an older woman.

"What is it?" he asked Caleb between deep breaths.

Caleb gestured to the fiftysomething woman. "This is Annette Lowell. She came to the Crab Shack looking for Tasha. She says she's her mother."

Matt didn't know how to react. Could Annette's appearance have something to do with Tasha being gone? "Hello."

The woman flashed a friendly smile. "You must be Matt Emerson."

"I am." Matt glanced at Caleb. He was beyond confused.

"Annette came to visit Tasha," Caleb said, his subtle shrug and the twist to his expression telling Matt he had no more information than that.

"Was Tasha expecting you?" Matt asked, still trying to pull the two events together. Was Tasha avoiding her mother? Matt knew they were estranged.

"No. I haven't spoken to Tasha in over a year."

"Not at all?"

"No."

Matt didn't really want to tell the woman her daughter was missing. He wasn't even sure if Tasha was missing. There could still be a logical explanation of why he couldn't find her.

"I saw the coverage of that terrible fire," Annette said to Matt. "I hope you'll be able to replace the yachts."

"We will."

"Good, good. I'm *so* looking forward to getting to know you." Her smile was expectant now. "I had no idea my daughter was dating such an accomplished man."

Dating? Where had Annette got the idea they were dating?

Then he remembered the picture in the national news, his arm around Tasha's shoulder, the expression of concern captured by the camera. Annette must have seen it and concluded that he and Tasha were together. It was clear she was happy about it.

"I'm a little busy right now." He looked to Caleb for assistance.

It wasn't fair to dump this on Caleb, but Matt had to concentrate on Tasha. He had to find her and assure himself she was safe. He was trying his house next. There was an outside chance she'd gone up there for a rest and turned off her phone. It was a long shot. But he didn't know what else to do.

Caleb stepped up. "Would you like to meet my wife?" he asked Annette. "She's pregnant and resting at the house right now, just up there on the hill. We're having twins."

Annette looked uncertain. It was clear she'd rather stay with Matt.

"Great idea," Matt chimed in. "I'll finish up here, and maybe we can talk later."

"With Tasha?" she asked.

"Of course."

The answer seemed to appease her, and she went willingly with Caleb.

Once again, Matt owed his friend big-time.

Without wasting another second, he called Melissa and discovered Tasha hadn't been to the Crab Shack in a couple of days. He checked his house but found nothing. So he asked the crew and dockworkers to check every inch of every boat.

They came up empty, and Matt called the police.

They told him he couldn't file a missing persons report for twenty-four hours. Then they had the gall to suggest Tasha might have disappeared of her own accord—because she knew she'd been caught committing arson.

It took every ounce of self-control he had not to ream the officer out over the phone.

His next stop was the security tapes from this morning. While he was reviewing them in the office, Caleb came back.

"What was *that* all about?" Caleb asked Matt without preamble.

"I have no idea. But I have bigger problems."

Caleb sobered. "What's going on?"

"It's Tasha. I can't find her."

"Was she supposed to be somewhere?"

"Here. She's supposed to be here!"

Caleb drew back.

"Sorry," Matt said. "I'm on edge. She's missing for hours. The police won't listen."

"The *police*?"

"The fire department thinks she's an arsonist."

"Wait. Slow down."

"She was the last person known to be on board *Crystal Zone*. They concluded some oily rags combusted in the engine room, and they blame her for leaving them there—possibly on purpose."

"That's ridiculous," Caleb said.

"It's something else. It's someone else." Matt kept his attention on the security footage. "There she is."

Caleb came around the desk to watch with him.

Tasha walked down the pier. By the time clock, he knew it was right after she'd talked to the fire investigator. She'd disappeared behind *Monty's Pride*.

Matt waited. He watched and he waited.

"Where did she go?" Caleb asked.

"There's nothing back there." Matt clicked Fast-Forward, and they continued to watch.

"That's an hour," Caleb said. "Would she be working on *Monty's Pride*?"

"We checked. She's not there. And she couldn't have boarded from the far side."

"I hate to say it," Caleb ventured. "Is there any chance she fell in?"

Matt shot him a look of disbelief. "Really? Plus the tide's incoming." He had to steel himself to even say it out loud. "She wouldn't have washed out to sea."

"I'm stretching," Caleb said.

"Wait a minute." The answer came to Matt in a lightning bolt. "A boat. If she left the pier without coming back around, it had to have been in a boat."

"The Crab Shack camera has a different angle."

Matt grabbed his coat. "Let's go."

Tasha's head was still throbbing, but at least her dizziness had subsided. She was thirsty, but she didn't want to say or do anything that might upset the man who held her captive. When he turned, she could see a bulge in the waistband of his pants.

It could be a gun. It was probably a gun. But at least he wasn't pointing it at her.

If she could get back to full strength, and if he came close enough, she might be able to overpower him. She knew instinctively that she'd get only one chance. If she tried and failed, he might go for the gun or knock her out again or tie her hands.

He'd been pacing the far side of the garage for a long time.

"You need something else to wear," he said. His tone was matter-of-fact. He didn't seem angry.

"Why?" she dared ask.

"Because you look terrible, all tatty and ratty. Your mother wouldn't like that at all."

"You know my mother?"

His grin was somewhat sickly. "Do I know your mother? I know her better than she knows herself."

Struggling to keep her growing fear at bay, Tasha racked her brain trying to place the man. Had they met back in Boston? Why was he wearing her father's favorite cologne?

"Why did you want me to get fired?" she dared to ask.

"Isn't it obvious? Your mother misses you. You need to come home."

Come home. It sounded like home for him, too. *He must live in Boston.*

"You thought if Matt fired me, I'd move back to Boston?"

"Ah, Matt. The handsome Matt. You wore a nice dress that night."

Tasha turned cold again.

"You must have liked it. You looked like you liked it, all red and sparkly. You looked like your sister Madison."

"Where's Madison?" Tasha's voice came out on a rasp. Had this man done something to the rest of her family?

"What's with all the questions?" he chided. "If you want to see Madison, simply come home."

"Okay," she agreed, trying another tactic. "I'll come home. How soon can we leave?"

He stared at her with open suspicion. "I'm not falling for that."

"Falling for what? I miss Madison. And I miss Shelby. I'd like to see them. A visit would be nice."

"No, no, no." He shook his head. "That was too quick. I'm not stupid."

"I simply hadn't thought about it for a while," she tried.

"You're trying to trick me. Well, it won't work."

"I don't want to trick you." She gave up. "I honestly want to give you what you want. You've gone to a lot of trouble here. You must want it very badly."

"First, you need to change."

Her heart leaped in anticipation. Maybe he'd leave the garage. Maybe he'd go shopping for some clothes. If he left her alone, especially if he didn't tie her hands, she could escape. There had to be a way out of this place.

"It's in the car."

"What's in the car?"

"The red dress."

She was back to being frightened again. "How did you get the red dress?"

He looked at her like she was being dense. "It was in your room. I took it from your room. I'm disappointed you didn't notice. You should take more care with such an expensive gown. I had it cleaned."

Tasha's creep factor jumped right back up again. At the same time, she realized she hadn't even noticed the dress was gone. When she'd thought back on that night, making love with Matt had been foremost on her mind. The dress had faded to insignificance.

The security cameras covered the marina but the staff quarters were farther back, out of range. He'd obviously slipped in at some point.

"I'll get it," the man said, heading for the door.

"I'm not changing in front of you," she shouted out.

He stopped and pivoted. "I wouldn't expect you to, dear. Whatever you think of me, I am a gentleman."

"What's your name?" She braved the question, then held her breath while she waited for him to answer or get angry.

"Giles."

"And you're from Boston?"

"The West End, born and raised." He seemed to expect her to be impressed.

"That's very nice."

"I'll get your dress. We need to go now."

"Where are we going?"

He turned again, this time his eyes narrowed in annoyance, and she braced herself. "Pay attention, Tasha. We're going to Boston."

She shuddered at his icy expression. He couldn't get her all the way to Boston as his prisoner. He'd have to drive. They couldn't board a plane.

It would be all but impossible to watch her every second. She'd escape. She'd definitely find a way to escape.

But what if he caught her? What would he do then?

Eleven

The Crab Shack security footage confirmed Matt's worst fears. The picture was grainy, but it showed Tasha being hauled into a boat and taken away.

"It's red," Caleb said, "but that's about as much detail as I'm getting."

"Probably a twenty-footer," Matt said. "There's no way they're leaving the inlet. That's something at least."

TJ arrived at the Crab Shack's office. "What's going on? Melissa said you were looking for Tasha."

"Somebody grabbed her," Matt said.

His instinct was to rush to his car and drive, but he didn't know where he was going. He should call the police, but he feared that would slow him down. He had to find her. He absolutely had to find her.

"What do you mean grabbed her?" TJ asked, his expression equal parts confusion and concern.

When Matt didn't answer, TJ looked to Caleb.

"Show him the clip," Caleb said.

Matt replayed it.

TJ swore under his breath.

"Matt thinks they won't leave the inlet," Caleb said. "It's a red twenty-footer. He might have pulled it onto a trailer, but maybe not. Maybe it's still tied up somewhere on the inlet."

"There are a lot of red cartoppers out there," TJ said, but he was taking out his phone as he said it.

Matt came to his feet. "We should start with the public dock." He was glad to have a course of action.

"What about the police?" Caleb asked.

"Herb?" TJ said into the phone. "Can you get me a helicopter?"

Matt turned to TJ in surprise.

"Now," TJ said and paused. "That'll do." He ended the call and pointed to the screen. "Can someone copy that for me?"

"Melissa?" Caleb called out.

She immediately popped her head through the doorway.

"Can you help TJ print out what's on the screen?"

"I'm going to the public dock," Matt said. "You'll call me?" he asked TJ.

"With anything we find," TJ said.

Under normal circumstances, Matt would have protested TJ's actions. But these weren't normal circumstances. He didn't care what resources it took. He was finding Tasha.

"I'll talk to the police," Caleb said. "What about Tasha's mother?"

Both TJ and Melissa stared at Caleb in surprise. "She's up with Jules. She suddenly dropped by for a visit."

"Yes," Matt said. "Talk to her. It's really strange that she's here. She might know something."

Matt sprinted to his car and roared out of the parking lot, zooming up the hill to the highway and turning right for the public dock. He dropped his phone on the seat beside him, ready to grab it if anyone called.

The sun was setting, and it was going to be dark soon. He could only imagine how terrified Tasha must be feeling. She had to be okay. She *had* to be okay.

It took him thirty minutes to get to the public dock. He leaped over the turnstile, not caring who might come after him.

He scanned the extensive docking system, row upon row of boats. He counted ten, no, twelve small red boats.

"Sir?" The attendant came up behind him. "If you don't have a pass card, I'll charge you five dollars."

Matt handed the kid a twenty. "Keep the change."

"Sure. Okay. Thanks, man."

Matt jogged to the dock with the biggest concentration of red twenty-footers.

He marched out on the dock, stopping to stare down at the first one. He realized he didn't know what he was looking for. Blood on the seat? He raked a hand through his hair. *Please, no, not that.*

Even if he found the boat, what would that tell him? He wouldn't know which way they went. Did the kidnapper have a car? Maybe the attendant was his best bet. Maybe the kid had seen something.

His phone rang. It was TJ, and Matt put it to his ear. "Yeah?"

"We see a red boat. It's a possible match."

"Where?"

"Ten minutes south of you. Take Ring Loop Road, third right you come to."

"TJ." Matt wanted him to be right. He so wanted him to be right. "I'm looking at a dozen red twenty-footers here."

"He hit her on the head," TJ reminded him. "I don't think he'd risk carrying her unconscious through the public dock. And if she was awake, she might call out. This place is secluded. And the boat is only tied off at the bow. The stern line is trailing in the water, like somebody was in a hurry."

"Yeah. Okay." Matt bought into TJ's logic. "It's worth a shot."

"We'll keep going farther."

"Thanks." Matt headed back to his car.

He impatiently followed TJ's directions, finally arriving at the turnoff. He followed the narrow road toward the beach, shutting off his engine to silently coast down the final hill.

He could see a red boat at the dock. The tide was high, pushing it up against the rocky shore. There was an old building visible through the trees.

He crept around to the front of the building and saw a car with the trunk standing open. He moved closer, silent on his feet, listening carefully.

The building door swung open, and he ducked behind a tree.

Tasha appeared. Her mouth was taped. Her hands were behind her back. And she was wearing the red party dress. A man had her grasped tight by one arm.

She spotted the open trunk. Her eyes went wide with fear, as she tried to wrench herself away.

"Let her go!" Matt surged forward.

The man turned. He pulled a gun and pointed it at Matt. Matt froze.

Tasha's eyes were wide with fear.

"You don't want to do this," Matt said, regretting his impulsive actions. How could he have been so stupid as to barge up on the kidnapper with no plan?

"I know exactly what I want to do," the man returned in a cold voice.

"Let her go," Matt said.

"How about *you* get out of my way."

"You're not going to shoot her," Matt said, operating in desperation and on the fly. He could not let the guy leave with Tasha. "You went to too much trouble to get her here."

"Who said anything about shooting *her*?" The man sneered.

Matt heard sirens in the distance, and he nearly staggered with relief. "The police are on their way."

"Move!" the man yelled to Matt.

"No. You're not taking her anywhere."

The man fired off a round. It went wide.

"Every neighbor for ten miles heard that," Matt said. "You'll never get away. If you kill me, that's cold-blooded murder. If you let her go, maybe it was a misunderstanding. Maybe you drive away. Maybe, you let her go, and I step aside, and you drive off anywhere you want."

To Matt's surprise, the man seemed to consider the offer.

Matt took a step forward. "The one thing that's not happening here is you leaving with Tasha."

The sirens grew louder.

"Last chance," Matt said, taking another step.

The man's eyes grew wild, darting around in obvious indecision.

Then he shoved Tasha to the side.

She fell, and Matt rushed toward her and covered her with his body.

The kidnapper jumped into the car and zoomed off, spraying them with dust and stones.

As the debris settled, Matt pressed the number for TJ. Then he gently peeled the tape from Tasha's mouth. "Are you hurt?"

"He's getting away," she gasped.

"He won't." Matt put the phone to his ear.

TJ had a bird's-eye view, and he was obviously in touch with both Caleb and the police.

The call connected.

"Yeah?" TJ said.

"He's running, red car," Matt said to TJ. "I've got Tasha."

"We see him."

The helicopter whirled overhead.

"There's only one road out," Matt said to Tasha. "And TJ can see him from the air. There's no way for him to escape. Now, please tell me you're all right."

"I'm fine. Frightened. I think that man is crazy."

"Did he tell you what he wanted? Why are you dressed up? Never mind. Don't say anything. Just…" Matt removed his jacket and wrapped it around her shoulders. "Rest. Just rest."

He wrapped his arms around her, cradling her against his chest. All he wanted to do was hold her. Everything else could wait.

The small police station was a hive of activity. Matt hadn't left Tasha's side since he'd found her, and everything beyond him and the detective interviewing her was a blur of motion, muted colors and indistinct sounds.

"You said you might have recognized Giles Malahide?" the detective asked her for what she thought was about the tenth time.

"Why do you keep asking?" Matt interjected.

The detective gave him a sharp look. "I'm trying to get a full picture." He turned his attention to Tasha again. "You said he seemed familiar."

"His smell seemed familiar. He was wearing the same brand of cologne as my father. And he talked about my mother."

"What did he say about your mother?"

"That she missed me."

"Tasha, darling." It was her mother's voice.

Tasha gave her head a swift shake. She was in worse shape than she'd thought. She tightened her grip on Matt's hands, waiting for the auditory hallucination to subside.

"I *need* to see her." Her mother's voice came again. "I'm her *mother*."

Tasha's eyes focused on a figure across the room. It was her mother and she was attempting to get past two female officers.

"Matt?" Tasha managed in a shaky voice.

She looked to him. He didn't seem surprised. Her mother was here? Her mother was actually in the room?

"You called my mother?" she asked. "Why would you call my mother?"

"I didn't call her. She showed up asking for you."

"You said Giles Malahide talked about your mother?" the detective asked.

"Is that his full name?" Tasha asked. Not that it mattered. She really didn't care who he was, as long as he stayed in jail and got some help.

"What is *he* doing here?" Tasha's mother demanded.

Tasha looked up to see Giles Malahide being marched past in handcuffs.

Matt quickly put his arms around Tasha and pulled her against his shoulder.

"Annette," Giles called out. "Annette, I found her. I found her."

"Bring that woman here," the detective barked.

"Can we go somewhere private?" Matt asked the detective.

"Yes," he said. "This way."

They rose, and Matt steered Tasha away from the commotion, down a short hallway to an interview room, helping her sit in a molded plastic chair.

"What is going on?" Tasha managed.

"We're going to find out," the detective said. Then his tone became less brisk, more soothing. "I know you've gone through this already. But can you start from the beginning? From the first instance of what you believed to be sabotage?"

Tasha was tired.

"Is that necessary?" Matt asked. His tone hadn't moderated at all.

She put a hand on his forearm. "I can do it."

"Are you sure?"

"I'm sure."

She reiterated the entire story, from the water found in the fuel in *Orca's Run*, to her eerie feeling on board *Crystal Zone* before the fire, to her terror at the prospect of being thrown in the trunk of Giles's car.

As she came to the end, there was a soft knock on the door. It opened, and a patrolwoman leaned her head into the room. "Detective?" she asked.

"Come in, Elliott."

"We have a statement from Giles Malahide. It's delusional, but it corroborates everything Annette Lowell is saying."

"My *mother* knew about this?" Tasha couldn't accept that.

"No, no," Officer Elliott was quick to say. "Malahide acted on his own." She glanced to the detective, obviously unsure of how much to reveal.

"Go on," he said.

"Giles worked on the Lowell estate as a handyman."

"Estate?" the detective asked and looked to Tasha.

Officer Elliott continued, "They're the Vincent Lowell family, libraries, university buildings, the charity.

"Giles claims he's in love with Annette," Officer Elliott said. "And he believed her fondest wish was to have her daughter Tasha back in Boston in the family fold. He tracked Tasha down. He thought if she got fired from the Whiskey Bay Marina, she'd come home. When that didn't work, he took a more direct approach."

Tasha felt like she'd fallen through the looking glass. The officer's summary was entirely plausible, but it didn't explain how her mother had turned up in the middle of it all.

"Why is my mother here?" she asked.

"She saw your photo in the newspaper. The one taken at the fire. The story talked about Matt Emerson and his business and, well…" Officer Elliott looked almost apologetic. "She said she wanted to meet your boyfriend."

Tasha nearly laughed. She quickly covered her mouth and tipped her head forward to stifle the inappropriate emotion.

"Are you all right?" Matt's tone was worried.

"I'm fine. I'm…" She looked back up, shaking her head and heaving a sigh. "It's my mother." She looked at Matt. "She thinks you're a catch. She thinks I've found myself a worthy mate who will turn me into a responsible married woman." Tasha looked to Officer Elliott. "Her fondest wish isn't to have me back in Boston. Her fondest wish is to see me settled down, not rattling around engine parts and boat motors."

"Do we have a full confession?" the detective asked Officer Elliott.

"He's denied nothing. We have plenty to hold him on."

The detective closed his notebook. "Then we're done here. You're free to go, Ms. Lowell."

"Are you ready to see your mother?" Matt asked as they rose.

With all that had happened today, facing her mother seemed like the easiest thing she'd ever been asked to do. "As ready as I'll ever be."

"You're sure?"

"It's fine." Tasha had been standing up to her mother for years. She could do it again.

They made their way back to the crowded waiting room. Melissa, Noah, Jules, Caleb and Alex were all there. Tasha found herself glad to see them. It felt like she had a family after all, especially with Matt by her side.

Jules gave her a hug. "Anything you need," she said. "All you have to do is ask."

"I'm just glad it's over," Tasha said. "It would have been nice to have a less dramatic ending."

The people within hearing distance laughed.

"But at least we know what was going on," Jules said. "Everything can get back to normal now."

"Tasha." Her mother made her way through the small cluster of people. She pulled Tasha into a hug. "I was so worried about you."

"Hello, Mom."

Tasha swiftly ended the hug. They weren't a hugging family. She could only assume her mother had been inspired by Jules to offer that kind of affection.

"You look lovely," her mother said, taking in the dress.

"Thank you."

"Are you all right? I had no idea Giles would do something like that. Your father fired him months ago."

"It wasn't your fault," Tasha said.

Matt stepped in. "It's time to take Tasha home."

"Of course. Of course," Annette said. "We can talk later, darling."

If her mother had truly come looking for a reformed daughter with an urbane, wealthy boyfriend, she was going to be sadly disappointed.

While Tasha slept, Matt had installed Annette in another of his guest rooms. Then Caleb, the best friend a man could ever ask for, invited Annette to join him and Jules for dinner at the Crab Shack. Matt was now staring at the clutter of Christmas decorations, wondering if Tasha would feel up to finishing the job in the next few days, or if he should simply cart them all down to the basement for next year.

He heard a noise, and looked to find her standing at the end of the hall.

"You're up," he said, coming to his feet. Then he noticed she was carrying her gym bag. "What are you doing?"

"Back to the staff quarters," she said.

"Why?" He knew she had to go eventually. But it didn't have to be right away.

"Thanks for letting me stay here," she said, walking toward the front door.

"Wait. Whoa. You don't have to rush off. You're fine here. It's good."

The last thing he wanted was for her to leave. He'd hoped… Okay, so he wasn't exactly sure what he'd hoped. But he knew for certain this wasn't it.

"No, it's not good. The danger has passed, and things can go back to normal."

"Just like that?" He snapped his fingers.

"Just like nothing. Matt, what's got into you?"

He followed her to the entry hall. "Your mother's here, for one thing."

Tasha dropped the bag at her feet. "I know she's here. And I'll call her tomorrow. We can do lunch at her hotel or something. I'll explain everything. She'll be disappointed.

But I'm used to that. She'll get over it. She has two other perfectly good daughters."

"I mean she's here, here," Matt said, pointing to the floor. "I invited her to stay in my other guest room."

Tasha's expression turned to utter astonishment. "Why would you do that?"

"Because she's your mother. And I thought you were staying here. It seemed to make sense." He knew they weren't on the best of terms, but Annette had come all the way across the country to see Tasha. Surely, they could be civil for a couple of days.

"That was a bad idea," Tasha said.

"She told me you hadn't seen her in years."

"It's not a secret."

"Don't you think this is a good chance?"

Tasha crossed her arms over her chest. "You know why she's here, right?"

"To see you."

"To see *you*. She thinks I found a good man. She thinks I've come to my senses, and I'm going to start planning my wedding to you any minute now."

"I think she misses you," Matt said honestly. He hadn't spent a lot of time with Annette, but her concern for Tasha seemed genuine.

"She came out here because of the picture in the paper."

"The picture that told her where to find you," he argued.

"The picture that she thought told her a wealthy man was in my life."

"Stay and talk to her." What Matt really meant was stay and talk with him. But he couldn't say that out loud. He hated the thought of her going back to that dim little room where she'd be alone, and then he'd be alone, too.

"I'll see her tomorrow," Tasha said.

He couldn't let her slip away like this. "What about us?"

She looked tired, and a little sad. "There isn't an us."

"There was last night."

"Last night was…last night. Our emotions were high."

He didn't buy it. "Our emotions are still high."

"The danger is over. I don't need to be here. And I don't need you taking my mother's side."

"I'm not taking her side."

She put her hand on the doorknob. "I appreciate your hospitality, and what you've done for my mom. But my life is my own. I can't let her change it, and I can't let you change it either."

"Staying in my guest room isn't changing your life."

"No? I already miss your bathtub."

He couldn't tell if she was joking. "That's another reason to stay."

"No, that's another reason to go. I'm tough, Matt. I'm sturdy and hardworking. I don't need bubbles and bath salts and endless gallons of hot water."

"There's no shame in liking bath salts."

"This Cinderella is leaving the castle and going back home."

"That's not how the story ends."

"It's how this story ends, Matt."

"Give us a chance."

"I have to be strong."

"Why does being strong mean walking away?"

"Not tonight, Matt. Please, not tonight."

And then she was gone. And he was alone. He wanted to go after her, but it was obvious she needed some time.

Through the night, Tasha's mind had whirled a million miles an hour. It had pinged from the kidnapping to her mother to Matt and back again. She'd been tempted to stay and spend the night with him, and the feeling scared her.

She'd been tempted by Matt, by everything about his lifestyle, the soaker tub the pillow-top bed. She'd even wanted to decorate his Christmas tree.

She was attracted to his strength, his support and intelligence, his concern and kindness. She'd wanted to throw every scrap of her hard-won independence out the window and jump headlong into the opulent life he'd built.

She couldn't let herself do that.

"Tasha?" Her mother interrupted her thoughts from across the table at the Crab Shack.

"Yes?" Tasha brought herself back to the present.

"I said you've changed."

"I'm older." Her mother looked older, too. Tasha hadn't expected that.

"You're calm, more serene. And that was a lovely dress you had on yesterday."

Tasha tried not to sigh. "It was borrowed."

"That's too bad. You should buy some nice things for yourself. Just because you have a dirty day job, doesn't mean you can't dress up and look pretty."

"I don't want to dress up and look pretty." Even as she said the words, she acknowledged they were a lie. She'd wanted to dress up for Matt. She still wanted to look nice for him. As hard as she tried, she couldn't banish the feeling.

"I don't want to argue, honey."

"Neither do I." Tasha realized she didn't. "But I'm a mechanic, Mom. And it's not just a day job that I leave behind. I like being strong, independent, relaxed and casual."

"I can accept that."

The answer surprised Tasha. "You can?"

Her mother reached out and covered her hand. "I'm not trying to change you."

Tasha blinked.

"But how does Matt feel about that?"

"Everything's not about a man, Mom."

"I know. But there's nothing like a good man to focus a woman's priorities."

Tasha was nervous enough about Matt's impact on her priorities. "You mean mess with a woman's priorities."

"What a thing to say. When I met your father, I was planning to move to New York City. Well, he changed that plan right away."

"You exchanged a mansion in the Hamptons for a mansion in Beacon Hill?"

"What do you have against big houses?" Annette asked.

"It's not the house. It's the lifestyle. Would you have married a mechanic and moved to the suburbs?"

The question seemed to stump her mother.

"I'd do that in a heartbeat. It would suit me just fine. But I can't be someone's wife who spends all her time dressing up, attending parties, buying new yachts and decorating Christmas trees."

"It's not the same thing. I'd be moving down the ladder. You'd be moving up."

Tasha retrieved her hand. "I'm on a different ladder."

Her mother's eyes narrowed in puzzlement. "Not needing to work is a blessing. When you don't need to work, you can do whatever you want."

"I do need to work."

"Not if you and Matt—"

"Mom, there is no me and Matt. He's my boss, full stop."

Her mother gave a knowing smile. "I've seen the way he looks at you. And I can't help but hear wedding bells. And it has nothing to do with wishful thinking."

"Oh, Mom. Matt doesn't want to marry me."

Matt wanted to sleep with her, sure. And she wanted to sleep with him. But he was her boss not her boyfriend.

"Well, not yet," Annette said. "That's not the way it works, darling. If only you hadn't left home so soon. There's so much I could have taught you."

"Mom, I left home because I didn't want to play those games."

"They're the only games worth playing."

"Oh, Mom."

It was an argument they'd had dozens of times. But

strangely, it didn't upset Tasha as much as it normally did. She realized, deep down, her mother meant well.

"I want you to keep in touch, honey. Okay?" Annette said.

"Okay." Tasha agreed with a nod, knowing it was time to move to a different relationship with her family. She wasn't caving to their wishes by any stretch, but her mother seemed a lot more willing to see her side of things. "I will."

Her mother's expression brightened. "Maybe even come for Christmas? You could bring Matt with you. He can meet your father and, well, you can see what happens from there."

Baby steps, Tasha told herself. "You're getting way ahead of yourself, Mom."

"Perhaps. But a mother can hope."

Twelve

Matt sat sprawled on a deck chair in front of his open fireplace. He normally loved the view from the marina building's rooftop deck. Tonight, the ocean looked bland. The sky was a weak pink as the sun disappeared, and dark clouds were moving in from the west. They'd hit the Coast Mountains soon and rain all over him.

He should care. He should go inside. He couldn't bring himself to do either.

Tasha had asked him to back off, and he'd backed off. And it was killing him to stay away from her.

Footsteps sounded on the outdoor staircase a few seconds before Caleb appeared.

"What's going on?" he asked Matt.

"Nothin'." Matt took another half-hearted drink of his beer.

Caleb helped himself to a bottle of beer from the compact fridge. "Where's Tasha?"

Matt shrugged. "I dunno."

Caleb twisted off his cap and took a chair. "I thought you two were a thing."

"We're not a thing." Matt wanted to be a thing. But what Matt wanted and what he got seemed to be completely different.

"I thought she stayed with you last night."

"That was the night before. When she was in danger. Last night, she went home."

"Oh."

"Yeah. Oh."

Caleb fell silent, and the fire hissed against the backdrop of the lackluster tide.

"You practically saved her life," he said.

"I guess that wasn't enough."

"What the heck happened?"

TJ appeared at the top of the stairs. "What happened to who?"

"To Matt," Caleb said. "He's all lonesome and pitiful."

"Where's Tasha?" TJ asked. Like Caleb, he helped himself to a beer.

"I'm not doing that all over again," Matt said.

"What?" TJ asked, looking from Matt to Caleb and back again.

"Trouble in paradise," Caleb said.

"It wasn't paradise," Matt said. Okay, maybe it had been paradise. But only for a fleeting moment in time, and now he felt awful.

"You were her white knight," TJ said as he sat down. "I saw it from the air."

Matt raised his bottle to punctuate TJ's very valid point. "That jerk shot at me. There was actual gunfire involved."

"So what went wrong?" TJ asked.

"That's what I asked," Caleb said.

"I asked her to say. She wanted to leave."

"Her mom really likes you," Caleb said.

"That's half the problem."

"Did you tell her how you feel?" TJ asked.

"Yes," Matt answered.

"You told her you were in love with her?"

"Wait, what?" Caleb asked. "Did I miss something?"

"That's your wild theory," Matt told TJ.

He didn't even know why TJ was so convinced it was true.

Sure, okay, maybe someday. If he was honest, Matt could see it happening. He could picture Tasha in his life for the long term.

"You moved heaven and earth to rescue her," Caleb said.

"She was my responsibility. She's my employee. She was kidnapped while she was at work."

"I've never seen you panic like that," TJ said.

He pulled his chair a little closer to the fire. The world was disappearing into darkness around them, and a chill was coming up in the air.

"A crazed maniac hit Tasha over the head and dragged her off in a boat." How exactly was Matt supposed to have reacted? "You were the one who hired a chopper," he said to TJ.

"It seemed like the most expeditious way to cover a lot of ground."

"That doesn't make you in love with Tasha." Matt frowned. He didn't even like saying the words that connected Tasha with TJ.

"What would you do if I asked her out again?" TJ asked.

Matt didn't hesitate. "I'd respectfully ask you not to do that."

Caleb snorted.

"See what I mean?" TJ said to Caleb.

"That doesn't prove anything." Although Matt had to admit he was exaggerating only a little bit.

And it went for any other guy, as well. He didn't know what he might do if he saw her with someone else. She was *his*. She had to be his.

"I can see the light coming on." Caleb was watching Matt but speaking to TJ.

"Any minute now..." TJ said. "Picture her in a wedding dress."

An image immediately popped up in Matt's mind. She looked beautiful, truly gorgeous. She was smiling, surrounded by flowers and sunshine. And he knew in that instant he'd do anything to keep her.

"And how do you feel?" Caleb asked. The laughter was gone from his voice.

"Like the luckiest guy on the planet."

"Bingo," TJ said, raising his beer in a toast.

"You need to tell her," Caleb said.

"Oh, no." Matt wasn't ready to go that far.

"She needs to know how you feel," TJ said.

"So she can turn me down again? She doesn't want a romance. She wants her career and her independence. She wants everyone to think of her as one of the guys."

"She told you that?" Caleb asked.

"She did."

"Exactly that?" TJ asked.

"She said her life was her own, and I wasn't going to change it. She said this was how our story ended."

Caleb and TJ exchanged a look.

"Yeah," Matt said. "Not going to be a happily-ever-after." He downed the rest of his beer.

"Wuss," TJ said.

"Coward," Caleb said.

Matt was insulted. "A guy shot at me."

"Didn't even wing you," TJ said.

"That's nothing," Caleb said.

"It was something," Matt said.

TJ leaned forward, bracing his hands on his knees. "You still have to tell her how you feel."

"I don't *have* to do anything."

"Haven't we always had your back?" Caleb asked.

"I asked her to stay," Matt repeated. "She decided to go."

"You asked her to stay the night." TJ's tone made the words an accusation.

"I meant more than that."

"Then tell her more than that."

Caleb came to his feet. "Ask her to stay for the rest of your life."

"That's…" Matt could picture it. He could honestly picture it.

"Exactly what you want to do," TJ said.

Matt stared at his friends.

TJ was right. They were both right. He was in love with Tasha, and he had to tell her. Maybe she'd reject him, maybe she wouldn't. But he wasn't going down without one heck of a fight.

"You'll want to get a ring," TJ said.

"It always works better with a ring," Caleb said.

"It worked for Noah," Matt agreed. "Do you think I should ask her in front of everyone?"

"No!" TJ and Caleb barked out in unison.

"Noah was sure of the answer," TJ said.

"You guys think she's going to turn me down." That was depressing.

"We don't," Caleb said.

"Maybe," TJ said. "It would probably help to get a really great ring. You need a loan?"

"I don't need a loan."

Matt might not be able to purchase two new yachts on short notice. But he could afford an engagement ring. He could afford a dazzling engagement ring—the kind of ring no woman, not even Tasha, would turn down.

Tasha had found the solution to her problem. She hated it, but she knew it was right. What she needed to do was glaringly obvious. She wrote Matt's name on the envelope and propped her resignation letter against the empty brown teapot on the round kitchen table in her staff quarters unit.

Somebody would find it there tomorrow.

She shrugged into her warmest jacket, pulling up the zipper. Her big suitcase was packed and standing in the middle of the room. She'd stuffed as much as she could into her gym bag. Everything else was in the three cardboard boxes she'd found in the marina's small warehouse.

She should hand him the letter herself. She knew that. A better woman would say goodbye and explain her decision. But she was afraid of what would happen if she confronted him, afraid she might cry. Or worse, afraid she'd change her mind.

She'd dreamed of Matt for the past three nights, spectacular, sexy dreams where he held her tight and made her feel cherished and safe. She loved them while she slept, but it was excruciatingly painful to wake up. She'd spent the days working hard, focusing on the challenges in front of her, trying desperately to wear out both her body and her mind.

It hadn't worked. And it wasn't going to work.

She gazed around the empty room, steeling herself. Maybe she'd go to Oregon, perhaps as far as California. It was warm there. Even in December, it was warm in California.

She looped her gym bag over her shoulder and extended the handle on her wheeled suitcase. But before she could move, there was a soft knock on her door.

Her stomach tightened with anxiety.

Her first thought was Matt. But it didn't sound like his knock. He wasn't tentative.

It came again.

"Hello?" she called out.

"It's Jules," came the reply.

Tasha hesitated. But she set down the gym bag and made her way to the door. She opened it partway, mustering up a smile. "Hi."

"How are you doing?"

"I'm fine."

"I thought you might come to the Crab Shack to talk."

"I've been busy." Tasha realized she was going to miss Jules, as well. And she'd miss Melissa. Not to mention Caleb and TJ. She barely knew Noah, but what she knew of him she liked. It would have been nice to get to know him better.

"Are you sure everything's okay?" Jules asked, the concern in her eyes reflected in her tone.

"Good. It's all good." Tasha gave a rapid nod.

"Yeah? Because I thought you might…" Jules cocked her head. "Do you mind if I come in?"

Tasha glanced back at her suitcase. It wasn't going to stay a secret for long. But she wasn't proud of the fact that she was sneaking off in the dark.

Jules waited, and Tasha couldn't think of a plausible excuse to refuse.

"Sure," she said, stepping back out of the way.

Jules entered. She glanced around the room and frowned. "What are you doing?"

"Leaving," Tasha said.

"Are you going home for Christmas?"

"No."

Jules was clearly astonished. "You're *leaving*, leaving?"

"Yes."

"You quit your job?"

Tasha's gaze flicked to the letter sitting on the table. "Yes."

Jules seemed to be at a loss for words. "I don't get it. What happened?"

"Nothing happened." Tasha picked up her gym bag again. "I really need to get going."

"Matt knows?" Jules asked.

Tasha wished she could lie. "He will."

Jules spotted the letter. "You wrote him a Dear John?"

"It's a letter of resignation." Tasha made a move for the door.

"You can't," Jules said, standing in her way.

"Jules, don't do this."

"You're making a mistake."

Jules took out her phone.

"What are you—"

Jules raised the phone to her ear. A second passed, maybe two, before she said, "She's leaving."

Tasha grabbed her suitcase, making to go around Jules.

But Jules backed into the door, leaning against it. "Tasha, that's who."

"Don't be ridiculous," Tasha said to Jules.

"Right *now*," Jules said. "Her suitcase is packed and everything."

"Seriously?" Tasha shook her head. This was getting out of hand.

Jules's eyes narrowed on Tasha. "I don't know how long I can do that."

"Jules, *please*." Tasha was growing desperate. She didn't trust herself with Matt. There was a reason she'd quit by letter.

"Hurry," Jules said into the phone. Then she ended the call and flattened herself against the door.

Tasha glanced around for an escape. She could jump out the window, but it was quite a drop on that side. And her big suitcase wouldn't fit through. She'd probably sprain an ankle, and Matt would find her in a heap on the pathway.

"What have you done?"

"You'll thank me," Jules said, but she didn't look completely confident.

"This is a disaster. We made *love*."

"You did?"

Tasha gave a jerky nod. "Do you know how embarrassing this is going to be?"

"I promise it won't be."

"It will." Tasha was growing frantic. "We have chemistry. We have *so* much chemistry. He practically saved my life. Do you know what that does to a woman's hormones? I'll never be able to resist him."

Now Jules looked baffled.

"Why resist him?"

"Because I'm not going to be *that* woman."

"What woman is that?"

"The woman who had a fling with her boss, who lost all credibility. I'd have to quit eventually. I might as well do it now while I still have my dignity. It's important to me."

"But at what cost to your future? Don't you want to be happy, Tasha?"

Someone banged on the door.

"Open up," Matt shouted from the other side.

Tasha took a step backward, nearly tripping on the suitcase. The gym bag slipped from her shoulder.

Jules moved to the side, and Matt pushed open the door.

He took in the suitcase and the empty room, and then zeroed in on Tasha.

"*What* are you doing?" His expression was part worry, part confusion.

"I'm resigning."

"Why?"

"You know why."

His eyes flashed with what looked like desperation. "I have no idea why."

"We can't go on like this, Matt."

"On like what? I did what you asked. I backed off."

"Yes, well…" She knew that was true, and she didn't dare admit that it hadn't helped. She still wanted him. She missed him. She…

Oh, no.

Not that.

She would *not* love Matt.

His expression turned to concern. "Tasha?" He closed the space between them. "You just turned white as a sheet."

"Go away," she rasped.

"I'm not going away." His hands closed gently around her arms.

Caleb appeared in the open doorway. "What's going on?"

"Shh," Jules hissed at him.

"Tasha." Matt's voice softened, and he stroked his palms along her arms. "Do you need to sit down?"

"No." She needed to leave, that's what she needed.

But she didn't want to leave. She wanted to fall into his arms. She wanted him to hold her tight. But she couldn't do it. It would only make things worse.

She loved him, and her heart was breaking in two.

He took her hands. "Tasha."

She gazed at their joined hands, feeling tears gather behind her eyes. Her throat went raw and her voice broke. "Please let me go."

"I can't do that."

TJ's voice sounded. "What did I—"

"Shh," Jules and Caleb said in unison.

Matt glanced over his shoulder. Then he looked into Tasha's eyes.

"They told me not to do it like this," he said. He lifted her hands, kissing her knuckles. "I'm not sure of your answer, and it would definitely work better with a ring."

Tasha squinted at him, trying to make sense of his words.

"But I love you, Tasha. I want you forever. I want you to marry me."

A roaring came up so fast in her ears, she was sure she couldn't have heard right.

She glanced past Matt to find Jules, Caleb and TJ all grinning.

"Wh-what?" she asked Matt.

"I love you," he repeated.

"I hate dresses." She found herself saying the first thing that came to her mind.

"Marry me in cargo pants," he said. "I don't care."

But she knew there was more to it than that. "You want someone to go yacht shopping with you, to take to fancy balls, to decorate your stupid Christmas tree."

He laughed softly and drew her into his arms.

"I'll go yacht shopping with him," Caleb offered.

"I'll go, too," TJ said. "After all, I'm the guy fronting the money."

"Let her speak," Jules said to both of them.

"You haven't thought this through," Tasha said.

"This is why you don't do it in front of people," Caleb whispered.

Jules elbowed him in the ribs.

"I've thought it through completely," Matt said.

She could see he was serious, and hope rose in her heart. She wanted to dream. She wanted to believe. Her voice went softer. "What if you change your mind?"

He arched a skeptical brow. "Change my mind about loving you?"

"About marrying a woman in cargo pants."

He drew back and cradled her face between his palms. "Tasha, I love you *exactly* the way you are."

Her heart thudded hard and deep inside her chest. She loved him, and she felt sunshine light up her world.

"I can't imagine my life without you and your cargo pants," he said.

Her heart lifted and lightened, and her lips curved into a gratified smile. "I suppose I could wear one more dress." She paused. "For the wedding."

His grin widened. "Is that a yes?"

She nodded, and he instantly wrapped her in a tight hug. A cheer went up behind him.

"Yes," she whispered in his ear.

He kissed her then, deeply and passionately.

"Congratulations," TJ called out.

Matt laughed in clear delight as he broke the kiss. He kept one arm around Tasha, turning to his friends. "You could have given me some privacy."

"Are you kidding?" Caleb asked. "We were dying to see how this turned out."

"It turned out great," Matt said, giving Tasha a squeeze.

Jules moved forward. "Congratulations." She commandeered Tasha for a hug.

"You were right," Tasha said to her.

"Right about what?"

"I do thank you."

Jules smiled. "I knew it! I'm so happy for you, for both of you."

"I can't believe this has happened," Tasha managed, still feeling awestruck.

"I can't believe she didn't say it," Caleb put in.

"She did," Matt said. He pointed to his friends. "You all saw her nod. That's good enough for me. I have witnesses."

"The I-love-you part," Caleb said.

Matt looked to Tasha, showing surprise on his face. "You did. Didn't you?"

"I don't remember." She made a show of stalling.

"You don't remember if you love me?"

She teased. "I don't remember if I said it." She felt it with all her heart, and she couldn't wait to say it out loud. "I do love you, Matt. I love you so very much."

He scooped her up into his arms. "Good thing you're already packed." He started for the door.

"I've got the bags," TJ said.

Tasha couldn't help but laugh. She wrapped her arms around Matt's neck and rested her head against his shoulder. She was done fighting. They were going home.

It was late Christmas Eve, and Tasha stepped back to admire her handiwork on the tree.

Returning from the kitchen, two mugs of peppermint hot chocolate in his hands, Matt paused. He'd never seen a more amazing sight—his beloved fiancée making his house feel like the perfect home.

"We finally got it decorated," she said, turning her head to smile at him. "Yum. Whipped cream."

"Only the best," he said.

She was dressed in low-waisted black sweatpants, a bulky purple sweater and a pair of gray knit socks. Her hair was up in a ponytail, and she couldn't have looked more beautiful.

He moved forward, handing her one of the mugs. "It tastes fantastic."

"Thanks." She took a sip through the froth of whipped cream.

"And so do you." He kissed her sweet mouth.

"And not a ball gown in sight."

"This is better than any old ball."

"Music to my ears." She moved around the coffee table to sit on the sofa.

It was the moment he'd been waiting for. "Look at the time."

She glanced to the wall clock. "It's midnight."

"Christmas Day," he said.

She smiled serenely up at him. "Merry Christmas."

He set his mug down on the table and reached under the tree. "That means you can open a present."

Her smile faded. "We're not going to wait until morning?"

"Just one," he said, retrieving it.

He moved to sit beside her, handing over a small mint-green satin pouch. It was embossed in gold and tied with a matching gold ribbon.

"This is beautiful." She admired the package for a moment. Then she grinned like a little kid, untying the ribbon and pulling open the pouch.

His chest tightened with joy and anticipation.

She peeked inside. "What?" Then she held out her palm and turned the little bag over.

A ring dropped out—a two-carat diamond surrounded by tiny deep green emeralds that matched her irises.

"Oh, Matt." Her eyes shimmered as she stared at it. "It's incredible."

He lifted it from her palm. "You're what's incredible."

He took her left hand. "Tasha Lowell. I love you so much." He slipped the ring onto her finger. "I cannot wait to marry you."

"Neither can I." She held out her hand, admiring the sparkle. "This is perfect."

"You're perfect."

"Stop doing that."

"What?"

"One-upping my ring compliments."

"The ring can't hold a candle to you." He drew her into his arms and gave her a long, satisfying kiss.

By the time they drew apart, they were both breathless.

"So, what now?" she asked, gazing again at the glittery ring.

"Now we plan a wedding. You want big and showy? Or small with just our friends? We can elope if you want." Matt didn't care how it got done, just so long as it got done.

"My mom would die for a big wedding."

He smoothed her hair from her forehead. "You called her back, didn't you?" He hadn't wanted to ask, not knowing how Tasha was feeling about her mother's renewed interest in her life.

"This afternoon."

"Did it go okay?"

Tasha shrugged. "She hasn't changed. But I get it, and I can cope. She's completely thrilled about you, remember? I imagine she'll be taking out an ad in the *Boston Globe* in time for New Year's."

"Do you mind?"

He'd support whatever Tasha wanted to do about her relationship with her mother.

"It feels good to make peace." She paused. "I suppose it wouldn't hurt to make them happy."

He searched her expression. "Are you actually talking about a formal wedding?"

A mischievous smile came across her face. "We could let Mom go to town."

Matt put a hand on Tasha's forehead, pretending to check for a fever.

"I could dress up," she said. "I could do the glitz-and-glamour thing for one night. As long as I end up married to you when it's over."

"You would look stupendous." He couldn't help but picture her in a fitted white gown, lots of lace, shimmering silk or satin.

"You'd like it, wouldn't you?"

"I would not complain."

"Then let's do it."

He wrapped her in another tight hug. "When I picture our future, it just gets better and better."

"Next thing you know, we'll be having babies."

"With you," he said. "I definitely want babies." He pictured a little girl in front of the Christmas tree looking just like Tasha.

Maybe it was Jules's being pregnant, but he suddenly found himself impatient. He put a gentle hand on Tasha's stomach, loving the soft warmth. "How soon do you think we might have them?"

"I don't know." She reached out and popped the top button on his shirt. Then she opened another and another. "Let's go find out."

* * * * *

LET'S TALK
Romance

For exclusive extracts, competitions
and special offers, find us online:

f facebook.com/millsandboon

🐦 @MillsandBoon

📷 @MillsandBoonUK

Get in touch on 01413 063232

For all the latest titles coming soon, visit
millsandboon.co.uk/nextmonth